Legends

A Literary Journal from
Grey Wolfe Publishing

Paranormal Pursuits 2016
Edited by Earl W. Wolfe

Grey Wolfe Publishing, LLC
PO Box 1088
Birmingham, Michigan 48009
www.GreyWolfePublishing.com

© 2016 Grey Wolfe Publishing
Published by Grey Wolfe Publishing, LLC
www.GreyWolfePublishing.com
All Rights Reserved

ISBN: 978-1628281712
Library of Congress Control Number: 2016958624

Legends

Paranormal Pursuits
2016

A Literary Journal from
Grey Wolfe Publishing

Edited by Earl W. Wolfe

Legends is a literary journal produced by Grey Wolfe Publishing.
Each year, talented writers from around the globe lend their work to this showcase of short stories, essays and poems for your reading enjoyment.

Some of the stories and poems within these pages may help you revisit memories you thought you'd forgotten. Others may reawaken emotions long dormant. And still others may reacquaint you with the laughter of your childhood. Regardless of which piece of poetry or prose you find most appealing, we are certain that these authors will quickly become some of your new favorites.

Grey Wolfe Publishing is an independent publishing house, headquartered in Michigan. We are committed to walking through the paths of the publishing forest with our authors as equals; never leading, never following… always side-by-side, with the strength and confidence of the Pack.

Ni Bóna Na Coróin.

Acknowledgements

The production of this book each year could not be accomplished without the expertise, literary passion and dedication of our amazing Pack. Each is a writer as well as a company team member; and each lends their unique perspective to serve both the company and our authors with integrity and creativity. We are grateful for their daily contributions to the growth of the Pack.

Contents

1.
A Child Is Born
John Grey

That the child be born healthy,
was all she asked of God.
Boy or girl,
that didn't matter.
Okay, so antichrist
was a bit of a stretch
but she loved that fruit of her loins
as deeply as if
the baptismal waters
hadn't burned "666" into his brow.
He had his father's eyes,
her mouth,
though the horns
growing out of his head
were new to the family DNA.
She remembers the first
words out of the little one's mouth.
"Dada" he gurgled.
Her husband beamed with pride.
But then his second word
was "patricide."

2.
Adept as Cornell, Evil as Degas
William Doreski

Beyond the public area
sprawl eighty haunted bedrooms
dusky with drawn shades. Paid to clean
the public space I sometimes roam
the entire mansion, savoring

the dusty elegant furniture,
ceramics, paintings, tapestries.
Today I choose the room in which
the crabby old duchess departed
in mauve armor of makeup,

crying for her legal team. I lie
on the bulky featherbed and feel
the duchess embrace me with glee,
the first man for many decades.
She presses on me postcards

of Niagara Falls and Mozart
at the clavichord, an angel
spun from pink and green silk, a bell
so tiny a mouse could wear it.
She arranges these in a box shaped

like a coffin, which she then wraps
in strips of hand-painted wallpaper

she discovered in the attic. Maybe
she failed as an artist in life,
but now she's adept as Cornell
and evil as Degas. She leaves
heavy tracks in the carpet,
unseemly for a ghost. Her touch,
when she pushes the finished box
into my hands, is delicate

and cunning, concealing its fire
under an arctic epidermis.
Back in the public area
I unwrap the box and find instead
of postcards, angel, and bell

a mummified beetle as big
as my thumb. Indian summer
blushes a flesh-pink sundown
as I lock up the building and sigh
for the lost duchess. I'll vacuum

up her footprints tomorrow,
but no matter how nicely she asks
I won't lie down with her again
to share that precious little sorrow
only the greatest art can name.

3.
Aeolus-The God of The Wind
Mark Hudson

After Odysseus escaped the land of Cyclopes,
he came to the Land of Aeolus, god of winds.
One of the most interesting of stops,
Aeolus lived here among family and friends.
Fragrant smoke filled pipes to the tops,
and roast meat being chewed to the ends.
Aeolus would eat meat and lick his chops,
and Odysseus set sail as Aeolus sends.
But greedy Odysseus opened a box,
thinking treasure would fill his hands.
The wrathful wind caused storms non-stop,
and off they drifted to dangerous lands.
The lands were full of giants and cannibals,
and some of the men were eaten like animals.

4.
After Taste
Edward Ahern

It began with the toilet seat. It was down. Roger never left the toilet seat down- it had been one of the sore points with Joyce before she divorced him. He squinted early morning eyes and propped the seat back up.

His cell phone beeped as he slid a razor down his cheeks. Roger glanced at the heading -a message from Joyce's sister. He finished shaving, wiped his face, and looked at the text, a broadcast to about twenty people. Joyce was dead. He called the sister without putting the phone back down.

"Sarah, Roger. What happened?"

Sarah was crying and stuffy nosed. "Oh, Roger! You didn't know? I- I wish someone else had told you. She died in a car wreck last night. They said she was dead before they reached the hospital."

"My God. Did somebody hit her?"

"No. She went off the road and into a gully. Apparently, she and Larry had a disagreement, and she went for a drive."

They talked a few more minutes. Roger and Sarah had never been close, and the conversation strained to a dry finish.

Roger held the phone in his hands. Joyce. Forty-three, no, forty-four years old. No kids with either him or Larry. He sat down. How hard they'd been on each other, how rasping. Yelling back and forth, but then, sometimes, wrestling down into sex in the kitchen or living room. *We were best together when we didn't talk.*
Autonomic movements took over. Drinking juice and coffee. Finishing dressing for work. He reached up to the closet railing for a favorite tie. It was missing. Roger rummaged around the closet floor. No tie. *Great.*

Just before leaving, Roger flipped open the lid of the garbage pail, dumping out the coffee grounds and watched the black grit splatter onto his missing tie.

I couldn't have thrown the tie in there, not without remembering. How the hell did my tie get into the kitchen garbage can?

Joyce had despised that tie, saying that the spaghetti stains might make it less ugly. She'd threatened several times to throw it out. She'd won post mortem.

Roger sat at his office desk quietly, a file opened before unfocused eyes. *Joyce. Brown hair cut in a bob. Quick in mind and movement. Petite framed, with heavy breasts that ski sloped over two ribs into pronounced nipples.*

He'd never remarried, never had another relationship that strengthened into living together. *I guess I was waiting for you to come back. Bad luck.*

Roger sat alone in his apartment that evening. Carrie telephoned, but he kept the conversation brief, unable to focus on another woman. Only two other people called. Joyce had taken most of their friends with her into the new marriage. And Larry was the widower, responsible for the arrangements. Roger looked up the number and called him.

"Larry? It's Roger Previs. I'd like to help out in some way…"

"Previs, leave me alone. I don't want your help. You can go to the wake and funeral, but don't pretend to comfort me."

"Look, Larry I…"

But Larry had hung up. *What the hell. I haven't spoken to him in two years, and he rips me up over the phone. He won after all. Joyce went with him.*

Roger drank infrequently but decided it was called for. He sat in the silent living room with a large scotch. He wanted to feel sorry for himself but instead felt that aggravated anticipation he so often felt with Joyce.

He was half asleep when the television blared and flashed. He stared at a sitcom about thirty-somethings that Joyce had loved, and he hated. The remote lay on the coffee table in front of him.

How the hell did this crap turn on? Did I put my foot on the table?

He grabbed the remote and punched off the television, then stared at it suspiciously. He'd dropped the remote on the sofa and walked the empty glass out to the kitchen when the TV reignited with the same crummy show.

Piece of crap short-circuiting remote. Roger bent behind the television and yanked out the electric plug. The thirty-somethings shut up.

That night, Roger dreamed about Joyce. He roiled in and out of sleep but kept falling back into the same topics- acid drippings about what was wrong with their life together. For all his anger, Roger could never have physically hurt Joyce,. Instead, he'd held her tightly as if the squeezed bodies would somehow wring out their argument. In the serial dreams, he held her to him three times. It felt good.

The next two days in the apartment were even more disorienting. The picture of he and Joyce trekking out west was back on the shelf, although he couldn't remember putting it there. The bed was remade both evenings when he returned from work. The toilet seat was always down, despite his persistently leaving it up. *It's like she's moved back in.* Roger retreated into mindless games on his computer, sitting with the uneasy sensation that Joyce was in the next room. His dreams about her persisted both nights.

I'm losing it. Got to talk to someone. Going bat crap sitting here alone. Shrinks are quacks. Maybe Father Louis. Roger called the church he and Joyce had haphazardly attended and made an appointment.

****

The morning of the fourth day after her death he put on a suit and went to her funeral. As behooved a used-to-be, he sat toward the back, away from the clustered groups of family, associates, and friends. Sarah noticed him and walked over.

"Roger, please don't go up to Larry to offer condolences."

"Why not, Sarah? He was mad at me a few days ago when I called him, but there's no reason for it."

"Apparently, he and Joyce had another blowup. She told him she was leaving and going to your place. He thinks you two were having an affair. Please don't go near him." Sarah threw Roger a speculative look, a glance that conveyed her own suspicions.

"Good God, we were nothing to each other anymore. I hadn't seen her in a year, maybe longer."

"Whatever Roger. Just please stay away from Larry."

Roger had been content to hover in the background, but now angrily considered bracing Larry. *I only wish we'd gotten together, it would have been worth the confrontation.*

****

That evening, reclined in front of a blank television screen, some of the good parts seeped back into his mind. The sideways glance and half-smiling lips when she was amused at one of his absurdities. How she carried her body when she knew he was watching. The way she could finish his thought and embellish it.

Enough. Quit hanging out in the lost part of the lost and found.

Roger picked up the phone and pulled a number out of its memory.

"Carrie? It's Roger. Thank you. Yeah, it's sad that she died so young and needlessly.

"Listen, I'm having a hard time being alone. Would you want to come by tomorrow evening for a little dinner?

"Great, see you then."

Carrie was an old friend who Roger could open up to about his problems. Joyce had hated her, suspecting that Carrie and Roger were dabbling in more than conversation. She'd been wrong. Roger had begun to have occasional comfort sex with Carrie only well after the divorce.

As soon as he put down the phone, Roger noticed a raspy, dry-rot smell that started him coughing. The odor persisted until he went to bed. The next morning, after a Joyce nightmare rather than a dream, Roger drove over to the Rectory at St. Thomas.

"Father Louis?"

"Yes. Roger, is it? We don't see you very much."

"I know Father, I haven't been very good about attending mass since the divorce. Father, I need to talk about some strange things that are happening to me."

Father Louis sat Roger down in a chair across his desk. "Do you wish confession?"

"Not confession exactly, Father, more getting your advice."

Father Louis said nothing as Roger described the happenings since Joyce's death. *I wonder if he thinks I'm crazy or just suffering from guilt.*

"Roger, after the death of a loved one, and she seems to have still been loved by you, it's normal to be hyper-sensitive, to loosen our grip on reality a bit." Father Louis went on to describe other grieving parishioners who had successfully emerged from anxiety and uncertainty.

"Father, fair enough, grief might explain my unease and the dreams, but what about the TV, and the picture, and the bed making, and the tie, and the toilet, for God's sake!"

They talked further. Finally Father Louis said," Look, Roger, I still think that you're going through a natural, very sad process that's unsettled you. However, everything you describe seems to take place at your apartment. There is something I can do that might provide emotional help."

"An exorcism?"

Father Louis laughed. "Nothing so dramatic. Some people who feel uneasy or threatened ask us to bless an item or a person, or, in your case, an apartment. It seems to help sometimes in getting rid of what concerns them."

"Let me think about it Father. And thanks for listening to me."

****

Late that afternoon, Roger began preparing lasagna for him and Carrie. The meat sauce simmered as he went in and out of the kitchen, tidying up the apartment. He mouthed the wooden ladle for a taste before spreading the sauce on the noodles and spit it out. *My God, there must be a whole jar of hot sauce in this. I couldn't have done that!* But an empty hot sauce bottle squatted on the counter.

Roger rummaged through his cupboard and found a prepared bottle of sauce he could substitute. *Keep focusing, stay calm, don't panic.*

When Carrie arrived her body language was blatant. She'd arrived prepared to spend the night. After dinner, they drank more wine in the living room. The CD player squealed into breakdown halfway through a mood-inducing track, and they talked gently across background silence. Roger described in clinical phrasing what had happened in the apartment since Joyce's death, and his worry that what was really happening was his own breakdown.

He felt uneasy, queasy almost, but moved over next to Carrie on the sofa, the prelude to the heavy petting prelude. As he leaned forward for a kiss, the apartment imploded.

Books launched out of their shelves and smacked into them. The television tumbled into the wall next to them. CD jewel cases spun into their faces, cutting both of them.

Carrie was cowering, screaming, at the end of the sofa. Roger grabbed her and pulled her out of the apartment, onto the landing. They were showered with debris as they fled.

Carrie screamed for another minute, then began to whimper. They inspected each other for injury as they crouched on the floor. The open-doored apartment behind them was silent.

"What happened Roger? Was it an earthquake?"

"I don't know. I don't think so. I don't know."

"Call the police."

"And tell them what? That the apartment threw us out? I'm just relieved that you're okay. And, in a way, relieved that you just saw what I saw. Whatever else is happening, I don't think I'm crazy."

They held each other for several minutes. "Come on," Roger said, "I'll take you home."

Roger, occasionally shivering, drove below the speed limit. When they reached her house, Carrie begged Roger to stay.

"I can't. I left the apartment open. I've at least got to go back and shut things up."

They kissed chastely, and Roger left. When he reached the apartment door, still ajar, he could hear the resurrected CD player making soft post-mayhem music.

Roger thought about just locking up his apartment, but needed to see, to verify. He walked in carefully. The television, screen cracked, was back on its stand. The books were on the shelves. The jewel cases in their slots. *It's a back-handed apology after an argument.*

There was nothing to clean up. Roger picked up the phone, which worked, and called the telephone number Father Louis had given him. He was sure that late on a Friday night he'd get a recording, but couldn't wait until morning.

"May God's blessings be upon you. This is Father Louis Pintye. I am away on retreat this weekend and unavailable, but please leave me a message, and I'll call as soon as I get back."

"Father Louis, it's Roger Previs. Things have gotten much worse since we talked. I think… I think I need that blessing you said you could perform. Could you possibly come by on Monday? Pray for me please, Father."

Now what do I do? I'm afraid to stay in my own apartment. Get a room somewhere? Move out? I've got the spiritual fumigator coming. Joyce, God damn it, this is my place now.

Roger cautiously prepared for bed. His last two actions were to down a liquid sleeping pill of scotch and double check that the front door was unlocked, just in case he had to run out again.

But his sleep was featureless and untroubled. As he awoke he smelled fresh, hazelnut flavored coffee. *Joyce, you know I hate that hazelnut slop of yours.* And then he remembered that Joyce was dead.

The coffee pot was full, the coffee freshly made. Roger decided not to remake it. *Adulterated coffee a la Joyce. Can you taste what I taste? Is that why you made it? Or are you just tormenting me?*

Roger plugged in the television, but it was injured beyond the CPR of electricity and stayed dark. He shaved, dressed and started out on his Saturday errands. His sense of Joyce dropped away as he went through the door, leaving a space empty.

When he returned to the apartment, Joyce re-enveloped him like a bathrobe. *What're you doing here? You left me, remember?*

Roger prepared and ate a cold supper, and then tried to read. It was hopeless. Stray, aching thoughts kept short-circuiting the text. What he should have said to Joyce that gave his meaning without hurting her. Her tenderness with the children and animals of others. The indelibly graceful way she could leave the bed nude to go into the bathroom. He finally put the book in his lap and talked aloud to the room.

"Okay Joyce, look. You know I've always loved you, even when I showed it badly. You can play your games with me but don't scare people like poor Carrie, who only tried to give me a Raggedy Ann to cuddle. Do your damndest, Joyce, having you near and surly is better than your absence."

The room seemed to go pastel. Roger's frustration softened as well, into an awareness that something strongly feminine was near him. Roger's dream that night was of he and Joyce in the bed he slept in, the bed they had shared for years. They were engaged in pre-marriage sex, the kind that ebbs and flows for much of a tide change.

Roger woke pleasantly exhausted to the smell of coffee- good, black coffee- no hazelnut. "Thank you," he muttered. He sat in the Sunday morning kitchen and read excerpts from the newspaper aloud, not sure how Joyce absorbed things. He savored his movements, thinking that Joyce might share in them.

He left the apartment once, to buy a television. When he'd set it up and turned it on he tuned to a depressingly chipper sitcom that Joyce had liked. After he'd put down the remote, the television switched to a football game. He left it there. It was her gift.

****

Joyce joined his sleep again that night, and he sensed the burbling river flow of her thoughts without words needed. They loved each other again, this time softly, as though they were both sore from prior injuries.

That Monday morning, a few minutes after 9a.m. Father Louis called.

"Roger I got your message. Are you all right?"

"Ah, Father. I'm okay, I think." Roger started pacing nervously from room to room.

"You sounded strained. Look, I can be over at your place a little before noon. It shouldn't take more than a half an hour to sanctify it."

Roger had fetched up in the bathroom. "Father, I don't know. I'm getting over the shock of what's happened, as you said I would. I'm more comfortable with things. Let's defer the blessing for a while."

"Okay Roger, your call. But I'm always here if you want to talk."

"Thanks, Father, I appreciate your calling."

As Roger clicked off the phone, he reached down and gently lowered the toilet seat.

5.
Brooklyn Ferry, A Ghost Story
William Doreski

After taking my daily pills
I fall from the ferry and drown.
The Brooklyn Ferry, Whitman's beard

plowing the river in sparkles
of sun. The engine smuts
the yellow sky with coal smoke.

The passengers in smelly woolens
clump like clots of moss on rock.
Manhattan without skyscrapers

exudes a rattle of carts, drays,
and wagons. Whitman tosses
a life preserver to save me,

but I'm so old and stony I sink
with pitiless glee to the bottom.
The mud engorges me. I'm fish

food before I've finished drowning.
This isn't funny, but the crowd
on the ferry laughs a huge gray

nineteenth century laugh designed
to drive its victims insane.
I can hear it while the fish nose

and nibble and my lungs pump
like sump pumps and the fresh
but oily water mingles with salt
to brew my future in the stars.
The Brooklyn Ferry hasn't run
since John and Washington Roebling

completed their gothic bridge
with diagonal harp-strung cables
and walkway down the center.

I'm walking that walkway right now.
I wave at the crowd of ghosts
on the ghost ferry steaming across
the East River with coal smoke
the color of Whitman's beard
and a school of grim suicides

paddling in its wake, every one
determined to reach Manhattan
before it finally drifts away.

6.
Darker Than Barker
Mark Hudson

Clive Barker is no Peter Parker,
he's a scarier thing than Stephen King.
His illustrations and imagination,
make Halloween look like a sunny vacation.
Even his books for children are bizarre,
I wonder if his comic books go too far.
So who am I scared of on Halloween?
That monsters might jump out of a magazine?
Last night, my mind was full of confusion,
but real-life issues were the big delusion.
So these monsters that crept into my brain
symbolize scenarios I can't explain.
There are things to fear in real life,
but I shouldn't let that fill me with strife.
I woke up this morning, and I felt okay,
but looking back on it, the sky was gray.
A nightmare I had made me awake,
I made some coffee and planned to feel great.
Like my Chinese fortune cookie I read yesterday,
"Pretty soon, you'll have sunshine, many rays."

7.
Death Of A Mermaid
A.J. Huffman

Shoreset.   Tangled and topless,
death-gripping conch shell, last
lifeline to deeper world.   Silver
scaled drying in mid-day's glare,
flaking, falling, brittle as autumn
leaves.   Distant tides begin
to rise, trickle in, teasing, twisting
tail in final surge of strength.
180 managed.   Bitter-sweet triumph
allows final view, seascape
crashing, reflective gaze
locked in suddenly sightless eyes.

8.
Ghost Hunter's Daughter
Brittney Corrigan

Don't ask me if it's true, if they exist.
I'm not sure how to tell you what
it's like in the shadows of each house,
the other hum beneath the appliance
hum, the way the walls lean in at me,
the vibration everywhere I put my feet.

Mostly I like to stand still, listen
to the clicks and knocks and my father
adjusting his knobs, pressing the padded
headphones tighter to his ears. Watch
my mother sway with her eyes fluttered
shut, her fingers gathering the air.

My father sees in green, sifts through
the static, rounds corners with his lens,
his metered tools. He walks right into
cellars,
basements, attics, untouched rooms, his
eyes
on the pull of the needle, the digital rise
and fall. Right past as I inhabit doorways,

press through the paneling and lathe.
Sometimes I blow a kiss to my mother,
send it out as a cool, spectral puff across
the hallway to her trembling cheek. Or place
my lucent fingers on her back, try to encirle
her with my body as she balances in the
dark.

They are always looking for the others:
the ones who throw spoons or creak
floorboards, nudge faucets or upend the
chairs.
The ones who lift children from knotted
bedclothes, whisper in sonar-ping echoes,
frighten by putting on their fiendish skins.

They bottle and banish, exorcise and incant.
Smudge and cleanse and burn and cast
away. But oh, how I want to tell them not
to send me over, too. I don't want to go. I
want to stay where the electric air surrounds
us. Where the light doesn't flicker and call.

9.
Deep Into The Woods
Debasree

The forest glowed with an eerie red light that pulsated every few seconds as if the wild tangle of foliage had a common breath of life that raced through unseen veins running in unison along everything that was there in it. Mongke knew that whatever it was that throbbed in there, it was poisonous, maybe even lethal. The trees had eyes in the Blood Forest and no human had ever dared venture inside, which was until now. Mongke knew that he had decided to play a big gamble by coming here; one that might cost him his life, but more importantly, his defeat would mean the death of the whole of his clan. He was their only trump card, so he had to do it. He had to win the negotiation, whatever it took to do that. But, would he be able to get an audience with the Queen? She was so reclusive that no one even knew how she looked; and that made her even more dangerous. Mongke clutched the diamond encrusted sabre and pricked his ears to catch the slightest of noises that might alert him to danger. He put his hand into the folds of his shirt where he had a handful of flares. What other things did he carry? He was armed with loads of gunpowder, some oil, wicks… in short, he was carrying everything to start an inferno, but this wasn't just any forest, and he wasn't going to bust into the home of any normal being, he was going to meet *Khünbish.*

****

They were a clan of cattle herders; the terrain they inhabited was something of a Martian landscape, and their tribes were known for their perseverance on such lands through the rigors that accompanied the grinds of surviving on livestock. The hills were covered under tonnes of snow for more than four months, and there were times when the sun didn't rise for days on end. Those were the days when packs of wolves came meandering for fresh meat, and those were the most trying times for the men to protect their sheep and goats from them. It had been centuries since these men had been living this way and they had grown quite adept at protecting their animals from the vicious onslaught of the carnivores at the end of each summer. It was a difficult life, but it was the best they had ever had, and would ever think of having. However, for centuries there had been strange happenings during the long winters. In spite of night guards prowling over the whole area, there had been incidents of missing cattle. Strange though it was, the elders called these accidents as the spirits' ways of taking sacrifices from them. When Mongke grew up, he knew that he had lots of responsibilities towards setting the sacrificial practices right. If the spirits wanted sacrifices, there ought to be a customary festival whereby they themselves offered those sacrifices; it would be better than losing their men who stood guard during the winter nights.

Every year there had been more than one manslaughter, mostly the young men who kept watch over their cattle. However, since the last three years, the violence and magnitude with which the wolves had made the vicious attacks had instilled fear among the elders. They even believed that it was the work of the Devil himself. Mongke had asked for the Elders' permission to arrange for an annual Bloodfest when they would make offerings to the spirits of land, air and the woods. The ceremony had been going on in full swing three years ago with the men drinking and making merry. They had made a sacrifice of ten goats and ten sheep. It had been customary for their tribes to let the blood dry out on the stone whenever they made a ceremonial offering to the spirits. Mongke knew that there were tribes elsewhere who didn't spill even a drop of blood, which they collected in vats and churned to be made into biscuits later on. But not them, they let the blood be washed away by winds and sand and be mixed with the essence of the air they breathed. The meat and the skins, they took away for their own consumption. Such were their beliefs and their way of life. But three years ago, Mongke's leadership was put under the scanner of scrutinization and disbelief all because the idea of such a ceremony had been his, and the massacre had occurred that very night.

****

Mongke parted the veil of vines that covered the entrance to the forest; he felt angry that he had to surreptitiously enter into the forest that was their land. Thankfully, these were the summer days, and it was light outside. He knew that a lot of his perception would change as soon as he entered. The wilderness would close in on him the moment he set foot inside the enchanted realm. He had the occasion to venture into the outermost bounds once, and he had been acutely aware of the unnerving darkness and absolute stillness around him. He could hear the sighs and breaths of lots of unseen creatures that lurked in the foggy darkness around him. It appeared as if the sun had never cast a single ray inside the forest, and it smelt of wilderness, marsh, fungi and something more feral. Mongke understood only later that he had come to associate that smell with death and sacrilege. To think that their own land had been taken away from them inch-by-inch, and they had been pushed off to search for newer pastures and meadows was not only vilifying but outright humiliating.

The moment he set foot in the forest, he felt his feet go ankle deep into something slushy, and he could feel numerous little fingers of vine trying to close in against his feet. They were trying to trap and swallow him; however Mongke also knew that these unknown dangers actually tasted your fear; the more fearful you were of them, the more imposing they appeared. He struck the ground near his feet with his sabre and immediately felt the pressure release, also aware of a strange whisper making its rounds up the various gigantic trees that caved in to create the illusion of a duplicate and sickening black sky above him. He also felt the smell grow stronger; they were closing in; the lust for fresh blood would draw them towards him automatically. He couldn't stop them forever, and so, it was upon him to hurry and search for Dhampir and his family before they found him.

****

As he trudged into the forest, the scene came crashing before his eyes; how Yuanshi had been the first to notice the six dead men in the morning. Well, it wasn't like there was some strict demarcation between night and morning during the winters, but she certainly found the corpses buried beneath loose snow right outside the animal pen. It was strange to see how the spears that the men had carried had been stripped off the iron head. At first, it appeared as if the snow had clotted the blood too soon, thus preventing too much bleeding, but on closer inspection, everyone was baffled to find the men devoid of any blood at all! The throats had been slit, and the men looked like stuffed mannequins who had been given flesh and bones but no blood.

Their bodies didn't bear any other marks, and their dead faces had been frozen into an expression of surprise rather than pain or fear. It wasn't evidently the work of a wolf or any other wild animal. Some human being had been responsible for the deaths, and it was upon Mongke as the leader of the tribes to hand out retribution to the perpetrator. He had been unsuccessful in doing that; in fact, no one had any clue as to who had been playing such ghastly games with them. After an inquest, the elders had concluded that some alien tribe had been responsible for the killing, and they would have to be more careful. Maybe, some other tribes had moved in, and they were trying to claim their own territory. That summer, one of their herders had gone missing while collecting berries from the forest. Days later, his body was found right outside the forest and in exactly the same condition as the earlier ones.

The incidents had marked off as series of backstabbing and the tribesmen had started wagging fingers about Mongke's lack of experience in leading them. Some even went so far as to say that his relationship with Altantsetseg had been the reason behind his neglect towards his duties. He had tried to tell those critics that he, as a young man, had as much right to fall in love, get married and start a family as anyone else in their tribe did. And as far as his love for Altantsetseg was concerned, she had always been his second priority behind his responsibilities as the leader. And it hadn't been his fault that she had been accepted into the clan by none other than Bat-Erdene himself, who had found in her every sign to be a worthy member of their tribes. The girl had been living alone deep in the forest all those years; she was the daughter of one of their own, a family that had died sixteen years ago in the blizzard along with the dozens of others. Altantsetseg had stated that she didn't know of a human settlement so near to the forest, and she had come looking for them as soon as she had come to know.

On having correctly answered all their questions, she had been accepted as one of them. The elders always said that she was a rare combination of beauty, brains, and courage. She had shown her courage the day when the great revelation came in the form of another episode of sacrilege following Bloodfest the last year. Numerous animals had been torn to bits, and two of their men had also been killed. It was Altantsetseg who had first noticed Dhampir, his wife and the four children lurking among the cliffs. How she had managed to decipher that they weren't human, was beyond Mongke's comprehension. But the valour she had shown at the time was hitherto unforeseen in their womenfolk. She had reacted in a split second, pinning the two adults to the ground and ready to slice off their heads. Everyone still talked about how she had tackled the vampires who seemed to be cowering in front of her fury. They had been begging and whimpering to let them go, but Altantsetseg's daggers were unrelenting.

Somehow, it had been difficult for Mongke to grasp the fact that those were not human, and their pleas for mercy were also devoid of human emotions. They had confessed to killing their animals and their men for years, but they had said that not always did they kill for themselves. They had the responsibility to feed the Queen too. Nonetheless, Mongke took pity on the children who hadn't quite developed the primal ferocity that was evident on the adults' faces.

Therefore, Mongke had decided, as the leader of their clan, to spare the creatures their miserable lives, at least for that day, but had taken a promise from them about never again hurting their men or animals.

Altantsetseg had vehemently opposed his decision, but he had gone on to say that he believed in the concept of peaceful co-existence. If the family did them no more harm, he saw no reason to kill them. After all, it was their nature to kill people, and they couldn't be expected to behave outside the primary compulsion of blood lust. He had also asked Dhampir to enter into a blood bond with him, so that he tasted a drop of Mongke's blood and carried the scent to all the others in the forest. It was to be a sort of passcode that they were never to behave offensively again; the forest would be their territory, but the human settlement would be out of their bounds, where they were no longer allowed to venture.

Mongke had been positive that his decision was for a greater good; it would ensure the safety of his men and their animals, although Altantsetseg had protested against the show of his 'unnecessary' mercy.

They had been living happily for months after the incident, but the killings had started again; this time, even more vicious and certainly containing elements of mockery. It was as if the vampires were challenging the men to dare stop them. Mongke had no other option but to step into their area and claim what was legitimately theirs; their lands. But for that, he needed to find Dhampir and his family as a sort of shield against the vile whispering creatures who were moving about the top branches of the giant trees, whispering, sighing, sneering and calling his name.

Mongke suddenly saw a group of women, they were simply beautiful; their pale skins emitting an aura around them, the long golden tresses sweeping the forest floor in abandonment. Their youth hardly covered by the flimsy negligees that clung to the inviting contours of their bodies. It was as if they were calling him to be all theirs. Mongke knew that this was certainly some kind of trick, but he felt drowsy and unable to resist his primal urges. He seemed to be losing his grasp on the sabre, his eyes growing heavy with the sweet scent of desire until he was ready to fall down on his knees and beg the women to assail his senses. The whispering was nearer than ever, as if drumming right into his ears. The heat that was brewing inside him made it impossible for him to tolerate his clothes any longer. He had to get naked...

****

A sudden vicious scuffle around him brought him back to his senses, and he saw that he was on his knees. As he stood up, he could see flashes of motion around him, until something was hurtled down, hundreds of feet away from where he was standing. He gradually understood that the scuffle had been between the women and Dhampir and his family, and the things that went hurtling past him were the fair maidens. He focussed his eyes upon them to see them changing forms vigorously, as if they were unable to decide what to look like, until they again settled back into their shimmering and beautiful forms, but not before Mongke had seen their fangs and red eyes boring through him.

Dhampir whispered to Mongke that he wouldn't be able to hold off the others for very long; the blood bond had been about protecting them from the dark forces inside the human settlement; this was the woods; their own territory where the bond ceased to exist. Nevertheless, their acquaintance with Mongke's scent had prevented them from getting outrightly violent, but eventually, their lust would overpower the pact of the blood bond.

Mongke wasn't immune to the Queen's blood lust. In fact, the vampire clan had lived in seclusion mostly feasting on animals and birds and occasionally slaying humans for hundreds of years, but that was before *Khünbish* arrived. She wasn't just a vampire, she hailed from a powerful family of warlocks who had been at war with the vampires for a very long time, until they had discovered the means of subduing them into slavery. As centuries passed, the two clans cross-bred and gave rise to a new family of vampires who were stronger and more cunning than all. However, by this time, the advent of modern civilization and electricity had begun posing special threats to the vampires and the real lineage of the warlocks had been lost in the interbreeding with the vampires. What remained of their legacy were but a few older warlocks who had almost lost their will to live any longer. As such, the vampires had decided to finish them off and reclaim their supremacy by ending their slavery.

They were successful at wiping out everyone except for a girl who fled with the help of her mighty magical skills. It wasn't for a couple decades that she resurfaced, although the vampires knew that she was there. Different inexplicable events told them that she was gathering her powers and would one day be back, and then she returned. She had been all around the world, but hadn't been able to find the clan of vampires who were ancestors from her father's side. It was her calling, she said, to search for them and be their queen. And thus, she one day found this vampire clan and claimed them as her servants. They took the whole forest for themselves; it was to be their own area, and when the goat herd had ventured for the berries inside, she herself had slain him and drank his blood. She didn't believe in surreptitiousness; she liked to challenge the humans by slaying them right in their homes. Dhampir sounded frightened when he said that he was betraying the most evil, jealous and darkest force in the world now.

****

Even before he had finished the sentence, and before Mongke had the occasion to understand one bit of what was happening, he saw Dhampir's head roll off and then his wife's, before being reduced to cinders. The children followed suit. Mongke must have let out a yell at the ghastly sight, but his voice was caught in his throat with the arrival of a dark hurricane that swept past him on all sides. The whispering and sneering were growing so unbearable that Mongke tried to shut the noise by pressing his fingers into his ears; he shut his eyes because the hurricane seemed to be giving them cold burns. His body had gone numb, and he could feel the group of beautiful women closing in. He crumbled to the ground, but suddenly, everything went still. He opened his eyes just a slit and saw a woman with long dark hair standing with her back to him. Although it was impenetrably dark all around the forest, she appeared to be glowing with some kind of shimmery phosphorescence. Mongke's sexual stirrings grew stronger than before; he felt like he was about to explode. The woman slowly turned around, and Mongke's sabre fell out of his grasp in amazement.

"Altantsetseg!" he muttered.

She spoke with a strange coldness that seemed to retch his heart, her eyes dug into his head so that it throbbed. Her perfect breasts heaved like two inviting mounds of pleasure, as she let her robe of black and red drop.

"My dear Mongke! So self-righteous... I have seen men cower with fright when they learn of us. I have seen men kneeling down in supplication before me, before their desires. And then, I find you; someone who doesn't even kiss the woman he loves. Oh! How much have I lusted to be taken by you, so that I could satiate myself with your nectar, your life force; *your blood*! You remember how vehemently I expressed my wish to kill the damned blood-sucking leech you called Dhampir? Because I knew that vampires have never been able to completely kill off all vestiges of their human emotions, and I expected the fool to enter into such a pact with you, as a sign of gratitude for sparing the life of his family. I knew that would indefinitely postpone my plan to turn each one of your clan into one of them, my slaves. If I couldn't do away with their leader, it would be impossible to start with any of the others. I have lived long enough bearing with the legacy of my mother's side, but magic no longer comes to me. I seem to have taken to blood more than magic, and it leaves you the moment you develop a love more intense than magic itself. But that has made me weaker, and I intend to rejuvenate myself beginning with your life force. Now, my dear Mongke, come to me and I'll grant you an eternal life".

Mongke felt the extreme force that seemed to pull him towards her pale white skin, he wanted to suck her nipples, kiss her belly button, savour the sweetness of her luscious red lips and delve deep into the pool of her desire. It was irresistible, but Mongke knew that he would be a goner as soon as he did that. The little cogs in his brain had started ticking, but he had to think fast.

"What is your real name?" he croaked.

She jangled with laughter, revealing pearly white teeth, and said, "Lilith. And that was a good question. My righteous little lover ought to know that much, and you're the lucky one to have learnt that". She had begun wriggling and squirming invitingly while the fair-faced maidens inched closer.

Had she said that she had grown weaker? Mongke was processing all the information he had received so far. *If she were no longer capable of superior magic, she was just a vampire now, albeit a strong one. So, she must have the same contingencies like the other vampires. Silver, fire, stake through the heart, and.... Sunlight!* He had to do it. He couldn't let his own desires trap the lives of all his clansmen in jeopardy. He knew that it was upon him to ensure their safety, and even the safety of the whole of humankind. Today was his calling. He knew what to do, and he was happy to be the one. It was a sacrifice that was worthwhile.

He crawled up to Lilith, acutely aware of the coldness of her body against his own heat. He let his lips brush against her revoltingly cold ones. He felt nauseated as Lilith's kiss grew in intensity; her fingers dug into his back, and she moved on to start removing his clothes. He had to be fast.

"Come on... don't waste your time fiddling with the damned clothes. Let's do it! Now! Take me! Turn me into one of your own! Come on!" Mongke sounded desperate and Lilith jangled with the shrill laughter again.

"So be it!" she said as they fell down upon the forest floor, engaging in a physically unequal feat but in a battle of wits, where Mongke had the advantage of anger and desperation. He realized that he was no match for the ferocity with which she urged him to perform, and he had to end this ghastly game as soon as possible. So he took out his dagger and also the box of matches and gunpowder from under his shirt.

He made a quick slit on his wrist and immediately felt the whole forest quivering as if in some morbid anticipation. The trees started swaying violently, but he was surprised to see specks of sky through the gaps among the leaves. *How was it possible?* Lilith had enchanted the woods. Then he remembered, magic didn't come when the performer found something more interesting than magic itself. Lilith's magic was wearing off as a result of her sexual overtures. So, the moment she would notice his blood and start drinking, her magic would completely wear off the forest, but he would start changing too, though it would take some time. He had to act fast, lighting the flares and the gunpowder and starting a fire, all within the short span before he changed completely; it would be a difficult task, but not impossible.

It is said that the human mind travels at astronomical speed, because he had all these thoughts within the split second before Lilith hungrily broke down upon his wrist, licking off his blood. Immediately, Mongke felt an enormous pain starting to jar his whole being, he hardly could keep his hands steady. Lighting the match was like the most gargantuan task he had ever undertaken, and he then touched it to his waist, where he had strapped the flares and more gunpowder. The sudden pain of burning brought back his sense of purpose, as he threw the packet of gunpowder upwards with force, so that it shot above the tallest of the trees and then fell back again, creating a hole amid the branches. He suddenly noticed that his plan had worked; as the magic wore off, the forest didn't appear as marshy and dark and damp as it had before; the tree branches had caught fire, and a hole was starting to burn amid the canopy overhead. Lilith let out a sudden growl of pain and anger, and Mongke noticed that her teeth that had been pearly white and inviting just a few minutes earlier, were now sharp and jagged, and her eyes seemed to be consumed in a redness that was inhuman. She snapped her fangs once and then dug them into Mongke's neck.

"Thank you, Lilith,", he whispered into her ear. "The fact that you aren't human, and the sorry fact of your miserable existence and your primal urges have been your undoing. You have done exactly as I wished for, I'm changing and it's for the better. Come to me, my darling", Mongke engaged in a tight embrace with Lilith.

The fire around his body started burning off bits of her skin as well, and her shrieks were unbearable. She pleaded with him to let her go. She reminded him of her promise to give him an eternal life.

"Eternal life? Oh, you must mean an eternal damnation!" It was Mongke's turn to laugh, though the unbearable pain of burns that wracked his body or whatever human was left of him prevented him from savouring the glory of his heroism. He grimaced, but didn't let Lilith go. All the better for his superhuman strength. Now the only thing that was left to be done was to drag both of them to the clearing that had burnt amid the canopy. *The sunshine*!

He realized that he was losing his purpose and the strength of his will; he had to be fast. He clung on to Lilith even more fiercely and rolled upon the forest floor, Lilith was tearing away his flesh now. She was trying to kill him before he transformed completely. As she dug her long nails into his neck with an intent of tearing away his head, Mongke was aware of the warmth of the sun's rays digging into his flesh. Lilith's expression changed to one of fear as she looked upwards. Mongke started laughing as they both fell down in a burning heap.

****

As the villagers saw the whole forest burning in an inferno, they hardly noticed specks flying off into the sky. They weren't birds, those were some lucky vampires who thought they could escape the blaze by flying off, but they made a spectacular show of fireworks in the sky before melting off into nothing...

10.
Después de la lluvia
Franco Strong

It appeared only after the rains, after the shriveled and corroded eye of the desert finally blinked. It appeared only when she was alone, when her husband and son were gone because these were only her sins to carry.

The sun rose and the early rays of light bent and shifted into a familiar outline against the clear horizon, it was a town, a *pueblo* she knew well because it was the village of her birth and her childhood. The unmistakable hacienda and its ceaseless rows of crops alongside a rusted railroad and single-story houses manifested atop the dry plains, like ephemeral remnants of the grey clouds. But the vision was only a phantom, a specter from her past that only she could see. No one else ever saw it, not her husband Arturo, nor her son Diego, not even any of the countless ranch-hands working the land. No, the town was utterly hers, a lurking apparition from her former life.

Pooled water splashed at her feet as she took uneasy steps towards the end of her property. Her muscles were old, tired, weathered from too many years in the Northern desert, the vast maw of the Sonora. She passed the workers scattered throughout, their faces different yet their eyes an echo of one another's because they all gazed into the same sun. Somewhere, far off behind, she heard the exhausted cry of a horse. Dry mud caked onto her ankles as she edged closer to the fence line demarking the end of her property. Ahead, the vision grew solid, coalescing into a perfect replica of the town that no longer existed.

Her hands swept from her forehead, down and across her chest, invoking the sign of The Lord as she prayed to Him, The Father, The Son, and the Holy Spirit. A hushed ringing of mission bells floated in the distance, a murmur that traversed over land and through time, announcing the arrival of her ghosts, these dead souls that regained a trace of life after every rain. She clutched the wooden cross that hung from her neck and let the familiar words of the prayers slide off her tongue. How many prayers could this land hold? Or were they always destined to be forgotten, as all things are when trapped between the sky's abyss and the broken, beige echo of the desert?

A single dirt path, its color a bit lighter than the surround gravel, cut through the open and placid lands, extending from her ranch into the horizon. She waited and kept her gaze set on the road. Atrophying pools of water simmered in the sun, reminiscent of scattered jewels left behind from an unspoken giant.

Finally, a small silhouette appeared on the road, hunched over, limping slightly. The sun hovered directly above and cast no shadows. The figure approached and came close enough for her to see his face, perfectly preserved, no wrinkle out of place, his eyes carved out exactly as they had been all those years ago. She had grown old though, age had taken its fingers and massaged the desert into her tired joints, but her sins were not yet finished, not yet dead and buried.

****

She remembered the words of her father, that men weren't crucified any longer because it was easier to tie a rope around a man's neck and hang him from whatever was available, a bridge, a tree, a balcony, a telegraph pole. And that's exactly how her young eyes found him, his limp and naked body dangling from the balcony of their hacienda, head slumped to the side, swollen tongue creeping out of his dead lips. Grey stubble still dotted his cheeks. The bandits had come early in the morning, before the old man had a chance to shave. And now his swaying body, caressed by the wind, served as banner of flesh announcing that the *Revolucíon* had dug its filthy claws into the town, the peasants' *Revolucíon*, Villa's *Revolucíon*, Zapata's *Revolucíon*, Carranza's *Revolucíon*, it mattered little who owned the Revolution because they were all criminals in Ofelia's adolescent mind.

She tried to keep her eyes down, focused on the field with its long rows of sweet potatoes that needed to be worked. Orders had been sent to the peasants to not cease work, that food needed to be produced for the Revolutionary army, then the land would be theirs to keep. She labored alongside the others in the field, attempting to fit in, trying to move and breathe like them, the peasants, the servants of this land who made their lives just above the plowed dirt, whose lungs were coated in a thin film of dust. She had to be something other than what she truly was: the young, virgin daughter of a rich hacienda owner. Her mother had been gunned down alongside the roads while trying to escape, her father stayed to defend his property (his lifeless eyes still gazed upon it), and Ofelia hid among those faces that were all scarred by the sun. Her own face was still young, her cheeks soft and round, her eyes a light brown, unpoisoned by the nocturnal darkness of a life bleeding of daily hardships.

The other women throughout the filed gasped and crossed themselves at the sight of the dangling, limp body. She heard other voices also, hushed whispers that slipped into her ears.

"Good riddance."

"Let him hang."

"His bones will be exposed to the truths of this parched land and swelling sun."

"Our *abuelos* know it, and now he knows is just as well."

No one dared to take a blade to the rope around her father's neck, and so she was forced to watch his frail body decay, his skin turn to leather in the undying heat, and she prayed that those lurking vultures wouldn't finally swoop in.

Her own body failed her as she struggled to imitate the others beside her in their grueling work, her bones had been estranged from the earth for fifteen long years, and even her shuffling footsteps seemed to require an immense effort, her muscles disobeyed commands, her fingers swelled, her palms bled. But she hid that thick, crimson liquid that spilled from her skin by piling layer upon layer of dry dirt over her moistened blisters, as though she were trying to give herself another skin, one that contained the same rough and calloused contours of the thirsty, jagged expanse of stones just beyond these fields. Her thoughts turned to the land, this country named Mexico, and how it seemed to be clawing at itself, searching for a soul, convulsing and regurgitating a sea of dead bodies in her sickness. Ofelia wondered if her own fate was already prescribed because of a life she never lived, for the scars she didn't possess.

A set of hands, leathery and heavy, fell upon Ofelia's shoulders. Doña Ramona stood beside Ofelia. The woman was old, short, and round, with deep crevices on her face as though a personal drought had taken hold of her skin since childhood.

"*Mija*," she said, "Tonight you come with me. I have room in my humble home."

"*Gracias, Doña Ramona*," Ofelia whispered.

"Your father was a good man," Doña Romona said. "Try to remember him as he was, not as he is now. No tears, *niña*. Don't let them see your sadness."

"*Sí*," Ofelia said as she let her tears return to the corroded heart that murmured in her chest.

Doña Ramona was one of the few peasants who knew Ofelia by face and name, a lonely widow who sometimes had to live off the charity of Ofelia's family and others. Her husband had died years ago and her sons had perished as part-time bandits and ghosts in the mountains.

"Here, child, like this," Doña Ramona said, using her powerful, taut forearms to dig and pull the crops from the ground. Ofelia mimicked the old woman's arms and tried to recall another time when her father was alive and well, his smile slightly askew, his voice deep and earthy like the coffee he drank.

But the sun was collapsing into the horizon, currents of light painted the panorama of lined fields in a yellow tint that gave everything one last breath of life before the nocturnal swell, even the limp body dangling from the hacienda balcony. For a moment he seemed to sway then exhale a thick, black breath of simmering ash.

Then gunshots pierced the sky of gelatinous purple. *Gritos* echoed through throats then against the nothingness of the horizon. The metallic fingernails of the rail line scratched along the earth, announcing the arrival of even more soldiers of the Revolution. An orange glow smoldered in the distance, emanating around Ofelia's old home, the hacienda, and she watched with her innocent eyes as the lips of the fire grew and consumed the white walls of her childhood.

****

She studied his face, perpetually stuck in time, exactly as it had been when she first saw it as a young woman, and she remembered how the rising sun had no effect on his cavernous pupils, how his face and all the others held a dense silence. Now she was an old woman, deteriorating in a mixture of sun and dormant sin, and he was still the same, Juan-Carlos Negrete. She knew him well, his name cauterized in her memory. He staggered over to her outreached arms.

"I've been traveling. For how long, I don't know. Please, if you have water…"

"Of course," she said. "Come this way, we have a well, Juan-Carlos"

The man repeated, "Juan-Carlos…" and hesitated, "That's my name…"

"*Sí, no es asi?*" she said.

The man paused, his straight brow line curled as though he were sifting through the grains of sand blowing through his memory.

"Yes, I am Juan-Carlos," he finally said.

Ofelia never got used to his voice, always sounding as if it were strangling itself against his lips. "*Mi nombre es Doña Ofelia,*" she said. "Let's get you some water and food. You have come a long way, no?"

She led him across her property to the well. He followed but with his gaze focused on the horizon as though the sun's warm current was the only thing he recognized amongst the sea of stones. His light-cotton trousers ruffled like the breaths of a sleeping child. And there was the slight stagger in his stride, a dragging left leg, that Ofelia had never forgotten, a sliding yet even tempo that had been ingrained within her memory.

She began to pump water from the well, her brittle muscles straining to lift and push and repeat.

"*Señora*, here, let me help," the man said.

"No," she said and pushed his hand away. "Let me. I owe you this much."

The water trickled out at first, small, crystalline droplets that caught the sun's light, and the man cupped it in his calloused, almost granite hands, and drank a mouthful. Excess water dribbled off his mouth and was absorbed by the wrinkles around his lips. She studied his face, his hands, so similar to the land he had come from, carved by the same winds, yet he never aged, eternal as all sins of the desert are. Ofelia's once sharp and angular cheeks were forfeited to Time's hands, replaced by loose and eroding angles.

"T*e gusta agua*?" she asked.

"*Sí*," the man said, "I was so thirsty, *Señora*. All I remember is the road, and walking and walking."

Ofelia nodded and reached her hand into the running water and drank. She let the moisture soak into her tired throat, and for a moment the liquid seemed to hold memories, pristine images of her son, Diego, naked and baptized as a child, his sins cleansed except for one: that of being born to his parents. And she saw Arturo, her husband, and how he refused the church all these years because he claimed that nothing is ever forgotten in this land where nothing grows, that his sins were never finished.

"You must be hungry," she said.

"*Señora*, you have been generous, but I cannot put that on you. I must go now."

"Nonsense, it's nothing. And where is it that you're headed to?"

The man seemed to sink into his thoughts yet return with no words, nothing.

Ofelia led the way to her house, the small mansion of Venetian blinds, oak woods, and gold trim that her husband loved so much. Ornate, wooden crosses hung upon the walls, Ofelia's collection, but they seemed absurd, almost lonely, two crossed lines that meant nothing because God's reach didn't extend this far.

She cooked eggs, chorizo, potatoes, and fresh tortillas for Juan-Carlos, his favorite meal, simple yet tasty, a typical peasant dish, a meal she had made numerous times before. Lumps of food slid down his throat, his rough skin reminded Ofelia of a reptile's scales. His bones probably ached with fatigue, his stomach was most likely starving. He had journeyed through the empty regions and placid time of the desert, a frontier of oblivion, a region devoid of shadows.

After the meal Ofelia served her guest a steaming cup of coffee which he drank in silence, mouthfuls at a time. Ofelia recognized it, the twitch upon his eyebrows, like invisible needles were lodged into his skin, and the raised corners of his mouth that announced the slow trickle of memories returning to him.

"Doña Ofelia I thank you, but I must leave. I have…" his lips wrestled with the words, "my family, they are waiting for me."

"I see," Ofelia answered, "And where are they?"

Juan-Carlos hung his head for a moment then said, "At my home. They're across the way."

"Of course."

"*Lo siento, Señora*, the sun, the walk, it must have done something to my thoughts, they come and go, they're here and then they aren't."

"You've come a long way. And the sun, it is warmth and poison in equal measure."

"*Sí, es cierto*," the man said, then added, "My wife is wise too, like you. Beautiful also. I can still see her eyes. Her face has grown hard since her younger days, but her eyes still seem to see all the beauty in the world that I sometimes forget."

"She sounds like a treasure," Ofelia said.

"One of the few I've had in my wheezing life," the man said. He spoke slowly, with long breaths in between fragmented sentences, as though he were reassembling a shattered mosaic or retracing an echo, his spoken words lifting the haze settled between his temples, endowing the man with a solid past, but a past that Ofelia knew well because she had heard it countless times. He spoke about his children, twin daughters, how they seemed happy although they went to sleep with growling stomachs because that was the only life they had known, and their brother, his son, who carried the burden of his father's failed dreams, a younger brother to protect his two older sisters, the twins, but the young boy had died, always sick since birth, his slight frame unable to support the immense weight and solitude found in a life caught beneath the open sky and prismatic plains of dry sands, but there was another, an even younger daughter, one who mimicked her older sisters and tried to grow up too soon, three girls, more precious that the Holy Trinity itself, and his son who never aged but still watched over his sisters from the other side of death, that was his family, that's who he needed to get back to.

"Your girls, they are blessed to have a father and husband who loves the as you do."

"Yes, but I pray for them, *Señora*. We are poor and my girls only have themselves to offer to the would-be-husbands. Offering only yourself is sometimes never enough. They'll need money, and I don't want them to do sinful things for money."

Ofelia nodded her head in agreement.

"And you, *Señora*, where is your family? Or is this ranch all yours?"

"No, I am too old and I don't have the strength to see these affairs all by myself. Maybe when I was younger, but not anymore. I have a husband and a son. The Holy Father has seen to it that I have only one child. But one is enough.

"Shall I meet them, *Señora*?"

"No, they are out and away, business out there across the plains."

The man squeezed his eyebrows together with his fingertips as though a pain had slithered in through his ears. "I think I remember seeing them, *Señora*, two riders on horseback, one old and one young."

"That was probably them," Ofelia said as she took the empty mug from Juan-Carlos with her bony fingers, aged yet still delicate.

"And you, Doña Ofelia, your face, the way your head tilts, the way your hair flows like a flooded river, I remember you also, from somewhere I don't know, like an echo I can still barely hear. Do you ever feel that way, *Señora*?" he asked as his calloused fingers scratched at his chin and throat.

"More than you know, Juan-Carlos. But it's probably someone else you remember, a different girl from a different time." She let her exhausted eyes fall upon the man. "*Vamos*. Let's get you outside and into the fresh air."

He followed her outside but his eyes were focused downward, on his steps, his feet, and the quickly drying mud that cracked beneath is toes, studying everything closely.

The sun was cooling itself off in the lower regions of the sky. Shadows elongated and groped at one another. Ofelia knew time was short, Juan-Carlos was remembering more, his memory would fully return before nightfall.

Small, dying pools of water still clung to the surface of the earth, and the rippling water caught Ofelia's reflection but the liquid seemed to bend, twist, warp across time, into different aspects of her life, images of her young lips devoid of wrinkles, her sharp cheeks, her mother sleeping in the midafternoon, her father's bruised knuckles, her first grey hairs, her infant eyes, images of her past as though it had shattered into a thousand jagged pieces and strewn across the land. Could he see them also, those scarred and ghostly images that composed her life, bleeding and black, aquiline moments that she only wanted to forget? Out here, in the parched plains, sins were never forgotten, they only lay dormant, just beneath the surface, seething, waiting for the rains to come so they could regain a bit of life.

The fatigued sun turned the sky into stratified layers of purple, red, orange, and Ofelia felt the creamy glow against her skin as she recalled another orange glow from her past, a fire on the horizon, flames that swayed in an amnesiac dance and consumed the life she had once known and gave her another, a different life, the one she had now, a small inferno whose embers still glowed in the nocturnal frontier of her soul.

****

Throughout her young life she had never slept like this, outside the beige walls of her hacienda, away from her mother and father, away from her home, cold, exhausted, with aching muscles constricting her chest. Doña Ramona had given Ofelia a small mat to sleep on and an even smaller cotton blanket littered with holes, which the cold night-air slipped through and rapped against her skin like a thousand invisible insects.

Voices, shouting, lone gunshots out in the distance kept Ofelia from sleep. It was the smoke too, slithering in through the broken window of Doña Ramon's hut, that kept Ofelia awake, the charred scent that rose in her nostrils, up to her temples, and she could envision her childhood, her family, a life burning away. She stood and peered out the window towards her old home, still smoldering in the darkness of night, a steady orange glow of embers sighing their final breaths. The revolutionaries (no, they were thieves, bandits, murderers, *assesinos, cerdos*) were still moving beneath the moonlight, eating, drinking, fucking, singing *corridos* about themselves and the best man amongst them, Pancho Villa, *Viva Villa, Viva Villa, Viva Villa!* We sing it three times because he is our New Father, he will live through Your Sons, but he has ridden into the mountains unseen like a Holy Spirit. Three days, three months, three years, it mattered little, he will return and we'll be waiting for him.

Tears dripped off Ofelia's cheeks, falling into the thick, blue night, as though the tears were never hers to begin with, but always the great, dense night that weighed upon every soul. She limped back to the mat, the dirt, the bitter cold, the whispered wind, the ragged blanket, and she prayed for liquid sleep to finally take hold of her.

It was as long while, an almost infinite pause in time, before Ofelia heard the earth's murmuring heartbeat, subtle at first, the cousin of an echo, but it grew louder, closer, and morphed into the unmistakable rhythm of horse hooves approaching. Voices followed, men, two, three, four distinct voices, then a knock at the front door.

"*Señora*, who lives in this house?"

Ofelia heard Doña Ramon's steady voice, "We live alone, my daughter and myself."

"*Donde esta ella?*"

"*Durmiendo.*"

"*Aqui?*"

"*Sí.*"

The door to her room lurched open and Ofelia smelled the men standing in the doorway more than she could see them, their sour breaths, their leathery skin, but most of all she smelled the blood these men has spilled, the blood that slowly trickled within them, the blood that coagulated into the heavy, red bricks within their souls, bricks that they would have to carry as long as they lived and made everything heavier, their breaths, their steps, their dreams.

One of the men grunted more than he spoke, calling for Ofelia to be awakened. Doña Ramona's voice broke in, "No, please, we were sleeping in peace. Leave us. We worked those fields for you all day and now we are tired."

A raspy voice emanated from the night, "Those who do not comply with our orders will be executed immediately."

Faceless, bodiless hands yanked the blanket off Ofelia and pulled her slight frame off the sleeping mat. The hands were rough, strong, palms like ancient gravel, fingers of reptilian scales which dragged Ofelia outside and pushed her along to start marching, voices commanding her to follow the man on horseback, up the slight incline, back to the wheezing embers of the burned hacienda. Other men were outside also, clutching rusted rifles and revolvers, faces only slightly illuminated by the moon, young, old, ageless faces of an equally ageless revolution, ageless because the sin that resides in the hearts of men is eternal, and Ofelia knew this revolution was nothing more than human sin enveloping the land.

Ofelia began to pray to the Virgin Mother like her own mother had always instructed her to whenever life seemed impossible, but the words seemed hollow, vague, a bitter mist pouring from her mouth. A dusty voice choked out that she better pray louder because all the priests had evacuated the church, leaving their precious flock behind, yet there wasn't a crumb of gold left within the holy walls.

"It's okay, *niña*. It's okay," Doña Ramona said in a hushed whisper.

Each step toward the glowing embers, each sigh of the cracked earth beneath her feet was like an inverted echo, a sound being refracted, leading to the life she could never reclaim, her mother's soft voice that carried the comforts of sleep, her father's eyes that seemed to carry a hushed solitude within, pulsating echoes of memory cascaded through her mind.

The dying glow of the smoldering, smoking hacienda walls was reminiscent of a million candles on the verge of being extinguished, yet out across on the other side of the desert. The group drew closer, the steady pounding horse hooves reverberated in the back of Ofelia's throat. Other silhouettes were gathered alongside the burning building, poor, ragged, unarmed men, women, children, the peasants of the land. The man atop the horseback shouted orders, for everyone to line up shoulder to shoulder, backs to the hacienda, eyes up so he could see them.
    "There are enemies of *La Revolucíon* still here, hiding amongst us, filthy descendants of landowners who became rich off your sweat, blood, and work," the man shouted as he climbed off his horse, his boots stomping with restrained anger against the ground. "I am *Commandante Alfonso de El Division Del Norte*. We've come to give you the land back. We only ask that you give us the filthy enemies of our cause."

A whispered murmur passed through the group gathered, a drone of empty syllables that Ofelia didn't attempt to decipher. She only remained silent, placid, hoping the dry air would quickly evaporate the tears clinging to her bottom eyelid, hoping her face would become as still as those points of light hovering in the liquid sky. She barely noticed Doña Ramon's hand clasped around her wrist as the murmuring died down.

"*Nunca? Nada?*" the commander asked. "Ah, it matters little."

He and two other men began to examine each peasant one by one, lifting a dim lantern to their faces, peering at their solemn eyes that seemed to exist more within the shadows than the dismal light. The commander stopped at a lonesome man within the line and yanked his hands towards the lantern.

"You're hands, their soft. Tell me, young man, what is your job here in town?" the commander asked.

"I'm a carpenter. I work with wood," the young man said, pulling his hands away from the light.

"I see," the commander said, hesitating. Then he threw his head over his shoulder and shouted, "Ignacio!"

"Si, Commandante!"

"*Eres carpintero?*"

"*Sí. Andes.*"

"Were your hands ever soft like a newborn's?"

"*No, Señor! Mi esposa* reminded me every night. Said she couldn't make love with a pile of coarse stones grabbing her body."

Laughter emanated through the gathered troops, their throats sounded just as rusty as their rifles.

Then a loud rupture split open the night, like a stone taken to still waters, and Ofelia saw the young man that had been interrogated by the commander slump over, clasping his stomach, huffing in the dirt. The commander stood over the wheezing body, *pistola* in hand, the metallic muzzle catching bits of fragmentary light. Voices gasped, some women tucked in *rebozos* offered prayers. A child cried out. The commander continued down the line of peasants, examining hands, faces, eyes.

Ofelia felt herself dissipating, whatever she had within her internally evaporated through her pores, until all that was let was an ephemeral ghost left behind. The commander stopped and examined Ofelia's hands, the fresh scars, the dying skin, the slender fingers, hands that betrayed her, devoid of callouses, hands that couldn't hide the blood that flowed within and the sin of never toiling in the earth, unlike all the others gathered here in the afterglow of a dead hacienda.

"*Señorita,*" the commander said, his massive hands enveloping hers. "You are beautiful, but your scars are fresh. Perhaps only from today?"

"No, I-"

"She is my daughter," Doña Ramona broke in.

"*Silencio!*" the commander said. "I'm speaking only to her."

Ofelia struggled to pull her fatigued and lifeless hands from the commander's grip but he latched onto her wrists with a single hand and un-holstered his revolver with the other. Her eyes peered at the commander's face, the orange flow and his dark skin coalesced into a thick purple, his hefty moustache was like a nest and Ofelia expected a slew of insects to come crawling out of his mouth at any moment. The pistol crept up, closer to Ofelia's face, and she could almost taste the metal barrel pointed at her.

"No, put the pistol down," a voice called out, a voice that seemed to be trapped between two unseen mountain tops. "Enough games, commander. You know we don't kill women. We don't kill the mothers of our unborn sons."

"They are not our sons if they come from the bloodline of the *hacendados*," the commander said.

"No more killing tonight. Celebrate. Drink. But not more blood, not tonight."

The weight of the empty sky dissolved off Ofelia's chest and she gasped for air. A figure appeared, a man, broad shoulders with right arm that slumped lightly. He seemed to be composed of both flesh and smoke in equal measure.

"I'm taking the girl with me," the unknown man said and led Ofelia away from the smoldering hacienda walls, away from the dim yellow glow that still seemed to whisper her name.

****

Her old bones retraced the steps the same way her soul retraced her sins. Juan-Carlos followed beside her. The two were like a stream, differing water but always flowing down the same path, always following the same riverbed to the same end. Juan-Carlos walked unconsciously, as though his thoughts were trapped within the gleaming pools of water scattered across the muddy ground, as though he were trying to extract the secrets that lay within the earth. Ofelia knew those secrets would come soon enough.

They passed a small plot of land lined with rows upon rows of wood crosses stuck into the earth. Ofelia thought about them, those two crossed lines, and how they meant almost nothing against the backdrop of solitude amongst the empty land. And she thought of those who lay beneath, the bones that soaked up the rain-water, the souls that weren't quite ready to rest.

"There was tragedy here?" Juan-Carlos asked.

"*Sí*, it still is," she answered.

"*Lo siento*," he said. "*Señora, yo tengo otra vida*. Somehow I knew you when you were different. I know them, too." He pointed to the rows of crosses.

A little farther off they came to a chapel, small, barely taller than their heads. She told Juan-Carlos to wait as she ducked into the small sanctuary. There was only a single bench inside. An image of the Christ-Child with the Eternal Virgin adorned the front, along an intricately carved wooden cross with gold trim etched along the sides. Bullet holes littered one wall and the dying sunlight that filtered in recalled stands of the finest silk. Ofelia prayed for an impossible forgiveness, until the final breath of sunlight exhaled from the horizon. Beneath the bench she felt for the cool metal of a rifle and checked to make sure it was properly loaded before she exited the chapel.

Outside Juan-Carlos was still waiting, but his eyes were transparent, his face intense, like slow burning lighting on a clear night. As Ofelia approached he said, "I remember, *Señora*, I remember everything."

****

His face was young, like hers, but his eyes were old, as though he had spent his days staring into the sun and his nights searching the darkness. He introduced himself as Arturo, commanding officer of the once great *Division Del Norte*, scattered now though, fragmented and broken. His words were composed of some unknown ash stuck in his throat.

"The men, they still want blood. They always do. Flesh is the currency now. Blood is the great equalizer of the Revolution. It matters little whose blood it is."

Fatigue infected his words, his truths, and Ofelia wondered what sins had been sliced, scabbed over, and scarred into his memory. Yes, blood had become the great equalizer and it mattered little whose was spilled because all blood evaporates just the same within the dry gravel.

They were alone, Ofelia and Arturo, a young man and young woman, in a hut made of dried mud bricks, like a brown mole rising from the earth's gravel skin. The chair beneath Ofelia creaked and groaned, and it seemed just as tired as the young man who moved through the candlelight before her, his gestures empty, reminiscent of the prism of stones that encircled this small town.

"It reminds me of home," the young man said as he stroked the wall. "Do you have a home, *Señorita*?"

"No," Ofelia said. "It's burned to the ground, gone."

"*Yo tambien*," the young man said. He went on, "I'm weary *Señorita*. I just want to go back to the lands I know. We all do, every man here. But the single line of the horizon, the incision of sky and earth, the endless sand, the jagged jaws of the mountains, they do something to you, *Señorita*, they make you forget things, secrets that you can't remember any longer."

"It's God. He speaks in ways we don't know, he weights our sins," Ofelia said.

The man laughed. "God's reach doesn't extend this far. No, it's something else I heard out there," he said in a sure, even voice, as though he had already weighed his own sins.

"What do you want from me?"

"I said already, a home."

"I have nothing," she said. No, she still had the smoke in her lungs, the ashes of a home, a family, another life, a faint taste that remained.

"You have your blood, the blood of a *hacendado*."

"That is still nothing. My home has been purged, my family is dead, by your Revolution."

"I own nothing of *La Revolucíon*. It's owned me for years now," Arturo said. "But your kind has made homes throughout the country. That's all you've done, settle lands and build homes for your families. Help me, *Señorita*, help me build a home, a family, you and I together. I've been listless for too long. I can feel the sands of the desert invading, pouring into my ribcage, suffocating my lungs, the emptiness is overwhelming, choking. It's in your blood. You can help me build a home, something that I can return to, something that we can return to."

His words, his presence was intertwined within the flickering light, displacing something within Ofelia, a ripple emanating across the still waters within her, his presence pulled at her, a slight ebb, like the tide to the invisible waves that composed her soul, no, not liquid, only waves of course, dry, infinitely shifting sands.

"I can't be like you. I wasn't made to be anything like you," she said.

"No, *Señorita*, my sweet girl, don't be like me, nothing like me, be something else, something truly different, my savior in a *vestido blanco* I have dreamt about."

His face was barely older than Ofelia's, but is eyes bespoke of an ancient solitude, an unchanged landscape. What burrowing sins lay within the marrow of this young man's bones that caused him to need her, Ofelia, a woman just barely the age for marriage, to act as a savior, a reprieve from his days of tireless sun, devoid of shadows which inhabited him? Maybe their paths were similar, maybe her prayers were identical to his because they died against the echoing silence of the wheezing earth and placid sky. She thought about his words, *un vestido blanco*, the white dress she only possessed in this man's dream.

"What are you asking of me?"

"We give the men what they want. We give them blood, any blood, it doesn't matter. Then we leave this tired town together, you and I. Can you do that, *Señorita*?"

"Whose blood? There isn't any left to give."

"Anyone's. It doesn't matter. Those peasants just outside, those faces who you've never really looked at until today. They mean nothing, a few more drops of blood mean nothing to the sea we've already swam through, *Señorita*. Those men of the *Revolucíon*, they want more, they want to see you turn on some of your own. They'll believe anything if it comes from your mouth. We, you, you and I, together, we just sacrifice a few more to the *Revolucíon* so we can be gone of it."

"But they've done nothing. It'd be a lie. They are innocent."

"No blood is innocent," Arturo said. "They'll kill you if you can't give them another." He went on, "I've seen things. I've seen a way out. And it's you I've seen beside me."

"You'll take me away from here?" she asked.

"*Sí.*"

Ofelia nodded her head. Maye that was all she needed, an escape, a way to burrow out from beneath the ashes of her past. She glanced up at the young man in front of her, at his face, at his eyes that seemed so intimately familiar. Maybe she had seen him before, maybe she had dreamt of them together already, in another time, in another life. They were memories that weren't her own, that belonged to another, to the land and the earth that preserved everything in a muted whisper.

****

"I remember everything," he said once again.

Her withered and atrophying muscles held the rifle, the razored-line of the muzzle aimed directly at the chest of Juan-Carlos. She had done this too many times, rains had fallen and dried, years had slipped away, yet her arms were steady, her aim unwavering.

"*Eres un assesino,*" Juan-Carlos said. "You killed us, you killed all of us," he said as his steps closed closer to Ofelia.

A breath of dying, purple sunlight settled over Juan-Carlos's silhouette, and he moved more like the apparition he was. Ofelia kept the rifle raised, the barrel ready to lick the white cotton covering Juan-Carlos's chest.

"Forgive me," Ofelia said. "I've lived with these sins for too long. Forgive me this once."

"*Quieres que,* forgiveness?"

A jagged rage manifested over Juan-Carlos's features, a pain and torment Ofelia had witnessed countless times. His face twisted upon itself, his cheeks hardened, eyes solidified, like the sharp mountains that rise up from the earth and seem to be groping for the sky. He was reaching for answers that Ofelia could never provide.

"Me, my family, you gave us to *La Muerte.* You killed them. My daughters, *Jesuscristo,* I remember now, their deaths. Not only us, but all the others. I couldn't even hold my familuy as the bullets ripped apart their flesh. *Mi esposa, oh, mi esposa, pobrecita.*" His hand moved to his flesh, his chest, where the bullet holes had pierced his body in a previous life.

"I prayed for them, Juan-Carlos, I prayed until my knees bled, until my own blood joined theirs," Ofelia said.

"You can't still feel them like I can. You can't still hear their gasps for breath as I do."

"Forgive me for my sins. Let me atone for them, this once, Juan-Carlos, so you don't need to return to torment me. I've paid for my sins a hundred times over!" Ofelia yelled.

Juan-Carlos cried out, an animalistic growl that almost shattered the prismatic desert air, and lunged towards the barrel of the rifle. A single volley ruptured from the tip of the gleaming metal. Then another three shots rang out, Ofelia's muscles pumped the lever-action rifle each time, one, two, three.

Juan-Carlos fell limp onto the dry earth. A pool of crimson trickled from his chest, expanding outward, soaking the white cotton. Labored, wheezing breaths siphoned from his lungs as he groped and clawed at the moist mud of the earth. But the earth was groping at him also, the dampened dirt already reclaiming what it was rightfully owed, the flesh of this man who had retrieved a bit of life, a bit of memory, if only for a day.

Ofelia crept closer to the body sprawled out across the ground. He gasped for air and bled like any other man, but Ofelia knew he was only a ghost, a sin that would never die, a memory that the desert kept hidden from Time's amnesiac gaze. She watched him die, slowly, like all the others. He'd return through, always after the rains, once the fickle layer of sand trickled away to reveal the reminiscences just below.

Ofelia ducked into the small chapel once again and placed the rifle beneath the wooden bench. Her skeletal hands navigated the darkness with ease. The gold-trimmed cross sat stoical beside the image of The Virgin, her downcast eyes searching for her lost child amongst the earth and the muddled pools of infinitely dark, yet still faintly reflective pools of water. There was nothing to see out here though, Ofelia was sure of it, God's reach, his Divine sight was absent and had vacated these lands long ago, leaving only a wasteland of sin, an open labyrinth of echoes from the past. No matter how long her virginal eyes searched she'd find nothing, that fragment of salvation would escape her, always; and Ofelia wondered if her own gaze overlapped with that of Our Virgin, if there was a point of congruence between them, if they somehow both longed for the same impossible forgiveness.

She took a wooden cross from the wall, her hand just as still, her fingers just as rigid and dead as the wood itself. Outside the body of Juan-Carlos was already beginning to decay and fester, an oozing, bubbling black liquid seeped from his mouth, ears, eyes. The life he had regained from the rains was gone now. His body wouldn't last long, dissolved and vanished, submerged within the earth long before the first morning light. The apparition of Juan-Carlos weighed little, nothing more than evaporated rains, and Ofelia began to drag the lifeless body across the slogging mud. Her old, aching muscles still had enough strength for this. She stopped at the small oasis of crosses that stood erect in the moist ground and placed Juan-Carlos and the new cross amongst the others. How many times had she left him there, like this, left to rot into the ground along with all the others, all those other ghosts who returned to torment her after the rains, how many times had she replayed this scene, how many sins had she endured? They were here, all of them, *hermanos, madres, esposos,* unknown faces that only gained a name and a voice after death.

She wondered if her ghosts would outlive her, or if they'd be extinguished when Ofelia herself perished beneath Death's choking embrace. Or could they only be waiting for her, hands extended with claw-like fingers ready to drag her lifeless body into their realm of immeasurable sand and echoing nothingness?

The crosses strewn across the earth were barely visible in the dying, last light, yet Ofelia thought about how little they meant now, two crossed lines that signified nothing against the placid, oncoming night and the distant horizon, that single incision that kept earth and the heavens alighted yet also separated. Still, she dropped to her knees and clasped her hands together, praying, begging God for a Divine amnesia to settle over the desert, for Earth to forget the seasons, forget the rains, leave only the sun and it's solitude; she pleaded for a drought that would last a hundred years.

****

Their faces had the same lines, contours, and wrinkles, as though the winds and rains that carved the hillsides and valleys also engraved their faces. They all looked alike in the early morning like a single extended family of some sort. The swelling yellow light brushed their cheeks, chins, jaws, but seemed to never reach the deep crevices that held their brown eyes. They were lined up against the one remaining wall of the hacienda that survived the flames of last night, about twenty souls, men, women, children, whole families that Ofelia had pointed out earlier in the day, her young fingers working as the blind hand of fate. She had pointed them out without looking, without wanting to know. And now they were gathered here, condemned souls, along with the men of the *Revolucíon*, their rifles drawn and aimed at the line of unarmed peasants. Beside Ofelia stood Arturo, her silent, uneasy savior, the man who spoke with the promise of another life.

Then everything happened swiftly, hazily, like Ofelia was peering through a yawning cloud of dust. A man on horseback shouted orders, that these people were traitors of the peasant's *Revolucíon*, hacienda owners, filthy scum, and he ordered them to be put to death. More shouts, rifles fired, cocked, aimed, fired again, hissing reminiscent of the rattlesnakes Ofelia would sometimes come across as a child.

They all fell, each one collapsing, yet silent, as though they had been born into silence, lived in silence, and their deaths would be no different.

"A woman shouldn't witness these sights," Arturo whispered into her ear.

"My fate should have been theirs, alongside them," she said.

"No, you owe them nothing."

Arturo left yet Ofelia stayed, waiting, listening for a groan, a voice, a curse that would claw towards the heavens. She yearned to see their gaping mouths open, throats strained, lips parted in agony as they damned her to hell, a twisting purgatory, yet no calls pierced the air to acknowledge her existence, no voices escaped through their bleeding mouths, only eyes stared back at her from crevices where no sunlight could reach. There was a glossy familiarity that covered their pupils as if they knew they'd see her again, saving their words for another time, long into the future, when solitude would be Ofelia's only company.

She listened and heard a small mosaic of extinguished breaths shuffled against one another, murmurs born of a dead earth, each exhale that brushed past her ears reminiscent of something she had known before, of her childhood and those late-summer rains she had loved once in another life.

11.
Fame Can Be Lame
Mark Hudson

I had been invited by Grey Wolfe Publishing to appear at one of their Summer Festivals. Being from Chicago, and being rather bad at directions, And furthermore, by not being a driver, I had taken a train to Michigan, and gotten close to Detroit, but when I got off, I realized, "Wow, I'm Here in Michigan, and I am lost."

I called Diana, and she came and picked me up. I was to spend a weekend promoting my latest book of short stories to the Michigan crowd, for one of their summer book-signing festivals.

I arrived for the weekend, and I was staying in a comfy lodge In town. The book-signing event was to go on all weekend, and I was thrilled. I'd been working on a book of short stories, and with the help of the editors at Grey Wolfe Publishing, I had produced my Masterpiece.

The first day was a thrill. I met local Michigan residents, all lovely people. They were so kind and encouraging, that I knew the trip was worthwhile.

Then up walked a slender blonde, a country girl with that look of innocence, yet definitely not naivety, and she approached my table and said, "Are you Mark Hudson? I'm your greatest fan!"

I was flabbergasted. My face turned beet red. My pride and ego soared like an eagle, while my insecurity bubbled at the surface. "Really?" I stammered.

Later that night, Grey Wolfe had a campfire in the woods. The blonde and I shared marshmallows over a campfire. "You didn't mean what you said, that you are my number one fan, did you?" I asked.

"Yes, I did. And I want to show you my dedication to your craft. Follow me into the woods," She flirted.

With adolescent enthusiasm, I followed her into the woods. We kissed under the moonlight. Then, came the kicker.

"Oh, Mark Hudson, we'll you join me in the circle?" And with that, she shape-shifted into a wolf! She chased me 'til the break of dawn, but I got away.

I told Diana about the experience in the morning, and how traumatized I was.   Diana looked me dead in the eye and said, "Well, why do you think we call it Grey Wolfe Publishing?"

12.
GEORGE AND THE DEVIL
(ANOTHER LIKELY STORY)
Charles Stern

The Devil sat down on the bench at the bus stop to his right. George gave him a sidelong glance, smirked to himself, and thought, really? This guy is dressed like Satan! He was obviously supposed to be the Devil. He had the traditional red face, slicked back black hair complete with widow's peak, and receding hairline on the sides. He even wore red clothes and a cape. There was the definite odor of sulfur and his red eyes appeared to be in flames. Is this guy for real? Is there really such a thing? Am I hallucinating?

As if he was reading George's mind, the Devil said, "yes. You are correct, I am Lucifer. You may know me as Satan, Beelzebub, Azazel, and many other names."

"Of course, you are," George said with a very sarcastic tone accompanied by a smirk.

"You don't believe me?"

"Well, you have to admit that it's pretty strange and frankly unbelievable." From what asylum did this guy escape? On second thought, am I seeing things? Maybe I need psychiatric help.

"I heard that!" he yelled. George jumped, and goose flesh shivered down his spine. Could this idiot be the real thing? Can he read my mind?

"Oh yeah? What was I thinking?"

"You called me a crazy person and then you tagged me as an idiot! I really do not appreciate that! In fact, you could go to hell for less than that you know." After a moment's hesitation, the Devil began to calm down and sounded more self-assured. He lowered his voice a couple of octaves. But you are ignorant. So I'll let it slide this time.

George thought, what does this old Jinn want?

"I want your soul," he said, reading George's mind again. He said it with an air of certainty as if it was a foregone conclusion. He was out collecting souls today, and this was just one more victim. No big deal. In fact, he sometimes got bored and set out to present a challenge to the target of his fancy.

George stifled a laugh that tried to gush forth from the deepest reaches of himself. It tried to force its way past his teeth and through his lips, but he clamped his mouth tight trying to hold back the pressure, but it was re-routed and went for his nose. So he held his breath to prevent the inevitable exhale. In the end though, he merely uttered a squeak and a snort. This small crack in his composure created a breach in the dam, and a full-blown flood erupted into uncontrollable gut-wrenching guffaws. "Ha, ha, ha... Oh, oh, oof...!" George tried to settle himself several times before he finally stopped. Once he regained a small bit of composure, he blurted, "What!?"

The Devil calmly reiterated, "I want your...."

"I know. I know! George interrupted in the most sarcastic tone he could muster, "You want my soul. That tired old saw? Can't you do better than that?"

The Devil was unruffled and stared calmly at George. "However you want me to say it, I want your soul."

George said nothing while his eyes were fixed on Lucifer. Is he serious? Can he be the real thing? "How do I know you're who you say you are?"

"People These days! No one believes in the Devil!" He pointed to a nearby trash can followed by George's gaze. He shrugged and sighed. The can spontaneously combusted. The Devil raised his hand, and the flames grew taller. George's eyes expanded to three times their normal size. He felt a knot tying off in his stomach.

"Well," he said, "You could have set that up in advance with some incendiary device like magicians do. Maybe you're a magician."

Beelzebub took a deep breath. "You are a difficult one. I can't wait to get you into my domain. You'll submit to my wishes then!" He stretched out his left hand toward George and moved it up slowly. George felt a strange sensation as if he had become weightless. He looked down and saw the bench five feet below him with nothing holding him up.

"Ayyyeee! Let me down!"

"Okay," said the Devil. With that, he closed his hand into a fist as though he was taking something back.

George crashed on the bench. "Ouch! Oh my God!" he said with tears in his eyes telegraphed from his butt to his brain.

The Devil said, "Don't bring Him into this!"

"Oh. Sorry!"

"Do you believe me now?" the Devil sneered.

"Okay, okay! I get it! You're the Devil incarnate. So why did you choose my soul?"

"You're such a worthy opponent; a challenge." Satan thought for a moment while a tiny piece of eternity trundled by. "I'll give you something before I take your soul home."

Lucifer offered George three wishes in exchange for his soul. "All you have to do is sign this document… in blood, of course."

George couldn't believe his ears, but there was no longer any doubt, this is the Devil. There was no mistake. He looked the part with his horns, tail, the trident, the whole ugly mess!

"So, just sign here." The Devil pointed to the signature line at the bottom of the last page just above where the name Lucifer was already conveniently inscribed.

George looked at the document. He hesitated, looked at the Devil and back at the paper three times. Lucifer waved a knife in front of George. "Just stab your hand and sign it with your blood. It won't hurt. I promise."

George thought, *what the hell*. My life is nothing to write home about anyway! He nodded and took the knife in his right hand, hesitated with the knife hanging in mid-air above his left palm. "How exactly does this work. Do I die right away or what?"

"Oh no! You get to live until I decide to collect you. I'm just taking your soul for now. Besides, you need time to enjoy the consequences of your wishes."

George stood there for another two minutes.

The Devil became increasingly impatient. "You really are a pain in the ass, aren't you? No wonder you have no friends!" Well, you'll be a perfect addition to my collection. I like to dominate and punish smart asses like you and make you realize just how helpless you really are!

The knife was still suspended over George's hand.

"Go on! The devil urged and pushed the paper forward. "I told you, it won't hurt."

George stabbed the knife into his left hand. "Ooooooo! That hurt a lot! I thought you said it wouldn't hurt!"

"I lied," Azazel said, "You do remember that I am the Devil do you not? What did you expect? " It's a knife after all." The Devil snickered under his breath, what an idiot! "Now sign it before the blood dries up and you have to stab yourself all over again.

George dabbed the index finger of his right hand in the pool of blood that had formed on the palm of his left as if it was an inkwell. He reached out and signed it simply, George.

"That's good enough. It's simply a formality anyway."

"Don't you need a date?"

"A date! You must be kidding. What difference does it make? This is eternity we're dealing with. Time has no real meaning. What a doofus! The Devil smiled with a sardonic smirk. "It's just insurance."

"Insurance?"

"Yes. In case you try to get out of it later, I have your signature to bind you to it in the Court of Cosmic Justice."

"Court of what?"

"Yeah. I know it sounds stupid, but the Big Guy wanted to be more contemporary. I suppose it sounds better than the old medieval-sounding Heavenly Court. You think I'm a nasty punisher, you should see the Big Guy! I mean demanding people sacrifice their own kids and sending plagues, famine, and locusts, etc. And that's while they're still alive! At least I wait for them to die to do His dirty work!"

"His dirty work?"

"Well, you don't think that I'm the one who condemns people to Hell do you? No. He makes the decisions. I'm just the jailer and punisher. I get all the blame, and he gets the glory! It's my punishment, my sentence, to do this job. Don't you see?" Lucifer looked a little sad, but quickly regained his composure. "I'm supposed to tempt everyone and get them to sign these papers as a kind of guilty plea. It avoids a protracted and messy trial, and it keeps the traffic down and the cue shorter at the pearly gates. The problem is that Hell is getting overcrowded, and I've had to reject some souls until I can expand it. Some souls are so bad that I can't even stand them. I have to lock them up in maximum security. The rest of the overcrowding ends up in purgatory for a while during renovations. But, believe me, that isn't exactly a walk in the park either. Did you ever read Dante? Whew!"

George felt a sudden jolt of fear. What have I done? What does this mean?

Reading George's mind, Lucifer said, "It means your soul is mine as soon as your three wishes are fulfilled. Now, what is your first wish? You can take your time," he lied.

George thought for a long while he paced back and forth in front of the bench. Sweat was running into his eyes from his forehead, and the sting of the salt was becoming unbearable. His heart was pounding, and his head was swimming. Am I already suffering the pains of Hell?

The Devil, reading George's mind said, "You ain't seen nothin' yet!" he laughed and laughed, doubled over in rib-shaking mirth, and nearly fell off the bench.

George finally said, "My first wish is for unlimited funds."

"Granted!" Azazel said with a huge grin.

"How can I be certain that you granted it? All I know is that you said so."

"Look in your pocket stupid!" He grinned with such gusto that George felt waves of sardonic humor passing over him.

George reached into his pocket and felt something. He slowly extracted it and saw a wad of cash in large denominations along with a checkbook that read One billion dollars. Next to it was written, unlimited funds.

Lucifer said, "Go ahead check it out! Go to the bank and withdraw whatever amount you like."

George got up and walked two blocks down the street to the bank and withdrew ten thousand dollars and placed it in a bag that seemed to materialize next to him. When he looked at the bank receipt, it indicated the withdrawal, but the balance had not changed.

"Wow!" I never thought I could do anything I wanted. Now I can!" He felt a surge of excitement course through his body. It expanded and filled the bank, stretched out the door and invaded the universe.

As he exited the building, there was the Devil sitting on the bench that wasn't there in front of the bank before. "Well?" the Devil grinned.

"It worked!" George said with a smile.

"I told you it would." What a putz "Now. Your next wish?"

George began to feel the anxiety rising again. I have to choose wisely. I can't squander this opportunity. He paced around again, sat for a while, paced some more and finally stopped directly in front of Lucifer. I want unlimited knowledge."

"Granted!" The Devil looked pleased with such a superior specimen.

George instantly knew everything, all possible knowledge was available to him. "Holy Shi…"

"Be careful using foul language around me!" The devil was miffed.

"What foul language? I stopped before I said shit. Wait! You're the Devil! What is it to you?"

"No, you idiot!" Lucifer shook his head, "Not shit, the H-word!"

"H-word?" George was puzzled for three beats of his heart. Oh! I see. Holy!"

The Devil cringed. Smoke drifted out of his left ear. "Stop it! You asshole! Just you wait until I get you in my domain!" son of a bitch! he whispered under his breath while he rubbed his ear.

With an exasperated sigh, Azazel said, "Okay, what is your last wish? Make it a good one. It's the final one, and there are no returns, no refunds, and no cash back. You're stuck with it."

George sat on the bench for an hour thinking of all the possibilities. Then he looked up, turned and looked the Devil in the eye for a silent moment with a smile on his face. Then he spoke with a firm and steady voice, "I want all of your power."

The Devil blinked and his mouth dropped open. He was speechless for a full minute. This one is clever SOB! Then he smiled. "No," he said.

"Okay. The deal's off! You're not fulfilling your part of the bargain." George was smiling now.

Lucifer realized that George had signed the contract without reading the fine print. He took the opportunity to wave his hand over it and added the fine print. He thrust it into George's hand. "Here," he pointed to the fine print. "It says you can't ask for that."

George wrinkled his face so much that it almost appeared to fold in half. He got up and paced around for another thirty-five minutes. A river of sweat was running down his back and from his forehead. He wiped the perspiration from his stinging his eyes. His knees were feeling weak and his legs felt like boards. Then his face smoothed out with a twinkle returned to his eyes, and he smirked. "Okay, I'll change my wish. I want to live a youthful and zestful life forever."

"But that means you'll never die!"

George smiled and nodded slightly. "Yes indeed! Let's just say that my soul belongs to you, but it's on lease to me forever. That way you keep your power, and I get what I want."

The Devil acted as though he felt defeated. His shoulders shrugged in a posture of surrender. He was silent for a long five minutes. Then he smirked, "Okay you clever fellow." The Devil seemed to realize he had met his match.

Beelzebub began to pace back and forth thinking how to get out of this bind. He came to a sudden stop.   He stood stock still for three minutes. His eyebrows flew to the top of his widow's peak. A huge grin spread across his face. He nodded slowly in a self-congratulatory gesture, "You asked for it kid!" the Devil seemed elated.

George began to worry. A sober expression replaced his smile. "Wait! What are you smiling about? Why are you so happy now that you lost the game?"

Satan turned slowly to face George. Looking him in the eye, he said, "Oh you'll find out! Ha Ha Ha Ha!" Then he yelled, "Your wish is granted!" and he disappeared in a blast of smoke and a shower of sparks leaving George alone in the street

Geez! Such theatrics! George felt good. He had cleverly defeated the ultimate opponent. He had unlimited money, knowledge, and life. What couldn't he do with all of that?! He walked down the street with a confident, grandiose air, and upright posture.

A woman was approaching in his direction and, as she passed, he smiled, nodded and said, "Hello," but she seemed to ignore him. She didn't even flinch and walked on looking straight down the street.

Just my luck! The first person I meet is deaf. He thought he heard the faint sound of lugubrious laughter somewhere in the distance. He followed the lady down the street waving his arms in front of her and trying to gain her attention to no avail. Irritated, he walked further down the street frantically trying to gain the attention of everyone he saw. But no one responded to him. Frustrated, he tried to grab a passing gentleman by the arm, but his hand passed right through him.

George could have everything and knew everything now, but no one could see or hear him. He couldn't touch anyone either! He reached into his pocket and retrieved the checkbook, and it still read unlimited funds.

Damn! Thought George.

13.
Geraldine Hall
Dabasree

The hansom cab drove along the cobblestoned path leading up to Geraldine Hall and Mary Anne couldn't help but notice the general look of neglect that surrounded the gigantic structure of masonry and stonework and gabled windows. Lights issuing from a certain upper story dormer window told her that the fables she had heard about Abraham Geraldine were mostly true. The eastern wing of the house that nested the mistress' room and the nursery was said to have caught fire during the spring of 1863, and had been reduced to cinders. Mistress Amelia Geraldine and little Anthony had succumbed to the inferno, and the master of the house, Abraham, who had been out at the time, returned to find the blaze still in progress. It was said that Miss Bethany, the housekeeper, and Stuart, the cook, had since been unable to persuade the master to put off the lights in the eastern wing. And so, they kept the lamps burning, because Master Bram insisted that little Anthony detested darkness, much the same way he did.

The small fluttering light cast by the gaslight hanging upon the rail hook in front of the hansom cab made the surroundings appear even darker. The building set against the backdrop of an inky blue sky, and peeking out of dense foliage covering it on three sides presented a vivid picture of spookiness. Mary Anne shuddered at the thought that this house was going to be her home from now on; the only comforting thought was that Charlie would be staying too! She nudged him with her elbow to his ribs, and he started awake, glancing in all directions before setting his eyes on Geraldine Hall. Letting out a low whistle, he raised an eyebrow in her direction. Evidently, the surroundings didn't quite affect him the same way they did Mary Anne.

"Hope we have dinner of stewed beef and mashed potatoes and lots of sweet peas and carrots," he whispered to his sister, who looked at him with an ostracizing glare. She, however, knew that for orphans who had spent most part of their teenage years in an impoverished and underfed environment, the most comforting thought that could surpass all uncertainties was hopes of a grand meal. In some ways, Charlie's cheekiness was what had earned them the good fortune of being adopted by Master Geraldine. He had made quite a show by declaring about his bogus clairvoyance skills, and the Fathers had certainly cast him in good light to their benefactor, so that their adoption papers were finalized within a week.

As they trudged along the six steps leading up to the giant oaken doors, carrying what little belongings they possessed, the children were welcomed by a tight-lipped and stern looking rotund little lady in a grey woolen frock and a white apron. She grimaced in what must have been a semblance of a smile and directed them up the corridors that were so steeped in shadows that Mary Anne felt suffocated of the darkness and the stillness around her. She turned back to see Charlie trying to pick up things as he walked behind them. He rapped her on the shoulder and whispered, "May the spirits of Amelia and Anthony rest in peace, Mary Anne. We must be disturbing their slumber by walking up to the eastern wing." Then he broke into a laugh.

"Shut up!" Mary Anne said. She looked forward to meeting the master during dinner, and wanted to be washed and ready for her appearance. She remembered Master Geraldine to be a very amiable and jovial young man with a handsome face and an athletic and tall physique. However, he had taken to frequent bouts of illnesses since the last three years, and after the fire episode, he had looked positively unwell. Having been on the board of benefactors for the orphanage, Mary Anne had often had the chance of seeing him there.

"I have got two of the smaller bedrooms arranged for you; remember never to walk into the nursery or into the master bedroom on the eastern wing, and don't fool around with the lamps. You will see that no one puts out the lights there, not since the mistress and…", it was comical to see the stern-faced Miss Bethany wipe off her tears and blow her nose on her apron.

****

Master Geraldine sat at the head of the table, the fluttering lights casting shadows on his hollowed-out cheeks. The matted hair and tangle of beard did little to make his sallow countenance appear any brighter. Mary Anne and Charlie, who had settled on both sides of the Master per his orders, looked at each other. The man looked possessed by some grave trouble, and the children saw that he hardly ate anything while they polished off the lamb casserole and mash, and vegetables like hungry wolves. At length, when they were too full of the excellent vanilla and carrot pudding, he let out a sigh and said, "Welcome children. Even though Geraldine Hall isn't what it used to be some years ago, I have taken it upon myself to rid it of its desolation. It's upon you to help me in such endeavour. As you see, I haven't been keeping too well of late, I would expect you to abide by what Miss Bethany asks of you, and never EVER speak to strangers. The house is full of them.".

Mary Anne felt a shiver running down her spine and noticed that Charlie's usual dauntlessness had also been marred.

****

It was very dark and completely noiseless, no crickets, toads or night birds. Everything was as still as if the whole house had been plunged into the bottom of the ocean. Mary Anne was jolted awake from her uneasy sleep, and she wished for the comfort of the orphanage dormitory housing forty beds. She crept out of the covers and pulled on the long coat; the floor was so cold that her feet seemed about to be frozen until she found the slippers. She literally ran out towards where she thought the door was. As she pulled it open, her eyes hurt with the light drafting out of the nursery and the master bedroom.

"Charlie,", she called out, and was about to push open the door to the room right next to hers, when someone tapped her on the shoulder. She turned around to find a woman smiling down at her. She must have been in her twenties and was extremely beautiful with tranquil blue eyes.

Her sudden appearance had made Mary Anne jumpy, and she backed away a few steps. "Who are you?" she asked.

"I'm Clara, Miss Bethany's niece. Didn't she ask you not to meander here and there at night?"

"She did, and the Master asked us not to speak to strangers,", answered Mary Anne.

"Well, why did he decide to adopt you two, all of a sudden?"

Mary Anne started feeling at ease with this woman, and shrugged implying her ignorance. Clara scanned the corridor before whispering into her ear, "Be careful… Master Bram isn't physically well. He has got a lot going on in his mind. He sometimes even mumbles incoherently; looks like he made a pact with someone powerful and reneged on the deal later, only to be hounded to madness".

"Pact? But how do you know Clara?" asked Mary Anne.

"Look, I don't have much time, and if someone finds us together, the Master is going to raise hell. Miss Bethany might even go on to pronounce me mad, but if you and your brilliant brother want to know the truth, better read Doctor Faustus. It's there in the library."

Clara quickly ran towards the staircase, and Mary Anne called out, "You stay in Miss Bethany's cottage? How am I to meet you again?"

Clara looked back and said, "Go through the family albums as well and the history of the Geraldines."

****

It had already been a week since the children had arrived and everything had been fine so far; except the fact that it seemed their movements were always closely monitored, and they had to abide by too many impositions. Mary Anne was kept busy in the kitchen and with the scullery maid after their meals, while Charlie was engaged with the horses and with the gardener. As such, they still hadn't found the chance to visit the library. Charlie insisted that he had seen movement in the nursery too many times and had even heard an infant crying somewhere nearby. Mary Anne, on the other hand had once seen Clara walking along the rose garden with a bundle in her arms.

It was just after lunch when Charlie came panting to his sister. His expressions told Mary Anne that he was frightened, which was unusual for him. "You won't believe it, Mary Anne. I have seen the Master's photo dating back to 1831."

"What's so unusual about that?" Mary Anne asked.

"He looked just the same as he does now,", answered Charlie.

"What? And what about the book I asked you to bring?" Mary Anne's voice was excited too.

"Here," Charlie extended his hand that had been kept covered under the folds of his coat. He held out a book, and then he extracted something else with is left hand with a triumphant look on his face. It was a photo. "I knew you wouldn't believe me, so I just tore off these photos. The legends said – Abraham Geraldine, 1831 and Abraham, Amelia and Anthony Geraldine, 1862."

As Mary Anne took a look at the photos, she felt faint and nauseated.

****

The room was stuffy and morbid; the many lamps did little to alleviate any of that. The wicker cradle, the cot, and the rocking horse stood in expectant silence. Both the children didn't know how the news of their supposed little adventure and sleuthing had reached the Master, but they had been summoned to the nursery for an interview with him.

They didn't know what to expect anymore; the whole house seemed to emanate an omen of foreboding. Mary Anne insisted that Amelia Geraldine was the woman who had introduced herself as Clara.   Also, how could the Master have been as old three decades back as he was now? Charlie had also gone into the kind of trance he sometimes went into, when he spoke incoherently. Mary Anne felt frightened.

"You, boy! You really are up to any good at seeing?" Master Bram's voice had an icy edge.

"Sometimes," muttered Charlie absent-mindedly.

"Great. I can feel the vibes in you. Now, tell me if the Dark One is coming for me. Tell me what do you see about me in ten years from now?" Geraldine sounded almost hysterical.

Charlie was swaying back and forth, and his voice was hardly audible; "Nothing" he whispered.

Mary Anne tried to stop shivering but couldn't. Something macabre was on its way. She turned around towards the window; outside was a full moon night. She almost fell down from her seat upon seeing Clara roaming about the grounds with a baby in her arms. She stopped and smiled straight at Mary Anne. She whimpered, "Oh… there she is, Charlie… Amelia is walking Anthony in the garden."

"Garden? Amelia? Why, I set fire to their rooms myself. The Dark One wouldn't let me love anyone more than Him. All too good for he had given me eternal youth like he granted Faustus his wishes, but how could I give myself to him for eternity? I felt too tired of my youth and didn't want to die because I loved my family more. So, I killed them. But the Dark One won't leave me still. Now, I'm going to sacrifice you two; maybe he will be satisfied then… tell me… tell me how happy you see me in my future," Bram Geraldine advanced towards Charlie.

"Nothing," he spat out in his trance, this time, his voice was steady and firm.

"Why, you little rascal," Abraham Geraldine flung himself at Charlie, but was shocked to see Amelia standing right beside Charlie's chair. Everything happened in slow motion then; even before he could stop himself, Geraldine was thrown out the third story window down onto the cobbled path that ran along the house.

The two children ran for their lives not knowing where, the servants might have followed them, but they were aware of Amelia's presence until they fell faint against the door of a farmhouse a couple of miles away. They had hardly realized that it had been Christmas Eve until they were taken in by the kindly couple whose house was abuzz with the preparations. As they were able to start coherently relating their experiences, the children noticed that a blaze had started spreading in the sky right where Geraldine Hall stood.

14.
Ghosts
A.J. Huffman

after Blue District, artist Osnat Tzadok

The blue light district comes alive
at midnight, when the water is still
and the underlying current of
discontent claws at the skin like a viral
beast in a cage with no lock. I have chained
myself to the radiator of my 13th floor
apartment to prevent myself from following
in their tracks. I howl at the moon
till the frustration ebbs, block out
the whispers of nighted winds, their song
of absolute escape burning in my ears.

15.
Haunted Staircase
A.J. Huffman

I remember when we moved into the old inn. I was five when my parents bought it at a Sheriff's sale. For a long time I thought that meant it used to belong to someone who had been sent to jail.

It was an old house set back in the country, but it was in pretty good shape. My parents gave it a new coat of paint – "eggshell" is what they called it. And, of course, my mother had to update the kitchen. "No use living in the dark ages when you don't have to," she told me as she plugged in the new microwave. But the place didn't need what my father referred to as "major renovations." And the first guests were registered a little over four weeks after we moved in.

Personally, I absolutely adored my new home. It held endless fascination for me. Every time I wandered into a new room, I felt like an adventurer. Like Columbus, I had discovered a whole new world, wanted to explore every inch of it. And I did. But no matter where my daily excursions led me, I always ended up playing on the central staircase.

The staircase was in the Grand Foyer – my mother's words – and was the central feature of the inn. In other words, it was the first thing the guests saw when they came in the main entrance. It was the biggest staircase I'd ever seen. It was wide enough for five people to walk down it, side by side, and not be crowded, and it was forty-two steps high (I counted them once). If that wasn't impressive enough, my mother had it carpeted with three-inch-thick, blood red carpeting. The staircase quickly became the pride and joy of the inn.

It was really no wonder I loved to play on those stairs, even though I always got in trouble for having my toys lying around where the guests could see them, could trip or fall over them. "Why do you always play in the foot traffic?" My mother would ask. "You have a huge room to play in upstairs, out of sight."

"Because the ghosts like the stairs best, mommy," I would patiently try to explain. I never understood why she couldn't see them. I saw them all the time. We played together. They were my friends.

"I see, dear," she would say, giving me that look. You know the one I mean. The look that says 'oh how cute, the baby has an imagination.' That patronizing look that I now understand to be a typical adult reaction to things they just don't believe in. Of course, I believed.   I had no reason not to.   There were ghosts.

There was the little girl I used to play with when I was six.   Her name was Mandy.   She died in the third room on the left side of the hall on the second floor.   Mandy told me that it had been the nursery when she lived there.   She had been really sick from the time she was born. She died of pneumonia when she was five and a half.

I met Jonathan when I was ten.   He died when he was eleven.   His parents were staying at the inn while they were in town visiting his mother's sister, who was ill.   Jonathan was riding his bike out front when a truck driver fell asleep behind the wheel, weaved off the road into the driveway.

I ran into Janis, literally, on my thirteenth birthday.   I was running late for dinner with grandma so I couldn't stop and talk, but Janis was waiting for me the next morning when I came down for breakfast.   We talked for hours.   She died in a car accident when she was thirteen. She and her parents were coming back from a wedding.   A drunk driver hit them.   They all died instantly.

Finally, there was Natashia.   She was the only one who didn't like the staircase.   I hung out with Natashia in my room, which was fine with me.   I was seventeen when I met her, and more than a little too old to still be "playing" on the staircase.

Natashia didn't like the staircase because that's where she died.   She and her boyfriend had snuck into the inn for a romantic weekend, but they got into an argument – something about what she was wearing, a skirt that was too short or too tight or something.   Her boyfriend got really mad when she arrived wearing it, screamed at her for "flaunting her goods."   He chased her down the upstairs hallway with a knife, stabbed her seventeen times before pushing her down the stairs.

I didn't blame her for not liking the stairs.   I still don't.

Sadly, I haven't seen any of them for over a year now.   Not since my accident.   Last year I was helping mother decorate for the annual Christmas party.   I was wrapping red and green garland around the banister of the staircase when I fell.   Actually, I slipped.   A piece of red garland was lying on the third step from the top.   My feet went out from under me, I couldn't catch my balance.   I tumbled down thirty-nine steps (couldn't help but count them as I fell).   I was pronounced dead by the paramedics as soon as they arrived.   I had broken my neck, died instantly.

My parents couldn't live at the inn after that.   They sold it two weeks later.   It's been empty ever since.   There is no one left but me now.   I just sit here on the staircase, waiting for someone to come and play with me.

16.
Head Sorcery In The Andes
Michael Berton

phantoms you all
mischievous delights
of a macabre triumph
crushed skulls and bone
powder inhaled performing
herculean tasks
sweat the skin
glory to those
who bring drum
blowing smoke
from whom they kill
skills the Jivaros
claim for manhood
hallucinogenic raids
in acquiring another's
soul moving from
one warrior to warrior
in a bluff trance
pounding trophy
fingers and palms
blistering moist
blood caresses
kissing wounds
the sensory passion
for human viscera
in a climax
thunder on the hemisphere
savored spectacle
of ornamentation

17.
Hell Hospital
Gail Galvan
(Short story from book titled:
Texting Smash-Ups, Mishaps, and Laughs)

"What do you mean transported? Where the fuck am I? How do I get out of this Hell hole?" Paul asked the long blond-haired teenage girl sitting beside him.   He darted his eyes here and there to try and take in all he was seeing.   "It's all black and white in here.   Everything in this room—and what's with the devil heads, pitchforks, and NO TEXTING poster wallpaper all over?"

"Jesus, stop! How many questions can a girl answer at once, Mister?" She took a puff off of a straw.   "Let's see… just what I said, transported.   This is a Hell Hospital and you're in it. There ain't no way out, not for a year anyway, until you've served you're sentence and changed that stinky attitude of yours. You're sick, I'm sick, supposedly, we're all sick, all of us scoundrels….the only cure here is to learn the evils of texting while driving.   Jeez, and how do I know why there's no friggen color in this Hell hole joint… wish I had a joint, you got any buddha on you? Anything 'sa-weet' in your pockets?" She ran her slender fingers through her hair and took another puff off of her make-believe cigarette.

"Is that straw really doing it for you? How much nicotine is there in a straw, anyway cutie?"

"Don't call me cutie.   My name's Dar Lisa…..and you're name is mud, 'cause like I said, you're stuck here along with the rest of us." Instead of laughing, she just stared at Paul awaiting the fear to erupt from within his brain.

"So like… prisoners, you mean? I'm only twenty-four years old and I'm a prisoner?"

"Yeah, buddy, now you got it.   You killed three people, right? What do you think, they give a texting murderous idiot an Academy Award? You should get three awards then.   Me? I only get one.   They say it's my fault this old lady died and all because she had a bad ticker.   Her granddaughter says me crossing over, heading for their car, gave her granny a heart attack at the wheel.   Just 'cause she had a bad heart, I'm stuck down here… It's like they say, life just ain't fair." This time she smiled and laughed wickedly while tapping him on the right shoulder.   "I'll tell you what.   Why don't you go out that door there, down the hallway, and get one of the nurses at the Nurses' Station to help you out." She pointed toward the stark white door.

"That's just what I'll do, by God. And I didn't kill anybody on purpose. It was just one of those things. Could happen to anybody." His six-foot tall body ran out the door and down the long hallway. He saw figures at what seemed to be a Nurses' Station. The white uniforms and old-time nursing hats gave him hope.

As he got closer, though, his heart started racing even faster and he jolted into a panic mode. None of the nurses had faces—complete blanks—no eyes, no noses, no mouths so somebody could tell him what the hell was going on. Most importantly, how he could stop it all and return to his good life as a computer analyst back in Portland, Oregon.

"I'm in the friggen Twilight Zone. Oh God, please help me. Wizard man, I wanna go home. Please God... I really want to go home now." He ran back to the room where he had talked with the girl, but she was gone. So back down the hallway, he took a closer look at the mannequin-like nurses and saw huge buttons running down the front of their uniforms. A sign at the desk read: *Push the top button for instructions to proceed.* His hand shook violently but he pushed at it and heard a click, then a caring, clear voice.

"Continue on down this hallway, turn right and enter the room with a door marked A." He took some long deep breaths trying to calm himself down, then bolted down the hallway. He entered the A-Room and saw nine people sitting in chairs formed in a circle. The blond-haired girl was among them. She motioned for him to sit down beside her.

"Thanks a lot for the help," he said sarcastically.

"No problem. Now shut up and listen."

"My name is Dar Lisa, I'm a text addict. I'm here, I guess, because I caused the death of some old lady with a bad heart. The police put it all on me, but it was raining, too, and that could have been a part of it all. I don't know. I'm trying to take responsibility, but it's hard and I want out of this HELL HOLE!" She screamed the last two words.

The middle-aged lady on her right began to talk next. "My name is Rosemary and I'm a text addict. I'm here because I caused the death of a mom and her 4 year old daughter. I was just trying to text my husband real quick, to tell him I had a dental appointment in the morning and he would have to take off work and drive me home...Before I knew it, I crashed into the car in front of me. Their stupid car was a lightweight and mine's a tank, a Ford Queen Victoria.....so, of course, my car barreled down on the other lady's car and that was it...my life is over. Well, theirs, too....but mine, too."

And so it went—all tragic deaths, all caused by texting, a driver who was distracted and not paying attention.

When it came time for Paul to speak, he just sat there, swallowed hard, fidgeted endlessly, and asked for a glass of water.

"No, no water. No food. We eat, drink once a day. You missed it by getting here after three p.m. You have to share or you'll be here without food and water until you do. If you talk, you'll get to at least sleep on a bed tonight in a ten by five foot cell. So fess up, Mister," the blond-haired girl with a pretty name urged him.

After a long silence and looks that could kill—as easily as a distracted texting driver—he told the others like it was.

"Alright, all right. My freakin' name is Paul Sanders, and I fucked up. I was driving and wanted to text my girlfriend to tell her to meet me. I was gonna give her a key to my apartment. I told her to meet me at my mom's house. But she had forgotten the address; she'd only been there once before. So I went to type in the street number...and honest to God, that's all I remember. Next thing I know, I was lying in a hospital bed with this gash in my forehead and blood all over my right arm. My mom was there and told me the gruesome news. She said, "Son, I don't know how or when, but you will learn to live with this. People saw you texting. There was a crash. Three people are dead because of you. Oh son, how many times? How many times did I warn you, my dear son?" Then my mom just freaked out and started praying crazy-like over my body."

And so, the new prisoner got his orientation. The next day, he pushed a second button on another still-life nurse. It assigned him to Room B where he would choose the skills that he would learn.

He had choices. He would serve an internship and assist in one of the following professions: a Plastic Surgery Clinic, Burn Unit, or Grief Center. He was warned that the Grief Center was the toughest, because parts of bodies might be able to be improved, repaired to a certain degree, but the mind—nobody was ever certain about the mind, how much healing could be done or how much damage seemed to always remain, no matter what.

Failure, bad attitudes, unwillingness to accept responsibility, if these were the results of his presence, then it simply and ultimately meant eternity in Hell. No way out, ever. If prisoners managed to get back to their lives and texted again while driving, once again—ZAP—eternity in Hell it would be.

Mister Sanders seemed to be making progress, dealt with his consequences, showed remorse, learned a skill. Once he got back to his life, he worked at a Burn Unit. But on the way home one day, he heard the music—Pearl Jam—which meant his cell had just gone off. He wanted to know if he had gotten a promotion, if he could cut his hours at the Burn Clinic and go back to his other job.   Paul had always kept the cell phone safely in the glove compartment to remind him that Hell awaited him again if he weakened at any point in time.

Who knows why people do things when they know what the dire consequences will be? Hell has no fury as it does with those stupid and weak enough to choose eternity by repeating the same mistakes.   Paul mumbled, "Ah, fuck it," leaned over and reached to open the glove compartment, got the phone out, answered it, and crashed into the car in front of him.   One more fatal statistic to add to the disastrous count.

Ron's mother stood in the hallway hospital after seeing her son, she dropped to her knees, flung open her purse and desperately opened a zippered compartment, took out a Nitroglycerin pill, and popped it under her tongue.   She held onto her chest and felt as if her heart would flop out onto the floor if she didn't press against it and hold it in.

She sat down, pushed herself up against a wall and veered back at the hospital unit she had just come from.   For six months now, Paul remained mostly in a coma…actually regained consciousness at one point and mumbled something about a blond-haired girl and being a prisoner, doing penance.   He also whispered once in his mom's ear that he wanted to live in the olden days when there were no telephones or cars, just horses, buggies, and telegraph offices.

Paul's mom looked up again and read the sign above the unit's entrance doorway.

Chicago Cook County Hospital Coma and Near-Death Life Experience Unit.

18.
Honey Hollow
Bobbie Groth

Me, Hannah Willett, fifty years old now, and I can remember the summer I was fourteen like it was yesterday.   That was the summer I fell under the power of untold secrets.   And when I learned I had lived before.

Pennington is a small village in rural New Jersey, surrounded by centuries-old farms and miles of stonewall.   The bones of my ancient relatives are scattered in little Quaker and Dutch cemeteries dotting the fields and dank woods of those Jersey midlands.   Our town celebrated its 300th anniversary almost ten years before the bicentennial celebration rocked the rest of the nation.   Its neat colonial English and Dutch houses, built to be heated by massive central fireplaces, hint of its great age, along with the bronze plaque mounted on the graveyard wall that I passed every time I walked into the center of the village as a child.   It said, almost as an afterthought, that British soldiers "exercised their horses over this wall during the American Revolution."

I always thought those words reduced the horror of a terrible bloody revolutionary time to a tidy, neutral statement about exercising horses.   Like the relentless Jersey honeysuckle that covered and obscured abandoned buildings with the swiftness of a few seasons, it hid an atrocity that had scarred the little town for generations.   Prior to that summer when I was fourteen, my childhood was a blur of muddy childish pleasures.   After it, I don't remember ever looking again at the world with less than perfect clarity.

****

We got up early that day, my dad and me.   I was going with him over to the Van Zant's farm.   The place was built in 1699, the impressive house laid out around two central chimneys that rose up from their colossal stone bases in the bowels of the foundation.   All the above-ground floors had walk-in stone fireplaces.   The hulking chimneys continued skyward, radiating their heat through the house right up until they erupted through the slate roof and towered over it to release their smoke, soot, and sparks above the danger level.   Pieter Van Zant had decided earlier that year that he was too old to chop wood and sold his woodlot to a housing developer. Two-hundred fifty years was long enough to wait for central heating.   My dad was going to help him put it in, and I was going to—well, maybe help my dad, but more likely just sit and drink lemonade and eat Mrs. Van Zant's cookies.

It was one of those typically hot and muggy New Jersey summer days when the sun burnishes the foliage with a sharp silver sheen and sweat drips and drips with no possibility of evaporation. My father's face was moist and puffy with waterlogged misery. He wore a bedraggled once-white T-shirt and grease-stained chinos, his tread heavy in the thick work boots that were his only other footwear besides the black oxfords he wore to his white shirt job. His weighty wood toolbox swung from one hand.

I walked beside him vaguely aware of the faint perfume of white clover blossoms almost lost in the reek of week-old mown field grass, intensely fetid with mildew and humidity. We trudged through the back orchard, down the lane that skirted the old African cemetery, and across a fallow field to jump the creek that ran into Van Zant's farm pond.

We then cut along the back of the fields towards his house, past the deep creaking dark of the open barn door. A waft of molasses horse feed was still carried on the air currents years after the structure housed horses. It drifted out the doors and followed us through the hen yard and to the back door.

Mrs. Van Zant smiled and clucked us in, dashing out two tall glasses of lemonade and her famous ginger snaps. I sat dipping my sharp snaps into the lemonade and sucking them until they crumbled away in my mouth.

My father and the Van Zants slipped right into their typical repartee of dry jokes and innuendo. They laughed a lot, and Mrs. Van Zant occasionally took a swat at her husband in mock exasperation. I did not understand what made adults laugh, so I just dunked and sucked until my cookies and lemonade were gone. Van Zant slapped both his knees,

"Willy," he commanded, "There's nothing for it. Gotta git it done," and stood up.

We all four made a beeline for the basement then. Old Van Zant had a crowbar and other tools to break their way through the stonework of the chimney block so he could vent the new furnace up through the old flue.

"Hell," Old Van Zant declared, "It's such a mighty thing—I bet it was the first indoor brick shithouse ever made. Makes me wonder about what kind of reading material we'll find inside."

"Maybe a few milkmaids in yards and yards of diaphanous material," my father intoned saucily, then widened his eyes in my direction, as if he had just realized I was there.

Mrs. Van Zant hooked my arm and led me around the corner from where they were working to tour the root cellar. We could hear the clinking of the men's hammers and chisels on the chimney stones. We felt their blows deep in our chests, like an internal clock striking. Mrs. Van Zant pointed her flashlight into the cracks between the solid granite foundation stones that lined the murky crawlspaces under the house.

"This place was built to hide from the Indians," she said. I nodded and ran my flashlight over the crevasses filled with rubble, here and there setting off a glint from crockery shards. A small white clay pipe with a broken stem lay within eyesight, but far out of reach unless I burrowed into dirt, floor joists, and moldering brick to get to it.

"Harry! Lord, look at this!" came old Pieter's voice, wheezing through the dark. I looked quizzically at Mrs. Van Zant, and she smiled crookedly, "Harriet. My name is Harriet. The old fool just does that to annoy me."

We trundled back to where the lantern's glow illuminated my father and Mr. Van Zant sweating in the dank cool of the basement. Their faces and forearms were crisscrossed with belts of red clay slip where they had wiped sweaty brows with dirtied limbs that had touched the floor or the foundation stones.

Van Zant was crouched on his knees before a small hole in the base of the chimney foundation, my father hanging over him with the battery lantern to light his work area. One stone, whose tuck-pointed mortar had been hacked away and left crumbled on the damp floor had been grasped, pulled out and pushed to the side.

Van Zant blinked up into the darkness and, hearing our proximity, stuck his hand up to the elbow into the hole.

"Look, it's a room, Har--it's a whole room. I can't touch anything."

"Well," I said to no one in particular, "This cellar was built to hide from the Indians." Mrs. Van Zant added her thin light to the lantern.

"C'mon old fool, heave ho and get the rest out."

"Room, hell, it's probably a sauna," said my father. He had the small curved crowbar and alternately chipped away at the mortar and hauled at the stones to dislodge them. Van Zant took a few mighty swings with the sledgehammer and between the two of them and all the energy released from the cacophony of grunts and groans and gritty thumping, they, at last, had broken enough of a hole for a man's head and shoulders. Van Zant propped the flashlight from the Missus on the floor just inside the opening and stuck his head and one shoulder through the dark slash.

"God damned shit oh my God," came his rasp, dulled by the dead air and stone.

"Good Lord, Pieter, watch your mouth!" snapped the Missus, "It's a child here."

Van Zant pulled his head out, his wispy gray hair standing crazily up, plastered with red mud from brushing the edges of the stone. His face was pale, even in the dark, and his pupils expanded to make his eyes black holes of surprise in his white cheeks.

"Willy, git over and take a look here," he said, shifting stiffly onto his knees and faltering, using his arms to push himself up over non-cooperative seventy-five--year-old joints.

My father was already crouched down before the altar of stone. He reached through the maw with the lantern and put it inside on the floor. Then he stuck his head and shoulder through; you could hear nothing but the sharp express of his breath in exclamation. He drew his head out,

"Van Zant, whattya got here, man?"

Mrs. Van Zant bent over and took his place, adding her own oaths to the encyclopedia begun by her husband and my father. Finally, my father motioned to me,

"Hannah, come over here and tell me what you see."

I crouched down, and being younger and smaller, could push my head, shoulders, and arms through the opening they had made. I rested my forearms on the floor and gazed up, my eyes adjusting to the stark brilliance of the lantern against the heavy darkness.

It was a room indeed, hardly big enough for the small table and chair it contained. A single-handled stoneware jug, the heavy locally-made kind hundreds of years old, sat on the edge of the table and another lay broken on the floor.

Sprawled in the chair was a skeleton, its limbs still encased in the tattered dust of its garments, some bones and rotting cloth yet defying the laws of gravity and retaining the living shape of their host. One boot held leg bones erect, the other spilled over crazily to one side. The empty eye sockets stared right through me, jaw wide open and resting on its crumpled rib cage.

There, my eyes caught the glint of the sword held erect by the bones from which its hilt protruded. One long arm dangled to the floor, its hand lying flat in a nest of finger bones. Glints of dull brassy gold caught the light on the buttons, some still lodged in the shelves of ribs, others scattered on the floor.

"It's a Hessian, Dad, I can tell by the buttons." I pulled my head out of the crack and regarded the adults. Their mouths gaped and eyes registered unexpected surprise at what I had said, and then all three broke into hoots of laughter. Bending at the waist they guffawed and slapped their knees, terror inflaming their hilarity until they coughed and snorted and their eyes ran. Finally they stopped, wiping dripping tears with clay-smeared forearms. Like I said, I did not understand what made adults laugh.

"What's so funny?" I demanded.

They laughed again, but Mrs. Van Zant grabbed me to her and squeezed my awkward fourteen-year-old bones heartily.

"It's not funny—you do your homework little girl!"

"God bless Mrs. Hurlbut," intoned my father reverently, "She's left her nit-picking mark on yet another generation of the young!"

Mrs. Hurlbut indeed.   She was the history teacher in junior high and the star of all things historical that were honored in numerous grade school, high school, Girl Scout and Boy Scout festivities.   The year of our 300th anniversary she had been Queen of Operations, demanding authenticity right down to the buttons of the re-enactor Hessian soldiers.

The adults put their heads through the hole a few more times before retrieving the lantern.   We clambered back up the wooden ladder that served as basement steps and through the half-door into the kitchen.   There they threw themselves into chairs around the old wooden table, rehearsing their expletives together in a group appreciation of the unusual experience we had just shared.

I sat on the floor, my back against the kitchen cabinets, and stared at them while they debriefed.   Without comment, Mrs. Van Zant rose from her chair, opened a cabinet and brought forth a flask of homemade cherry brandy.   The Van Zant's cherry brandy was legendary.   My father called it "the nectar of the Gods," and could be enticed by Van Zant to do any kind of dirty work with the words, "And after that's done, we'll take a wee nip of the cherry--for medicinal purposes only, of course."

They each poured a shot and turned to me in unison, raising their glasses and pledging as one: "For medicinal purposes only." I had no interest in such weak-willed adult crutches. I hissed at them.   They downed the brandy and thumped their glasses on the table.

"So, Van Zant," my father broke the silence of their studied drinking, "So you had the Lindbergh baby all along." Van Zant spat his brandy back into his glass and swore at my father. The missus didn't even bother to admonish him.   She furrowed her brow at me, and I rolled my eyes in adolescent disgust.

They picked up their normal teasing banter, this time focusing on the mystery that had riveted the town for years.   When the baby of Charles Lindbergh had disappeared, kidnapped, his small remains were finally found by an old man who lived in the row of small houses that had sheltered the town's African American population for some three hundred years.   Some were former slaves who had escaped north courtesy of the Quakers.   They joined an enclave of Africans who had come over with the earliest French trappers, and had never been slaves in

America.   Van Zant noted the body had already been found, but my father continued to embellish a tale of Van Zant boggling the kidnapping so long that the child grew up, still imprisoned in their cellar, and had finally died of old age.

"He has a sword through his heart," I stated.   They turned to me in unison once again. Van Zant coughed.

"Good God, Willy, this can't get out.   The cops and the whole FBI will all be over here tearing the house and barn apart looking for my other victims."

"It's a Hessian," my father said firmly.

"That doesn't mean anything.   That young idiot copper can't wait to try to put himself on the map." Van Zant was right.   When the old police chief passed away, the young officer who took his place had an attitude that was a far cry from the way law enforcement had ever been done before.   The old chief grew up in town and knew everyone there.   A simple reminder or a chat at the Dutch Treat Café used to be enough to bring our most hardened provincial criminal around.

But the whippersnapper was of a new generation with a big pistol and fresh out of police academy training.   He had a dubious reputation already, having drawn his gun at the squeal of fugitive adolescent tires, managing to discharge it into his groin in the process.   I don't think a gun had been drawn in Pennington by a man in uniform since the American Revolution.   He became the laughing stock of the whole town.   Consequently, he was always looking for blood now.

My father fell silent and ran his finger up and down his shot glass, filled with brandy again.

"We can't leave it in there--eventually you'll have to get the furnace worked on, and it'll be seen."

"We've got the burial ground," said Mrs. Van Zant.   They all nodded.   Back behind the barn, nestled next to the woodlot, was a small family burial ground with headstones and markers going back almost a hundred years before that Hessian had met his maker.   Trees grew up between the headstones, shading and shrouding the plot, providing excellent cover.   Hardly anyone even knew it was there except the family.

We spent the afternoon removing the bones to a plain three-foot square pine box Van Zant put together while my father dug a hole six feet down, just big enough to hold it.   He had placed it toward the back of the burial ground, far from the house, where it would be easily lost among the other graves.

I passed the bones and the tatters of uniform and buttons out the hole in the wall to Mrs. Van Zant, who stacked them solidly in the box, along with the broken crockery and the sword. We left the old table and chair to be bricked up again when work on the furnace was done. Before Van Zant nailed down the lid, Mrs. Van Zant took out one button and pressed it into my hand.

"This'll be for you," she said, and gave me the single-handled stoneware jug as well. "You keep these for your part--we'll always know the truth."

Before sunset, we carried the pine box out behind the barn into the old graveyard and lowered it into the odd square grave. The adults stood in a moment of silence, then I threw some day lilies down into the hole. We silently filled it in, tamped the loose dirt down, and shoved more soil and rocks in it until the dirt was even with the rest of the ground.

My father and Pieter Van Zant had dragged a boulder from the old stonewall in the wheelbarrow and dumped it onto the gravesite. The boulder settled nicely over the disturbed earth.

"That's the headstone," said Van Zant. "Nothing on it because we don't know anything."

We were all strangely quiet, the oddness of the day sitting on our tongues like an unexpected clump of salt in the midst of a sweet cake. My father threw the last of the dirt displaced by the pine box into the undergrowth in the woods. We poured buckets of water on the disturbed ground around the boulder to wash away the crumbles of rock and soil. A few rains and you wouldn't be able to tell the earth had been disturbed at all. By next summer, vines would own that boulder.

****

It was after dark when my father and I trudged back the way we had come that morning, weaving in and around the familiar landmarks with a knowledge that required no light.

"Dad," I said, "Why would a soldier end up stabbed like that, in somebody's cellar, all bricked up in the wall?" He was silent for a minute. I could barely hear where his feet trod the soft ground. The sound of the foliage swished by his body and tool box as he walked through the path narrowed by lush summer growth reassured me that he was still there.

"I don't know," he said at last. "There was a lot of fighting in this area--maybe he was found on the battlefield and--"

"But Dad, they would have buried him with the others."

"Yeah--I don't know.   Maybe the Van Zant family was hiding a Hessian in their cellar--you know, hiding him from their neighbors.   Their neighbors might have been for the Revolution and the Van Zants against it.   Maybe somebody found him and murdered him and they just closed him up in there to keep it all quiet."

"Maybe," I said.   But it still nagged at me.   I swung the jug, its weight bumping hard against my thigh as we walked.   I fingered the button in my pocket with my other hand.   None of the explanations seemed right.

The day kept replaying in my mind, confused and dreamlike.   Twelve hours gone by seemed like a century, and we had nothing to show for the remarkable experience except the button and jug I would probably just set on my dresser and stare at for the rest of my life, wondering.

When we got to the house, my mother was throwing herself into the nighttime routines of my brothers and sister.   I could hear my younger brothers squabbling as they got into their pj's, my sister splashing in the tub and my older brother hammering out in the garage.

My father and I pulled the leftovers from the fridge and ate cold hamburgers and potato salad, tomatoes, string beans and corn on the cob.   This was standard summer fare at our house. While the garden gave birth day after day, we ate it without let-up, or froze it, or canned it.   This was the time of fresh food that wouldn't come again 'til next summer.   Hot or cold, we ate it.

When my Mom came down from reading to my little sister, I slipped away while my parents talked.   I took the jug and button up to the room I shared with baby Sarah.   I called her "Bug."

Setting the jug on my mirrored dresser, I dropped the button through its mouth.   The sound it made as it hit bottom was an oddly muffled thud, rather than the metal on stoneware clink I expected.   My sister stirred in her trundle at the sound and started to sit up.

"Lie down, Bug," I whispered, and gently pushed her back down.   "If you're quiet I'll tell you a story." I heard her latch on to her two middle fingers and suck contentedly.   I knew that she stroked the ears of her favorite stuffed lamby.   No story was necessary, she was back asleep.

I took my pj's into the bathroom.   In the shower I scrubbed my hair with White Rain and soaped the red clay smears away.   Stepping out into the steam bath created by the hot water on this muggy night, I dried myself as best as I could in the humidity.   Finally, I pulled on my shorty pj's and combed the snarls out of my hair.   My clothes were done for.   I pushed them down the laundry chute along with the bath mat that bore traces of red clay from my feet.

When I tiptoed back into my room, I could hear Bug's soft nasal snore.   I turned on the lamp on my dresser, right next to my bed, sure it wouldn't wake her.   She sighed and turned over, cramming her two middle fingers deeper into her mouth and strangling her lamby even tighter.

I plumped up my pillows and sat on my bed, pulling the jug over to have a last look. I turned it over, but there was no mark on the uneven bottom--nothing on the sides but the rough, dark brown glaze. As I righted it, I heard the button rolling on the inside, its sound a soft rustling. I tipped the jug over again to dump the button out, but though it clattered towards the opening, something got in the way of its exit. I kept trying to shake that button out, but it just wouldn't come.

Finally, the need to sleep won out. I put the jug back on the dresser, shut off my lamp, and pulled my pillows down to the bottom of my bed, where I could lie next to my bedroom window as my eyes adjusted to the dark. Gradually the night stars appeared to me and darkness slowly melted into the shapes of leaves and hedges and trees. I stared out into the night world basking in the soft blue haze of the moon, punctuated by one streetlight marking where a street ran perpendicular into ours. A light breeze blew in on me, and the rustling of the leaves lulled me to sleep.

****

I woke sweating, though the night air was cool. My chest was tight and cold with fear; my stomach clenched in the grip of a nightmare. My eyes opened to the pre-dawn gray that muffled everything into a gauzy haze of indistinct shapes and colors. I was turned back around in the bed, my pillow slipped over the side onto the sleeping Bug, my sheets knotted and twisted around my legs.

In the half-conscious panic that gripped me, I kicked to free my feet. I shook my head to disperse the dark dream terror: being chased, glimpses of a soldier's face, sweating, dirty, up close, leering as I desperately tried to flee. A wild anguish reached to pull me back into the nightmare, terror that coursed through my ribcage leaving me breathless.

I flung my elbow out to turn over. Pain exploded through my arm as my funny bone hit something cold and hard on the bed. I struggled up, despite the numbness of legs that had fallen asleep in the tangled web of the sheets. I switched on my lamp.

I was panting like I'd been running. My heart felt as if it would burst. Beside me was the jug, somehow on the bed despite my putting it on my dresser the night before. This was what had so viciously attacked my funny bone as I thrashed about in the aftermath of the nightmare.

Below the mouth of the jug, the button, finally freed, lay glinting on the bed. I picked it up and turned it over, tracing the miniscule unreadable letters on the back and raised design on the front. I reached over and slid it into my jewelry box on the top of my dresser. I didn't want Bug to get my button.

I waved my feet back and forth, trying to force the pins and needles out of them. Sitting up straighter, I leaned over and fetched my pillow off of the comatose Bug, slipping it behind me against the headboard. Bug continued to sleep unmoving.

I picked up the jug and shook it, hearing the soft rattle inside. Paper? I turned it over and shook harder, but the contents lodged in the neck once again. The button was out, but my curiosity swelled.

Rubbing the last of the nerve pain out of my feet I swung them over the side of the bed and stood up. They held. I reached back and hooked my index finger through the jug handle, then silently and awkwardly stepped around Bug's trundle bed. Quietly I let myself out the bedroom door.

The house stood ticking with silence. Downstairs I heard the soft bonging of the mantle clock: four o'clock in the morning. My little brothers weren't even awake yet or engaged in their early morning ransacking of the cereal cabinet and pouring buckets of sugar on their pre-sugared breakfast cereal before anyone came down to stop them.

I padded down the hallway feeling the smooth wood floors on the bottoms of my feet, and descended the stairs noiselessly, avoiding the creaks and groans. Passing through the downstairs hallway into the kitchen, I refilled the cat food bowl and stroked Mamakitty's ears as she bumped her head frantically against my hand. I opened the cellar door and went down through the faintly musty dark into the damp coolness of the basement.

My father's workshop took up the better part of the basement, heaped with tools and wood and odd pieces of hose and fence and wires. I switched on the workbench light, put my jug down, and scanned the wall of tools. Picking up a foot long piece of doweling I thrust it through the jug opening, trying to trap the contents. No luck. I threw the dowel down and searched for something else.

A pair of needle-nose pliers was almost long enough. I shook the contents down as far as I could into the neck and grasped a small bit of the edge with the very tip of the pliers. But when I attempted to pull, a faint ripping sound stopped me. I tipped it up again and tried the dowel, but it scraped the side of the flask catching nothing.

"Why don't you just break the jar?" My older brother Ethan's voice was matter of fact, but the suddenness of its arrival made me jump and shudder.

"What're you doing up?" I knew better. Ethan had a job at the hardware store. He came and went on his own time.

"No, what're YOU doing?" he countered.

"There's something in here," I pushed the jug towards him.   Ethan was the mechanical brains of the family, and whether put to good or evil, his skill was legendary.

"I said, why don't you break it?"

"No, I want it," I replied.   "But I gotta get that thing out."

He held the jug upside down and shook it, then squinted into the narrow neck, tilting his head one way, then another as if sizing up his own escape through the little hole.   He shot me a ferocious glare and wiggled his eyebrows up and down like a cartoon villain.   I banged on his shoulder with my fist.

"Cut it out," I said.

"You quit it, you'll make me drop it," he said.   "Go upstairs and get me a chopstick." Ethan had the commanding assurance of the oldest child.   I was halfway up the stairs to the kitchen before I even realized I had broken my vow to stop running and fetching at his command.   I yanked open the junk drawer to the right of the kitchen sink and rummaged noisily among utensils, old batteries, and other flotsam and jetsam, my hand groping for the tattered bamboo chopsticks that always lay at the bottom of the drawer.

I grabbed one and ran lightly back down the stairs to Ethan.   He stared at me intensely and then switched his gaze to the end of the chopstick.   Suddenly he thrust it into his mouth and drew it out with a pale pink wad of chewing gum impaled on the end.   He plunged that through the narrow neck of the jug, manipulating it back and forth until he let out a short satisfied "Ah!"

"Gotchya! C'mere Grub," he said, precariously balancing the stick and jug.   "Grub" was short for "Grubworm" his favorite nickname for me.   He said I was always grubbing around in the garbage looking for treasure.   That was pretty literally true, so I accepted his name as much as I accepted his authority: immediately, unconsciously, acquired at birth.

I reached over and grasped the jug with both of my hands so that he could use both of his hands to reel his prey into the mouth of the jug.   A tiny corner of paper finally appeared.

"Get it, Hannah." He whispered excitedly.   My slender fingers entered the jug mouth and I began to pull and twist, rolling the tiny sheet of paper up tighter until it passed easily through the mouth of the jug, and slipped out into my hands.   I unrolled it and instinctually offered it to Ethan as if it were his prize, not mine.

"Go ahead, Wormy," he said.   "That's what you wanted."

I unrolled the paper scrap and stared at it in the dim cellar light.   It had a short, small message scratched on it by some ancient quill pen, blotched and spotted with ink.   "By the grace of God my hand is innocent and the hand of all who herein dwell.   My book tells the truth before God and all.   May God rest his soul, but he is of the devil."   It was signed, Hannah Willett, in the year of our Lord, September 19, 1776, Honey Hollow.

A queer feeling entered my head through my eyes, which gazed down at my own name, familiar, yet unfamiliar in some strange forgotten handwriting.

Dumbly I handed the paper to Ethan, whose eyebrows shot up when he saw my name on it.

"What did you put this in there for?" he asked.

"I didn't," I replied.

"Then what the heck is it?"

I hesitated.   My father had said not to tell anyone of our find.   But surely he had told my mother, which to me meant surely I could tell Ethan.   After all, he was my protector and my friend.   He could be trusted.

I began to tell him what we had found at Van Zant's basement.   Ethan's expression was seriously stoic.   As the story unfolded, he did not once question its veracity.

"So this is the jug that was next to the soldier?" he asked finally.

I nodded, and we both looked down again at the paper.

Finally, Ethan shrugged his shoulders.   "I guess you gotta go to Honey Hollow," he said. "That's where her book is." He turned and walked away then, and I heard his sure tread go up the cellar stairs.

I looked back at the paper that lay in my outstretched palms, lit vaguely by the dim cellar lighting.   In one moment we had captured this elusive prey, and in so doing, its mystery only deepened.   I rolled it back up and carried it, and the jug, up to my bedroom.   Setting the jug on my dresser, I squirreled the note away in my wooden jewelry box next to it.   I had to keep it safe from the little boys and Bug.

****

Honey Hollow was the name of a ruin back in the woods off Fiddler's Creek Road.   I had been there a few times with Ethan, when we stopped to explore it during bike trips from our house over to the river.   It was all that was left of a small village that, being deserted well over two-hundred years ago, had succumbed to the camouflaging affects of the New Jersey jungle of honeysuckle and Virginia Creeper.   Four or five chimneys still stood, though not intact.

Basements caved in under stone foundations, and we knew to be very careful to look for wells. In the fall the abandoned foundations had a sad, moldering look. But in full high summer greenery you wouldn't even know it was there.

I ate breakfast, took my bike, and trekked along the back lanes that crisscrossed the hills over to the river. Farms and fields spread out on either side of me like a patchwork quilt. Today I ignored the cows and the horses, and went straight for the stretch of road that held the sheltered path that burrowed back into the woods towards the Hollow.

I ditched my bike in the trees by the side of the road. Then I picked my way carefully through the high grasses and stones, wading through little creeklets that ran across the trail that wound up into the woods, over the top of a ridge, and finally began the descent into the hollow on the other side.

The locals said Honey Hollow was originally a Dutch settlement, built more than three hundred years ago, and hidden from the mainstream when the area became English, and then American. As the children moved away, the families died out; no one had lived there as long as anyone could remember.

The kids at school talked about it all the time. There were supposed to be ghosts there, or maybe pirate treasure. Ethan and I were happy looking for arrowheads or horseshoes when we went up here.

I rounded a bush, and the trail opened out into the settlement. As my eyes adjusted to the filtered early morning sun, I could make out the dark ghosts of the old stone chimneys. I cut across the bottom of the hollow, then stopped and stared down into the first basement hole, a trap of tree trunks and old leaves caught in the corral of the four walls. I walked to the next, and the next, trying to get an idea of the shape of this little village for the first time.

Following a deer trail behind the third house I found a gravestone. When I squatted, a few more came into view. Here was the family cemetery, quiet, peaceful in the dapple of the summer woods. The standing stones had a few marks, which might once have been letters, but lichen and rain had nearly washed the old slates clean.

Some were lying flat, and when I turned one over, I found I could still read its inscription. One by one, I turned them up to the light of day, wondering what families had so forgotten their ancestors that their tombstones had fallen into disrepair.

Apparently, one of those families was mine. As I pulled one stone up and turned it over I was faced with my own obituary: Hannah Willett, April 3, 1762 - November 11, 1846.

There she is. The note-writer. The girl in the jug. I recalled the youthful scrawl on the old parchment—1776—when she wrote that note, she would have been very nearly my own age.

I dropped the stone in surprise.   It fell on its back, its inscription facing the leaf canopy over me. So, here she is.   This is Honey Hollow: she lived and died here.

That day I went home, and my brain fairly burned with my new information.   I lay on my bed, resting from the long bike trip, and fingered the button as I thought about her--about me, the other me, the girl with my name who lived so many years ago.   The girl who begged in her note to be forgiven.   The girl who was born and died in Honey Hollow, but who wrote with fear and left the note in the Van Zants' house all the way over here, in our sleepy little town.

Every day that I could, after that, I took my bike and rode over to the Hollow.   I went into each of the ruins, and searched for her book.   I didn't really think I would find it--this place had been abandoned for so long.   How could a book last? But I did find it, or maybe I should say it found me.

＊＊＊＊

It was late August.   In New Jersey, it is so hot and sultry at this time of year that even the Delaware River lies low on its banks.   So low we could walk across it splashing and leaping from rock to rock, but always being able to touch bottom.

My Mom was in bed a lot with heat headaches; my Dad was gone all day at work; Ethan was at the hardware store, the kids went to my grandma's house.   I was cleaning stalls out at the horse farm, and after I was done I would bike by the Hollow and look for Hannah's book some more.

One day, I had been up the night before reading and had to be at the barn at seven o'clock in the morning, so I guess I was sleepy.   I hid my bike, walked over to the Hollow, and found my favorite knoll of grass.   I put down a beach towel I still had in my bike pack from taking Bug and the little boys to swim in Stoney Brook.   I spread it out on the grass, and lay down with my forearm over my eyes to shield them from the stray rays of sun that made it through the leaves.

I guess I was asleep.   I felt drowsy and the next moment, the ruins around me had become houses with walls.   I could smell the waft of wood smoke and hear the low creaking query of chickens.   I was no longer in woodland, but in a dooryard, and I was walking into one of the houses--my house, it was my house.   I knew it.

I went straight to the fireplace, and opened a slit of a cupboard door where the kindling was kept.   I ran my hand down the side into its depths and checked to see if the box was still there.   I felt the stone that covered it cold against my hand, and an anguish gripped my stomach, hurling itself up from the box, through my arm and into my body until I thought I would suffocate.

I lurched up straight with a yell, gasping for air. I looked around--I was on the towel, in the woods, the chimney stones as dank and ruined as ever, and my chest tight with fear and dread.

I got up, wound the towel into a bundle and tucked it under my arm. I was no more sleeping than I was awake. I walked straight across the little clearing the way I had in the little snippet of dreamtime. The foundation I went for was notable because it was more complete than any of the others. I passed over the front door sill, and picked my way across the forest detritus that clogged its interior.

Straight to the chimney I went, straight to the kindling bin. What had once been hung with cupboard doors were now square holes. I reached my hand down into the dead leaves that filled it, and scraping, almost as in a dream, I peeled away layer upon layer.   My hand hit stone. I brushed it off; it was a piece of slate, not too big, nor too heavy for me to lift. I used two hands to slide and jostle it out of there. It covered a stone chamber.

The metal box was in there. It was cool and dry, and I wondered what fluke of nature had kept it undisturbed all these years. I carefully pried the lid off, and inside was Hannah's book.

It was small, and covered in leather, dry, dusty now with age and cracked, the color rubbed and faded. I realized that the note I had was torn from this book. I carefully turned over the old pages, afraid they might crumble in my hands.

In the beginning I saw where Hannah had practiced her letters, then she had inscribed prayers and Bible verses, and childish poems. She must have been hardly older than Bug. Near the end I saw the gap where the page had been torn out, and opened to it.

My eyes burned and watered, for the script was small, and the quill blotchy, and the language strange to me, though not foreign. On the page after the ripped out leaf, she began.

****

This is my last entry and God preserve my soul, for what I have done I have done for the preservation of good and not for evil intent. I have been a good girl and stayed home as they told us to, locked up in the house and I have only gone abroad in the company of Father.

We had heard that the foreign soldiers were come down from New York and they would rap upon the door in the dark of night and break it to enter, beating and killing and robbing all within, and so we were upon our guard. We Friends have been of a target for our refusal to bow to the authority of the enemy, and even an elder, Brother Payne, has been sorely tested to fight his enemy with his own hands and do damage that our Lord bids us not. Though Sister Morris bids us relieve the suffering of all, these are terrible times and goodness does not seem to conquer evil.   I have been a Friend since birth and have attended Meeting with my family since I was a babe in arms. In all ways I have tried to walk with God's light in me and upon me, and I have been a good and obedient daughter to my parents.   I have raised neither fist nor harsh words to those around me or my household and I have fulfilled my duty to God such as it has been taught to me.   Dear Lord, you have given me the test you gave to the Hebrews, and I shudder that I know not whither I have followed your word or blasphemed it in the most heinous way.

Me, a Godly young woman, went with the others as instructed when we heard the soldiers were marching soon to be in town.   'Twas there that I was visiting my cousin Rebekkah but nine years old to help her with her letters, and a sweet girl who likewise has walked in the Way and obeyed both mother and father.   With my dear Aunt we ran quickly from the town to the forest having nothing but the clothes on our backs, and me with my book which I am never without. There we met near a dozen other women and girls. We all sought to hide, thinking to come back to our animals when the danger had passed.

The men of the town were gone to soldiering or the Friends into hiding as they would be kilt we knew.   But in that wood we were found and sorely treated, and upon us came a crowd of the Hessian soldiers, I know not how many, but they were rough and yelling, and their faces red with the whiskey, and those awful faces clouded my fear.   I heard my dear Aunt's screams as she went down under one who began to rip upon her clothing for they were determined to molest us and lie with us.   I pulled my small cousin's hand who in her fear for her mother was stiff and not moving, but I pulled her and in our fear we ran to preserve our lives and our bodies.   I pulled her and tried to quiet her screaming but this she could not do and for all that running one of the ruffians was behind us as we broke the woods.   I saw the Van Zant farm, and I ran pulling my cousin as this beast behind us began to grab for our skirts.   He unbuckled and dropped his weapons as he cornered us before the great front door, and his trousers were untied.   He reached for my little cousin Rebekkah.   She screamed like as to I've never heard, and I grabbed his sword that was fallen. Raising it I said 'Come not further!' but he laughed like the very devil and still came.   Then he stumbled upon the flagstone step in his drunkenness and fell upon us both and roared.   Suddenly all was still, but we were pinned underneath him. My cousin sobbed, and she had relieved herself and was wet and frightened, but I could not move under his terrible weight, then I realized he had stopped roaring and was still and I began to move and push him aside.

The door behind us opened, and Mistress Van Zant exclaimed 'Dear Lord preserve us', and she began to pull upon his arms and wrestled him off us and picked us girls up hugging us and kissing us and brushing away the tears though by God she did not know our names nor the names of our fathers.   I saw then that the sword held in my hand was plunged deep into his chest and he instantly went to our Lord with eyes turned up in the sockets and a bit of blood escaped his lips.   I screamed and screamed, and Mistress Van Zant covered my mouth and held me crying and also Rebekkah, and finally said 'Stop!' in a terrible voice and I stopped.   She said we must hide the wicked soldier or we would all meet our maker at the hands of that army.

We pulled on him, even Rebekkah, and we pulled him into the house and to the door to the cellar hole and threw him down, then went ourselves there, and Mistress Van Zant had us push him into the stone cupboard by the chimney block where the preserves are stored, all hers hidden now from pillage. We pushed him into the chair, and I tore a leaf from my book and wrote a note to excuse all who might find him. We shut the cupboard door, and went up to clean whatever blood we could find. And then we gathered rocks from the wall and hid in the cellar with Mistress Van Zant while she piled them into the door and mixing the mortar she slopped it on and soon there was a wall where the cupboard had been.

All the while we prayed and she told us that we must never tell what we had seen for it would come to no good for us or her. And she said that God knew all and had preserved us from our terrible fate by placing the sword in my hand and I was not to think I had sinned, for surely, I could see that I had saved my Rebekkah's life and virtue to say nothing of my own. Mistress Van Zant said God had even preserved her in the house waiting for me, when the rest of the family had gone down to Philadelphia to hide with relatives, but she had stayed back in her sick bed with one horse hidden and even now had just begun to pack to leave.

For this, I thank the dear Lord for her kind words and our preservation for we know not if our mothers live or die, but I beg you, Lord, if I have done wrong in your sight to strike me down that I may not live to see. Signed by herself September 19, 1776, Hannah Willet, fourteen years old.

****

Here the words tattered off in a blotch of ink. I held the book in my hands, also the cover and the box it was in, that had preserved it from the damp. It was dry and not rotted, just the leather powdery with age. I hugged it to my chest, and wept for my poor namesake, Hannah Willet, fourteen years old like me, and frightened beyond anything I could have imagined— frightened as I had been in the nightmare the jug brought me the first night I had it. I thought of the many times we girls at school complained of our parents warning us not to be alone, not to go out in the woods without company, to come home before dark. We laughed and pooh-poohed their over-protection of us, for what could happen in such a small town as ours? Nothing had ever happened here, we laughed.

But it did. Hannah Willett says so.

I lingered, not knowing if I should take Hannah's book, or if I should return it to its hiding place, where she herself had placed it all those years ago. At last, I put it back, thinking that I knew where it was, and I would decide later whether to keep it for my own, my own namesake.

****

September comes upon the Jersey midlands with all the deadly heat of August. Then, as the air dries out towards the end of the month, the leaves begin to turn and the grasses bleach out to tan. By the time the first frost winds of October blow in, the colors on the maples and oaks make you catch your breath.

It is my favorite time of year, for all the lush growth of the summer has acquired a jubilant color, and unlike a slow sad dying into winter, it is a mad explosion of triumph. I spent many hours on my bicycle in the fall, revisiting my old haunts. I went to Honey Hollow so many times then, and pulled the book out and read it again.

School had started and I, of course, hated school with a passion. I gazed out the old double-hung panes of the school windows at the distant beckoning fall trees. I spent my Saturday mornings volunteering at the library. In the last sunny, warm days, I had those mornings virtually free of distraction, as no one came in when the other choice was the deliciousness of a mid-Atlantic fall day.

The library was crowded into the back of the old firehouse, an ancient brick building trimmed with white and decked out with nooks and crannies and gingerbread, like all the buildings of that ornate age just before the turn of the 20th century. The small rooms were shelved floor to ceiling with books. They held me in thrall.

I could spend hours just loafing from shelf to shelf, reading titles, picking up books, scanning through them. A world lay at my fingertips. There was nothing more wonderful for me than my job re-shelving: I got to look at all the books that others had taken out, books and subjects I might never think to look for on my own.

One Saturday there was nothing for me to do after some perfunctory shelving, so I read behind the circulation desk. Miss Reed, the head librarian, was there on Saturdays, and I heard her greeting Mrs. Hurlbut as she came in.

"What is it today, Eleanor?" she said in her reedy bird voice.

"The Evening Post, Gwen, I want to re-check the Evening Post." The two elderly women tick-tick-ticked their way to the back of the library in their black sensibly heeled shoes, their flowered jersey dresses swishing around them like a breeze. At the door to the mysterious always-locked room that had a small neatly hand-inked card reading "Employees Only" taped to it, Miss Reed turned and beckoned me.

"Hannah, come with us, dear." She unlocked the mysterious room, and I dutifully went in. Floor to ceiling were shelves, and on them were stacks of old newspapers, journals, and books that looked as if they had been made by Moses himself. A strange dry smell emanated from the room; it was close, dead air in there.

"Sit here, dear." Miss Reed motioned me to the old wooden table that took up the entire center of the room.   "I want you to stay with Mrs. Hurlbut and should she need anything, you come out and tell me."

I sat down obediently.   Mrs. Hurlbut always knew exactly what she wanted, so this might turn out to be a demanding morning.   Going over to a pile of newspapers, she lifted a short stack of them covered with slips of paper with handwritten notes, obviously something she had been working on.

I sat silently, and she situated herself across the table from me.   I remembered her well, and she me, and we chatted some about what I would be doing in high school.   I was in that strange, sullen period of all fourteen- year-olds where everyone you have known for your entire life suddenly becomes suspicious.   I held back some.

Mrs. Hurlbut was nothing if not an experienced teacher, so she soon dropped the pleasantries and bent down to her work.

"Hannah," she said presently, looking up, "there is no reason for you to be bored.   Here, have a look at these pages.   I have an extra pair of gloves you can wear.   Turn each page slowly and carefully, avoid touching them with your fingers.   If something is too hard to turn, just do it slowly."

She opened her purse and took a pair of white gloves out of a little cellophane bag, and I put them on.   They were strange to turn paper with, for they made me clumsy.   But I began to peruse the first salmon-colored old newspaper.   The Pennsylvania Evening Post it said, and I saw the date, 28 December, 1776.

I began to read, and suddenly something caught my eye.   Extract of a letter from an officer of distinction in the American Army… "Since I wrote you this morning, I have had an opportunity of hearing a number of the particulars of the horrid depredations committed by that part of the British army, which was stationed at and near Pennytown under the command of Lord Cornwallis.   Besides the sixteen young women who had fled to the woods to avoid their brutality, and were there seized and carried off, one man had the cruel mortification to have his wife and only daughter (a child of ten years of age) ravished.   This he himself, almost choked with grief, uttered in lamentations to his friends. They told me of it, and also informed me that another girl of thirteen years of age was taken from her father's house, carried to a barn about a mile, there ravished, and afterwards made use of by five more of these brutes…."

The words seemed to jump all over the page, for Hannah Willett's note kept coming before my eyes, the cramped, desperate handwriting, the terror it expressed.   I found a later issue, April 24, 1777.   In Congress, April 18, 1777.   The Committee appointed to inquire into the conduct of the enemy beg leave to report…Fourth, the lust and brutality of the soldiers in abusing of women….

So it was true.   It was here in the old newspaper, what had happened to the girls and women of our town, Pennington, back when it was Pennytown.   At that time, Honey Hollow was a thriving village, during those terrible years when the peaceful Quakers and other settlers of this area had been torn by war.   This was not what we had learned about the Revolutionary War in school, and not what our village had turned out to celebrate.   We had only learned about George Washington, and marching soldiers, and the bravery of the crossing of the Delaware. That was only a thin veneer that masked the ugly truth.   Nothing had ever been said to us about what happened to the women and girls in a colonial America occupied by Hessian and English troops.

"What is it, Hannah?" When Mrs. Hurlbut asked the question, I realized I had been staring at her, holding her responsible for the secret.

"Nothing," I said, "It's just that--when you read it in the paper here, it seems different than we studied it in school."

Mrs. Hurlbut's face broke into a delighted smile.   "Yes, Hannah Willett, things are not always what they seem in school.   If you are going to find the truth, you must do it on your own." She turned back to her work, but I could see the smile on her face for many minutes more.

I wore that same smile, years later, teaching college, when a student told me that the version of women's history I had just introduced to the class "was all the out-takes from anything I've ever learned about history in school." I knew that was a student who would be searching on her own from then on.

After that Saturday with Mrs. Hurlbut in the library, I returned again and again for the rest of my high school years to help her with her research.   Then I was seventeen, and almost ready to leave for college.   I didn't know what lay in store for the slowly decomposing structures of Honey Hollow.   Hidden by vines and the woods, they disappeared a little each year.   Around them, farmland was being eaten up by housing developments.

****

In the end, I took Hannah Willett's box and book out of the chimney cupboard in Honey Hollow.   I took her things to Mrs. Hurlbut.   We met in the library, as usual.   I walked in one Saturday morning with the box and the book, and I knocked softly on the research room door.

Mrs. Hurlbut was always glad to see me.   I pushed the box and book towards her.

"What have we here?" she asked.   So I told her.

I suppose I could have kept the book and box with me everywhere I went for my adult life—across the continental United States, to Europe, and back again.   I could have gotten a lockbox at the bank, where the controlled air would preserve them as well as could be. But I wanted a place that could be their permanent home.

When I left Mrs. Hurlbut that morning, slipping quietly out of the research room door so I wouldn't be late for work, her eyes and cheeks glistened with tears as she read Hannah's book. I found Hannah's things a home with her, in a library situated in the lush Jersey midlands where both of us Hannah Willets grew up. A safe place for telling secrets that should be told.

19.
Hooked On Bionics
Mark Hudson

The Elvis impersonator was trapped in the Japanese robotics factory. How he got there, was a story worth explaining. But isn't everything that is true about Earth, true as well beyond Earth?

Nobody had heard of Elvis Presley in the future. In fact, America as whole was left powerless over the superpowers that ruled the world. The Elvis impersonator had come to Japan to pretend to perform, but really he was a secret spy.

The Elvis impersonator was an odd relic of the ancient days, before machines ruled with an iron fist.

The robotic judge summoned the Elvis impersonator before it. He was shackled in chains. "Speak or sing, Elvis impersonator!" the robot said.

The Elvis impersonator sang, "Love me tender, love me tender," in a human, melodic voice.

The robotic judge listened, and a silver tear came out of its robotic eye. Then pretty soon, his robotic face got wet and the machine malfunctioned. As his wires crackled, he screamed out, "Who loves you, baby?" and died.

The Elvis impersonator threw his disguise off, and said, "Come on, Kulak! There's no time to lose! Grab the laser guns! We're heading into the pit of the factory!"

Suddenly, a big face on the screen appeared. It was a Japanese woman, or was it a robot that was a look-alike? "You will not escape from me! I'm Big Sister!"
"Big Sister? Whatever happened to Big Brother?"

"That was my brother. But I killed him, and now I'm in charge!"

"What's your position?"

"I'm playing chess, and you're the chess piece! I will take you to the prison of this factory, where I use my special torture devices to create running colors of red, your blood!"

The Japanese matriarch, Big Sister, led the Elvis impersonator down the robotic factory steps into a dungeon. Once there, she tied him up to a medieval torture device.

"What is this?" he stammered.

"It's a form of torture. I press this button, and feathers come and tickle your feet. Are you ticklish?"

"I don't know. I guess I never gave it much thought."

"Well, who do you work for?"

"Myself."

"That's a lie. I'll torture you till you confess." She pressed the button. But it didn't turn on.

"Oh, darn! The batteries have run out!"

"Well, what kind of torture is tickling someone's feet, anyway?'

"Just one we use. But I guess I'll just have to resort to water-boarding."
"Sorry, the only surfing I do is on the internet."

"You'll be lucky if you ever see so much as a calculator again!"

"That's what my high school algebra teacher said."

"I know. I kidnapped her once. She cooked some great sushi for the Ambassador from Mercury."

"You mean she's dead?"

"No, she's just in a very deep sleep. But there are plenty of robots that look like her, talk like her, act like her! We cloned her DNA! And she is our model for a decent algebra teacher."

"So what does that mean, the robotic teachers are just as good at torturing kids with homework, as their former human teachers?"

"Who said anything about children? We work so hard here in the robotics factory that we don't have any time for children. If anybody has children, they are given the maximum tutoring available in a locked-down environment."

"What about recess? What about breathing air, seeing nature?"

"Air? Nature? What are these things?"

"All right, you are losing me here."

"Well, you're in luck," said Big Sister. "We can't find the water board. But you're going to have to deal with the robotic hand!"

"Oh, I'm so intimated." said the Elvis impersonator.

"You will be, once you see it. Dubbed It after a famous American TV show, this electric hand has a mind of its own. It can tickle you, probe you, punch you, and it is a master torturer with needles. Are you going to tell me who you work for, or do I need to bring out the hand?"

"Give me a hand, lady."

You're very smug! All I have to do is press this button and the floating hand will come flying out of the ceiling!"

"Hurry up, I'm getting bored!"

"Men! They're so egotistical! Come to me, my little hand!"

A robotic hand came flying through the air from a little hole in the ceiling. For three hours, it beat, poked, prodded, and stuck little pins in the Elvis Impersonator. Finally, he just wimped out. "Okay, fine, I'll tell you who I'm working for."

"America."

"That's not specific enough. Be more specific."

"Okay, fine. I'll admit it. Sharky Malone's Bar and Grill. I was doing karaoke as Elvis to try and pay back the mob boss who ran the whole operation. But it backfired. I couldn't make a dime doing my Elvis impersonations. In fact, people paid the bar to refuse to let me sing. So Sharky said if I went as a spy to Japan, he'd forgive the debt I owed him."

"Why did he want to spy on Japan?"

"Well, because Japan and America are at war."
"No, we're not! You Americans are so dumb! Don't you ever read the newspapers?"

"No!"

"Sounds like they played a really cruel practical joke on you! How would you like to get revenge?"

"I wouldn't. Sharky is really sneaky. If I tried to screw him over one more time he might make me eat sand again."

"Sand? What does he live on the beach?"

"Yes. We're talking about Miami beach, Florida."

"Is he a gangster?"

"Well, he tries to be. But he's better than me. I'm just an Elvis impersonator. I can't even drink a shot of tequila without throwing up."

"But does he have a lot of money?"

"Yes. But he gets it all illegally. Look, why are you interested? Aren't you Big Sister? Don't you have all the money in the world?"

"No, just most of it. But you've given me some ideas. We can rob Sharky and steal his money, and be rich. And you can maybe be my lover, if you take off that goofy Elvis costume."

"Sounds like a plan that won't work. Besides, I love my Elvis costume. I go to sleep in it. The only time I take it off is when I shower."

"Well, let me take your Elvis wig off and see what you look like without it."

"I'm bald, and I have sunspots from global warming."

"Okay. We'll leave the wig on. Come to think of it, I like your wig. Did you know I wear a wig? Take a look at what I look like without a wig." Big Sister removed her wig, revealing an electronic visible mass of swirling circuits of neurons all connected by some higher-up genius in some unknown location.

"You mean, you really are a robot? Gross! I'm out of here!" The Elvis impersonator busted open the door, went racing down the hallway, and Big Sister sent the electronic hand flying after him. It put a stranglehold around his neck, and he fell to the floor.

"You will not escape as easy as you think." said Big Sister. "I can make you do anything I want. But you've made me mad. Tonight we'll sleep in private bedrooms. But don't try anything funny. I've got the whole room monitored by cameras. Good night."

With that, the Elvis impersonator seemed to be transported to a cold, iron room with with a bed and a toilet, and just a sink, but not even a shower. How could this be worse? He was a captive of a robotic woman who had a crush on him, and if he didn't obey, her machines would crush him! He began to toss on his bed. Why did Sharky send him here? Was it punishment for singing out of tune? For driving his customers away? For the money he owed the bar for his gambling and drug debt?

He had no answers. Maybe Big Sister was right. He should want revenge. But was this what the world had come down to in 2050, you never knew who was a robot or a human, and humans always seemed to be the ones who were constantly befuddled?

A line from an Elvis song came to the Elvis impersonator,

"I'm caught in a trap, I can't look back, because I love you too much baby."

The impersonator thought of Big Sister taking off the wig, and showing that display of circuitry connecting all those robotic wires, and he said out loud, "Yuck!" and with that, he fell asleep, as Big Sister watched him from a hidden camera, looking for body motions that would symbolize signs of betrayal.

"Wake up, elfin scumbag!"

"That's Elvis, to you!"

"Here, wake up and have a shower." Big Sister dumped a bucket of water on Elvis.

"Hey, ow! Why'd you do that?"

"Time to rob Sharky. Let's go to Miami."

They got into a space capsule against the better judgment of Elvis. The space capsule went down a tunnel, and flew out into outer space, with the darkness of space only lit by dimly visible stars.

"I'm scared." said Elvis.

"That's why I'm wearing the pants in this operation," said Big Sister. "Do as I say, not as I do. Or perhaps, do as I say, and do as I do. Learn how to do crime like me. We can be like Bonny and Clyde."

"But Sharky will kill us!" complained Elvis.

"I will have nothing of giving Sharky the upper hand," replied Big Sister. "We are partners now. Now, give me a big kiss, baby."

A mechanical tongue that looked like a silver lizard-like tongue crept out of Big Sister's mouth, and twirled around in the air, reminding Elvis of the scene in 101 Dalmatians where two mutts kissed with spaghetti.

Elvis lost his lunch, and a plethora of vomit floated though the air, and landed on Big Sister's face.

"What is that vile fluid?" screamed Big Sister. "It's in my eyes!" Big Sister put her hands to her eyes, and realized the vomit had blinded her eyes. She fell to the ground, writhing in pain.

Suddenly, the space ship lurched and went through a black hole. Big Sister writhed in pain, and it was apparent that her brains were short-circuiting. Elvis wasn't paying attention to the controls of the space-ship, so horrified was he by the disfigurement of his captor.

Big Sister's body flinched back and forth, and then it became perfectly still. Elvis could tell she or it was dead. He was so full of relief, that he forgot that he was in an unpiloted spaceship. He turned around and let out a shriek. He was entering a black hole, or a time warp, beyond his human reckoning. He put his space ship in auto pilot, went and got into his bunk, and strapped himself in, going to sleep, and preparing to wake up to the absolute worst.

The Elvis impersonator woke up millennium later, and he wondered where he was. He put on his spacesuit, grabbed his laser gun, and left his spaceship. He wandered off, forgetting his spaceship in the place he crashed.

He walked a little ways, and a bunch of space aliens approached him, and they revered him as if he were a god. They all looked like human beings.

"Where am I?" said the Elvis impersonator.

"You have landed on the planet of eternal reruns," said a space alien. "We've been expecting you. It's been pre-destined that you come here to be king. And here is the woman to be your wife, Lucille Ball."

A Lucille Ball impersonator appeared and a wedding began to take place, before the Elvis impersonator knew what was happening. "What's happening? I never wanted to get married. Whatever happened to Ricky?"

"He's married to another rerun hologram," said Lucille Ball. "But lover, you're all mine!"

So the marriage took place, and a different Elvis impersonator sang, "I'm caught in a trap." And the Elvis impersonator was. He was another prisoner on the planet of eternal reruns, never to escape. But each day would be like Groundhog Day, but would he really know? Who knows? Sometimes, it just felt like the Elvis impersonator had taken one step beyond into "The Twilight Zone."

20.
I Am Frankenstein
A.J. Huffman

Electric life
        pumping
         light, beckoning
through the dark. I am child
of maniacal mind, but I have
purpose. I focus. I am energy
contracting, releasing, the lightning's
crack, injecting. I am the intersection
of breath
and brain
death. I am walking body
parts. I am monster
             of everyone else's making.

21.
I Am Ghost
A.J. Huffman

of raven wings, a blinding black hologram
haunting deserted planes of my own mind.
I am flightless, condemned
to flutter like a charred butterfly,
inches above grassless fields,
infinities below flowing skies.   I am miles
beyond salvation, condemned to an eternity
in a transparent hell.   My only reprieve
is a repeated act of desperation,
a forward thrusting, splaying my body
as if it were becoming
part of the glass.

22.
In The Shadow of Sasquatch
Michael Berton

walking evolution's footprint
one size fits all predators
a world of giants & gnomes
human migration
tracking bone & dung
shedding skins
hunting magic
savage intoxicants
earth's backwash
all that is ingested
recycles as nutrients

graphite pixels
supernova sonar
high definition dna
organic tuning
a new constellation
frontal lobe sweating
an etch-a-sketch pattern

tumble in the belly
suicide reverb
in the gargantuan's ear
secret lives of inanimate
objects diagrammed
on the blackboard
dead screen echo
cerebral humming

23.
Intergalactic Guests
Norbert Gora

Silvery glow,
like a meteor shower,
flashed in the sky.

Flying leviathan
appeared in the front of his eyes,
burned his heart on the fire of dismay.

Rumor of the rotating engines,
made of alien technology,
choked his throat claws of fear.

Festival of lights, show of emotions,
ignorance tapped into his heart,
like a drum roll.

Intergalactic guests from distant reaches of
galaxy
fell down from the sky on the forest ground,
wanted to say hello to the new world.

His scream pierced the air like a needle
material,
seeing this thing from the depths of cosmos,
it had no head, just a bloody pumpkin, eyes
radiated the scarlet.

In his brain stabbed the message,
telepathy curtain obscured his mind,
with a stranger existence tried to tame.

Guest from the planet of wonders
had no intentions of good,
from the pumpkin dripped the blood.

His last thoughts were deadly for us,
for them it was the beginning,
for us it meant the end of the theatre of
existence.

24.
Investigation
Norbert Gora

The walls of home closed his invisible eyes,
the smell of crime penetrated them,
like a ghost, shape created of the energy,
unable to solve unresolved.

Commissioner moved his gaze,
trying to pierce the body,
trying to find the definitive proof.

The fumes of horror hung in the air,
the feeling of the next wave of blood spilling,
waited in a corner, like a monster.

The soul did not want to go
through the gate of eternity,
in the body, like satanic virus, has jammed.

Policeman leaned over the dead,
then it happened,
pale hands touched his neck, wanted to
wrap it like a silk scarf.

Shout of horror tore the air, at a thousand
parts,
heart speeded up,
beating as fast as a car engine.

Was he undead or resurrected?
It was for him nothing more,
then the snow dust in the wind dancing.

The eyes from the dead arose,
looked at him angrily,
thousands of questions was moving over his
head, like a battle ram.

Investigation with the nightmare in the
background,
his heart was knocking with the power of
piston,
mind was yelling: "get away from there, get
away from there!."

25.
Jean Jacques
Moshe Sonnheim

We met Jean Jacques by chance. New to the city, we asked him for directions. Tall and slender, he cut an impressive figure.

His aquiline nose was set in a handsome face, topped by grayish-blonde hair beneath a white fedora. Impeccably-dressed, with a silver-topped walking stick, he seemed reminiscent of an earlier era.

His dulcet voice calmed our fears of a new life and a new place. He invited us to dine with him in an outdoor café and chatted amiably with us for hours. Thus began a friendship which could last for years.

As we settled in, Jean Jacques continued to meet with us in the same café. His blue eyes sparkled with nostalgia as he regaled us with tales of days gone by---of beautiful women and handsome men, of Grand Balls and gay soirees.

Winter approached; the beginning of a new year and a new century brought an invitation from Jean Jacques to farewell the old, and ring in the new. Oddly enough, we had never visited his apartment. The door would be open, he said, and he gave us detailed instructions how to get there.

Snow fell gently as we carefully crossed a boulevard teeming with speeding cars. In the middle was a great swath of green, bordered again with a teeming boulevard. As we crossed, an imposing Victorian building loomed opposite us. In the hotel was Jean Jacques' apartment. There was, however, no doorman and no elevator boy. Nor did the elevator work. As we trudged up the stairs to the eighth floor, we noticed no signs of other people. Moreover, there was a strange odor of decay beyond the magnificent exterior of the building.

As promised, Jean Jacques' door was open. He was not yet there. On the wall hung a framed photograph of a beautiful young woman lying vampishly on a sofa. In a corner, a Grand piano stood ready for playing. On its top stood a framed photograph of a wizened old woman who once may have been beautiful. The rest of the apartment was empty; Jean Jacques was nowhere to be found.

At the stroke of midnight, the hotel came to life. Lights were everywhere. Sounds of music, singing, laughter, and dancing reverberated through its empty halls. Jean Jacques was still nowhere to be found.

Then, all fell silent.

We never saw Jean Jacques again!

26.
Joy of The Worm
William Doreski

The chill in the barn this morning
reminds me of your handshake.
"I wish you all joy of the worm,"
you joked at the corner of Seventh
and Thirty-Third. I schlepped my bags
to Forty-Second, caught the bus
to Boston, and have seen you since
only in People magazine
with lovers dangling like rosaries.

You wished me joy of the worm,
but you were Cleopatra and I
the clown, my uncouth antics
the rage of Manhattan although
no one remembered me from one drink
to the next, our black-clad mob
smitten with the Warhol aesthetic
that rendered private ego moot.

Now on a skittish April Sunday
I feel the ghost of your ghost
fluttering in the rafters where
already mud-daubers work
their papier-mâché wonders.
Your unlisted phone number rattles
in my head, but I'll never call.
The worm, the deadly aspic,
coils around my tender organs,
but after all these sullen decades
has grown too decadent to strike.

No joy but in the unraveling
of the many tiny mysteries
that inspire the daily grind:
the wasps at work, your shadow
in the rafters, the hard light
rusting through the hayloft, the lisp
of snowmelt in roadside ditches,
and the linger of that handshake
more fatal than any bite.

27.
Legally Dead
Chris Scattergood
A Fool's Guide to Salvation

It was bizarre. I fell off the roof. If I had to die young, why wasn't it saving some kid in a fire? I'd have settled for being run down by a drunk. At least that would have been tragic. All I had was a dining out story. 'Did you hear? He did a triple axel off the roof while putting up the Christmas lights. The French judge gave him five point eight.'

I have to say it didn't hurt; I guess souls don't feel pain. My head bounced off the sidewalk, and that was that. The next I knew I was standing outside my body, watching Marion hover around it and scream. There was a neighbour with a cell phone, then the sirens and after that, two paramedics came and scooped me up. It was then I panicked. I didn't want my body taken from me so I tried to get inside the ambulance. It was too late. I heard the heavenly choir and after that I was zooming upwards, going to the light.

It took some time to get myself together, but once my mind cleared I could see this massive archway. Above it was a clock with just a minute hand, now at sixteen past the hour. I heard the choir sing a final perfect note and then came utter peace. The air was still and warm and smelt like sage behind the rain, and I could hear this calming voice explaining that around a hundred people die each minute, and here we were. That was why the clock had just the minute hand. All across the world, time had stopped for us at sixteen past. For some strange reason, I thought about Newfoundland with its half hour standard time; and wondered if the people there died thirty minutes later. Perhaps they had to use another entrance? I giggled with embarrassment. This place felt far too holy for my jokes.

Soon enough I sensed that we were moving forward, all of us who died at sixteen past the hour. We were being swept towards this giant, solemn figure guarding two pathways. Some of us were ushered to the left but most flowed smoothly to the right. At first, I felt quite reassured to be among the larger group, I must be in the chosen, but soon the shapes beside me started to get agitated, their shadowy faces mouthing silent screams. Then the light began to fade, and the path turned down. The smell turned sour, and the air grew cold and filled with grit that stung my face. Next, this wall of utter blackness rushed towards me, and I panicked. Was I going to hell? Now travelling even faster and screaming in terror, I slammed into this net.

Instantly I rebounded, careening backwards and spinning violently. At first, there was an overwhelming sense of speed and chaos, but then all motion ceased and everything went back to being calm and warm and scented as before. I was in this formless, all-white room and there beside me was this smallish, shimmering presence. For a moment we had silence then it seemed to speak inside my head.

"Hello," it said, "don't be afraid. You're safe now, you're in my care. My name is Halaliel. I'm a scribe, an angel who keeps records, and I work with recalls. There's been a glitch. We moved you here too soon. As of now, you're only legally dead so you'll need to go into holding."

For the first while, I just gaped but then I managed to stammer, "Is this some crazy dream?" When I tried to speak it felt like I was shrieking, the terror of hell still on me.

"Just relax and keep focused on me. You're confused right now as well as frightened. It might help you understand your situation if I took you on a field trip. Come with me."

He motioned in my direction, and we rose together, gliding from the room and just as quickly, we were flying above a huge but unfamiliar city. He guided me to what was obviously a hospital, and we floated through its structure, coming to a stop inside a sombre, half-lit room overrun with cables, tubes and hoses, glowing monitors and LED displays. I could hear a ventilator wheezing and the hum of more equipment, and I caught the smell of disinfectant mixed with urine. Everywhere I looked was stainless steel and plastic, but in among the clutter was my body hooked to anything that didn't move.

"What's going on here?" My terror was subsiding but not my confusion.

"When you hit the concrete, you sustained a head injury. That's what killed you. The rest of your body is fine, hardly damaged, lots of useful parts. You were quite young, late-thirties, a non-smoker, reasonably fit, no Olympic athlete but still in decent condition. You'd fetch a good price in many cultures."

"What do you mean?"

"You're being harvested. They have a match for both your heart and your lungs though neither recipient is fully ready at this time. As you may know, these are organs that depreciate rapidly once they leave the host. Outside your body, there's about a six-hour window before they risk becoming useless, so you'll be kept on life support until the others reach the operating room. Left to yourself, you would have died, but since there was a pressing need for your organs, the surgeons put you back on life support then signed off on irreparable brain stem damage. That's why the confusion, up above we don't call time of death until the heart stops."

"You mean they're carving me up for parts, and I'm not yet dead?"

"That's a fine point to argue. Most medical authorities are comfortable with brain stem damage. You've been declared legally dead; ethical enough for what they need to do. Don't complain. If you'd been actually dead, you'd now be in hell."

"Who said they could carve me up?"

"Marion, of course. As your wife, she has standing."

"Marion said that. Why would she say that?"

"Well, given how badly your head was injured, nobody wanted an open casket."

"What's that got to do with them cutting me up?"

"She's also ticked at you. Don't forget, you have a history. Remember when you broke your arm trying to jump your bike onto the curb. Then there was the time you set fire to the garden shed by brazing copper tubing next to a can of paint thinner, you still have the scars from that, and when you wrote off the car by using cruise control on an icy road. You were often careless, and in the end, that attitude has cost her your companionship. Right now she's angry with you. I think her actual words were – 'take whatever you want, perhaps he's useful now he's dead; he was a waste of skin when he was alive.'"

"That's a bit over the top, isn't it?"

"Perhaps she over-reacted, but anger is a valid part of the grief cycle. You must admit that yours was a foolish way to die. I'm certain she'll come round soon, she cares about you deeply, but surely you can see her point."

No, I could not. I was furious. Saying what she did was completely disrespectful and as for carving up my body, the doctors should be caring for me. Priming myself to wallow in self-righteousness, I was about to tell him how I felt but got cut off when Halaliel said, "Now that I've explained your situation, we must return. At this moment, your journey to hell is on hold but in a few hours, they'll harvest your organs then terminate life support. Once that happens, you'll die almost instantly and resume your descent unless there's now some reason not to. That gives you the chance to save yourself but only if you take it."

We went back to the all-white room and hung around for a while. At first, I just stared at him. I knew he was expecting something from me, but I'd no idea what it was. In the end, he gave up waiting and asked, "Were you surprised to find that you'd been sent to hell? More than just afraid of going there, had you always thought you'd be in heaven?"

"Honestly, I'd never really given it much thought."

"Don't you think you ought to since you're at the gates of hell?"

It was the wrong thing to say. When I heard that, I froze. If I had a hundred pieces of brain, three were working on my situation, but the other ninety-seven were drowning in fear. I think he must have guessed that since he followed up with, "I can see you're struggling. Let me try to guide you through this, if that's okay with you?" It was okay with me, I was desperate for guidance. In the past I'd never thought about such things; I'd always seen them as a waste of time. It seems that I was wrong, and now I had to learn new skills. If we were going anywhere with this, he'd have to take the lead.

He spoke again. "I'm guessing that however you imagined heaven, you've never before doubted you'd be going there."

That was true. While I'd never thought too much about God or the afterlife, some part of me had always assumed there was a heaven, and that I'd be in it. *What was heaven like?* I'd no idea but it had to beat the competition. *What did it take to get there?* I wasn't sure, but it must be about being good. *What else was there, but if that was how it worked, why had I been rerouted?* I'd never done anything really bad, not like some people. I'd always tried to be a decent person. Surely that was good enough, or so I told Halaliel.

"So you think you're not a bad person, not perhaps as good as Gandhi or Mother Teresa but certainly better than Stalin or Charles Manson. Morally, you're kind of average so everything depends on where God draws the line."

"What do you mean?"

"Well, it's like you're saying heaven must have some grading system, and you believe you'd done enough to get a pass mark. It seems not since you and most of your intake were bound for hell, which itself raises an interesting point. Do you think God ought to be doing that, sending people to hell?"

"Now you mention it, no I don't."

"Why not?"

"Well, isn't God supposed to be about love? If hell's this awful place, why would a loving God send people there?"

"So, in your view, being a loving God means having no standards? He ought to be this nice old guy who just wants everyone happy."

"I never said that."

"Actually, you did. You said He should let in everyone however badly they'd behaved in this life. Why would He do that? Heaven is His home. Doesn't He get to say who He wants for company? In a way, you share that view."

"How do you mean?"

"You loved your kids, didn't you, but you wouldn't let them do whatever they wanted. Part of love is discipline and standards. You certainly believed that though in practice, except when you were angry, you mostly let Marion be the bad guy."

"Now you're just winding me up." I felt myself becoming irritated.

Halaliel stopped talking and stared at me until I calmed down. Eventually he said, "You'd better tell me what you do believe. Let's start with the basics. In your opinion, how do you think a person gets to heaven?"

"Well, I don't believe you do it by hanging around in churches and all that nonsense. They're just a bunch of hypocrites, acting so holy. They're no better than anyone else."

"So you never actively worshipped God in the company of other people."

"You don't need to go to church to connect with God."

"But you do believe in God?"

"Oh yes, I think there's more to this world than what we can see." I felt strangely righteous as I confirmed the existence of God.

"Without putting words in your mouth, would you perhaps describe yourself as being spiritual but not religious?"

I thought that over and liked it. "Yes," I said, "I'd go with that."

Halaliel seemed to sigh as if he'd heard that said too often. I was thinking he might want a better attitude but before I had the chance to tell him he began again. "Can we start by ruling out certain options? For the sake of argument, let's assume you eat pork, you were never circumcised, and you've never been to Mecca. Is that correct?"

He didn't wait for my answer; he knew it anyway. "Okay," he said, "Let's rule out Islam and Judaism. So moving on, we need to deal with the accident."

"What are you talking about?"

"Perhaps I should backtrack. Your claim to be spiritual implies some sympathy perhaps with Eastern beliefs?" He paused for me to contradict him. When I said nothing, he resumed. "However, being spiritual in the Eastern tradition is intimately involved with developing your higher consciousness, transcending its various levels until you can comprehend the working of the divine plan. Such development requires a regimen of spiritual practices so I have to ask, did you do much meditation?"

"I was always too busy making a living."

"Hmm," he said and waited for me to speak. Again, I had nothing to add so he resumed. "There is a second problem. Many from the West mistakenly assume reincarnation is always onwards and upwards. In reality, the path to enlightenment is a constant struggle involving many hardships and setbacks. The nature of your demise, dying while young in a freak accident, has the flavor of bad Karma so if you did reincarnate, you understand it might be as a rodent."

That was one insult too many and I let him know I'd had enough. It was followed by a minute of strained silence before he said, "I can see I've hurt your feelings. That is an odd position for you to take. You are standing on the brink of hell but choosing instead to focus on your bruised ego. I would say my work is now complete. I shall pass you to Gamaliel."

That suited me; I was happy to have someone new. For one thing, Gamaliel at least looked like an angel. He was tall and stately and had an air of mystery, not like the undersized Halaliel who'd also done nothing except insult me. Maybe this guy could move things forward. "Okay," I said, "what happens now?"

"You'd be surprised how much progress has been made. Most of the clutter is gone. I should tell you Christianity will be your only hope for escaping hell. All the other religions looked for effort from you in your earthly life, and as you said, you weren't much into that. Salvation through Christ remains possible as long as you still breathe, which also means we need to hurry. My expertise is in grace and forgiveness which is where your hope lies, though I can see your ego is going to be a problem."

"What are you telling me now?" I could see this guy was every bit as pompous as the last one. Perhaps all angels have to take a special course in arrogance.

"Let me explain. You admit you were irritated by Halaliel. Irritation implies some felt need to defend self-concept. Defensiveness does not suggest humility, and in your situation humility is essential."

"I don't know about being defensive. He started it. He kept talking down to me, trying to make me look shallow and stupid."

"You understand you are about to petition the maker of the universe for your salvation."

"That's different. I'll be respectful then. I know how to behave."

"So you say. I would remind you that a precursor of humility is personal honesty. Is there any basis for the charge of being shallow? Remember, we are trying to save your immortal soul."

That remark stung but he had a point. If I were honest, I'd have to admit I hadn't thought enough about this sort of thing while still alive. I apologized and promised I'd try harder in future, an offer that I'd often made before in life.

He accepted and continued to explain. "Imagine a ladder leading from earth to heaven. By your good works in this life, you hope to climb the ladder. Incidentally, you're quite right about not needing a church in the way you conceive of church. While all religions share a common desire to be good, if a person can climb this ladder by his own efforts then they contribute little to the process. So far, does that make sense?"

It did, it made perfect sense. If souls can nod, then I nodded.

"So the issue becomes – how far up this ladder must you climb to prove to God you've earned the right to be in heaven? Now since it's His heaven, it's His rules for entry, but given that a loving God wouldn't keep the rules secret, you should expect to find them in His holy book. We'd said earlier that Christianity applied in your case, which makes the Bible the holy book of record. What are your thoughts about the Bible?"

"I never read it much, the language was too weird, but it seemed to be full of smiting and funny names, and things you weren't supposed to do."

Gamaliel appeared to sigh but then continued. "The Book of Isaiah claims it was written no later than the reign of Hezekiah, king of Judah, and as we all know, he died in 687 BC." He paused for effect, but that didn't work. I hadn't found it funny. He started again. "In chapter 45, Isaiah writes that someone called Cyrus would free the Israelite captives from slavery and help them return and rebuild Jerusalem, and in fact, Cyrus the Great of Persia did exactly that when he conquered Babylon in 539 BC, one hundred and fifty years later. Here's my point. The Bible didn't just guess at these details; it got the man's name right. That's beyond all coincidence leaving you with only two possible explanations – either the Bible is divinely inspired, or it is a fraud written after the fact, and my question to you is which do you believe?"

"I don't know. I never thought about it."

"I know I'm not supposed to prompt you but do you recall going to the light and then being in the company of angels?"

"What are you getting at?"

"Does that perhaps speak to the supernatural?"

"I guess."

"So there is a supernatural?"

"Sure."

"And about the Bible, do you think there could be divine inspiration?"

"Okay, I see what you mean. Yeah, sure."

"Is that your final answer, or do you wish to call a lifeline?"

That crack got to me. "Don't be snarky," I said and felt the better for saying it. Being condescending seemed to be their way of doing business, but he must have made some progress as he followed up with, "Can I now assume that you'd be willing to accept the Bible as the word of God?"

"I guess so."

"In that case, would you like to know what it says about ladder climbing?"

"Yeah, sure."

"You won't like it."

"Just get on with it."

"I know you'll remember that one of the Ten Commandments is that you shall not commit adultery. How do you feel about that?"

I felt good about that. I hadn't committed adultery.

"I'm sorry to tell you but in the Sermon on the Mount our Lord explains that anyone who even looks at a woman lustfully will be judged as having committed adultery with her in his heart. His expectations I'm afraid are rather more severe than yours."

"That's ridiculous. No one can meet that standard. What's the harm in checking out a good looking woman if you don't take it any further?"

"Please listen carefully. If you accept the Bible as the word of God, then the Ten Commandments list what are acceptable behaviors and what I just told you is how He interprets that Commandment. More to the point, He follows up by stating that if anyone fails any of the Commandments in even the smallest of details, that person has failed the whole test and is now barred from entering heaven by his own efforts. Earlier, we talked about you climbing the ladder through your own good works. Since these are the standards you needed to meet, you can appreciate your efforts would have failed. That was why you were being sent to hell."

"I don't believe you." I was angry and frustrated. It felt as if this was some giant cosmic game whose only purpose was to make a fool of me. It was an unfair test. The expectations were too high and far too much was resting on them.

"What is it you don't believe?"

"This test is ridiculous, and the standard is ridiculous. No one can pass it. It's just set up for failure."

"Stop and think. You know that can't be true. You saw yourself that some of the souls veered to the left of the guardian. Since they were bound for heaven, there must be a way for people to gain entry."

Once he said that I went silent. He was right. *Some of us had been saved. It couldn't be they met this standard. No one could meet it, so God must have given them special status or exemption. Perhaps He plays favorites and if so, how would I get a piece of that?* I asked the angel, "How was that done? What was special about those people?"

"The fear of the Lord is the beginning of wisdom."

"What does that mean?"

"It means we're going on a journey. Watch and learn." In an instant, the scene changed, and we were hovering over a schoolyard. It was my middle school. As we looked on, Brian Routledge, one of the regular bullies, walked over to Kevin Allcott, a harmless nerd and said, "I never hit a guy with glasses." He then pulled off his glasses and for no good reason punched the poor guy in the face.   I could see me as a teen, standing beside them and collapsed in laughter. I thought the insult was hilarious. Whenever I met other people, I told them the story. I even told the story back to Kevin Allcott.

"That was tacky," said Gamaliel.

I felt embarrassed and started to bluster. "Come on," I said. "I was just a kid. It's the sort of stupid thing kids do. It was no big deal anyway, and it was years ago, long forgotten. Who cares anymore?" There was no doubt I'd done a rotten thing, and part of me hoped that Kevin's ego hadn't suffered any long term damage.

"Not good enough," said Gamaliel who knew my thoughts. "Are you ashamed because it was morally wrong, or just concerned you might be held responsible for what you did? If I was to tell you Kevin was unharmed, would you promptly forgive yourself?" I was irritated by his fancy word games so I swore at him. He seemed unfazed by that.

We moved to a new scene. I was older now and sitting in the back of a car with some girl I couldn't remember, trying to make out and hoping to talk her into sex. She didn't want to do it, but I kept on yakking anyway. I didn't grab at her or keep her there, nothing physical, just me nagging and constant pressure. It was pathetic. "What do you think?" said Gamaliel.

"I guess I could be a jerk."

"I know you weren't a rapist or a murderer, but lack of respect is an ongoing theme with you. Watch this." We were in a parking lot. A lady was struggling with her three kids while loading packages into her car. I was driving by with Marion. This lady had blocked the roadway and was holding me up. I gave her two seconds then leaned on the horn.

Gamaliel froze the frame then asked, "Do you remember doing these things?"

"Sort of, now you've brought them to mind."

"Do you sometimes get flashbacks of things you've done you'd rather forget?"

"Not too often but now and again."

"And when you get them, do you just shrug them off?"

"I guess so. They're all in the past. They can't be changed now. Life goes on."

"So mostly you live in the present."

"I guess. What's wrong with that?"

"The unexamined life is not worth living."

"Who says?"

"Socrates."

"What does he know?"

There was a pause then Gamaliel said, "I think we've reached ground zero."

The next I knew we were flying above this village. Below us were these little low houses with whitewashed walls and flat mud roofs. As we neared the ground I could feel the blast of hot air rising, the atmosphere was filled with dust and the sun beat down on a landscape drained of colour. There were donkeys tied to a water trough, and were those other things camels? People were crowding the village streets, but Gamaliel picked out this group of dirty, bearded men with covered heads and coarse brown robes. As we watched, a woman in a long black robe came into view. She was walking far too quickly for this heat, her body stiff, her head erect and she was pointing at their leader.

"Teacher," she said, "where were you? We sent for you days ago? Why did you take so long to get here? You knew he was desperately ill. You should have been here. You could have helped. It's like you didn't care." He met her fierce gaze but gave no answer.

I was impressed. In what must be a traditional culture, she'd taken on this higher status male. I like people with guts. Still pointing at him she told the world, "If you had been here, my brother would not have died." *Good for you,* I thought. *She's wearing her grief in anger. She's holding him responsible for failing to show up,* except she then said, "But I know that even now God will give you whatever you ask."

That remark disappointed me. I'd guessed this teacher was a faith healer, and despite the obvious, this woman still believed he could do something. *Let it go girl, dead is dead.* The man was standing there, looking all solemn and dignified and telling her, "Your brother will rise again," like that was going to happen.

Here it comes I thought, get out the checkbook. The poor woman's desperate. She'll do almost anything. Given she still believed in what he was selling, he was setting her up to pluck her one more time, except she then said, "I know he will rise again in the resurrection at the last day," whatever that might mean.

This teacher came back with, "I am the resurrection and the life. The one who believes in me will live, even though they die; and whoever lives by believing in me will never die. Do you believe this?"

"Yes, Lord," she said. "I believe that you are the Messiah, the Son of God, who is to come into the world." *This is nonsense,* I thought; *what is she talking about?*

As soon as she'd finished speaking the woman left but then a second woman, this one sobbing came up and said the same thing. By that time a crowd had gathered and the teacher was crying too. Some of them said that showed he cared, but others said if he'd cared that much, he'd have done something. Next thing I knew we were at the grave site. The first woman was back again, worrying now how the corpse would smell but the teacher made them open the chamber anyway, and after that the brother came strolling out dressed up like the mummy.

Gamaliel guided me back to the all-white room. Once we got there I said, "What happened? I don't get it."

"I didn't expect you would, not yet anyway." He waited for a moment and then added, "You know that was Jesus, don't you?"

Now I felt stupid. I should have figured that out. Of course, it was Jesus. I'd been watching him do a miracle, bringing that woman's brother back to life. Maybe He was for real after all.

"Okay," said Gamaliel, "you asked how those others got saved. This is how. Surely you must understand by now you're riddled with sin and cannot earn your way to heaven, but if you confess those sins and ask for God's mercy, by His sinless life that He willed to you, and His innocent death that replaces your own, you can be saved. Do you believe that?"

"I still don't get it."

"You just saw it happen. Let me explain. Jesus Christ, the Son of God, also became fully human, came down to earth and lived here a perfect, sinless life, one that was good enough to climb the ladder to heaven, and then He chose death instead as payment for your sins so that you could inherit His pass into heaven. All that is being asked of you is for you to believe that."

"What do you mean?"

"You keep asking these questions. Stop stalling; you don't need any more information. Just beg His forgiveness, throw yourself on His mercy, admit to Him that you are a sinner, and once you do that, your sins will be forgiven, and you will be saved."

"That's all there is to it?"

"Yes."

"That doesn't make sense."

"Why do you keep on doubting? Being up here, you've seen far more than any person has a right to see. Look around you and know that this is real. Just have faith. Why do you insist that it all makes sense?"

"So, if Adolf Hitler did what you said, he'd go to heaven."

"Yes."

"I don't believe it. It's too easy. He has to be punished for what he did. He can't just step out of it at the last moment. That's not right."

"It's not your place to say who God will choose to save."

"And nothing I ever did counts for anything, like I was wasting my time trying to be nice to people?"

"It wasn't wrong to bring kindness into the world, but as I said, you still can't earn your way into heaven. That's not the way you get in."

"I don't know. It all seems kind of arbitrary and dictatorial to me. I'm not sure I buy into any of this."

Those were the last words I would speak. Instantly, I was back at the archway but this time, alone. I could see no clock, but the voice from before was telling me my time had run out, that my heart had stopped soon after they pulled the plug. I was now dead and since I'd rejected God's offer to join Him, He'd respected my decision and granted me my independence.

With that, it is utterly, totally black. The atmosphere feels cold and clammy and somehow sticky as if I'm standing in motor oil. It smells like motor oil too. I can move a little but only with huge effort, so much effort I figure I'm here for good. I also know I'm alone, and there's nothing beyond me to trigger my senses; that I now must live inside my head. Whatever is outside of me is so deeply silent it almost hurts.

Why am I here? There must some way to get this reviewed. All I've done wrong is fail to meet an impossible standard. They're acting too quickly; I make the right choices when I have enough time. It always takes me a while to process anything. This whole business is a mistake. It's unfair, and I'm being cheated. I find I'm starting to rave and repeat myself so I relax and empty my mind, but then I'm bored. Anyway, my mind is going again. I remember the silly stories that Gamaliel dumped over me. They all seem so trivial, not worth remembering, and anyway, it's not like the others aren't at fault. Brian Routledge for one is far worse than me.

This just isn't right. Whoever made this decision is over-reacting. The punishment needs to fit the crime, and anyway, God should be doing this better. It isn't as though He's blameless here. The test is ridiculous, set up for failure, nothing more than a trap for decent people. What loving God pulls a stunt like that? As I'm thinking about it, I'm angry and obsessing. The obsessing worries me; it's not how I should spend my time. *Now, that's a thought, how should I spend my time? I need a plan, something to keep me focused until I get out of here. This can't last forever, can it...*

28.
Listen
Moshe Sonnheim

Listen to the distant drums
Listen to the bugle's Calls
Listen to the wind-blown flags
Listen to the marching feet
Listen to the song of war
Listen to the cries of pain
Listen to the gasp of death
The Army of the Dead
Is coming near

Across the blood-soaked fields
Across the trampled towns
The gutted homes
The silent streams
The broken dreams
The Army of the Dead is moving on

You sent them off
With marching band
To fight the fight
For Mother/Father Land
To bring you back
The spoils of war
And crush the foe
Forevermore

Listen to the muffled drums
Listen to the bugle's Taps
Listen to the wind-torn flags
Listen to the trudging feet
Listen to the mournful cry
The Army of the Dead
Is coming near
The Army of the Dead
Will soon be here
Listen!

29.
Local Color
William Doreski

A disembodied foot stalks
the village, the ghost of a foot
from the Civil War, the residue
of Colonel Bass, struck by cannon fire
while running away from battle.

His regiment sent home his foot
to mock the town that fathered him,
but no one got the joke.   Now it tramps
from shop to shop to uncover
the remainder of the colonel,
but his atoms refuse to congeal.

We're used to this single foot,
this funereal oddity
that like the pot-bellied pigs
a woman walks leashed through town
passes for local color.

It never confronts anyone
but merely hobbles along,
leaving the bruised air tingling.

Because it leaves no prints in snow
anyone can tell it's a ghost.

It shows up on film, though.
I've often photographed it hopping
into the diner, the post office,
the bookstore café, where local
and visiting poets honor it
with rhymes that would jolt Poe mad.

Although I pity the Colonel
blown to particles, a cowardice
adrift in the world, his foot
displays a redeeming persistence
in its blind and clumsy search.

Still, I'd rather die in one piece
and lie as still as possible
and let the cosmos digest me
fully and completely, leaving
no stray metrical elements
to make the local dogs howl.

30.
Los Murals De La Arena
Franco Strong

He searched through the loose, convoluted images of his past. A layer of calloused scars had settled over his memories, concealing those events gone by. Maybe he had been too much of a man, not enough of a father.

He spoke into the telephone, asking how sure they were of the information.

"We're almost certain. The reports are reliable. If it stands as is, stateside your company is being liquidated tomorrow."

"Ah," he said. His deep voice lingered like the scent of cork soaked in tequila. He hung-up the golden rotary telephone and stretched his wrinkled fingers over the mahogany desk. The swirling, bleeding dark spots of wood matched his own leopard hands. If he kept them there too long the bones within might become brittle wood themselves.

Hanging flush against the office wall was a matching cross ornately decorated with intricate carvings and more gold trim. He hadn't prayed in years. Not since his wife died. Not since he last spoke to his son.

Everything else in the office had flourishes of gold, from the typewriter down to his fountain pen, like a dream taken from Hernan Cortes's mind. Arturo had accumulated wealth and the power inseparable from it. But that meant little now with his graying temples and wrinkled, almost viscous skin. He arrived in old age too soon like early rains left stagnant beneath the desert sun.

He left the building that he owned, the headquarters of the small business-empire he had built which consisted of construction, farming, shipping, and property holdings. The engine of the new '58 Buick gurgled to life and he drove off. The road stretched deeper into the regions of nowhere which compose Sonora Desert of Northern Mexico.

In his youth he had come here, riding north to fight, to join alongside Villa and the Division del Norte. And this empty desert is where he ended up staying. Once he had experienced the solitude of being caught between the two abysses of the open sky and parched earth nothing else could move his soul.

The road continued along, curving, swaying, the slowest of dances. Clouds hung low over the land, like the old man's own brow-line. There was a stillness pervading the atmosphere as though an imperceptible crack in the sky was ready to expand and shatter the blue into a million shards of jagged azul geMs.

The old man drove and thought about his son somewhere over there, in America, across the crystal and prismatic frontier of the border. In the States his son had a wife, a daughter, a life of comfort, things Arturo hadn't known at that age. His own youth had been so much different.

Beneath the keloid scars of his memory, images of the past began to bleed with life.

****

By now the words meant little coming from his young lips but he uttered them anyway. "Viva la Revolucion."

He gripped the elderly Indígeno's throat. The wrinkled skin felt like dried-out cactus. Arturo's young hands sunk the straight, razored-metal of his knife into the man's belly. The Indio's body went limp then slumped to the floor. Parched earth soaked up the pooling and warm liquid.

Gunshots went off somewhere beyond followed by a woman's shriek and horse hooves pounding dirt. The faint smell of smoke crept up Arturo's nose, continued rising, and gathered in his forehead, enveloping his thoughts in a dim haze. He stepped over the prostrate body and forced his way through the door and into the small house. The men needed supplies, anything. He cursed, the omnipotent dust of the desert crunched between his teeth and tongue. This house looked to have little to nothing in it. Hopefully the other men fared better, or God help them all. Ah, no. God's reach didn't extend this far. Arturo was sure of it.

The Revolution had been put on hold. The Division del Norte was scattered if it existed at all, the Villistas strangled by Carranza's forces. A handful of men tried to trek back up to the empty lands they called home. The horses dragged the living corpses of men through the skeletal rocks bleached by the sun alongside the ocean of ancient gravel. This small town of Indígenas made the stupid mistake of being in the way of Arturo and the desperate men, along with resisting Pancho Villa sometime earlier in this civil war. Or at least that's how the rumor went. None of the men knew for sure. It mattered little now. When the men rode into town words had been exchanged for shouting which had been traded for gunshots.

Arturo coughed with dry lungs and continued searching through the pathetically small, ramshackle house. There was nothing. This family too had been starving, the same as the land outside. He cleaned his bloody knife with an apron he found resting on the woodstove that was covered in a film of dust, unused. Even too poor for wood, Arturo realized.

More smoke slithered through the open door. Ah, his fellow men would burn this town into the already scorched earth. Then once the smoke stretched itself thin into the horizon he could forget this place just as easily as the desert forgets her sunsets. He sat and rested his feet and hands, heavy from travel and slaughter. Currents of thought dissolved in his mind until only a simmering black hole remained. And only that blistering black seemed real nowadays. He was young but weary. Too much had happened too soon, promises were broken and his dreams had unraveled in the ceaseless western winds.

A dull, blunt blow crashed into his temple tearing him from his partial amnesia. He hunched over, dazed, his fingers pressed against his throbbing and swollen head. Blood flooded into his cranium, on the verge of bursting through his ears. His arms shot up instinctively, protecting. Another softer blow landed against his forearms. This time he saw a woman, her hair impossibly dark, waving a cast-iron pan in her arms. He unleashed a quick backhand. She cried out, dropping her makeshift weapon. She scrambled for it but Arturo's boot sent it sliding away. His gaze met hers.

They both paused for an uncertain moment and Arturo silently prayed for the woman to just give up, don't be foolish now. Maybe in another lifetime he'd say she was beautiful. Her eyes seemed a shade of brown taken from the depths that preceded creation. A primal desperation secreted from the stained-glass irises, more singular, more encompassing than anything he had experienced in his tired life.

She cried out and lunged, her rough hands clawing, grasping, choking whatever they touched upon. Fingers gouged his weary eyes. Nails peeled off pieces of his rough and unshaven cheek. He tried to hold her powerful forearms at bay. The calloused hands squeezed and mangled his throat.

Coughing.

Vision blurred.

A sharp and deafening rupture rendered everything meaningless. Fingers released Arturo's throat. Air spread into his lungs. The woman collapsed and Arturo stood with his revolver in hand. She gazed up and her brown eyes that had a subterranean depth moments ago were now only absent pools of shallow water. He stumbled backward, his hands heavy with the weight of one more dead and severed possibility.

Women weren't supposed to die, not like this, not by his hand. He uttered a dry curse to himself. Ah, what did it matter now?

Arturo coughed, trying to clear his lungs of the stench of fresh death, and looked around. There, in the corner, he saw another set of brown eyes glowing in the orange light, waiting.

The swaying road came to an end and Arturo's wrinkled hands steered the Buick through the first gate, passing through the garden of palms and succulents. He entered another fence, an iron gate, the garage, and finally the padlocked door of his hacienda-style house. They were like consecutive boxes that Arturo continued to bury himself within as time lurched along. Soon he'd find himself in that final box, sealed forever, his heavy hands finally resting.

The house was old and empty. His footsteps echoed off tiled floors. The tapping weaved through more mahogany wood, piano, marble counters, decorative candles never lit, and a chandelier that always remained on. Outside, through the Venetian blinds, the clouds still hung low, compressing the sky with a grey, monolithic gravity.

Pedro-Juan, the lone butler of the house, appeared from one of the corridors, but Arturo waved him off and the young man disappeared just as easily as he had come.

Arturo dragged his heavy feet up the stairs passing the myriad of crosses hung on the wall. They had been his wife's collection when she was still alive. He needed her, Ofelia, right now. No matter how divinely decorated they were those two perpendicular lines meant nothing to him. His faith had been his wife. Once he stopped touching her flesh he ceased feeling Heaven.

In his study he poured a glass of mezcal and scanned over the legal documents pertaining to his company. By tomorrow morning the empire he had built would once again fall completely into his hands. But more blood needed to be sacrificed, his own. His son was idealistic and foolish, not a man of this world. Arturo had given his son, Diego, the keys to the empire. All Diego had to do in America was watch the books as their wealth grew. But his son would rather spit in his father's face and liquidate his shares of the company, sell it for pieces. Maybe it worked like that in the states, a man could sell most of the company, dismantle a small empire, and walk away unscathed. Not here in Mexico. There were too many greedy mouths to be fed, too many claw-like fingers extended and open. If the empire stopped producing then the thieves and murderers, smugglers, politicians and backdoor bankers, they'd find the father and son and the rest of their family. And he hadn't lived this long, raised himself from ruins, only to be slaughtered like cattle.

He fished through the top drawers of the desk until his fingers wrapped around the cold metal of a small key which he used to unlock the bottom cabinet of the tall bookshelf behind. Inside was a clay jar, unglazed and flat-tan, with circular symbols alongside zigzagging lines, and pictures drawn of half-man/half-animals with prostrate bodies reaching up to the sky. He swirled the jar around listening to the rotting, black-molasses liquid swish within.

He had done this too many times. His rusted mind was tired of Death and her slithering, choking finality. He tried to remember a time when life offered more.

****

The gun holstered in Diego's saddle was almost as tall as he was and the horse he rode was too large for the boy's adolescent frame. But Diego has insisted on riding like a true vaquero, like a man, like his father. Despite Ofelia's protests Arturo decided it would be beneficial for Diego. The boy needed to learn what it took to be a man. All of this would be his someday.

They rode off from their ranch and into the desert that offered everything and nothing in equal measure, enchanted and cursed. In the far distance jagged mountains seemed to watch and retreat back slightly as the horses pushed forward. Bundles of dry brush lay face-down while sporadic cacti reached their fingers over the lifeless boulders and into the sky.

Arturo watched as the boy fidgeted in his saddle, sweat glistening on his brow line, remaining silent in his effort to fix himself and the rifle strapped to the saddle beneath his legs.

"Hijo, need a break?"

"No, I can go on," the boy said shifting the moist kerchief around his neck and giant, rounded hat covering his head.

After a long while of pushing farther into the empty territories that belonged only to the oppressive sun Arturo stopped his horse. Both dismounted, father and son.

"Rest a little. And drink," Arturo instructed and the boy gulped down mouthfuls from his canteen. "Save some though. For the way back."

Diego took one last swallow then capped the canteen.

It was the hours of no shadows, the sun hovered directly above in the high sky. Arturo patted and caressed his horse while whispering sweetly into the animal's ear. He then motioned for Diego to do the same.

"Keep them happy out here and she'll keep you alive. They're like a wife. Remember that, Mijo."

The boy nodded and imitated his father's long caresses against the horse's powerful, taut neck and shoulders. "Is this what you did when you were younger, Papa? When you were fighting the other men out in the desert?"

The myriad of images were cauterized in Arturo's memory but he only answered is son simply. "No. We chased and fired at men we didn't see, ghosts. And sometimes the ghosts fired back." He patted his horse a few more times. "Pick up the rifle, it's time for you to learn." His lips cracked into a faint smile that quickly died. "In case those ghosts come back for me."

Arturo explained the Winchester and its lever action, how you were able to ride and shoot, how the Villistas won so many battles backed by such a sturdy and reliable weapon. He made sure his son held the weapon snug against his shoulders. Exhale. Squeeze, don't pull. Aim for something small on the target. Respect the weapon and she'll respect you.

A few rounds pierced through the brush in the distance. Diego lowered the gun and looked up with prideful, marble-brown eyes. The innocent glance reminded Arturo of another boy he had left behind, forgotten to the past. He straightened his black moustache then took his handkerchief and wiped the sweat from Diego's wrinkleless face.

A gentle then sharp rustling cascaded through the wind. The handkerchief dropped and Arturo scanned the horizon. A ways off he spotted the slinking movements of a coyote's fur. He tracked the animal a moment. Pointing, he whispered to his son, "Shoot."

Diego's small arms lifted the rifle against his face. One eye closed, the other aimed. The boys hesitated, lowered the rifle, then lifted the gleaming metal once again to his cheek.

"Papa," Diego whispered back, "es macho o hembra?"

"It doesn't matter. Shoot." Arturo's gaze didn't stray from the animal.

"I need to know."

"Aim. Shoot, Hijo."

The boy's slim arms quivered like the heat rising in the distance. "I need to-"

"Be a man!"

"Papa-"

"Vamanos, Hijo!"

The gun ripped through the open land. Diego's frail body jerked and recoiled from the blast. He let out a gasp of pain. The coyote spooked and sprinted off.

Arturo drew his own rifle. He hadn't forgotten, the movements were ingrained within his hands. Track. Aim. Adjust.

Three quick shots exhaled from the barrel. The coyote in the distance limped and dragged itself a few more strides before collapsing. Gun-smoke seeped into the blistering air.

Diego peered up at his father silently. The boy's eyes seemed to be a darker shade of brown, almost black.

"Saddle up, let's go," Arturo said.

"Are we going to find the coyote?"

"No need. She belongs to the desert now."

The two rode off even farther and crossed a hidden ravine where the mighty stallions sucked down precious water, then continued on. The sun began to set. Elongated shadows groped at the two lonesome riders. A silent eruption of orange and purple hung in the sky. The sun sank into the scorched earth to somewhere below their booted feet.

"Papa, are we going to sleep beneath the stars tonight?" Diego asked.

Arturo nodded as his horse trotted along. He told Diego about his nights in the Revolution where they had nothing, no supplies, and rode aimlessly beneath the stars with winds clawing at their faces, cold. No matter how much death had been inflicted upon either side these stars above still shined with the same intensity, indifferent to man. Stars have little use for human suffering.

"I like the stars," Diego stated. "Mama says the night is God's shroud over the world." He went on. "And the stars are tiny needlepoints poked through. The light is just Heaven glowing on the other side."

The desert was almost unconscious.

"Es muy bonita, ay Papa?" the boy added.

Arturo peered up at the nightly veil punctured with needlepoints of light. How close Heaven seemed just then.

He breathed in the whispers of the cool night air alongside his son while the stars floated in the placid ocean above.

****

His wrinkled and skeletal fingers held the clay jar once again. He had learned Death's dance well through the years, her swaying, his hands held against the hips of her ghostly silhouette. He sat in the burgundy chair of his office, the jar heavy in his lap. Ah, all empire had been built upon the sacrifices of innocent blood.   But he was still too tired for this, too much of a dying old man. And this time the blood spilled would be part of his own.

He dialed and the phone rang endlessly without anyone picking up on the other end. No surprise. Diego hadn't spoken to him in years. Today was no different.

The putrid black liquid sloshed and bubbled within the clay jar as though it wanted to be set free. It had fermented over the years, growing green, grey, then finally a thick black. A wrinkled palm cupped a handful of the liquid and Arturo sipped. Streaks dribbled off his chin as he chocked down the rotten fluid.

It started slowly, his head buzzed like a blanket of insects descending upon him. Then his consciousness seemed to expand, edging against infinity. The void violently pressed back compressing his mind into nothing but a pinpoint. Then everything within seemed to crack, shatter, rain down broken shards of mirror.

He relaxed in the sturdy chair and remembered the first time he had tasted this cursed poison.

****

The eyes in the corner had seen it all, witnessed Arturo's slaying of the Indio-woman. The brown irises belonged to a boy, hunched over and shirtless, his coffee-skin baked by the sun. The boy's protruding shoulders and ribs reminded Arturo of the rock formations that crawled out from the desert sands.

Arturo stepped over the nameless woman's body, which still leaked crimson, and approached the boy. Outside the village burned and the smoke grew heavy.

His hands hovered above his holster as he squatted to the boy's level. Held firmly in the young boy's hands was a book alongside an unglazed and tan jar. Both items had matching symbols of circles, zigzagging lines, and half-man/half-animal bodies decorating the exteriors.

"What do you have there?" Arturo asked.

The boy didn't waver or flinch as his eyes shifted between Arturo and the body which lay behind.

Arturo snapped his fingers and asked again. "Let me see." He reached out. "Comprendes, niño pequeño?"

The boy nodded and rose to his feet.

"Then hand it over," Arturo demanded. His fingers wrapped around the butt of his revolver.

"No. These aren't meant for you," the boy said. "Asesino. Cerdo."

The heavy steel of the revolver struck the boy's cheek. "You'd like to join her?" Arturo asked and gestured to the body that lay behind his feet. He pressed the barrel square against the boy's forehead and yanked the jar free. Inside was an impossibly clear liquid with a vague sea-mist and floral odor.

"Que es esto?" Arturo asked. "Agua?" He sniffed once more. His throat itched with thirst and he tasted a tiny sip.

The boy said nothing with the revolver still held against his skull. Sporadic gunshots from outside mixed with the smoke and setting sunlight that spilled like paint.

A slow buzzing crept into Arturo's neck, jaw, then lodged itself within his head. He tried to keep the revolver pointed ahead but he lost muscle sensation and it fell uselessly from his fingertips. Vision blurred as smoke slithered into his nostrils gripping his mind in a mass of hazy palms and fingers. He tried to concentrate, clear his mind. The boy pulled the jar from Arturo's limp hands. Thoughts weakened and expanded into blackness.

His vision grew sharp once again, focused. Smoke still burned in his nostrils. A lumbering achiness pulsed through his cheek. Something weighed in his hands. The clay jar, the book. He set both onto the ground.

His body felt strange though, limber, more serpentine. He examined the back of his hands but didn't recognize the veins or skin. He methodically clutched then released his grip in the air. Just beyond his fingers was a form, a body, clothes he recognized as his own. He rolled the limp body over only to see himself and the familiar mask of his own face. That was his body there, limp and lifeless, tattered and broken. He backed away in horror, touching and feeling the alien body he inhabited now, small, shirtless, cheek sore, protruding ribs, starved, young, the body of an Indio-boy. His own face and form still lay on the ground, almost mocking him in its limp unconsciousness. He groped at the starved chest, forearms, and stomach he occupied, but his fingertips only conveyed what he already knew.

He ran to the open front door leaping over another body, that of the Indio-woman. Smoke flowed in, choking the young lungs. He dropped to his knees then clawed at the foreign skin, trying to peel away this unfamiliar form that wasn't his own.

Gunshots close by echoed in his skull. He covered his ears, peered up, and was pulled out of his personal torment. Just ahead he saw it all with purified eyes, the village gnawed by the jaws of fire, choking smoke, spectral cries of agony, men, women, young voices, voices of the elderly, gunshots, men on horseback with revolvers drawn, women in rebozos clutching infants, men clutching bleeding arms, bodies collapsed under the weight of lead points, children crying in the dirt, the dirt soaked up tears that meant little to nothing, rider-less horses limping towards Death, prayers uttered, cries to The Lord, cries to forgotten gods in dead tongues, steel, knives swung, flesh severed, gunshots, silence, the smoke, the choking smoke. In the distance the exhausted sun gave up on the panorama of violence as she fell to earth.

He saw it all with those tender eyes, his sight renewed in innocence. And those marble-brown irises that weren't his own could only weep for this vision, the engulfing calamity that hangs between the borders of this world and oblivion.

The frail body collapsed into the dirt but the earth offered no reprieve. Even with his crying eyes closed he still witnessed it all with a prismatic clarity.

****

The poison had taken hold. Arturo was about to leave his old, fatigued body once again.

He concentrated on Diego, his son, as he floated between the echoing halls of nothingness. Where had that little boy gone? Why had he decided on a life across the crystalline border and left his father to wither away? Arturo remembered the times when they had ridden together, father and son, through the desert, before Diego had left his old man to grope aimlessly though the shifting sands. And now only those open expanses composed Arturo's existence, along with the fragile line of the horizon that kept the sky and the desert separated.

The buzzing in his temples ceased and he awoke beneath the folding, warm waves of white bed sheets. His knuckles and fingers curled then released smoothly. Gone was the achiness between his bones that has accumulated over the years like sand between unknown crevices.

Beside him, wrapped in the sheets, lay the sleeping outline of Florina. He gently pulled the blankets down revealing the curving line of her bare back and waist. She had always made a beautiful wife. His son had chosen well.

An undulating warmth seeped below his navel. Ah yes, he had almost forgotten what it was like to be young. The back of his fingertips followed the swooping line from her waist up to her back which finally ended at her neckline. She stirred slightly as his hand lingered above her throat. Fingers touched her skin and felt her trachea take in air. Then he gripped tightly, squeezed, his thumbs dug into the soft tissue beside her vocal cords muffling her gasps. She moaned, struggled. Her eyes fluttered open giving life to her perfect cheeks and beautiful lips. He smothered her exquisite face with a pillow. The floral-scent of her hair caressed the air. Helpless, soft hands clawed at his chin, hands of a mother. Her body flinched as he felt the life exhale from her throat. Her fragile neck reminded him of the chickens he had butchered as a child. She twitched once more then it was over.

He left her lifeless form beneath the sheets and walked down the hall passing door after door. Somewhere within the house Marie slept the easy sleep of a child. He let her dream while she still could. Tomorrow, at daybreak, she'd awaken with a different life.

He drove Diego's car through the town and into the single-lane highway that swayed hypnotically through the desert. Farther and farther he pressed, descending towards the land that lived a daily death only to be renewed at each dawn. The rain clouds above began to murmur as he crossed the border, the meeting point of two drifting worlds. This land is where his son belonged, where they had ridden long ago and gazed up at Heaven. A few glimmering lights where still lit in the sleepy border town. He passed through the barren and tiny streets. The road emptied into the desert beyond where a monolithic black surrounded and swallowed everything.

Arturo had come here before, ridden through the Northern lands when he was younger. And now he was young once again. How easy it would be to restart again, revive those dreams he had left in the churning winds and shifting sands of the desert. No, he couldn't, it was impossible. One lifetime of scars was enough. His sins were almost finished. The emptied desert had already settled within him.

He accelerated, the engine screeched. He gripped the steering wheel then jerked hard to the right. Wheels hit the dirt and the car tumbled, a box of crumpled metal, rubber, fragmented glass. Bones snapped, joints shattered, cranium splintered, metal punctured warm organs, gasoline mixed with blood and saliva.

He groaned with a crushed throat, still alive. He crawled out of the wreckage, pulling a broken body along the cold sand that clung to his open wounds. Dead brush and thorns scratched at him with infinitely small fingers, welcoming him to the dirt that reclaims all. His hands pushed against the entirety of the earth as he rolled onto his back to face the open sky. At least he could give his son this, an image Diego loved at one time, those needlepoints of Heaven up above.

Clouds slipped in and out of his vision. His fingers and lips grew cold. He coughed from the whispers of smoke, closed his eyes, and dreamed of being back home.

****

Arturo was within his old, fatigued body once again. The familiar walls of his study surrounded him, lined with bookshelves of mahogany wood. The clay jar with bubbling black liquid still lay heavy in his lap. He locked it away and wandered outside.

The desert was calling him, like she sometimes did in his lonely nights. Out here, across the night, he knew part of his blood was being consumed by the endless sands. His thoughts tumbled until they settled upon the smoke and Indian village that burned years ago. He never knew if the Indio-boy ever made it out alive. Maybe that boy was still out there alongside Diego, both waiting to be claimed by the wandering desert and nocturnal abyss.

The wind carved away at Arturo's cheekbones.   He peered up and searched the sky. Thick clouds had gathered above. They hovered, grey and motionless, covering those needlepoints of light which lay behind.

The rains came quick, falling fast and hard.

31.
Luminescence
Caitlyn Mancini

There were blurs of colors that appeared as she slid in and out of consciousness. Her head was pounding. She couldn't move. It was as if she was detached from her body. There were muffled voices that she could make out every now and again. It sounded like her brother and her dad talking, but she couldn't understand them.

What's going on? Is this a dream?

The pain certainly felt real. Although every time the voices started fading, the pain seemed to ebb away.

"Lil! Lillian!" her brother's voice echoed somewhere in the distance.

Cody?

He sounded panic-stricken.

Lillian's eyes snapped open. Her surroundings appeared fuzzy at first. She slowly lifted her body and realized in a panic that it was hard to move. She felt heavy and disoriented. Her muscles began to respond, and she instinctively brought a hand to the back of her head. The throbbing was still present, but it had dulled.

"Dad? Cody?" she called out hoarsely.

Lillian blinked and immediately her eyes widened. She was lying down in a field of grass. She stood up and saw that the field disappeared into the horizon as if it was endless. She was in the middle of nowhere it seemed.

"It feels so real, but it has to be a dream," she murmured.

Turning all the way around, Lillian realized that in every direction there were flowers, seemingly endless. She closed her eyes and willed herself to wake up. She didn't know how long she stayed like that, but eventually she became restless and concerned. She decided that her only option was to get up and explore and hopefully something would trigger her to wake up.

She gazed around not sure where to go until she discovered there was a small path of dirt leading through the flowers. It was the only path that she could see so she followed it. The path led up a steep hill, still covered in grass, and as she reached the top, she suddenly stopped. At the bottom of the hill was a house. It was a simple, large house with several windows. It was all white except for the door and windows, which were purple.

As she approached the house, she went to go walk up the steps and noticed she didn't have any shoes or socks on. Glancing down, she saw that she was in her new bathing suit. She reached for the handle, but before she even touched it, the door swung open. Lillian jumped back. The wind must have blown the door open.

"Hello?" she called out.

The place seemed rather devoid of furniture. The floor was a sleek, pale marble and there was a large staircase that curved to the left as it reached the second floor. Oddly, the entire room had no doors. The only windows were the ones by the front door. Lillian approached the staircase and began climbing it slowly. A loud sound echoed, and Lillian gasped and turned around. The door had slammed shut. Something moved in her peripheral vision, and Lillian wheeled her head back around. There was nothing there. Her mind was playing tricks on her.

She swallowed and wrapped her arms around herself. The stairs led up to a long hallway that was dimly lit. The white oval lights that lined the walls appeared brand new. One light on the end flickered every few seconds. She kept walking and walking. There were no doors or windows, just a long hallway.

Suddenly, she clutched at her chest and gasped for air. A cold chill struck her like an electric shock. She collapsed to the floor and tried to catch her breath. Her body was trembling uncontrollably. There was a pulling sensation in her chest that made it hard to breathe. Lillian lifted her head, and her eyes widened. There was a white door now standing at the end of the hallway.

Wait, there wasn't a door there before… was there?

Lillian stared at the door. She stood back up and took a step toward the door. It was just a dream; it couldn't hurt her. She never died in her dreams; she always woke up right before. Slowly, she reached out for it.

"No, don't go in there!"

Lillian screamed and wheeled around. The voice came from behind her. A young girl, no older than ten or eleven, was standing before her. She had long wavy, dark brown hair, pale skin, and sky-blue eyes. She was wearing a purple dress and oddly, she didn't have shoes either. It was the terrified expression on her face, however, that made Lillian jump away from the door.

"Why? What's behind it?"

"I don't know, but I know it's not good," the girl replied in a shaky voice.

Lillian stepped away from the door and toward the girl. "Who are you?"

The girl glanced at the door once. "My name is Azaria. Follow me. I know a safe place."

Lillian glanced over her shoulder at the door but it was gone. Lillian then followed her back down the hallway and downstairs. When they reached the bottom and turned left, Lillian was stunned to see a doorway that she had not noticed before. There was an arch leading from the entrance into another room. This room was nothing like the entrance. There was a beautiful crystal chandelier hanging from the tall ceiling, and there was a table with purple, glass jars. Five of them. Four of the jars were glowing subtly from the inside like there were candles inside of them. The last one wasn't glowing.

"Um, what is this place?"

"It's my sanctuary," Azaria said.

Gazing around the room, Lillian noticed there wasn't much. There wasn't even any furniture.

"I'm still fixing it up," Azaria said, "but I'm sure pretty soon it will be complete."

Lillian nodded. "So, do you know where we are? I mean I assume this is a dream, but it feels so real and normally I don't know when I'm dreaming."

Azaria's eyes dimmed, and she shook her head. "You're not dreaming. You're between life and death right now. You must be in a coma; that's what I was in too."

"Wait *what*? That's not true!" Lillian raised her voice. "This isn't real! I'm not...there's no way I'm in a coma. I..." she stopped mid-sentence when images flashed before her; images of Cody and the door and falling backwards.

It can't be true...

"Do you remember something?"

Lillian glanced at Azaria. She looked so small and sad; her eyes were wide and open – innocent even. It couldn't be true. Lillian rubbed her left arm. She didn't even want to think about dying or never seeing her family again.

"I… I remember falling down the stairs, but how do you know we're in a coma?"

Azaria cast her eyes down, and Lillian felt the urge to hug her. "Because everyone who comes here is in a coma."

"Everyone? How many people are here?" Lillian swallowed.

"Well, I've only seen four people, but I haven't been here long. I haven't left this house. I've been too scared. That white door… it appeared to me, and I think that door takes you away. And I don't want to die."

Lillian struggled to keep her balance. She fought hard against the tears that threatened to stream down.

I can't break down now. I don't want to scare Azaria. I guess it makes sense a white door would lead to heaven or wherever it is people go. But this place… between life and death, how can this exist? I wonder how long Azaria's been here.

A part of her still didn't believe this was real. There was no way she was in control of waking up or not, even if she was in a coma. The other part of her wanted to stay strong for Azaria.

"Okay, Azaria, we can help each other get back somehow." Her voice was steady, and she wondered if that was because she still hoped it was a dream. "If we don't go through the white door, then there's got to be a way to wake up from the coma, right?"

"Maybe there's a way out but I don't know what's out there," Azaria replied calmly, shaking her head. "One lady named Christine told me that she had been there for years trying to get back. She called this place the coma world. Christine told me that once you're in a deep enough coma, you get trapped here. The longer you're in a coma, and the closer you get to dying, the more real this place becomes. She said that when you get here, it's because you're detached from your body. I don't think we can leave this place."

Lillian went over and put an arm around her. "Don't worry. Maybe she's wrong. We'll get back together, okay?"

Azaria nodded against her. Lillian pulled away, and Azaria smiled. "I'm so glad I met you. I was here all by myself."

"Where did the others go? Where did Christine go?" Lillian wondered.

Azaria just stared at her blankly. "I don't know. I think she went through the white door. That's why I won't go near it. I don't know what happened to her."

"Are you sure that's not the way out?" Lillian asked, realizing she was gripping Azaria's arms rather harshly. She let go immediately.

Azaria's eyebrows furrowed. "No, it's not. Trust me."

"Well, how do you know that Christine didn't find her body through the white door?"

Azaria stared at her unblinking for a second and then she shrugged. "I don't know. I don't know anything about this world. Maybe we should go outside. If you're with me, I won't be scared."

Torn between wanting to find the white door again and exploring outside, Lillian finally nodded. "Okay. I guess maybe that's a good idea. I woke up in a field so maybe there is a way back somewhere out there."

Azaria's eyes widened. "You're not going to leave me, are you? Like they did?"

"No, don't worry. I'm not," Lillian reassured her.

"Promise?" Azaria begged, reaching out to grasp Lillian's hand.

"I promise. We'll find a way out."

Lillian's throat constricted.

What if it's not a dream? What if the longer we're here the closer to death our bodies get? How much time do we have? And what will happen if we don't get back in time? Please don't let it be too late!

It was such a surreal feeling. Lillian knew that something bad had happened to her, but she couldn't believe that she was really on the edge of death. She should have been panicking, but she just couldn't react; she felt numb.

"What's wrong?" Azaria asked.

"I just... I miss my family. I can't imagine not seeing them again, even my annoying brother," Lillian whispered, feeling her nose and eyes sting.

Lillian was silent, lost in thought. She remembered her fight with Cody. She remembered how angry she was at him. It seemed so stupid now.

"Don't worry, we have each other," Azaria said, holding out her hand.

Lillian grasped her hand and felt comforted by the fact that she wasn't alone.

They left the room with Azaria clutching Lillian's hand. Lillian moved toward the front entrance. Outside appeared to be the same as she remembered. There was no wind and endless fields. Lillian began walking toward the direction she remembered coming from. Azaria strolled alongside her.

"I think this is where I was when I woke up," Lillian said, searching around. It was strange, though. She could see the house from the distance, and she hadn't been able to see it from that point before.

"I can't remember where I woke up," Azaria said, picking up a flower to put in her hair.

There was something else Lillian hadn't noticed before. In the opposite direction of looking down the massive hill at the house, there was a strange cloudy mist that surrounded the area behind the hill where they stood.

"What is that?" Lillian asked.

Azaria shrugged. "I see that everywhere. I think it surrounds this world. You can't go through it, but it tingles when you touch it."

Lillian stopped just before it. Reaching out a hand Lillian's brushed her fingers against it. A spark of electricity erupted, and she snapped her hand back. It startled her more than anything else. It wasn't painful, but it made her whole hand tingle. It only lasted for a few seconds, but she felt as though she could still feel the sparks traveling through her fingers.

"Wow. That's weird," Lillian said, turning around. Azaria was smiling at her.

"Let's go," Azaria said. She sounded impatient. She probably wanted to get out of there as much as Lillian did.

Nodding, she turned and followed Azaria back toward the house only, this time, they veered off toward the left of the house. They seemed to walk for a while and at first, Lillian didn't see anything but fields out in front of them. Then suddenly, something appeared as if it was an illusion until it became clear. It was a forest. There were tons of trees clustered together. Walking through it, Lillian felt in awe although she heard no birds and saw no animals. The forest was very thick and when it cleared there was a beautiful lake that appeared to go on forever in the distance.

"Wow. Azaria, look at..."

She trailed off as soon as she noticed Azaria was gone. She turned around every which way but couldn't see a sign of her. She called out her name loudly, but there was no answer. She turned back toward the lake wondering if Azaria had jumped into the water. She hadn't heard a splash. Lillian glanced down as something tickled her feet. The grass below her feet was plain except for a few purple flowers here and there.

Lillian called out for Azaria again. She didn't want to be alone. Lillian frantically began running through the forest. On her way back out, in the direction she had come from, Lillian stopped. There was a strange path leading into another section of the forest.

Biting her lip, Lillian decided to follow the path. There must have been a reason for it. Lillian gasped as she was suddenly face-to-face with a wall of mist. She was now in the opposite direction of where the lake was. It was darker in this part of the forest. Her curiosity got the best of her, and she reached out toward the mist again. The second her fingers touched it she saw the white sparks that trickled up her hand. What she didn't expect was for the mist to part, revealing a thick, thorny bush.

Cautiously, she reached out a hand and felt a sting. She jerked her hand back. She tried to peer through the bush. All she could see was a path, but where it led, she had no idea.

Maybe this is the way out!

Glancing behind her, Lillian knew the only way back would lead her right to where she started. Lillian squatted down and tried to find somewhere she could squeeze into. She hesitantly reached out a hand again and tried to move the branch out of the way. The spark erupted again only, this time, the branch shivered. The same spark happened when she touched the mist. She tried it again and again, and she felt the familiar sting.

As she stood up, she thought about the computer games she played. *This is just like my puzzle games at home. I just have to figure out how to get past it.* She got the branch to move when she touched it. Then she remembered the lake and the forest. *Maybe things can appear and disappear in this world.*

Reaching out again, she was determined to break through. She wanted nothing more than for the bush to just get out of her way. The second her fingers touched the branch, a huge spark of electricity flowed. It crackled against her fingers spreading onto the bush. She watched in amazement as the blinding white sparks caused the bush to shudder. The bush flew apart giving her enough room to walk through it. Lillian hurried through it and was relieved when it didn't close behind her.

The path was completely different from the rest of what she'd seen. There was no grass and no flowers beneath her. There was only dirt. The path led further down towards a run-down house. It was brown and plain, falling apart, and looked much older than the house she had first encountered. She walked up to the front door expecting it to open automatically like last time. It didn't. She tried to turn the handle, but it wouldn't budge. She felt awkward knocking on it. She reached out her hand brushing it across the door. She held her hand, still picturing the sparks of electricity. When nothing happened, she sighed out of frustration and banged on the door.

"Open you stupid door! Open!"

She felt a shock and a sting like before. She backed up out of surprise, and the door creaked open. She turned to look behind her. The path was still open. The entry way was very small. There was a flight of stairs a foot away and a doorway that led into the next room to the left. She could see the kitchen on the other side of the stairs.

The door slammed behind her, and she screamed. She swiveled around to the door but was startled by a noise from behind her. Someone was coming down the stairs. Wheeling around, she was startled to see a familiar face.

"Azaria? There you are. How did you get here?" Lillian questioned.

Azaria didn't respond. In fact, she turned her head away as if listening, before she came down the rest of the stairs. Azaria walked right passed her toward the doorway into the other room. Lillian reached out toward her, but her hand went straight through her shoulder. She yanked it back just as Azaria tiptoed into the next room. Cautiously, Lillian followed behind her. They went through the living room toward another door that was partially open. Azaria stopped right before the door and pressed her ear toward the crack. Lillian was too anxious to get any closer so she couldn't hear what the voices beyond the door were saying. Azaria's eyes narrowed, and she clenched her fists. Lillian heard some movement from the other side of the door. Azaria dashed away from the door back to the stairs.

"Don't argue with me Don," a woman said as she walked out.

Lillian stared at the woman wide-eyed. A man followed behind her.

"Jill, I'm not arguing. I'm just saying that we tried. That's all we can do," the man retorted firmly.

"I know. I know. I just…" Jill sighed. "I don't know what I'm going to say to her."

"We've done enough! She's completely ungrateful with the way she's been acting. She's gotten so bad now, throwing those horrible tantrums," Don complained, shaking his head.

As they spoke quietly, they too moved through the living room passing Lillian without a glance. They reached the front entryway.

"Alana, sweetie, what are you doing out of bed?" Jill asked.

Lillian approached the doorway and peered around the corner. Azaria was standing on the second to last step of the stairs gripping the rail so tight her knuckles were white. The strange thing was that they called her Alana.

"You're still sick," Jill continued.

"It's not like you care!" Azaria yelled.

"Alana, don't speak to us that way!" Don barked.

"I don't care!" Azaria screeched, stomping her foot.

"Alana!" Jill exclaimed.

"Don't call me that! My name is Azaria!" Jill and Don just glanced at one another in confusion. "I hate you both! You just want to get rid of me!"

"That's not true. We would love to have you, but you keep acting up," Jill explained.

"That's an understatement," Don scoffed.

"Alana, sweetie, we want to make this work, but clearly you're not comfortable here."

Azaria's eyes were hooked onto Jill's face. The anger that showed on her face was alarming. "You're supposed to be my family!" Azaria screamed back.

"Hey, you little brat, it's not our fault that your mother dumped you on us!" Don shouted.

"Don, please!" Jill begged.

"No! She needs to be put in her place! Your sister dies of a drug overdose by her own hands, and the girl's father is a useless, unemployed slug who wants nothing to do with her, and now we're somehow responsible! Just because we're in the will and because we're the godparents!"

Don turned back to Azaria. "Do you have any idea what it's been like for us? We're too old for this. Our kids are in college, and we wanted the place to ourselves but out of the goodness of our hearts, we made sure you didn't end up with your loser father! And foster care would've been worse! And this is how you thank us?" he bellowed.

"I hate you!" Azaria screamed. She stomped back upstairs and slammed the door.

"I'm done with you! Your father can deal with you, brat!" Don yelled.

Suddenly, everything began blurring. It was whizzing past Lillian like flashes of a dream. Azaria was in her room now. She was pacing back and forth. Azaria released a loud, furious scream as she threw things on the floor. Her face was red, and her hands were clenched. Azaria didn't look very well. She was sweating and on occasion clutching her head as if it hurt. She grabbed a photo frame and threw it on the floor. Then she yanked open her drawer and pulled out a pair of scissors. With terrifying fury, Azaria stabbed the frame many times, screaming as she did so. Lillian was so frightened that she backed up against the wall.

Some tears were leaking from Azaria's eyes now, but she had stopped crying. Lillian watched her uncertainly. Azaria still couldn't see her. Azaria stood up quietly and wiped at her eyes. The pair of scissors were still in her grip. She went out of her room and walked down the hall. Lillian followed her toward the door at the end of the hall. Azaria opened it and stepped inside. Lillian's chest tightened as she gazed at the sleeping couple in the bed. Azaria's fingers tightened around the pair of scissors, and she walked quickly over to one side of the bed. Lillian screamed as Azaria thrust the scissors into the man's neck and yanked them out. Don flailed his arms helplessly unable to scream as blood burst from his throat. His fingers trembled as he tried to grasp at his neck, staring wide-eyed at Azaria. Then Azaria twirled on her heel, and somehow Don knew what was going to happen next. Although he was bleeding to death, he managed to reach out a bloody trembling hand to his wife.

Lillian cupped her hands over her mouth and sobbed. Jill managed to wake up and turn on the light as Azaria reached her side of the bed. She raised the scissors so fast that Jill could only let out a surprised gasp. Azaria lunged at her, and Jill put her hands in front of her face, screaming. Azaria stabbed her hands over and over. Jill tried to shove her body backwards, away from the attack and landed on Don. Jill was screaming for Don, and it wasn't until she turned that she saw him lying with eyes wide open covered in blood. Jill sobbed hysterically screaming for Don. Her hands were all bloody, and she could barely move as Azaria stumbled onto the bed to reach her. Jill fell against the headboard with her bloodied hands outstretched in front of her begging for Azaria to stop through sobs.

Azaria was out of breath. She was sweating more profusely, but she lashed out with the scissors again. Only this time, just as she lashed out at Jill, she stumbled. Her balance faltered, and she fell backwards on the bed. She attempted to stand back up, but her eyes rolled into the back of her head. Her fingers lost their grip on the scissors, and as Azaria fought to stay conscious, she saw the sobbing, injured Jill struggle to pick up the phone by the bedside and then it all went black.

The scene changed again only, this time, Lillian was taken some place familiar. It was the hospital nearby her dad's place. She remembered suddenly that she had been over at her dad's with Cody. That was the last thing she remembered. It was their dad's turn to have them for the weekend. The room was blurry as Azaria fought to wake up. Despite that the faces of the people in the room were blurry, Azaria heard every word.

"Her guardian says she just attacked them after a fight," a male voice spoke.

"If she wakes up, we need to transfer her to the psych ward and get a consult," the female responded.

"The tests came back positive. There's definitely encephalitis."

"Yeah. I managed to calm the woman down enough to get some answers. The girl had a virus right before, and she had been getting constant headaches, so she said she gave the girl Aspirin. I think it might be Reye's syndrome, based on the sudden personality changes and increase in violent behavior. We need to monitor her and get another brain scan right away. We need to get the swelling down, or she could lapse into a coma."

The female continued to talk, but her words were suddenly inaudible. The room began spinning, and darkness surrounded her. Lillian panicked, reaching out blindly to find a way out. Her body lurched forward, and she found herself lying on the ground staring up. She saw the house in front of her just as she had when she first approached it. Lillian scrambled to her feet and ran back the way she came.

When she got back through the strange path, she collapsed. All that blood. Azaria killed that man. She tried to kill his wife too. How could anybody do something like that? Azaria couldn't have been older than ten. The doctors mentioned some kind of brain condition. The girl that she saw in that memory was nothing like the girl she met.

Just then, the bright sunlight that seemed to be coming from everywhere was diminishing. Lillian gazed up at the sky, which was nothing more than the same strange mist that she had seen before. Somehow, it was changing, becoming darker. When her eyes moved away from the sky, she realized that Azaria was standing two feet away from her. Lillian's heart skipped a beat, and she couldn't suppress the gasp that escaped.

"Why didn't you come find me?" Azaria demanded.

"What?" Lillian forced out.

"I was playing hide and seek! I left you the trail of flowers to follow!" Azaria exclaimed.

Lillian recalled seeing strange purple blossoms in the forest, but she had ignored them.

"I'm sorry. I got lost," Lillian replied in a shaky voice.

Azaria stared at her. Slowly, her eyes rose to the path Lillian had just come from before they settled back on her. Lillian's heart was pounding so loud it echoed in her ears.

"I saw you come out of there," Azaria said. Her tone was different. It was more confident and firm.

"No! No, I didn't. I was just –"

"You're lying!" Azaria screamed.

Lillian jumped. Lillian couldn't find any words to say; her mouth was frozen into place. Finally, she forced herself to speak. "Please. I just want to go home. Don't you want to go home?"

Azaria clenched her fists. "This is my home! This is *my* world!"

"But it's not real," Lillian argued. "It's an illusion."

"No, it's not! You don't understand! I don't have a home! They were going to send me away," Azaria snapped, her voice trembling. "I won't go back!"

As she took a step forward, Lillian jumped to her feet. She needed to run but with Azaria so close she wouldn't get far. She had to distract her.

"Is Alana your real name?"

Azaria's eyes narrowed. "I'm not Alana. My name is Azaria!"

"Okay. I'm sorry," Lillian said, stepping backward. "Azaria, why don't you come with me? We can be together back in the real world."

It seemed to be working. Azaria unclenched her fists. "I can't go back."

"You don't have to go back to them. You can come back with me," Lillian pleaded.

"You don't understand! My body is gone!"

Lillian stared at her wide-eyed. Then she looked off to her right. If she ran through the forest, perhaps she could lose her.

"I've been here for too long now. But I don't care! I like my world! I can make things happen," Azaria said, reaching down to touch the grass. The little sparks of electricity came off her fingers, the same thing that happened when Lillian touched the mist. Purple flowers began blossoming all around Azaria, matching with her dress.

"How did you do that?" Lillian gasped.

"I can do lots of things," Azaria said, smiling. "And I can teach you. We can be here together and make this our world. Besides, it's too late," she hissed, narrowing her eyes. "You didn't go through the white door."

The smug tone of her voice sent a chill through Lillian's body.

No, it can't be! That was my way out this whole time! Azaria manipulated me from the beginning.

"Wait. Show me how you did that again," Lillian said as her body tensed.

Azaria smiled and bent down to touch the grass. Lillian dashed off the second she looked away. She didn't even look back. She ran as hard as she could through the forest and back toward the field. She just kept running in hopes that it wasn't too late. She wasn't going to believe Azaria. She was a liar. The white house seemed so far away, but she kept running. She had to get back home.

Lillian crashed into the door, scrambling for the door handle. She charged inside and almost slipped on the floor. Leaping for the stairs, she took them two at a time and dashed down the hallway.

"Please. Please! *Please*," she whispered frantically.

She heard the sound of a door slamming shut. Her whole body jumped. Maybe the door didn't appear in the same place every time! She ran further down the hallway reaching out for it. She tried to will it to come to her like Azaria had willed the flowers to bloom.

How long has Azaria been here? And how long did it take her to learn how to make things appear?

She touched a nearby wall dragging her fingers and trying to set off the electric spark.

Just then, Lillian crashed right into something. She was knocked backward, but she managed to catch her balance. The white door stood there in front of her. She didn't even hesitate. She jumped up and grabbed the doorknob. It flung open, and she slammed it behind her.

There was darkness all around her. She stepped forward blindly. Swirls of color erupted around her. It reminded her of what she saw right before she woke up in the world. Her hopes lifted, and she felt her stomach flutter with relief and anticipation. She shut her eyes and waited for the moment when she'd hear her brother's voice, or her parents. She waited for what felt like forever before she opened her eyes again. She blinked and saw that she was lying in her bed. She sat up and looked around. Everything was the way she remembered it. She ran out her door and down the stairs.

"Dad? Cody?"

She heard voices nearby. They were coming from the kitchen. Her feet never even made a sound as she raced into the kitchen to see her dad pouring coffee into his mug. Cody was sitting at the table eating breakfast.

"Dad!" Lillian shouted. She couldn't believe she was finally home.

"Hey, do you two want to go out in the boat today?" her dad asked.

"Yeah!" Cody exclaimed as he stuffed toast in his mouth.

"Oh. Sure. Um, dad, can you tell me what's going on? Was I in a coma?" Lillian asked breathlessly.

"I want to drive the boat this time too! Lillian got to do it last time," Cody whined.

Lillian stared at him in confusion. Usually, that would annoy her, but not this time.

"Lillian, do you want any more toast?" her dad asked.

Lillian just shook her head. She went over to the table and sat down. Maybe she had brain damage or some memory loss, and she couldn't remember getting home.

"I have to tell you guys something really freaky," Lillian spoke up.

"No!" Cody exclaimed glaring at her.

Lillian's eyebrows furrowed. She gave him a puzzled look. "You don't even know what I'm going to say, Cody. It's about what happened when I was in the –"

"That's enough you two, stop bickering."

Lillian glanced over at her dad. "We weren't bickering."

"She started it," Cody said.

She looked back and forth from Cody to her dad. "You guys come on. I'm really freaked out here. Don't you care to know what happened to me?"

"If you guys want to go out while it's still sunny, you should hurry up and finish your breakfast."

"Dad! Are you listening to me?" Lillian shouted. She glanced over at Cody who was gulping down his juice.

"Done!"

"Okay. Let's hit the road."

He took one last gulp of his coffee. Lillian stomped over to where he was and stood in front of him. He didn't even stop walking. He walked right through her. Lillian stood there staring out in front of her where her dad had just been standing. Slowly, she turned around and saw Cody walking out the door. Seeing them from that angle and recognizing Cody's new swimsuit brought her crashing back to reality. This had happened before. That's why it seemed so familiar to her.

"No! I went through the door! I should be home!" Lillian bellowed, craning her neck to the ceiling.

"You are home."

Lillian screamed. She wheeled around frantically searching for the source of the voice. Azaria appeared to her from the doorway.

"What is this?" Lillian demanded.

"A memory," Azaria replied calmly. "Isn't this what you wanted? To be home?"

"This isn't home! I can't even talk to them! It's not real!" Lillian felt the tears cascade down her cheeks. Her body trembled with fear. She didn't want to be alone. She just wanted to see her family.

Azaria just stared at her silently. She had an unreadable expression on her face.

"I don't want to repeat all these stupid memories!" Lillian shouted, clenching her fists.

"This can be our home together. You don't need them anymore," Azaria said. Despite that her voice was soft, her tone was emotionless, like she repeating a line she rehearsed.

"You said that it was too late because the white door was gone, but I went through it!" Lillian screamed.

"That's because I put it there," Azaria said.

"So that...that wasn't the real white door?" Lillian's breath caught in her throat.

"That was the same white door. It's not a real escape. I created it," Azaria replied coolly.

Lillian felt all the muscles in her body seize, making it hard to move. She was sad and scared, but she was also angry.

So the white door was a trick?

"Then why did you tell me not to go in it?" Lillian asked hoarsely.

"I needed you to trust me," Azaria said. "I know you're scared. I was scared too when I first came here and didn't know where I was. I was here all by myself for the longest time before I started seeing other people."

Other people. That's right! Azaria mentioned she had seen four other people unless that was a lie, of course. But if there were others, where did they go?

Lillian inhaled a shaky breath. "What really happened to Christine?"

"She didn't want to stay here either! Nobody ever wants me! Nobody ever cares how lonely I feel here! She said horrible things to me, and she said she would never stay here with me! She tried to find her way out. I trapped her in the white door like you. No matter what I did, she still wanted to leave just like all the others!" Azaria threw her hands up in the air. "I tried to make them see how great this world is," Azaria's voice rose.

Azaria's eyes glanced downward for a second. She clenched her fists. "They wouldn't listen! You have to touch the mist here. None of them would do it so they began to fade. They looked like transparent ghosts. I tried to save them! Christine was the first person that came here after me, and when she faded, she became a little ball of electricity. When that happened, I put her in a jar to keep her safe. She was just floating around. I even still talk to her."

A flashback invaded Lillian's mind. She remembered when Azaria took her into the strange room that had suddenly appeared, the room that Azaria had called her sanctuary. She had noticed the five jars on the table, four of which were glowing.

Is the ball of light their souls? Are their souls trapped here forever?

"Why aren't you fading?" Lillian whispered.

Azaria blinked and then smiled. "Because I'm part of this world now. I told you. You have to touch the mist. That's how you become connected. That's how the world gets your memories. I learned how to control things and make things appear. I've spent a lot of time making this house and everything in it. When I first came here, there was nothing but mist and the dirt beneath our feet. I remember I was so scared of all the mist around me, and I tried to push it away from me, and that's when I saw the sparks. And when I wished for a beautiful grassy field instead of the ugly mist, it just started to appear, like magic! I don't even know how long it's been since I've been trapped here, but I'm happy here. I've made this place like heaven!" she exclaimed brightly.

Suddenly, her expression changed to a frown. "The others could've been happy. They would've made this world their home, and they didn't. We could've been a family. They gave up, and that's why they faded. I had to wait for someone like you, someone who would touch the mist willingly!"

Azaria's smile widened. "So you won't fade now! We can be sisters forever!"

Lillian shook her head over and over. "I don't want to be here. You can't keep me here!"

Lillian dashed around her through the living room and up the stairs. When she got to her bedroom, she slammed the door shut and locked it. She wiped tears from her eyes as she backed up towards the wall.

She lashed out at the wall and was stunned when her hand slipped through. The door to her room shook, and Lillian pressed both hands against the wall. She stared at it and imagined a pathway out. She pictured what she wanted to happen in her head over and over. Small electric bursts zapped out of her fingers, licking at the wall. The wall vanished and in its place was mist.

"You can't run from me, Lillian," she heard Azaria's voice nearby.

Lillian threw herself at the mist hoping with all her might that if she couldn't go through it, maybe it would at least kill her and send her off to heaven. Instead of going through it, the mist exploded around her and spat her out. Scrambling to her feet, she saw that she never left the white house. It was standing in front of her. Azaria's cry of fury echoed from above her. Lillian dashed away from the house. The only thing she could think to do was to go back to the place where she had come from and pray that she could get out the same way she came in.

The sky darkened around her as if swallowing her up. She could barely see the grass beneath her feet. Lillian struggled up the hill towards the top where she remembered waking up. The mist was just feet away. Lillian stretched her arms out toward the mist. A spark ignited from her fingertips which lit up like a candle against the darkness. As she pulled her fingers back, the mist followed, still glowing from the sparks of electricity that continued to run through it up to her fingers.

"You can't escape!" Azaria shouted stomping up the hill from behind her.

Lillian backed away until her back was against the mist.

"I told you, you can't go through it so there's nowhere else to go. Just come with me, Lillian. We can have so much fun here." Azaria began approaching her.

"Stay away from me! Get away!" Lillian screamed.

Lillian thrust her hands into the mist trying to claw her way out. Sparks erupted around her, and the mist flew out and began spreading in front of her. An idea struck her as Azaria closed in. Lillian clawed at the mist again, willing it to surround her like a shield. Flailing her arms frantically, Lillian tore through more and more mist, guiding it in front of her. The mist swirled around her, shooting out electric sparks every few seconds. A lot of the mist was still attached to her fingers so she moved her arms in a circular motion to allow the mist to circle her body.

Azaria reached out to grab her hands and screeched as an electric shock blocked her from reaching through the mist. Lillian's entire body shook with anticipation.

Azaria's right. We can't go through the mist. But it can be manipulated! As long as the mist is around me she can't touch me!

"STOP IT!" Azaria bellowed as she stomped her foot. "It doesn't matter if you do that! You can't keep it up forever! Stop trying to run away!"

Lillian continued to swirl the mist around her. She wasn't even getting tired.

It doesn't matter. She's right. I can't do this forever.

As a last desperate attempt, Lillian shut her eyes and willed herself to go home. If things could appear and disappear in the world, then it should have been possible that she could make herself disappear. Lillian circled her arms faster and faster, spinning around to keep the mist swirling around her. She could feel the tingling sensation begin to spread throughout her arms.

"Lillian, stop! You can't escape! YOU PROMISED ME YOU WOULDN'T LEAVE ME!" Azaria screeched at the top of her lungs.

Lillian pictured her dad's house. She pictured Cody sitting with his Playstation game on the couch. She could see herself at home, excited that they would all get to go to the beach. She just bought a new bathing suit too. She could see herself racing into her bedroom to change, and when she came out, Cody was already dressed and racing for the door. She ran as fast as she could to try to catch up to him, to get to the door before him.

She jumped up the steep steps two at a time. Cody reached for the door, laughing that he won. In an attempt to make sure he won, an innocent mistake, he closed the door in her face. She wasn't prepared for that. Her forehead slammed into the door, which threw her body off balance. The last thing she remembered was releasing one high-pitched scream of shock before falling backwards.

Cody, she thought. *He must be so upset.*

"NOOOOOOOOOO!" Azaria screamed frantically.

The terrified scream caused the memory to disappear, and Lillian opened her eyes. What she saw before her made her gasp. The swirling mist around her was glowing a blinding white light. All the electrical sparks were fusing together creating an immense shield around her. Lillian could still see Azaria, but the mist was becoming harder to see through.

Hope coursed through her bringing tears to her eyes. Lillian grabbed at the mist more confidently, thinking about her family, picturing her real home.

Azaria screeched loudly and clawed at the mist. She pounded her hands against it but nothing she did let her break through the barrier.

"You can't leave me!" Azaria screamed. "I won't allow it! I'll make you stay! I can control this world better than you!"

Those words made Lillian's heart skip a beat. She was too close. As Azaria attempted to will the mist to move apart, Lillian noticed that mist would move and then come right back together. Every time it did that, Azaria become more and more enraged.

Azaria may have better control of the world but I want to go home more than anything. My will has to be stronger or I'll never see my family again!

Lillian watched in awe as the beautiful sparks began merging together, creating one solid form around her. The world in the distance beyond, the grass and the flowers and even Azaria herself was becoming blurry.

"NOOOO! NO! NO! NO!" Azaria bellowed in fury as she collapsed to the ground. She pounded her fists on the ground screaming over and over. "You have to stay here! You touched the mist! You *can't* leave me!"

Azaria began tearing at the grass, throwing clumps of it all around. Lillian watched speechlessly. Her arms never hesitated, and her hope rose even more. Azaria lifted her head from the ground. Lillian saw the tears streaming down her face. Anger and pain flashed in Azaria's eyes before she completely disappeared. Lillian could still hear her screaming, but she stayed focused. She twirled her entire body around and around. The shield became more blinding as it created a tornado of luminescence all around her. It became so bright that Lillian shut her eyes. She felt her nose sting, but she wasn't sure if tears actually fell. She was warm, and she felt so light as though she was floating.

The warmth instantly vanished as the breath was knocked out of her. Lillian coughed, completely taken aback. A horrible, throbbing pain sliced through her head spreading down her neck. She wanted to scream, but she couldn't stop coughing. She felt a sharp prick in her arm and Lillian's arm jerked in reaction.

"It's okay. Calm down."

The gentle female voice caused her to turn her head. Lillian struggled to open her eyes. Her vision was a bit blurry, and she felt so disoriented. There was a blurry face in front of her.

"Just breathe. It's all right."

Lillian hardly registered that she was breathing shallowly. There was another voice, a male voice.

"Is she awake?"

"Yes. She just woke up," the female voice answered.

"My head," Lillian croaked.

"Give her some pain meds," the man replied.

The pounding in her head made it harder for her to concentrate on the strange voices around her. The voices ebbed and flowed. She was suddenly aware of was someone touching her hand. Lillian's eyes snapped open, yanking her hand away.

"Lil," the familiar voice replied.

The fear of seeing Azaria vanished at the sight of Cody and her dad. Cody was the one who had touched her hand.

"Cody? Dad? Is that really you?" Lillian whispered hoarsely.

"How are you feeling?" her dad asked as he came up next to Cody.

"My head feels better," Lillian said, slowly reaching a hand up toward her head. That's when she noticed the bandage. It was in the back of her head.

"I'm sorry, Lil," Cody said. It was then she noticed that his eyes were red.

"It's okay. I'm fine, really," Lillian said, forcing a smile. She reached out a hand and placed it on top of Cody's head. "It's not your fault."

Just then, a small spark came from one of her fingers. Several pieces of Cody's bangs stood upright.

"Hey! You shocked me," he said, rubbing his head.

Lillian's eyes widened. She didn't even realize she had pulled her hand away.

"We're glad you're awake, kiddo," her dad said. "You have no idea how relieved we felt when they told us you were awake."

"How long was I out?" Lillian asked.

"You were only in a coma for a few hours. The doctors said you should be back to normal in a week."

"Just a few hours?" she asked. *It feels like days.*

"Mom's supposed to get here soon," Cody said, rubbing his nose.

"Mom's coming?" Lillian gasped.

Her dad smiled down at her. "Yes. You're fortunate to have been unconscious when I called her and told her what happened. She ran into some traffic, and she's been calling every twenty minutes for an update. Just rest up. They want to run a few more tests before they give it the all-clear."

Lillian nodded and leaned back against the pillow. She couldn't express the amount of relief she had that she was with her family. She was back.

They were at the hospital for several more hours, but she didn't care. Her mom arrived a short time later and, after making a fuss over her, proceeded to lecture them all about being more careful. The doctors sent her home with medication and she was told to come back if she experienced any dizziness or other symptoms.

As they all met up at her dad's house, she couldn't help but feel comforted by the fact that both her mom and dad were there together. Her mom was only planning to stay a few days since she had to get back to work but that was enough for her. Her mom and dad sent her straight to bed to get some rest. With the help of the pain medications, Lillian fell asleep immediately.

She could see the beautiful electrical light again. She remembered the warmth and the feeling of floating. When the feeling vanished, she found herself standing in front of the white house. Lillian's whole body froze.

"You're back!"

Clutching her chest, Lillian wheeled around to see Azaria standing before her. She was wearing the same purple dress as she remembered. "What do you mean I'm back? Am I in a coma again? You can't keep me here! I'll escape the same way I came!" Lillian exclaimed. Lillian shut her eyes tight. She gasped aloud as her body jolted upright in bed. Lillian looked around and saw that she was in her room. A knock came at the door.

"Lillian, sweetie, are you okay?"

The door opened, and her mom stepped inside. "I thought I heard you yell."

"I'm sorry, Mom. Was I asleep?"

"Yes. You just went to bed twenty minutes ago," her mom said. She sat down on the bed and put a hand on her forehead. "Are you having trouble remembering things?"

"No. I'm fine. I just didn't realize I was dreaming," Lillian said.

Her mom smiled. "All right. Well, get some rest. If you need anything, we'll be right downstairs."

"Thanks," Lillian said, sinking back onto her pillows. Glancing down she saw her hands were trembling. Taking in a shaky breath, she closed her eyes and relaxed her body. It wasn't an illusion. She wasn't in a coma.

"How did you do that?"

Lillian's eyes snapped open, and she turned to see Azaria standing before her again. She was back in the coma world.

"Am I dreaming?" Lillian asked aloud. "Are you real?"

"Of course I'm real," Azaria replied.

"I don't understand. I was just back with my mom. She said I had been asleep."

Azaria cocked her head to the side curiously. "You are dreaming," she said finally.

Lillian tried not to panic. Azaria had mentioned that they were intertwined with the world once they touched the mist.

Azaria's lips curled into a smile. "I told you, Lillian. You touched the mist. You can't leave me."

Lillian just stared wide-eyed at her as Azaria held out her hand.

"Now we can be sisters. Forever."

32.
Madame Zelda
H.R. Boldwood

June 12, 1975, dawned with an abundance of promise. Charlie Hunsacker and I lay on Rodanthe beach, watching fish-bellied tourists sacrifice themselves to the sun god. We marveled at the sight of well-oiled, bikini-clad girls and mentally untied the strings that stood between us and a small glimpse of heaven. But even thoughts of young, glistening breasts couldn't make thirteen-year-old boys lie still. We raced across the sand through a heady blend of coconut oils, dodged a kaleidoscopic collection of beach towels, and headed for our bikes.

I climbed onto Sancho, my trusty red Schwinn, and waited for Charlie. A hot summer breeze gusted a piece of paper into my leg. It was a flyer for the Barlowe Brother's Carnival. Had I simply brushed it away, having never read it, perhaps that day would have ended as splendidly as it had begun. Perhaps every night thereafter wouldn't have ended in nightmares. And perhaps Charlie Hunsacker would never have disappeared.

****

"Last one to Stricker's Grove's a rotten egg!" I shoved the flyer into my pocket and took off like I was being chased by the devil himself.

Charlie pedaled hard to catch me. "Why are we going to Stricker's Gove?"

"A carnival's in town!"

We tore through Rodanthe and into the woods, pretending to be knights upon our steeds, searching for a dragon to slay. Only when we reached the majestic tents of The Barlow Brother's Carnival did we finally stop, and there we found our dragon. She was a magnificent fortune-telling machine named Madame Zelda with a porcelain face and coal-black eyes that flashed yellow when she dispensed divinations on tiny strips of paper; her lips siren red, her head encircled with a silk scarf. She wore shoulder-length hoop earrings and sat cross-legged before a crystal ball, her gaze never wavering; head held high, an all-powerful clairvoyant, willing to share the future with those who dared seek it. People waited patiently under the sweltering sun for her pearls of wisdom, intriguing insights, and prophesies. She was a portal to the unknown. When had ten cents ever purchased more? Charlie and I were moths to her flame.

"Give me a dime," Charlie said.

I rolled my eyes. "If I had a dime, I wouldn't be standing here with you."

"Shit," Charlie said with a kick at the dirt. We took one last look at Madame Zelda, then with hands shoved deep into our pockets, we turned to leave. But the barker had other plans.

"Why the hangdog look, gents? Zelda loves her dimes, but she loves satisfied customers even more. They're the ones who keep coming back. Every good businessman knows that. One turn each, I'll give you. Just promise me you'll come back with money in your pocket. Fair enough?" He didn't have to ask twice.

Charlie muscled his way in front of me. Madame Zelda sprang to life and spit out his fortune. He read it and frowned. "Grave consequences await. What's that supposed to mean?"

"Who cares?" I asked, grabbing mine. It wasn't much better. "You will be consumed by your dreams."

The barker's eyes widened and his color faded. He shooed us away. "Off you go, you've had your turn. Never mind coming back. I wouldn't, if I were you. Madame Zelda sounds a bit peeved."

But of course, we were coming back. What choice did we have? Our fortunes provided more questions than answers. We devised a plan that had nothing to do with feeding Madame Zelda dimes. We would return in the dead of night, after the carnival closed, with handfuls of arcade room tokens. We'd slip them into her coin slot. She would never know the difference. Madame Zelda's knowledge would be ours, and ours alone! We each told our parents that we were spending the night at the other's house and swore to see our mission through no matter the cost.

It seemed as if night might never come, but when the time was right, we made our way back to the fairgrounds and crawled like commandos into Madame Zelda's tent. We'd brought flashlights but found we didn't need them. Madame Zelda's box was fully lit — as if she had been expecting us. The night was strangely quiet; the air heavy and still. I thought I heard a chuckle coming from inside the box. It's only your imagination, I thought. Ignore it. Sweat broke out on my upper lip despite the sudden burst of frigid air that washed over me. "Hurry up, do it already!"

Charlie put a token into the coin tray and pushed. The tray stuttered and caught. Charlie pushed harder. The screeching sound of metal against metal would surely give us away. "Stop! You're going to break it!" I said. Charlie ignored me and pushed the tray with all his might. A low growl hummed inside the box.

"What the hell was that?" I asked.

"What was what?" Charlie kept jimmying the tray to work it loose. "Madame Zelda's going to be one sorry bitch if she doesn't spit out another fortune but damn quick!"

A tiny scrap of paper fluttered out of the machine. Charlie's eyes grew wide, but then he smiled and bobbed his head like a bad-ass. "Guess you didn't want your butt kicked after all, did you, bitch?" He picked up his fortune and read.

"You were warned."

"Come on, Charlie. Let's get out of here," I said.

"Warned? You want warned? Suck it up, Zelda. This is going to hurt." He kicked her. "What'd you think about that, huh?"

The hair on the back of my neck stood up. "No shit, Charlie, we need to go."

"Not until we get what we came for – a whole night's worth of fortunes. And that's just what we're going to get." He reached into the mouth of the machine where the fortunes came out and stuck his fingers in as far as they could go. The box moaned. It sounded sexy, dirty.

"Charlie, come on. We're leaving, now!" I grabbed his jacket and pulled him toward me, but his fingers were caught in the machine.

"Oh Jesus!" he screamed. "Get it off of me!" It began to shake with Charlie's arm stuck inside. "Help me! Shit! Make it stop!" The lights inside the box flashed faster and faster. The room spun, slowly at first, then gyrated at dizzying speed. My thoughts tumbled. Please God, let this be a dream. The last thing I remember was watching Charlie's arm disappear further and further into the machine. And then the room went black.

When I came to, no trace of Charlie or the carnival remained, only the tattered flyer I'd shoved into my pocket – the same flyer I'd read with such joy only hours before. It was proof that I wasn't dreaming, that the carnival had been real. But when I pulled the flyer back out, it had changed. The date of the carnival was now June 12, 1925 – fifty years earlier. Charlie and I hadn't even been born. But Madame Zelda, spawn of some unnamed evil, had always been, and would forever be.

****

Madame Zelda's predictions were as true as north. These days, when sleep prevails, it's neither long, nor restful. Memories of that fateful night churn like an angry ocean. In the worst of my dreams, Madame Zelda, with her siren red lips and sultry moan, returns to visit me. She spits out a tiny scrap of paper that takes me to the brink of madness. In the dusky light of fitful dreams, my eyes make out the words, "Forever mine."

33.
Man Of Naivety Weaved
Norbert Gora

Horror tapped in the branches of trees,
spit the fear, laughed the wind,
seeing this man, soaked in naivety and arrogance.

Besotted by the courage, he wanted to
find the beast in the forest,
which froze the blood in the veins.

Born from the nightmare, no one could understand,
which mind has created it, devilish pact had to get it out of the earth,
revitalized by the promise of Satan.

Glow of the flashlight cut through the forest road,
the nightmare of nightmares danced around,
trying to push him into the dark.

Weary, disappointed, with the defeat was
almost shook hands, when the rasp behind him
enveloped his mind woven from the death breath.

He screamed and fell to the ground,
and the light pierced the sky, like a laser,
it's beam landed on those ruby eyes.

The devil's seed, the wolfish growl.
"Those, who seek, finally will find"
beast muttered the last words, until life got away from him.

34.
Medusa In The Mirror
Mark Hudson

Medusa's reflection in the mirror was not fair,
an ugly gorgon with snakes in her hair.
One of three sisters hated by mortal man,
to destroy these monsters required a plan.
The mirror was something she looked at alone,
 humans would gaze at her and turn to stone.
Perseus beheaded her by avoiding her gaze,
he looked in a mirror and his sword was raised.
He beheaded her, snake heads and all,
the loveliest sight for the mirror on the wall.

35.
Memorias de la Tierra
Franco Strong

The votive candles flickered with the light taken from a remembered dream. An image of the Virgin of Guadalupe sat atop the altar with her heavy gaze perpetually searching the earth for the son she had lost. There were other faces though, hidden amongst the blooming marigolds, photographic portraits all colored with the same somber grey. The outlines of their features—strong jaws, wide eyes, linear brow lines—seemed to be pulled by Time's eroding fingertips.

Tamayo kneeled in front of the altar and uttered a prayer to those faces, his ancestors. He imagined that the purifying salt atop the table was only a collection of dried and forgotten tears. Incense dripped into the air and in between the bending and shifting wisps of smoke, Tamayo heard whispers, sighs, moans, but they were faint and unclear as though the voices were coming from the opposite end of the desert expanse. Tamayo wondered how far his own words could travel, if those on the other side of Death could hear his prayers. His voice didn't need to travel that far, he only wished that it would reach his disappeared mother so he could tell her that even though he loved his abuelo he didn't want to live with the old man any longer. He wanted to tell his mother that he missed being with her, in her arms, how her hair smelled like flowers, how her hands were both rough and soft at the same time, and how her soothing touch was the only thing that could send him to sleep on certain restless nights. Maybe her voice was already there, alongside the others, murmuring to not be forgotten on this day, All Soul's Day, Día de los Muertos.

A voice, heavy and human, called out to Tamayo and he lifted his eyes to see his abuelo standing in the doorway. The old man always stood a little taller in the shadows of nightfall, as though once the oppressive weight of the sun was gone, his spine straightened out to its true length.

"Hijo, come. We have work to do."

"Tonight?"

"Sí," the old man said and walked out of the doorway, the orange candlelight making his image linger a moment longer. The old man never spoke much and Tamayo never asked many questions. Tamayo trusted the old man, and he trusted the old man's silence even more.

He peered up at the Virgin Maria and the other nameless faces upon the altar, and they seemed to beg him to stay, to hear their stories, as if they had recovered a little life from him and a second death awaited them once they were alone and forgotten.

The old man was already waiting outside in his rusted pickup, the engine wheezing in the placid blue air of night. They drove off, two men, one old and one young. Somewhere along the way, Tamayo lost track of their sleepy town, the constellations of streetlamps, the empty highway, the silent side streets, and he found himself on a crumbling road that trailed up a bald hillside. The headlights picked up the slowly swaying path, the curves a vague dance that only the hillsides knew. Low-lying, dead brush protruded from the otherwise barren soil and Tamayo imagined that those leafless branches were the hairs of a giant beast which hibernated just beneath the earth.

The old man parked the truck at the end of the paved road, then he walked a little farther off with Tamayo following, the ancient gravel sighing beneath their feet. The old man carried a small basket and Tamayo could smell the aroma of warm tortillas. They stopped at the edge of a vista overlooking the scattered light below. Tamayo whispered that the pockets of light looked like pools of water, maybe small oceans with invisible, black waves rippling through them.

"I've only seen the ocean once," the old man said, his voice course like burning embers were lodged in his throat. "But I've known her cousin, the desert. It's a waterless ocean, a sea of stones." The old man was quiet for a moment. "After a lifetime you learn to love it in your own way."

"It's pretty," Tamayo said. He thought about the old man and all those memories that must reside within that leathery, sulfuric skin of his. It was like peering at a dry riverbed and imagining the torrents of cold water that must have flowed through at one time. Tamayo only knew his grandfather had made a living as a ranch-hand his whole life, and if the old man stopped working his hardened hands would probably dissolve and be reclaimed by the parched soil, the same soil which had forged them with its inexhaustible sand and dirt.

They waited longer, Tamayo walked in circles to keep his legs warm, and time seemed to lurch directly alongside the light breeze.

The old man lifted a finger to the distance and said, "Beyond those hills is Mexico. You can't see it, but it's there."

Tamayo had heard the whispered rumors about that place, that his mother had crossed back over the prismatic, crystalline frontier and she'd probably never return. His fragmented thoughts coalesced and he wondered what kind of place Mexico must be, where women drift in only to be swallowed whole and never heard from again.

"Our blood first simmered over there in that black heap. It still simmers to this day. You can hear her prayers sometimes, carried through the winds and the rains," the old man said.

Tamayo listened and heard nothing. But maybe that was the prayer: a dense, monolithic silence. "Do you think Mama is there, like they say?" he asked.

"We pray for everyone on All Soul's Day," the man answered, "even those that are lost."

Images seemed to rise from the earth and saturate Tamayo's mental landscape, his mother's soft face, her hair, then a deep chasm that slowly opened like a sleepy eye, and a pupil that was filled with an ancient, granulated black.

The lights below and the stars above floated and danced, both pulled by the same invisible tide. He wondered how many lives these lights had presided over, indifferent witnesses to the sufferings of those below. Then, for a moment, the faint scent of incense pressed against Tamayo's nostrils, followed by the sound of hooves beating and dragging against the earth, but those noises seemed hollow, as though emanated from the shifting westerly winds more so than any real point in time.

"Ah, here we are," the old man said.

A tall silhouette approached from out the darkness and Tamayo recognized the unmistakable outline of a man on horseback. The horse trotted with a severe limp, almost stumbling over itself. A stench of stale and dry sweat proceeded the lonesome rider, and as he came closer Tamayo made out a floppy Stetson resting on the rider's back, gold yet rusted button's running down his legs, leather boots with crevices like veins, a frayed poncho over his chest with dark circles matted into the cloth like spots on aged wood. A thin moustache and high cheekbones graced the man's face along with deep set eyes reminiscent of precious metal that hasn't been mined yet. Desert dust covered his whole body.

Tamayo's abuelo spoke in an even-keeled Spanish to the rider, "Ella is muy bonita," he said and stroked the taut neck of the brown mare.

"Ay sí, pero her legs are hurt," the rider said.

"I see. Her legs," the old replied. "She needs rest. Come down and I can help you unsaddle her."

The rider hesitated and didn't move.

"You don't recognize me," the old man said. "It's okay. Yo soy un primo de su papa. You've been away from the ranch a long time."

The rider looked over the old man and then Tamayo felt the heavy gaze fall upon him.

"How long has it been?" the rider asked.

"Mucho tiempo. Un año" the old man said. "But you have the papers, of course."

The mysterious rider nodded his head. "Sí."

"Come, we'll help you get them to su padre," the old man said.

The rider dismounted from his ailing horse, which let out a deep, asthmatic breath. Tamayo peered at the rider and by the light of the moon he saw a face, young, barely on the cusp of manhood, yet vaguely familiar somehow, a resemblance to Tamayo's own face but unfamiliar also, like he was peering through the shards of a broken mirror.
"Who is he?" Tamayo whispered to his abuelo.

The old man lay an almost skeletal hand upon Tamayo's shoulder, "He's one of those lost souls we pray for on this day."

The rider faced them and asked, "Your hijo?"

"My grandson, Tamayo. Your distant primo," the old man said.

"Israel. Mucho gusto," the rider said with an outstretched hand, scars running across his knuckles.

Tamayo took the man's grip and an alien sensation tore through his body, like infinite grains of sand and stone penetrated into his skin, burrowing itself in his arteries. He felt the languished desert sun burn in his chest, shrieking echoes clawed through his ears, a coldness cleaved through and severed his psyche in half. He saw them with innocent eyes, crystalized calamities, memories that weren't his own.

****

He crossed over the border, that prismatic frontier of dry lands, the terminal point of two worlds: the United States and Mexico. The border-town was sleepy, a prevailing unconsciousness extruded from the peoples' faces, similar to those early-morning dreams one has just before awakening.

Israel pushed past the town and rode farther along into the depths of the forsaken lands. Here, the thirsty mountains loomed a little closer in order to carefully examine the solitary figure riding along their stone ribs. It felt like he had been through here before, as though he were also crossing that nocturnal frontier within his soul towards some preordained rendezvous on the other side of the horizon.

Israel's family used to call this land, Mexico, their country. But an invisible incision had been freshly sliced into the earth. After the war with the norteamericanos, Israel and his family found themselves stranded in Alta-California, strangers to their own land, foreigners of both the body and soul, motherless nomads. They tried to get along, make a life as they always had, but other settlers questioned the legitimacy of Israel's family properties: a massive ranch whose only demarcations were the natural wrinkles of the earth. Israel's padre, too old and too proud to leave his land, had sent Israel to ride into Mexico and retrieve the official documents that would justify ownership and the family's right to live on the ranch they had always called home.

The sun and its endless caresses of warmth seemed to conjure a dream within Israel's exhausted mind, one of stars collapsing, an ocean evaporated, documents and papers written with the shifting sands in a language he didn't recognize. The dream passed and Israel knew it was time to rest.

Inocencia, his horse, was strong but he could sense her muscles stiffening with fatigue. He remembered the words of his father: horses are like women, treat them right and they'll keep you alive.

Once he set up a small, makeshift camp he watched the sun fall as though it was tired of holding up the weight of the sky.

Long, symmetrical rows of crops lined the hillside and horizon, a signal that Israel was leaving behind a solitary expanse and entering the lands of other men. He rode past a crumbling church with men lazily working as though their limbs, faces, and bodies weren't their own, trying to reconstruct a distorted skeleton of walls and empty windows.

He arrived at the center of the small town around midday, the sun at its apex and the town devoid of shadows. Dust covered everything, the adobe walls, tiled roofs, iron bars, windows, and porticos. Even the townspeople's faces couldn't escape the omnipotent granules, they were there, between that old woman's wrinkled eyelids, and here, beneath this young man's tongue. The thin film of sand was a reminder that any lives built atop the exiled lands were condemned to Time's amnesic gaze.

The official governmental building was adjacent to the central square, which wasn't more than an open space with a few dead plants and one dismal, leafless tree in the center. Israel tied up his horse, and then once inside the building he spoke to an older gentleman, explaining the situation, the official documents required, who his father was (he was well known due to the sheer size of the family ranch), and the correspondences they had with their former country's government.

The older gentleman said that yes, they had been expecting the young sir form Alta-California, the paperwork would be ready in one, maybe two days at most, governmental bullshit, you see, and leaned his heavy body closer to Israel.

"The matter of time is important," Israel said.

"They'll have it ready when it's ready," the man shrugged, "governmental bullshit." Then he told Israel to enjoy this small town, that he would personally see that Israel found the finest accommodations, some lodgings where the young man could get some well-deserved sleep.

Israel agreed, helpless to do otherwise. He retrieved Inocencia from outside and followed the man to the lodgings across town. Once again, the outline of the ruined church reappeared in Israel's view and his sun-poisoned mind wasn't sure if he had seen the crumbled walls only once before or a hundred times.

That night Israel lay awake in bed. Acclimating to the world of men is difficult when one has found the ocean of solitude between the desert and the sky. Outside the thin window, he heard voices, murmurings of the town, then a woman singing a corrido about a drunken hero who buried his dead wife in the desert, but the sleek and slender body of the woman was actually only a large stone, and the man had never loved anyone in his tired life because the desert, that overbearing and jealous mistress, loved him too much and she would never let him out of her labyrinthine grip.

He idly listened a little longer to the sounds brought to his ear, before dressing and making his way to the stables out back where Inocencia was resting. She too seemed uneasy with this night and its noises. Israel patted the mare's thick neck and whispered sweet and soothing words into the animal's ear. She was the only connection Israel had to his home, the ranch, and its crusted hillsides he knew so well growing up that they were firmly embedded within his soul. He could almost see all the faces of the ranch, tías and tíos, hermanos, abuelos, nephews, cousins, all the faces that passed through their land, their features slight variations on the same theme because they were forged by the same blood, sun, and history. He envisioned his father, the old soldier, riding atop his caballo with his perpetually loaded rifle because the old man was still at war, with time, with nature, with his own soul. He envisioned his mother with her stoical gaze, which always peered into the empty spaces of life's shattered reflection. Could she see him as he was, a young man, tired, hungry, lonely, and maybe a bit older now because his soul allowed the bitter cold of the desert night to enter in? A fleeting, transparent notion crept across Israel's mind, that his loved ones had forgotten him the moment he cleared the border.

He whispered a prayer into Inocencia's ear, "Bring me home, querida," before leaving to rest once again.

He went searching for those nocturnal sounds he heard earlier, but the town was a semi-conscious specter. Then, from out of the opaque night, a silhouette appeared and only a moment later did Israel hear footsteps.

The feminine outline spoke to him, her voice seemed like the fingertips of a cascading shadow: "Are you alone out here also?"

"Sí," Israel said, then added, "It isn't safe for a woman to be out alone. People might get ideas."

The woman laughed and moved closer to Israel. "Everyone in town knows me and they know I'm not that type of girl. They think I'm mad, but they know I'm not like that. And I've found you, so I'm not alone now, am I?"

"No, I guess you aren't alone now," Israel said.

Thin yet strong lips above an angular chin with soft and slender cheeks composed the young woman's face. Her large and round eyes competed with the half-moon above. She was simply beautiful, but something in her eyes made Israel hesitate, as though instead of looking at the constellations in the night sky she peered into those black recesses of nothingness which separate the needlepoints of light.

"May I join you?" she asked.

Israel shrugged and they started along together.

"I knew I'd find you," she said. "It's like I had remembered it before it happened, or I had read it somewhere."

"You can read?" Israel asked, surprised that a woman of humble origins knew the writings of men.

The subtle wind seemed to laugh for her and she said, "No, not words. I read the same things everyone else does, the wind, the rain, the sun, all those things which carry the fate of men within them."

"Ah, I see," Israel said.

They walked along and she spoke more, about strange things, stories, the origins of this town, coyotes, empty graves, life, sickness, death, pyramids buried beneath the sand, the sun, the crumbled church, lost children. Israel tried to contemplate what she was saying but he lost her words as soon as she uttered them. Still, something in her voice was reminiscent of the hazy heat which woke Israel on summer mornings.

"We're both a little lost," she said.

"You don't know your town?" Israel asked and surveyed the adobe buildings flanking either side of them. His hand brushed against his knife, just to be sure it was still there. He had heard stories of conniving women who preyed on the souls of unsuspecting men.

"No, I know this town well. It's probably the only thing I'll ever know. But us, you and I, we're lost in a different way," she said.

"I'm not so sure," Israel chuckled. "I was sent here. I'm supposed to be here."

"Any stranger that comes to his town is naturally searching for something they've lost," she said. "I can tell by your longer left stride that you are searching for a home. And the way your head tilts you're longing for a mother."

Israel straightened his stride and stiffened his neck. "I have both, up North."

"Then why are you here and not there with them?" she asked. "But what I mean to say is that you are motherless, without a land, an orphan to the hillsides with no dirt to call your own. Except maybe out there somewhere," she pointed to the distance, "isn't that so?"

He didn't answer and they walked a long stretch in silence, the town also densely quiet, like it was on the precipice of collapsing into the cold earth, as though someone else were imagining it, and the dreamer was ready to wake at any moment.

"You can go ahead and tell me about yourself or I can continue listening to the night and it'll tell me everything I need to know about you," she said.

He spoke a little about himself, about his family, the hacienda, how he was sent by order of his aging father, how he had traveled through the desert without speaking a word, yet he heard more voices than he could ever dream to count.

"And they sent you alone? No tienes hermanos?"

"They have their own lives, families, wives, husbands, children."

"They sent their youngest?"

"I'm not the youngest. There were others. But winters are cold and help is far."

The two had circled the town and they were returning to the stables. Her eyes seemed to contain another story within, but the voice was too far gone, drowned in the edges of her transparent irises.

"I need to rest," Israel said.

"I know. I'll wait for you tomorrow, here, at sundown," she said, and Israel agreed.

"You can kiss me goodnight," she added, "I don't mind."

Israel leaned in and his lips pressed against warm flesh, inviting, soft and subtle like a thunderstorm a great distance away. Then her slight frame slipped into the tactile night, her body swaying to an ancient melody, and Israel was left alone with the ghost of a kiss that tasted so familiar.

The day leaked through Israel, one yellow, sun-streaked moment after another. The governmental papers hadn't arrived when he checked in the morning, and he found himself with nothing to do except wander amongst the town once again. He attempted to retrace his steps from last night while the sun painted his skin with its vibrant vitality. During daylight the thirsty town appeared smaller and insignificant, as all things are when flanked by a gravel abyss and omnipotent sun above. In the nocturnal darkness of last night though, beside that peculiar woman, the streets had slithered into a labyrinthine coil.

Droplets of white clouds diluted the blue sky throughout the day until the quivering horizon swallowed the last daylight. Israel visited Inocencia, brushed her coat down, and whispered that soon she'd be free and out of the stable, amongst the open land where her muscles could stretch to their full length.

The wait seemed long and empty until the aquiline silhouette appeared. The young woman wore the darkness like a shawl draped across her shoulders. Maybe she only existed at night, a tangential entity to La Luna.

"How long have you been waiting?" she asked.

"Not long," Israel replied.

"Here, I made these for you," she said and unwrapped a few warm tortillas from a bundle of cloth.

Israel bit into the warmed masa which melted and slid town his throat.

"Good?"

"Sí."

She added, "I'd made a good wife if I had the chance."

"Of course. Someday," Israel said and took another bite.

"No, fate will have it otherwise. I'll live like Our Virgin. She knows how similar we are."

"You haven't told me your name," Israel said. "I thought about it as I slept last night."

"You already know it. Maybe you dreamt it last night. It's Maria. Now, let's walk while we still have time."

He let her lead and the streets seemed to snake into new possibilities, stretching and shortening at will. They ended at the crumbled skeleton of the old church.

"Here again?" Israel asked.

"All paths, no matter where they are in the world, naturally lead to the river or a pile of debris, sometimes even both."

Israel said he had never heard that maxim before. His thoughts turned to the small streams that ran through the hills of his family ranch during the rainy season, and how he had mistaken the sighing water for human voices when he was younger.

"That's how things are. You'll find out for yourself, one day" she said and then continued on, telling the story of how the church collapsed, how some said the walls were sunk by an old woman, others claimed a child had opened her mouth and swallowed it, still others were adamant that it was simply the weight of forgotten sins.

"And which do you believe is true?" Israel asked.

"All of them. I wouldn't tell them to you if I knew they weren't true," she said.

A current of light from the half-moon flowed onto everything below, except for the woman's face, her skin allergic to the phosphoric glow. Israel wondered if there was a point of congruence between the two of them, if a space within their souls overlapped, or if they'd always long for one another like the desert longs for its ancient ocean to return.

"Vamos," she said. "There is nothing else to this town. Even if we search every day for a year, we'll still find nothing."

Israel didn't mind, he could have followed this woman through the ghostly streets all night, but her hand, calloused and maybe even scarred, pulled him along.

She told him to eat, finish the rest of the tortillas. "God knows you won't have any more home-cooked food."

They arrived back where they started, somewhere outside the stables where Inocencia slept. Israel thanked her for the food along with the walk and her stories, and he began to say more but she interrupted.

"You don't have to say, but I know you love me. I've heard it before, a remnant of your voice. And in my own way I love you, ever since you crossed that border up North. I know you can never take me to those lands up there, but for tonight you can be with me," she said with sad eyes, her vision focused somewhere beyond Israel, behind, in the darkness that stretches across time itself.

Once the two of them were in the room she began to undress, silently, her fingers and hands following some preordained action. The same wind which had carved out the hills and the plains also shaped her almost perfect curves, and he stroked her waist with trembling hands, yet the wispy sensations in his fingertips was familiar, a path he had navigated many time before.

"Probrecito, probrecito, my little lost angel. You haven't been with a woman before, I know." She kissed his neck. "Don't be afraid, there is nothing you can do, I'm barren."

No, she was an oasis of skin, flesh, and tangible scents. He pressed his body against hers, he embraced her supple skin, his salvation was there, within the diaphanous yet fractured edges of her soul. Her breath was a chorus unearthed from the dry soil, an echo finally arriving from years past.

"How many times must you perish in my arms?" she whispered.

Israel knew he loved her, maybe even at the simultaneous moment she loved him, the exact moment he stepped through the crystal frontier. He loved her because she was barren, encompassing in her absence. He closed his eyes and an entire night sky floated through his head, the stars liquefied and dripped down to the dry plains below.

The warmth of the sun gently stirred Israel awake like motherly hands. Daylight filtered in through the window, illuminating the bed devoid of a woman's flesh. Somehow Israel expected it, her absence at dawn, because she was a creature that existed within the lungs of the night. She could never live beneath the sun, and he knew it.

The official documents had arrived at the governmental building and he had no trouble retrieving them. Inocencia's muscles were well rested and relaxed, and Israel left the town simply like a whisper.

The days didn't pass by, rather, they replayed in a cyclical loop fueled by the sun's shrieking heat. Hadn't he already seen those hillsides, the ribs of the desert? Hadn't he already passed that creosote and cacti, the charred navel-hairs of these plains? He kept the morning sun to his right, the evening sun to his left, and Inocencia's nose pointed North towards the lands he had been born into.

Visions traversed over the backdrop of Israel's mind, the dark and potent coffee his father drank, the crisp hiss of earth as it was being shoveled, water dripping off balconies after a storm, his mother's joints that creaked like wooden walls on a cold morning. At nightfall he heard voices, the voices which whisper a man's fate and cause time to exist and then pass on by. In the aquiline moments just before sleep, he thought about her, that peculiar woman he had loved briefly in that unconscious town, the strange and sublime stories that poured from her mouth. At times he still tasted the ghost of her intimately familiar kiss, and he wondered how much longer it would linger upon his cracked lips now that he was out here in the amnesiac expanse. Her warmth was near also, hovering beside him, extruding from her ephemeral body. He opened his eyes, his reveries disappearing once he gazed upon the dying embers of his campfire and the ocean of stars above, indifferent to his presence below.

The sun was renewed once again as Inocencia trotted along. Roads, trails, other towns should have crossed Israel's path by this stage of the long journey, but the open landscape hinted at nothing except a continuation of its placid, beige coloration. His food was gone, the final droplets of water sloshed through his canteen, and Inocencia hadn't lapped up anything to drink in days. The papers he had been sent to retrieve were still stowed away safely within a wooden box and the tough leather of his saddlebag, the ink and paper thrummed with life and gained weight the farther he pushed towards the horizon. He dreamed of casting the papers into the lifeless sand and riding off, Inocencia in full gallop back home. No, he convinced himself he could survive these lands with the papers intact. He recalled the words his mother spoke to him ever since he was a small child, that his family blood had been forged in the choking dust and heat, that it was an inseparable part of his soul.

He dismounted and rested Inocencia in the shade of a rock outcropping. It was better to only run her at night from now on, when the cooler, blue air reinvigorated exhausted lungs. He looked across the dead plains and laughed at the shimmering, false water of the distance. With his right hand against the butt of his pistol he whispered to the cracked earth that he wasn't that dumb, that he knew her tricks well enough. His voice clawed its way from out of his body as he cursed himself, then aimed. One, two, three, gunshots disappeared into the phantom waters of the distance.

Inocencia's stride stretched across the nocturnal abyss, galloping along, chasing the silver mist cast by La Luna. He had found a path earlier in the day, a forgotten path overgrown and barely visible, and he hoped it lead to somewhere, a town, a village, the cool waters of a river. Crisp air with azul edges blew across his face and sliced open his brittle lips. If Inocencia kept up this pace they'd make it home in a few short nights, the work finally finished and his homecoming complete, a son worthy of his own name. His exhausted muscles were on the verge of shattering and his starving stomach was gnawing into his ribcage. He shed those agonizing thoughts and left them behind to the deprived earth. Across the infinite sands there were people, loved ones awaiting him, those who would appreciate the fresh wrinkles carved into his face. His poncho trailed behind and caressed the wind as he kept Inocencia moving across the night.

Two loud, jerking snaps tore through the air. The pounding hooves ceased instantly, Inocencia shrieked. The boundless night halted, an absolute transparency overcame Israel's mind. The desert whispered chorus of secrets to him, a revelation unfolded, and he saw each mountain, each forgotten crevice, each grain of sand, each thistle and thorn with perfect clarity, the images composing a panorama of desolation. Then he felt himself fall to the earth, his brittle body pummeled into jagged stones, his chest almost collapsing in on itself. He lay there, face down and cheeks bleeding, huffing the grains of sand that clawed at his parched throat. He slowly rose to his feet and attempted to brush off the dirt which clung to his body, trying to reclaim his skin as its own. His right arm and shoulder dangled uselessly, broken in more places than he could count.

Behind, a few paces back, lay the massive body off Inocencia, her hind legs kicking and scrambling, hooves scraping against the dry earth. She whimpered in pain and attempted to stand but her unsteady legs gave out and she buckled with a deadening thud. The whimpers continued, air siphoning out of her lungs as she lay inert. Israel drug his own wounded body towards his horse, his refuge, his sole connection to his home and his youth. The hazy dust-cloud between Israel's temples cleared long enough for him to examine Inocencia, and his fingers brushed upon her broken and mangled front legs. She couldn't go on, her stride would never return, her terminal point had been reached, here, on this lonely patch of land.

With his one functioning hand Israel stroked the neck of the animal he had loved like a member of the family he was desperately trying to remember now. She peered at him with her primitive eyes, terrified, unable to comprehend the numb cruelty of the night. Her shuddering hide calmed after Israel whispered words into her ears, "It's okay, relax, I'm here. Niña bonita, estoy aquí."

A throbbing pain swelled along the right side of Israel's shattered body and he kneeled down. The night churned in its indifference as Israel nestled Inocencia's head into his lap.

"You did good. You've always done good," he said. "It'll be over soon. Just rest, amor, rest."

He muttered a dry curse to the placid stars above, the points of light that traced out every constellation and mapped out the unknown fate of each man. Maybe this place, the desert and the sky, had seen too many deaths, knew the outcome of every man who wandered through with sin and innocence it his soul, and now this palace devoid of walls or windows had no use for the suffering of men.

A warm liquid seeped into Israel's lap and for a moment the thought it was he blue night itself spreading across his skin, but the sensation was too warm, too thick. His fingers followed the droplets up towards the source: Inocencia's flared nostrils. She huffed a few more heavy breaths. She wouldn't make it to the morning. Regret and unfulfilled memories settled over Israel, he couldn't give her one last sunrise, one last glimpse of the open land she had been born and raised to traverse. He unfurled his poncho and spread it over her head along with her eyes, those brown marbles that absorbed the mute heavens. The muzzle of the pistol briefly caught the silver light of the moon, trembling as Israel pressed it against the poncho. A single salvo ruptured the night before the opaque silence returned.

Israel grabbed the box of cherished papers with his hand, the left hand, the good hand. He staggered on, his aching body desperate to leave the negative expanse of land, sky, and the invisible incision of the horizon that separates the two and keeps the entire world aligned. Fleeting visions crossed the desert of his mind, forgotten as soon as they arose, fragments of lights, shards of sounds, voices, hands, warmth. Heavy feet barely slid over the sand, dragging dust along, each step seemed to cost him another lost night of his life, yet he lumbered on. How many steps had he taken, how many nights had passed? He peered behind to see how far he had gone only to gaze upon the limp outline of Inocencia still close, just barely out of reach. The desert wouldn't give him up.

The wind picked up and whispered a hymn to him, low at first, then it gathered into a chorus until he heard voices, distinct murmurings, and they relayed stories to his ear, about how he was meant to stay here, how he had always been here, year upon year the same fate, voices like his mother's, his father's, the woman from the sleepy town that he loved only in the dead of night, and even more voices, familiar, always familiar with their prayers calling to him.

The dry earth, anxious for her ancient ocean to return, swallowed the saline droplets that fell to her, her thirst quenched for the night. Opaque silence settled once again.

The rounded outlines of moisture vanished in the heat of the sun's rising tide.

****

Tamayo pulled his hand back from the caballero and the crystallized memories retreated into the night. He peered at the rider, Israel, and saw a face covered in dust, cracked lips and a sadness in his eyes that was washed out in the misty moonlight, yet Tamayo recognized all of these features as his own, like a reflection of his face filtered through a corroded mirror.

The familiar voice of Tamayo's grandfather broke in, "You must be tired, very tired."

"Sí," the caballero said.

"Are you hungry? We brought you food," the old man said and handed a few tortillas to the caballero.

"Me estoy muriendo de hambre. I can't remember the last time I ate," he said as he bit into the warm masa. "I just want to see my mother and then sleep."

"Sí, she has been waiting for you. You can give us the papers and then go on and rest. We'll take them to your father."

"Muchas gracias," Israel said, digging out the small wooden box from the worn leather saddlebag. He handed the papers to Tamayo who held them with uneasy hands.

The old man broke in and asked, "Did you see any others out there, also returning? A woman, lost amongst the border, searching for her son?"

"No, there were no others. The desert is a lonely place," the rider said, then he walked away. Dark splotches littered his torn poncho and the gold buttons of his pants shifted like reptilian scales. He lay a hand upon his horse's thick neck and led her off, the two of them, a lost son and a crippled horse, disappeared into the night.

Tamayo peered up at his abuelo but the old man kept gazing into the darkness as though his eyes gathered those things that one only sees in old age. The box of papers within Tamayo's hands seemed to yawn alongside the cool air.

"I saw things, Papa. Strange things," Tamayo said.

"Yes, you've seen the delicate tragedy that christened out blood. It's our collective memory, our collective fate. We become lost, Tamayo, always."

Tamayo opened the box and the brittle wood exhaled, but inside were no papers, no documents, only a pile of sand that sifted between Israel's fingers, warm somehow, reminiscent of a mother's caress. Images cascaded through his mind and he thought of her, her voice, her hands, her hair that flowed like a riverbed, her body and flesh the consistency of sand, her eyes the consistency of gravel. She was still out there, across the sea of stones, that ocean devoid of water. He could still hear whispered traces carried over by the warm winds.

They waited a long time upon that vista, two men, one old and one young, one searching for a mother, one waiting for a daughter.

"I don't think she's coming, Papa," Tamayo finally said.

The old man shook his head. "No. We'll pray for next year."

Tamayo followed his abuelo. The rusted pickup gurgled to life and they began their descent back downhill.

36.
Never Gone
Renata Dawidowicz

Solitary darkness with the moisture of droplets of rain turning this atmosphere very foggy
Slowly I walk alone and visit these ghosts asleep here from the twelfth century
I picture the mourning of their German ancestors laying them to rest in a religious ceremony
After World War II their country was divided and their families were forced out
Peacefully they lay as the history of their past generations was left behind in this cemetery
This could not last because greed took over and they could not even let them rest in peace
 A man came and took an axe to all the ancient monuments till only two tiny pieces are left now
He wanted to make money and built a park
The rumor was he built himself a fabulous house from these historical monuments
The ghosts had a peaceful resting place for generations in this lovely countryside they were born
It was utter chaos the ghosts were weeping and screaming as the axe went down on their graves
But a few days later the ghosts came to visit him as he was making a bench for the park
A piece of wood stabbed him in the heart and the ghosts held hands around him as he lay dying
They were dressed in their funeral attire and sang their ancient songs
Every night they visit his grave and sing ancient religious songs in a circle
He set them free to roam around at night in the dark ness of the countryside
Nothing was really taken away from them as their blood is still etched in the soil of generations
As I watched this evening darkness and felt the moist rain I saw a huge red umbrella left opened
I counted twenty empty whiskey bottles and snacks of chips and saw there had been a party
They drink themselves to oblivion in this cemetery park while the ghosts are free to roam
What he did not understand the ancient monuments were worth more money historically
He could of built the park someplace else because there are so many empty fields there
Instead he set the ghosts free by destroying there resting place

37.
Night and Death, You Are The Ones
John Grey

Night's a deep black stain.
Death grips like ice.
Sounds don't play well together.
My heart lacks the courage to scream.

Night's like the rat that
nibbles on the crumbs of wedding cake.
A voice asks the unanswerable question,
"Is anybody there?"

A presence will try anything.
A bedside clock is a co-conspirator.
Is that window really rattling
or is it just glad to frighten me?

Night takes something out
of its hidden meat locker.
Or is that someone?
It's being dragged across the floor.

Death is congealed in its red outer garments.
The space between beings shortens like breath.
Night is not just cold.
It's cold enough for death.

38.
Not A Ghost
William Doreski

Behind a locked panel, a slab
of concrete dusted with spiders.
No shelving, no hidden space.
Yet every night, water, blood, or slime
oozes through the seams and smuts
the floor. I keep it locked
to discourage whatever's trying
to embody itself. Not a ghost—
too generously hydrated
to slip through spirit dimensions.

You wonder that I can live
with this permeable surface
hidden by a few old boards.
You say you'd rip off the panel
and seal and paint the concrete
and leave this area exposed
and lit by a hundred-watt bulb
for a week to scare off the creature.
You don't believe it's human.
But I had the blood analyzed
and it's just as mortal as mine.

The creature, even materialized,
would never harm us. The faint
odor of its desire inspirits
the house with a woodsy air,
like music heard at a distance.
Let's wine ourselves and dance
a little in the cool autumn dusk.
Tomorrow I'll mop up the mess.

39.
Orienting To The Other Side
Jane Sloven

"More coffee?" Marco asked.

Only if you have more cream and sugar," Penelope said. "And how about a donut? Do you have any of those on hand? At five in the morning, my self-control is non-existent. Besides, familiar sustenance is likely to help me make sense of this place. What's next?"

Marco lifted a silver carafe and poured steaming coffee into a cup and saucer before handing Penelope the creamer, silver embossed with a dragon design. She looked at the dragon, poured, and flipped her eyes up to his with a question embedded in her gaze.

He smiled and passed the matching sugar bowl, complete with tongs. A platter of donuts warm from the oven sat in the center of the table next to a vase of pink roses.

When had they materialized? Penelope wondered. "Do I have to worry about my gluten intolerance anymore?" she asked.

"No," Marco replied. "Death has its advantages.

"So you've said." Penelope drained the coffee cup, polished off a sweetly glazed gluten-filled donut and pushed back from the table. "What's next?" She rolled her eyes upwards with disdain and was suddenly swept along with her gaze. "Marco! How do I get down?"

"First lesson," he smiled. "Lower your eyes, slowly, slowly," he warned as she descended, first rapidly and a bit off course, bumping her head into the chandelier and struggling to untangle her long curls from the candlesticks before trying again with a bit more subtlety. She landed with a soft thump.

"Honestly," she said. "How am I ever going to... whoops," Penelope's habit of rolling her eyes propelled her into one wall and then another before she just closed them altogether and prayed. It worked, somewhat. She hovered a foot or two off the ground. "Absolutely anybody could look up my skirt," she snapped.

Marco laughed that robust laugh she'd so seriously missed in the years since his death. "The living can't see you, honey, and the dead don't care."

"Whyever not? Can't we have sex on this side of the veil?"

"We sure can," he grinned. "And it's terrific... but we don't have the kind of bodies we inhabited on the Earth plane, so there is nothing to look at."

"Then what are my clothes hanging on?"

"A form, but not..." he sighed, "not a flesh and bone form. Here, touch me." He floated up to where she hovered.

"You're hardly palpable," Penelope said, and then she gasped. "My hand just passed right through you but it didn't change the shape or sensation of your arm. How can that be?"

"Give me your hand," he said, and she did. It felt like holding hands always felt—she'd loved holding hands with Marco ever since childhood. From the first day they'd met, when her grandparents moved into the big old yellow Victorian house next to Marco's parents, and Penelope found Marco sitting in her grandmother's kitchen eating a piece of blueberry pie.

****

"Look what our neighbor, Marco, brought over as a welcome present," Gram commanded, and Penelope had smiled shyly.

"Sit down honey. I'm cutting you a piece right now." Gram cut three more pieces, one for Penelope, one for Grandpa and one for herself, and all four of them sat around the round oak table having themselves a feast of blueberry pie.

When Marco next smiled, his teeth were blue, and so were Penelope's. They laughed and ran out to play, making forts under the front porch, climbing trees, rolling down the big hill of the front lawn over and over until it was dusk and time to go inside.

****

"Penelope," Marco's voice interrupted her reverie. "Stay focused for a bit, please. I want to show you the basics."

"What makes you think I'm not focused?

"You started to fade."

"What?" Penelope asked nervously.

"Look at yourself, Carefully!" Marco yelled. "You can't look at anything too fast, that's how we travel, how we move from place to place. You don't want to be smashing into walls or floors, or even ceilings," he smiled.

"I don't have a body that will get hurt anymore, will I?" Penelope groused.

"No, not really. But it's better to be in charge of how you move. You'll see. Over time, it will get easier."

"Marco, you've been here for so long now, haven't you? Is this your job, showing new arrivals the ropes, so to speak?" Penelope's focus was laser-like now, she saw Marco the way she'd always seen him — through the haze of friendship, deep affection, and admiration. She loved his curly black hair, wide smile, olive skin, laughing brown eyes and tender heart.

He returned her gaze—seeing Penelope as he'd always perceived her—curls not unlike his own—but reddish brown, eyes a funny kind of gray-green hazel, a smattering of freckles across her nose, and that ever-present dare in her affectionate stare. Time lost all meaning here, at least, the sense of time he'd had when still in a body. He couldn't compute the number of years that had passed since they'd last been together and it wasn't within bounds for him to ask that of her anyway. "It's not my job per se," Marco replied. "But when we know loved ones are coming over, we can put in a request to greet them and do the initial orientation."

Seeing Marco's smile reassured Penelope. "I'm so glad you did. It's all been a bit disconcerting," she paused and began laughing. "What an understatement!"

"We can talk about it, you know," Marco said. "If that would help you. I'm here to show you how to move about, orient you to the landscape, answer any questions, listen," he smiled, "And surround you with affection, caring, and compassion."

"Until?" she asked anxiously.

"Until you're ready to move on, meet other folks, those you knew on Earth and before that, and even before that—you know, from other lifetimes."

"And then what?" she prompted.

"Don't worry, Penelope. You'll be perfectly safe here. Way safer than you were when embodied. Although you had unseen guardians and companions on Earth, even though you didn't necessarily know it."

"Oh, I knew it all right," Penelope said. "Especially in the last year. I could feel them around me. It made it easier to come over, even though I didn't really want to."

"I know," Marco slid his arm around her and they floated to a comfy couch the color of sky. Had it been there all along, she wondered, or just materialized when they needed it?

"Do you want to talk about it?" Marco asked a second time, though neither of them were counting.

"Well, I felt so ill, you know," Penelope sighed. "And the longer it went on, the less tied I felt to my body. It was more like dreaming, even in the daytime, and I was often flying, flying over all sorts of terrain—as if I were a bird with a bird's view of things. Flying above, soaring sometimes. And that was nice. It gave me a break from the pain and the procedures. And when I refused to let anyone do any more procedures, I could feel my life force leaking out. It had been leaking out for quite some time, but all the procedures had supplanted that awareness with another kind of thing—a sense of alienation from my body and from life—and I hated that!" Penelope took a long, deep breath. Marco slid his fingers between hers and they clasped hands, palm-to-palm, the way they used to. "Over time," he said, "those feelings will fade. You'll remember the light in transit more than the suffering beforehand."

"It's already happening," Penelope nodded. "It's so much more about that peaceful pull toward the opening, almost like clouds parting but more like the ocean too—I can't really describe it." She held two fingers over her mouth for a moment. "Like ocean waves that are also clouds parting and moving and roiling. I knew it was the opening—the parting of veils—the space between worlds. And the light, it was fantastic. I wasn't afraid," she said. "I wasn't afraid at all."

40.

Overdone Legend
Mark Hudson

Oh, be aware of the woods so deep,
where headless horsemen roam and creep.
And if you get lost around the trees,
you might be getting Lyme's disease.
But need not fear a lethal tick,
the headless horseman is so quick.
He cuts off heads with great precision,
tonight you'll see him in a vision.
All hollow's eve is a time to cower,
you feel him watching you by the hour.
You try to sleep but you hide below,
your bed and see the eyes that glow.
How can eyes exist without a head?
The horseman is neither live nor dead.
You see him through your windowpane,
he slowly is driving you insane.
He hurls a pumpkin on your path,
you can't escape the horseman's wrath.

And then you see a buggy swerving,
and out pops the ghost of Washington Irving.
Who says, "Hey, I hate to wallow,
but I wrote the original Sleepy Hollow!
I've been ripped off to the maximum,
now from death I return for some!
To haunt the graves of the story thieves,
and all the people who don't believe!"
And so he gives some people fright,
come to reclaim his copyright.
Classic tale butchered for good,
totally destroyed by Hollywood.
On Halloween, the world contains
scary news for timid brains.
So let's take classics from long ago,
true horror like Edgar Allen Poe,
And let the subtle tales attract,
a difference between horror and fact.

41.
Paint Me Panicked
Jake E. Parker

I should have punched the jerk, he thought to himself as the lines began to take shape on the paper. Talking to himself aloud facilitated releasing some of the pressure that was building in the combustion chamber of his thoughts. A caricature of Troy's bloody and bruised face appeared distinctly on the page. His nose was deformed and pushed slightly off center.

Rory had a flair for drawing funny cartoons, and it came in handy when he was angry with someone. His hands moved rapidly across the sketchbook. Ooh yeah, he was angry.

"This will fix that innocent look, you two-faced jerk."

As the picture developed, Troy was lying on the ground in a fetal position with his face pleadingly turned up facing his assailant.

"This is what you deserve," Rory spoke aloud to the image on the page. Some of the anger had faded, and he began to smile to himself at his concocted retribution.

Rory decided to add a dark malevolent force to the drawing. A force no one should ever mess with. With a charcoal pencil, he formed a dark cloud hovering over Troy. It was menacing, but it needed more. He looked for a silver pencil, but it was missing from his supplies, so he went to his dad's room and selected a silver one from his set of colors. His dad was a graphic designer for an advertising agency, and he often created his designs at home. His art was more than just his job. When not working on a project for work, he worked on art as a hobby. His paintings were amazing, and his love of art was reflected in his work. His studio was one of the biggest rooms in the house, and Rory relished being in this room watching his father work. Father and son working side-by-side creating fanciful, whimsical, even beautiful images. Form, coloring, light, and shading were skills passed from his father.

Back at his desk, Rory created a silver fist, barely visible, in the dark cloud. The fist had red tones on the knuckles with a droplet of blood dripping from the center one. Rory had considered drawing his own face in the dark cloud with a fierce snarl but reconsidered. He'd never be able to actually punch Troy no matter how angry he got. Troy was his best friend.

For years, he and Troy had laughed and joked in secret about different people they knew. As they discussed someone they disliked, Rory would draw a funny scene of the person being humiliated in some way, and Troy would suggest some storyline with tips about what should be included. It was fun.

An even more secret project was conjuring a picture of some girl they had a crush on. The image usually involved a sexy female heroine or super girl in a very revealing uniform. The facial features were distinguishable, but the form was very exaggerated, especially in the bosom and the exposed long, muscular legs. Troy admired all these renderings and, unlike the other drawings that were destroyed, they placed the sexy pictures in a box they kept in Troy's garage in a storage loft behind some of the framing timbers.

And there lay the rub. Troy had taken one of the pictures of Susan, Rory's special subject, and shown it to her. He had even told her that Rory had a thing for her. It was a betrayal he could never forgive.

Susan was two years older, and she lived only a block away. There was no way to avoid her, and he would never be able to face her again without feeling humiliation and guilt.

"I wonder what she thought about the picture?" he couldn't help but think.

The next morning he was feeling better. He thought it was time to go to Troy's house and tell him how upset he was that Troy had shown the drawing. He would tell him that those drawings were a secret that only the two of them should know about, and if Troy couldn't understand that he would take them and destroy them and never share his drawings with Troy again.

He was resolved about what he needed to say as he knocked on Troy's front door a bit later. After a long wait, Troy's aunt answered the door.

"Rory, what are you doing here?" she asked.

"I came to see Troy. Is he here?"

"Oh, God. You haven't heard, have you?"

"Heard what?" Rory asked. From her expression and her behavior, he knew something was terribly wrong.

"Troy was assaulted yesterday. He's in the hospital, and he's in pretty bad shape. Why don't you go on down and visit him, I'm sure he'd want to see his best friend. He may be in there a while. I'm here watching Trevor while Judy and Don stay with him in the hospital. Please ask Judy to call me and let me know how he's doing," his aunt said.

"I will. Thanks."

Rory was stunned. What had happened? Who would have attacked Troy? But guilt was burning in his heart. He had imagined beating him up himself only yesterday, but that was an obscure thought on his part. He would never really wish to harm Troy. Still, it left him uneasy.

He hurried to get there. The small town hospital was located centrally in the community. The receptionist gave him directions to Troy's room. Through the open door, he could see Troy's mother and dad sitting near the bed. He knocked softly to announce his presence. Troy's mother looked up at him.

"Rory, thank you for coming," she said as she stood to hug him. Her eyes were swollen from crying, and her voice was shaking with emotion.

Rory looked at his friend's bruised and swollen face, and fear and guilt slowed his heartbeat. Troy looked up at him with his one good eye. The other was swollen closed. He smiled through puffy lips and tried to say something, but his words were garbled. Rory stepped closer to hear.

"You should see the other guy," he joked.

"Yeah. I'll bet he doesn't have a mark on him," Rory shot back.

"Rory, would you mind staying with Troy for a little bit while Don and I get some breakfast in the cafeteria?" his mother asked. "We've been with him all night, and while he was able to get a little Jello down, we haven't had a bite."

"Sure. I don't have to hold his hand, do I?" he asked as he looked back down at his friend with a grin on his face.

His mother smiled at him and shook her head. She and Troy's father got their coats and left.

When they were alone, Rory asked, "What happened?"

"I'm not sure I'm in the right mind to tell you. At least, no one else thinks so. They think my brain's been bounced around in my head and I'm imagining things."

"So who attacked you?"

"It wasn't a who. It was a what." Troy said.   Rory's stomach clenched.

"I saw a dark cloud forming around me, even though just moments before the sky had been clear. It scared the shit out of me. Then this silver fist the size of a bowling ball flew out of the cloud and punched me five or six times and then withdrew back into the cloud. The dang thing felt like it was made of stainless steel. I swear." Troy told him.

They looked at one another for several minutes. Rory was dumbfounded. He knew that fist. He drew that fist.

"What do you think?" Troy asked after a minute. He studied his friend's face and could see he was upset.

Rory withdrew from his thoughts and focused on Troy. A moment later he smiled.

"I think your brain's been bounced around in your head and you're imagining things."

There was no way he was going to tell Troy what he really thought or in any way describe what he had drawn. But he was worried. Have I done this without meaning to? It's silly to think that I could have, isn't it?

That night he was still pondering the events and was no closer to discovering the implications of his drawing. The events can't be connected, yet the things Troy described are too similar to what I drew to dismiss easily.

His father inquired about his preoccupation when he got home and saw his troubled son.

"Dad, I think I was the cause of Troy being hurt," he said.   Then he went on to explain what he had drawn and what Troy had told him had really happened. His father considered what he had heard for a moment.

"Show me the pencil you borrowed from my collection," his father said.

Rory retrieved the old silver pencil from his desk and handed it to his father. His father studied it for several moments in deep thought.

"Rory, many people believe there is magic in art. Have I ever told you of the legendary story of Maurice Devroe?"

Rory shook his head.

"Maurice Devroe was a French artist in the 18th century who it is claimed quelled a revolution. Mobs of angry citizens protested in the streets night after night, burning effigies of the king and threatening to overthrow the empire. The reigning king, upon the advice of his royal counselor, hired Maurice to paint a picture of calm and tranquility so powerful as to dispel anger for anyone who gazed upon it. Maurice fulfilled the contract. Overnight he painted his masterpiece, pouring his soul and magic into the scene. The next night, as the crowd began to gather again, the king had the painting mounted onto a wagon. One of his soldiers, posing as a protester, drove through the crowd chanting a message of peace and tolerance. The painting touched the very soul of the hundreds who gazed upon it. Anger faded from their hearts. And as the citizens who had seen the masterpiece stopped their protests and returned to their homes, others, even those who had not seen the painting, lost their zeal from lack of support. The rebellion ended."

Rory was fascinated by the story. "What scene did Maurice paint?" he asked.

"No one knows. Those who gazed upon it took it to their graves, and it is rumored that Maurice himself burned the painting."

"But why would he do that?" Rory pleaded.

"The legend is not clear about why. But it is rumored that Maurice later learned that hundreds of people died as a result of the neglect and abuse they suffered under the reign of the king. He was devastated and refused to be a part of any further assistance to the realm. But he designed his own revenge against the king. It is reported that he painted a secret portrait of the king, sick and dying of a mysterious pox. The king died just weeks later. When that painting was discovered later, no one understood how Maurice had ever observed the king on his deathbed to make such an accurate painting."

Rory considered what he had been told. "Dad, do you believe Maurice was able to do those things with just his paintings?"

"As I said earlier, Rory, there is magic in art. Anyone who has ever observed a masterpiece and felt its power and wonder must believe there is more to art than just paint and canvas. But until today, I have never experienced anything to indicate that someone could truly create a piece of art that would affect physical reality. But I think you did. You used a pencil that was claimed to have been once owned by Maurice Devroe. I bought it, doubting its authenticity. But I liked its age and potential history, and I was captivated by the possibility that it could be true."

"So you think I caused Troy to be hurt?" Rory asked. His voice wavered with the question. He wanted to know, but he feared the answer.

Dad saw the uncertainty and fear in his son's eyes, and he didn't want to produce any further suffering for his son. But he knew that lying to him could be even more damaging. And he was sure Rory would detect the lie even if he did. So he chose his words carefully.

"Rory, I know you didn't really intend to hurt Troy. You've been best friends for a long time. But I think something happened when you drew that picture. Something I never really believed was possible. I think that pencil recognized a magic in you, and I think it might have awakened and stimulated a power that neither of us knew was there," Dad answered. "That pencil was handled by many people over the years, but none have found it magical. Including myself. But in your hands, I think the magic surfaced."

"But I don't want that kind of power…or magic. Not if it can hurt people."

Rory was near tears, and Dad's heart was breaking to see him in such pain. He gently placed his hand on Rory's shoulder to comfort his son.   "Power…any kind of power…can be for good or bad, depending on the person who wields it. I guess you can have a power and never use it, but I can't see you being happy never sketching again. You love it and you're good at it. It would be like me deciding never to use my left arm again. I just don't think you can live your whole life without something that's such a big part of you." Dad paused and studied his son.

"I think that instead of trying to suppress your ability, you should master it. Control it. Use it for good."

Dad's words helped reduce the pent-up fear Rory was feeling. Can I control it? How do you control your feelings? Your desires? Aren't those things by nature uncontrollable? "How?" he asked simply.

"I don't think there's a simple answer to that, Rory. I think you may have to begin by determining your feelings when you draw something. When you're happy it will show in your drawing ,but not to the detriment of the subject. When you're awed by something, I think that will also show in your work. But if you're angry, grieving, or irritable because of what someone has done or said, you have to repress you desire to retaliate. If what you draw can hurt or manipulate another person, you have to ask yourself if it's the right thing to do. Would you want someone to be able to control what happens to you?"

Rory considered his dad's words. They made sense. I am going to have to be very careful. This is going to be very, very hard.

"I know you'll always make the best choices when you draw. You're a good boy," Dad told him.

I wish I had the confidence that Dad has in me.

42.
Possession
Briana J. Weiss

The demon lies in wait, each and every night
There is no sleep for either of them
"Little boy, little boy, I see you--"
He closes his eyes, fighting the tempting
voice
The trap, the lure, so inviting
But he will not permit the demon entrance

Yet the demon persists, insists on
cooperation
The demon will not be ignored
"Little boy, little boy, I'm still here--"
He grasps his head, covers his ears
But the voice is never gone
And demands to be heard

He could imagine the demon
Eyes like fierce embers, teeth glinting and
sharp
And how he wondered if his imagination was
reality

But he could not look, should not--
"Little boy, little boy, let me in--"
A shiver races up and down his body
The warmth sapped from his very being
And a shudder-y breath escapes
Misting before him in the cool air

He knew better, knew not to look
For that was how the demon entered
And stole you
Replaced you
In the end, became you
He knew not to look
But couldn't resist temptation

"Little boy, little boy, we are eternally one--"
He opens his eyes and sees the demon
Just as he'd pictured, frightening
Sees himself, accepting that
I was you all along

43.
Repression
Wm. Bernan

Huddled in his canyon, impish, brooding, the demon waited, toiling. Sharpening innumerable implements, grinding points to the narrow ends of salvaged steel with scraps of brick. Preparations for a confrontation he didn't know was coming, yet somehow felt inevitable. He sensed the draw. Felt it coming closer.

****

It was as if I'd been served a summons. A calling out of the aether. A craving. The sudden onset of the must-have variety. I haven't even liked chocolate milk, not since I was a kid.

It was a lazy Football Sunday. I hadn't showered, wasn't planning on leaving the couch, and was waiting for the night game--not that I cared about Redskins-Browns. I had the keys in my hand but something urged me to walk. Does anyone walk anymore?

Seventy degrees, a pleasant breeze set the leaves tumbling like brown paper confetti. All along Forest Street to the corner, old maples, up Alfred to the gas station convenience store, oaks. Barely a mile, the air fresh, none of the stale garbage smell I usually associate with sidewalks when the town hadn't collected the Hefty bags on time.

I desperately wanted chocolate milk and Doritos, first time in forever, like when I was a kid watching a drunk Jan Michael Vincent in Airwolf, not that I knew then why his slur changed from scene to scene. Before college, grad school, a seat in the firm. Before I forgot about being young.

I whistled the mile to the gas station. I never whistled.

Wishing the clerk, a cute redhead maybe eighteen, wasn't half my age, I paid for the junk food, adding a few impulse buys, and cradled the brown bag in the crook of my arm like a six pack. Gluttonously I grabbed the quart of chocolate milk and took a big draw as I stepped out of the store.

I shot to one knee, fighting the gorge rising in my throat. Instantly nauseous, heaving and gasping, the wind knock out of me like I was sucker-punched by Mike Tyson. Breathing in spurts, a balled fist attempted to clear my watering eyes, helping little. Seeing spots, I blinked, wondering if I was hallucinating. Colorblindness? Images of buildings I knew weren't there?

Everything was wrong. Monotone. Gray.

Terror-struck, senses on high alert, I was inexplicably aware that I was being chased or lured or both. I didn't know by what.

The urge to run, to escape the terror that I knew was watching me, without turning I tried to duck back into the store. I stepped backwards into brick. The glass door, the neon beer signs, the tape measure saying I'm a shade under six feet tall, gone. The pumps too. My whole suburb had been erased. I was cramped in a dark hellish cityscape--where I could feel a million eyes yet hear nothing. One half-conscious synapse told me I'd been here, dread told me I shouldn't be.

I panicked. Which way? Safety? Shelter? Where could the unseen something not find me? I wanted a couch to hide behind, a cop car to drive by, an umbrella, anything. Childish fears of boogie men and killer clowns, hellacious tortures and painful emptiness forced their way in to my mind, my soul.

A trap? I stumbled forward, a long step off the curb into a ghost town of leaves, cigarette butts, and hot dog wrappers in the gutter, and waited for the other shoe to drop. I felt like I'd tripped the stick propping up the Acme box, feeling it collapse around me, closing in, confining. Hunted, baited, trapped.   Just no Bugs, no Elmer.

The horizon seemed miles above me. I had no bearings. Buildings stood menacingly over me under leaden storm clouds, but no thunder, no lightning, no rain, the world on pause. Perpetual midnight.

A memory threatened to surface. I blinked it away, then bade it come. It obeyed neither, lingering at the edge of consciousness.

Run, I pressed. Where? Home? Which? I was pulled in a direction. Toward home? Not mine, I thought. Do I have more than one? I didn't think so. It felt like I knew of one. Can I get back to the house? There was no Alfred Street, no Forest, displaced by multistory brick edifices defaced by grime, decay, spray paint. Stately trees were swapped for rusting cars in various stages of disassembly. None moving. No people. A stench (familiar?) pervaded the phantom city, rotting dumpsters.

Get moving. My legs finally obeyed my reasoning, it could be no more dangerous than standing still when you don't know what's after you. Knowing without justification the path. Along the nearest tenement, through the abandoned warehouse, then up the alley--the shortcut. Toward home? Toward something I didn't know. I had to follow, it was all I knew.

If the destination was home, it didn't feel like safety.

The warehouse door scraped ominously. Steel, fire resistant, dented from innumerable kicks, hammered. A single broken link indicating at one time someone had cut away a chain or a padlock. A high bank of windows permitted miserable light. Feeling eyes on me every step, unsure if I was being chased or drawn deeper into a trap, petrified of both, my path laid out before me in my mind. I walked, hearing nothing but my heartbeat in my ears and the rustling of brown paper at my elbow. No other footsteps, no scuffling of mice, no drip of water. My footsteps kicked up dust I couldn't see, more than once I sneezed, the sound inexplicably swallowed. Surreal. The giant hollow space conspicuously absent any echo.

I shuffled to the broken roll-up I shouldn't have foreseen but expected would be there. A broken panel provided crawl space onto a truck height leap to the ground.

The warehouse backed up to another. The alley between was dismal. Narrow. A wonder any trucks once made it down. The buildings appeared to lean in. A sliver of steel-grey sky above, like storm clouds backlit by a full moon, barely illuminated. Loading docks, dumpsters, steel doors. A row of amber bulbs up high, burning yet generating no useful light.

Crying? A whimper?

Terrified, drawn by the penetrating phantom sound, I knew my course. Sending spent canned goods skittering like the rats who might have once infested them, I hurried up the dark alley to the box-end. Corralled.

The brick canyon was filled with all the detritus that I hate about cities; tires, shopping carts, a settlement of cardboard and newspaper--a homeless village seemingly devoid of occupants. Three walls, only one way out. In the box ghost-town I again heard the whine, plaintive, familiar, chilling. My legs became cement, neither obeying my bidding to proceed nor submitting to the desire to run. To say I had 'Goosebumps' doesn't begin to capture my state while craning my neck to listen, to peer around that last stack of cardboard, the tug of war between my need to see and my gut demanding retreat, to hide, fly, die, anything but pursue this course. Something was there. Something I didn't want to see, but had to. Furtively, somehow, my feet took a step.

He was a juvenile, a monochrome homeless waif. Opie from Mayberry in rags, as if he'd sheltered in the dark alley forever. He couldn't have been more than eight or nine, yet seemed drenched in thirty years of grime. He seemed light as a shadow when he turned.

"You?" he said.

"Me?" I replied.

"Yes, Me," he said, standing, revealing, shedding the whimper along with his newsprint cloak, victory spreading across eyes I hadn't seen in a long time, a smile I still sometimes wear when winning at poker.

I slowly placed the bag on the ground, the jug beside.

"The chocolate milk?" He asked.

My brow furled, unable to process what he meant, half-presuming I was dreaming, a state in which such absurdities exist without explanation.

"What about it?" I stammered, wary he knew more than me. Feeling I was in a game where I didn't understand the rules.

"Tall," he assessed me, then sharpening his glare, "It's my turn." His eyes burned manic, demonic, targeting the jug; saying he meant to get the milk, going through me if necessary.

I footed the jug behind me, knowing that to offer it would be bad. His lunge caught me by surprise. Whirling to evade, he landed on my back a lot more solidly than a shadow, his 'Eeeyaaahhh!' familiar.

The tone, that cry; I'd suspected but resisted recognition. Then, arms around my neck, heals spurring into my thighs, I knew. He was me. I was him.

His touch recalled the nightmares, a million visions resurrected from dark recesses, his mind to mine. The nights I couldn't sleep for fear of being trapped in the otherworldly city. The hellacious half-time when I seemed possessed, a terror, a problem child they called me. The therapy. Doctors, priests, my parents' divorce. Their overnight cure. The hypnosis.

I grabbed my younger self by the back of the neck and threw him into a wad of boxes, destroying what was his estate.

"How?" I pant.

"You. You left me here," he croaks, accusing, evilly, anciently, belying his young frame.

"But, how?"

"Yes, how?" Growling, saliva like a rabid badger. "How did you, the one who could be bullied, the one who runs. How did you? You. You escaped. Trapped me here. It's My Turn!"

Repressed memories kept pouring in, bad times suppressed by charlatans who'd inadvertently left a gateway for his return. A trigger object that could unlock all the malice they'd secreted away.

I knew if he got to the jug he'd leave, taking my life outside. I'd be trapped here. I grabbed it, clutching it to my chest as he leapt, again landing on my back. Half-rolling, using his momentum, I threw him against the wall, stunning him temporarily back to a whining stupor.

I violently gulped the chocolate milk. It does nothing. It brought me, but as if seeing into his mind, I inferred it would only let him out.

Only one of us could leave, and I wasn't the fighter. He was the impulsive, the angry, the violent. Everything I abhorred. I couldn't stop him.

He ran at me. I parried, accidentally tripping him into the wad of boxes. A screen of dust obscured his landing, his recovery, his rummaging through the debris. Keen, instinctual, fight or flight--with only the one option, I stared into the fog, hoping for a tool, an idea. I'd never used weapons.

I caught a glint in the periphery, barely a flash or a spark in the weak light, felt a sting, like being brushed by an arc of electricity. My cheek burned as I realized, throwing stars.

He stood in the midst of his fallen hovel, slipping on the dust covered cardboard, his aim off. A star had grazed my face, deeper than a scratch, blood warmed my cheek, my chin, trickled into the corner of my mouth. Another, flung sidearm, curled a path past my waist, nearly catching my shirt in the process. Seeing him clearly in the settling cloud, manic eyes, gleefully grinning, an armload of ammunition diminishing as he sent each downrange at me, giddily anticipating any of the five-pointed razors embedding themselves in my flesh. Certainly these first throws took barely a second, but it still took all for my brain to signal the word Run.

I sprinted down the alley, past dumpsters which rang like a gong when struck by his homemade shurikens. Past buckets, barrels, trash, the loading docks, I ran faster than I'd ever run in my life, knowing behind me was every evil intent I might have ever harbored, directed at me. Flailing my arms, the jug still locked in my right hand, chocolate milk spewed all over the black and white scene. As the jug emptied, feeling it was somehow slowing me, I pitched it behind a heap of garbage, not caring to note where.

I hurdled a fallen stack of used tires, flew by the broken roll-up I'd previously crawled under, hurdled more tires, hearing another clang as the stars kept coming. A glint whizzed by me, forcing me to question from which direction. I saw a dumpster, distinctively painted, I thought I'd seen before, but companies paint them alike, don't they? I slowed to a canter as the stars became fewer. Perhaps he was running out and was taking more careful aim. Ahead I could barely see, but I thought I was, well, I thought I was crazy. It looked the same. Another star zipped by me. This one definitely from the front as my jog turned into a slide for home plate to avoid the missile, dead-aim at my face, eye level. He was there, immediately in front of me. I'd run directly up on him. Into his box-end canyon. Same walls. Same graffiti. I hadn't turned, he'd turned the city.

I definitely didn't know the rules to this game, but it was clear; I died, or he did.

I searched around my feet while he rummaged again through his destroyed home. I crept back to the source of the first clang. The star hadn't impaled the dumpster, but the obvious dent showed me where the thing must have dropped. I groped at my feet until a prick of steel drew blood from my finger. Standing, I waited for a clear shot, thinking, "How do I even hold this thing?"

He stood in a half-crouch, a little plastic army man, fixed bayonet.

I tried to time my throw for between my breaths, but they were coming too fast and hard. My heart was going a thousand beats a second and my mouth swelled, dry and metallic, like I'd been sucking on an old penny. This is how it felt I to know you were about to die.

One shot. One throw I hoped I could make. I gripped the star between my thumb and curled index finger, cocked my arm and whole upper body in a wind up, coiled like a spring, and let loose the same 'Eeeyaaahhh' I'd heard come out of him moments before. Haplessly, the would-be lethal pentagram tumbled end over end, missing him by a mile.

He charged, leveling a pike of sharpened re-bar at my navel. Still turning from my errant throw, using reflexes I didn't know I possessed, I grabbed for the steel, jerking it forward in his grip and forcing it to the ground in one motion. Barely registering his gasp as his sternum crashed into the other end, momentum lifting him like a pole-vaulter, I'd blundered into the resolution. Seven feet of steel, he'd sharpened both ends. Face down above me, slowly sliding, letting his body weight do the deed, I crouched below holding bar upright. Black, oily blood ran down the pike, painting my forearm, dripped on my back, down my neck. I dared a glance as his face slid closer to mine. Demon eyes shot daggers, his last curses, forever wishing me fiery damnation. He wheezed a choking liquid sound, succumbing to the mortal wound.

Daylight exploded in an avalanche of color as I apeared back outside of the convenience store; complete with gas pumps, sounds, life, and breezes of a fall afternoon.

Dizzy. Stricken. Immediately I felt light, or light-headed. I again collapsed to one knee.

Pain, heartbreak, bolts of lightning shattering my core like glass, a hollowness coursed through me. Tears formed from somewhere untouched for decades--but the void was quickly filling. Panacea, ambrosia, a well-spring of happy emotion from somewhere else, brimming, soon overflowing a kind of bliss, soothing every crack, every shard.

A joyousness I hadn't felt since childhood. A freedom to be me. To play. I grabbed a handful of dried leaves and pressed them to my nose, to smell, to feel, some tangible earth, noticing there was no stinging cheekbone, no cut to my face.

I cried in elation.   Cried in sadness.   Cried for an unnamed loss.   An unnamable gain.   Or maybe namable.   Peace.   A cessation of three decades of warfare I didn't even know was being fought.   But I knew the homecoming.   I felt like a kid.

Though I've never again wanted chocolate milk.

44.
Scary Dreams
Mark Hudson

I told a friend of mine
That I had scary dreams
And he said unto me,
" It is not what it seems.
Because I have them too.
And I am in control.
No monster or a demon
Can take charge of my soul."
I said, " I guess you're right.
I wasn't really complaining.
I sometimes find bad dreams
Extremely entertaining."

45.
Self-Portrait As Unidentified Flying Object
A.J. Huffman

Suspended
moment of disbelief,
you see me as light,
flashing beacon of possibility
from another world.   Alien entity,
my body defies your nature.
I am unsolvable
mystery, an unexplainable moment
in a seemingly endless night.   The next
morning, I remain a hazy memory,
a post-drunk jumble of coincidences
and bad timing.   A blush of shame
no one will understand.   I am galactic
embarrassment, conveniently classified:
mistake.

46.
Shake And Bake
A Story Of Divine Intervention
Nancy Cole Silverman

Welcome to Tinseltown, the motion picture capital of the world, the home of glitz, glamor and where one can never be too rich or too thin. Where everyone has a story to tell and on every corner, there is a star waiting to be discovered.

Allow me to introduce myself.   I am your stage director, or as some in the industry like to refer to as God, he who wields almighty power. So, if you're ready, settle back and allow me to present, Shake and Bake, a reality play, happening before our very eyes.

Act One.

It's four o'clock in the afternoon. The California sun is setting low in the afternoon sky and Madeline Pensky, our protagonist, toddles with a wine glass in hand and her loyal four-footed companion, Alfred, to her mailbox. Behind her, a trailer sits on a bare desert mountaintop. Madeline's visit to the mailbox is the highlight of her day. The only communication she has with an outside world that has passed her by, an aged star whose light has long since gone out. Her mail, usually consisting of nothing more than brochures from the Neptune Society, advertisements for medical alert bracelets and invitations to luncheons on retirement planning, offer nothing of any personal interest. But today, there is a large, legal-sized envelope that causes her heart to quicken.

Splashed across the front, in bold red letters, are the words: Urgent! Important Information Regarding Your Sweepstakes Entry. Open Immediately.

Like a presenting actress at the Oscars, Madeline tears into the envelope and stares at the letter inside.

Congratulations! You have won the Big Readers Sweepstakes. Ten Million Dollars.

Madeline slaps her hand to her chest.   Her heart beats so fast she feels it is about to leap from her body. She holds her breath.   At last, she has won!

Arrangements are to be made for a special camera crew to film the presentation of the check to Miss Pensky, the lucky winner of the Big Readers Ten Million Dollar Sweepstakes! Until then, the letter warns, she mustn't say anything or forfeit her winnings.

Tonight, Madeline will barely sleep. She'll spend the night with Alfred, a dog of indeterminate breed and years, at the foot of her bed, counting her fortune, planning how she is going to spend her winnings. No more will anyone laugh when she states that her financial planning had included a lottery card and a receipt from the Big Readers Sweepstakes. Her luck has changed. She, Madeline Pensky, the former runner-up for Miss Hollywood, is about to reclaim her rightful position in the limelight. Dignity, fame, and fortune will be hers.

Madeline Pensky hasn't been a particularly lucky woman. Forty years ago, she moved from her hometown outside of Topeka, Kansas, to find herself in Hollywood. She likes to tell people she earned her living as an actress. Albeit, not a particularly successful one. Her one big break came years ago when she landed a role as Detective Borowski, a sexy young investigator, sidekick to a bigger Hollywood name, in a television series called Bay City Patrol. Unfortunately, the show was canceled after the third season when her co-star was arrested for smuggling drugs. After that, Madeleine picked up bit parts here and there—nothing ever quite as exciting as that of Detective Borowski—and subsidized her income, like many actors, as a waitress. She had been married three times; the first for love, the second for security, the third for companionship. Husband three had swindled her out of her life savings, and up until she visited her mailbox that afternoon, she had been living on her social security, less than seven hundred dollars a month and royalties, a petty sum she received each month for work she'd done as an actress. But with her sudden winning, she was as the police would later say, a target; the type of woman, for whom fortune seekers might be hunting.

And now, if you'll allow me, a little stage direction. Let's cue the camera. Day two. A long shot of a lone trailer, sitting on top a dry, dusty desert mountaintop. The awards crew approaches, the camera follows. The presenter, a young man, turns to the camera crew and knocks on Madeline's front door, then places his index finger on his lips.

"Shsssh. We're here today to present— "

You know the rest, but all the same, let me describe the scene.

Madeline answers the door. This morning she's looking more like a reincarnated Jayne Mansfield than the untidy, gray-haired lady who less than twenty-four hours earlier we watched as she ambled from her trailer to her mailbox with her dog, dressed in her housecoat and pink slippers. Her mousey gray hair is covered with a platinum blonde wig, bouffant style. Her cheeks are rouged rosy red, and her eyes are accented with lashes the length of spider legs. Around her body, tied firmly like that of a corset, is a frilly white apron. All things she has pulled from a stage trunk of old memorabilia. Madeline, like Norma Desmond from the movie Sunset Boulevard, is ready for her close-up.

The filming of Madeline's mock surprise and the acceptance of the monstrously large check—a four-foot long, two-foot high prop—with the words ten-million-dollars, boldly emblazoned up it, not only made the nightly news but also the front page of the LA Times. Talk of Madeline, a one-time actress and single, older woman, winning that much money was everywhere. On TV talk shows, on the radio, in aisles of supermarkets. Madeline was back in the limelight.

Now you may be thinking Madeline was planning on moving from her home. Taking her winnings and investing in a much more upscale location than the remote trailer site where she, Alfred, and her menagerie of small animals had been living. And if you were, you wouldn't be alone.

Enter stage right: one Samuel Peterson, former farrier, horse trader and recently turned struggling real estate agent. There is a knock on the door.

Knock. Knock. Knock.

Madeline opens the door and stares through the screen at the stranger on her doorstep. An older man, neatly dressed in blue jeans and boots, stands humbly with a cowboy hat in his hand.

"Ms. Pensky?"

The cowboy speaks with kind of a down-home Texas drawl.

"Yes."

Madeline opens the door wide enough to get a better view of the man. He is slim, with thinning blond hair and nicotine-stained teeth. A small cat races out from between her legs.

"Now, look what you've done. You've let Precious out! What is it you want?"

"Sorry to disturb you, ma'am. I uh...uh....I recognized you from TV. Not just the news about your recent Big Reads win either, but your face. Could never forget that face."

Madeline touches the platinum blonde wig, grateful she'd thought to put it on again this morning.

"I was a fan, or I guess, to be honest, still am."

Madeline exhales. It's been years since anyone has come up to her on the street and asked for her autograph and she doubts that's what he's here for now.

"What can I do for you?"

"Actually, I was hoping I might be able to help you. I'm a realtor. Allow me to introduce myself, Sam Peterson's my name. People 'round here call me Sammy."

Sam reaches into his pocket and pulls out a business card, then waits for her to open the screen and passes it through.

"I was wonderin', considering your recent win—not that I was being nosey, ma'am, but, you never know—I thought you might be interested in sellin' the place. Got a few clients who might want a spread like this. What ya got here? 'Bout an acre, maybe more? Place like this on a hilltop like it is, not too far from the city, why I bet you can almost touch the stars at night. Probably get you a really good– "

"You can stop right there, Mr? What did you say your name was?"

Madeline pauses and glances down at the card.

"Petersen. Samuel Peterson."

"I'm sorry, Mr. Petersen, I'm not interested."

She starts to hand his business card back to him but Peterson backs up and puts his hat back on his head and his other hand in his pocket.

"Well, I'm sure it's a bit too soon. You're probably overwhelmed with all the opportunity you have. Why don't you keep my card? Just in case, and if you think you might be interested, give me a call. Happy to help."

Samuel tips his hat and backs away from the door, determined he'll try again.

****

Now, ladies and gentlemen, that we've reached the end of Act One, I would like to share with you a little Madeline History. I don't expect Madeline would want you to know that in addition to her trunk of wigs, costumes, and Hollywood makeup hidden inside her trailer, that our Madeline had another little secret she's hiding. But why should I spoil it for you? You'll find out soon enough. Because, like you, Samuel Peterson's interest has been piqued by Madeline's refusal to sell her dumpy double-wide in the middle of nowheresville. And, as a new realtor in the area, it is to his benefit to get her listing. After all, that's all realtors really want. Or is it?

Welcome to Act Two.

It's mid-morning, two weeks later, and Samuel is again on Madeline's doorstep, hat in hand. But this time, our determined realtor has brought a gift, a bouquet of Southern California Poppies, wildflowers, he hides behind his back.

Knock. Knock. Knock.

Samuel knocks boldly on the door, then steps back and waits. In the background, we hear what sounds like slippers shuffling across a linoleum floor. The door opens.

"Ms. Pensky?"

Samuel shifts his weight nervously in his cowboy boots. As the door opens wider, he sees Madeline standing before him. But this is not the Madeline he'd seen the other day with her platinum bouffant hair and a frilly apron. The woman standing before him today is dressed in her housecoat, and carrying a large box. On her head, covering wisps of her gray hair is a bandana.

"Well, now, if it isn't Mr. Peterson. I see you don't give up easily. So, I'll tell you again. I'm not interested in selling. Good day."

Madeline shifts the uncomfortably large box to her hip and starts to close the door.

"Sorry to disturb you, Ms. Pensky, but I was in the area, and I thought I'd stop by and bring you these."

Samuel takes the flowers from behind his back and holds them out like a peace offering.

"Please, Ms. Pensky. These won't last the day without water, and it looks like you could use some help. At least, let me leave them and maybe help you with that box? It looks heavy, and it'd be a shame to let these beautiful flowers just wither and die here all alone on the mountain."

"Umph. Well, I could use the help, but if you're here to talk to me about selling, I promise you, you'd be wastin' your time. I'm not interested. Plain and simple. I like it here."

Madeline backs away from the door, and Samuel takes the box from her. Entering the trailer his eyes scan the living area, trying to get an idea of the condition and size of the trailer. He places the box on the coffee table, a cat scurries from beneath it. Across the room, three more cats sit in a cat tree, beside it, are two more boxes like that he has just put on the table.

"Doing a little spring cleaning, are you?"

"Don't get your hopes up, Mr. Peterson.   I'm not planning on moving. Just sorting through a few of my old theater things. Thought I might throw some it out."

"Mind if I take a look? I was a big fan, you know."

"Suit yourself. I was about to make myself a cup of coffee. You care for one?"

Without waiting for an answer, Madeline heads to the kitchen, a small utility affair at the far end of the living room. The trailer's living area is as bare bones as it gets. Aged, whitewashed, wood-paneled walls with cheap vinyl flooring, and accented with mid-century furnishings.

Sammy looks inside the box. It is full of wigs, scarves, eyeglasses and memorabilia from Madeline's theater days. He lifts a red wig from inside the box.

"You're not planning to throw this out? It was your signature look, Detective Borowski, from Bay City Patrol. My favorite."

"Well, you're hardly alone. My Ex loved me in that role.   It was my big break."

Madeleine joins him on the couch and places a tray on the table with two cups of coffee, a plate of cookies and a small vase with the wildflowers he had brought her.

"He was a lot like you. A salesman, but not a particularly good one. Poor man was driven crazy by my good fortune. Unfortunately, it ruined my marriage."

Madeline takes the wig from him and stuffs it back in the box.

"I'm afraid, things ended badly between us."

"I'm sorry to hear that. I loved that show. But certainly, you must have some good memories from then."

Madeline leans forward and takes a silver scarf from the box and wraps it dramatically around her neck.

"This. I wore it on the set with my second husband. He was a wonderful man. Not a terribly good actor and a bit controlling. But loyal as the day is long, until..."

"Until?"

"Until he passed."

"I'm sorry."

Samuel picks up his coffee cup up and sits back on the couch.

"It was rather untimely, I'm afraid. But then there was Roger. And I can assure you, I've no mementos in that box to remind me of him. Roger, damn his soul, cleaned me out, took me for everything I had, and now, far as I care, it's good riddance."

Samuel sips his coffee, furrows his brow and considers what to say next.

"You do have a lot of memories here, Ms. Pensky. Not that I'm pushing, but perhaps you should consider selling, getting a fresh start, somewhere else."

"Ah! There you go. You're exactly like my ex-husband. Always trying to tell me what to do. But I'm not selling. Besides, I have my menagerie of animals here. This is their home. How could I sell this place out from under them? Just because of my good fortune. Now that wouldn't fair, would it?"

Samuel smiles and puts his cup back on the table, then crosses his arms and looks her directly in the eye.

"Not to be rude, Ms. Pensky, but have you given any thought to what you will do with all that money you've won?"

"I thought I might travel. I've always wanted to but never could when my husbands were alive. Such stick-in-the-muds."

"Well then, there's no stopping you now then, is there?"

"I suppose not, Mr. Peterson, but I've never fancied traveling alone. I'm more of a together person."

"You could advertise for a traveling companion."

"A companion? With one those awful matchmaker services?"

"Well, you might give it a try. You never know. Lady like you, retired actress, moneyed. I'm sure the men would be lined up 'round your door for such an opportunity."

"With their walkers maybe. Most men my age are looking for a nurse with a purse. Not my interest, thank you."

"I'm sure there's someone out there, in plenty good shape, who would be delighted."

"And just where do think I should go, Mr. Peterson? If you could do anything you want, go anywhere in the world, where would it be?"

"I've never had the opportunity to think seriously 'bout that. But if I could, why I'd do one of those fancy river trips you see advertised on TV all the time. Maybe go to some exotic place like Budapest or the Taj Mahal."

"You surprise me, Mr. Peterson. You're much more of a dreamer than I'd given you credit for. You sure you're not pitching yourself?"

"Me?"

"Yes, you, Mr. Peterson."

"Are you suggesting, Ms. Pensky, that you might consider me as a traveling companion?"

"Goodness, Mr. Peterson, I think your assumptions are a bit quick."

From behind them, there is a scratching at the back door. Madeline gets up to let the dog in, then stops him abruptly. Quickly taking something from his mouth, she shoves it in her pocket and returns to the couch.

"I'm afraid it's getting late, Mr. Peterson. Perhaps we should continue this conversation another time."

Sam's stands up, the dog approaches him, and he pets him on the head.

"I'd love to Ms. Pensky, but please, if I come back, call me Sammy or Samuel."

"Alright, then, Samuel. Until next time. And you can call me Maddy."

Nice isn't it. Two older people making a connection? Our poor little millionairess Maddy, stuck up on that hill all by herself, too stubborn to move. And Samuel, a hapless bachelor whose beginning to think his life is about to take a turn for the better. Or is it?

****

Welcome, my friends to Act Three. And now, if you'll allow me, a little divine intervention.

It's dawn. The sun is beginning to break through the clouds after a long wet night of torrential downpours. A specialty of mine followed by another of my favorites, earthquakes. There's a violent convulsive shaking of the earth. The hillside behind Maddy's home begins to slip, trees are felled to the ground, and a portion of her backyard begins to crack open. But the trailer remains miraculously steadfast on its mounting.

Inside, Maddy is thrown from her bed. She grabs her robe and races to the window. The damage the earthquake has done to her backyard is overwhelming. The shed had collapsed. There are several sinkholes, three to be exact, that have opened up to reveal their contents. Like the past climbing from beneath the earth's surface, the bones of her former husbands lie exposed.

Without bothering to dress, Maddy rushes to the backyard, Alfred at her heels, barking. From what remains of the shed, she pulls a shovel from beneath the ruins and starts to fill the exposed graves with the loose earth. From behind her, Sam appears on the back steps of the mobile home. He looks frazzled.

"Maddy, Maddy. Are you okay?"

Maddy straightens herself and stares at Samuel. Clearly, she was not expecting him. The look of disbelief, her eyes wide, mouth open, written on her face.

"What are you doing here, Samuel?"

"I came to check on you. I was worried."

Sam jumps off the porch and comes to her, grabbing the shovel from her hands.

"Maddy, what are you doing?"

Even now staring at the three open sinkholes, it hasn't hit him. Before him are plots, crude graves and within those earthen walls are the bones of her –

"Maddy! Maddy! What is this?"

Maddy's heart is racing, her breath like panting, coming in big heavy waves.

"Oh, I wish you hadn't seen that."

She grabs the shovel back from him.

"I'm afraid this complicates things between us, Samuel."

"Maddy, what are you talking about?"

She laughs. The sound of her laughter like like that of a mad woman.

"All you wanted was a listing, you stupid fool. Why couldn't you just leave it alone? Stay out of my business? You're just like the others. Always trying to tell me what to do. And look what it got them. Go ahead, look. What do you think this is?"

Samuel stares at the plots before him and shakes his head.

"No. No, this can't be. You're not trying to tell me these are the bones of your– "

"My ex-husbands, Samuel. That's Thomas, he and I bought this place together. There's Michael, Mr. Boring, and that over there is that bastard, Donald, who ripped me off."

Maddy points to each of the graves and stands definitely before him. Her hands wrap slowly tighter around the handle of the shovel.

"I'm sorry you had to see this. But I suppose it's for the best. Sooner or later, you'd have figured it out. But it doesn't have to end this way. The decision's yours, Samuel."

Sammy stands frozen, unable to move, his eyes fixed on the open graves.

"We could have a good time together, Samuel. Think about it. What was it you wanted to see? Budapest? The Taj Mahal? With my money, together, we could do it all."

Without a word, Sammy stares into her eyes. The eyes of Detective Borowski, the woman he had fantasized about for years, the woman who was asking him to join her.

"I need your answer, Samuel. I don't have a lot of time."

Sammy reaches for the shovel. Determined to take it from her. To stop her.

They struggle with their hands on the handle, pushing each other back and forth. Then Maddy, being shorter and of a stout frame, the center of gravity to her advantage, twists and leans her hip into him, like she'd been taught to do when playing Detective Borowski on TV. Caught off guard, Sammy's hands break free of the shovel, and he topples over her, hitting his head on a rock, knocking himself unconscious.

Maddy stops, stares at the body, then rolls it into the grave on top of husband number three and covers them. Stepping back, with the sweat dripping from her brow, she exhales.

"Well now, that is a shame," she says. "But, tomorrow is another day. Perhaps I'll plant some flowers."

Such a sad state of affairs. Particularly for Samuel Petersen. Oh, I suppose one might say he has ended up with the property, just perhaps not as he had intended. And Maddy, poor Madeline, all alone again and without a traveling companion.

But this would hardly be the end of the story. We're barely through Act Three, and I so hate to end things on such a dour note. Let's flash forward.

Two weeks later. A Monday morning. Maddy's trailer.

There is a knock on the door.

Knock. Knock. Knock.

Maddy answers. She is dressed in a pair of tight-fitting jeans and wearing the red wig. An older, slightly bedraggled-looking fellow dressed in a Columbo-style trench coat, identifies himself as an LAPD detective. He is there to inquire about a missing person. It seems a local realtor, Mr. Samuel Peterson, has disappeared. The detective hands her his card.

"His appointment book shows he may have been canvassing the area for listings last month. Right before the earthquake. I thought I'd stop by and see if you remember seeing him."

Madeline stares at the card, shakes her head and tries to hand it back.

"Sorry, Detective."

"Keep it. And if you think of anything, give us a call."

The detective takes a step off the porch then stops. He looks a bit befuddled, then pointing a finger at her as he says–

"Excuse me, aren't you the woman who won all that money?"

"The Big Readers Sweepstakes. Ten million dollars. Yes. That's me."

Madeline fans herself with the detective's card. The detective smiles, his hands in his overcoat.

"So then, you must be that actress. Madeline– "

"Madeline Pensky. I played Detective Borowski on Bay City Patrol."

The detective takes his hands out of his pockets, and raises them, shoulder height, upward to the sky. A huge smile on his round face.

"They'll never believe this back at headquarters."

 Maddy winks and points her index finger, her hand like a gun, in his direction.

"Gotch ya, Detective."

 "Wow. I could sure use a Detective Borowski on this case with me now. She always got her man."

"Yes, well, I'm afraid I don't know anything about any realtor. After the news broke about my winnings, I found realtor cards in my mailbox and up and down the drive like desert locusts. Of course, I trashed them all. I'm not about to sell. So, if this Peterson's card was among them, if wouldn't know."

"Just my luck."

Madeline pushes a few of the red hairs back behind her ear.

 "Perhaps, Detective, your Mr. Peterson was just swallowed up by the quake."

The detective turns and looks out at the view in front of the trailer.

"Think so, huh?"

"It was just a joke, Detective. Just a joke."

 The detective shakes his head and starts to leave again, then stops and turns back to her.

"So, what's it like?"

"What's what like, Detective?"

 "Winning all that money. I can't imagine how that must feel.   Bet you get a lot of gentlemen callers up here, hoping to woo you away with all your winnings."

Madeline drops her head and smiles, her eyes staring directly into his.

"Men, Detective, have never been much of a problem, money or no money. The right one always seems to come along."

"I imagine so. Lots of lonely hearts. Well then, good day, ma'am."

The detective nods and starts to back off the porch. Madeline hollers after him.

"Detective, there's a bit of a chill in the air. I was just about to make myself a cup of coffee. Perhaps you'd like to come in and join me."

"I could use some coffee. That is if you're not too busy?"

"Nonsense. I was just playing around on the computer. Make yourself at home. I won't be a minute."

The detective takes a seat on the couch, his eyes scanning the room, as detectives do. Maddy's computer sits on the coffee table in front of him and is open to an online site, Seniors Seeking Seniors.

Maddy returns and places a silver tray, coffee for two and vase with wildflowers, on the coffee table.

"Do you prefer milk or cream with your coffee, Detective?"

He ignores her, pulls the computer closer to him and studies the page. Maddy stirs a pack of sugar into her coffee, studying him, her hands shaking.

"Interesting website. Always wondered how those worked. You've used it before?"

"Oh, that silly thing? Of course not. I was just entertaining myself. A friend of mine suggested I might try it. I really should put this computer away, before we spill coffee all over it."

Maddy reaches for her laptop. The detective puts his hand on top of hers. There's a moment. Remember, I did warn you this was a play of divine intervention. The two smile awkwardly at one another. And then the detective says—

"Please, don't. I find it interesting."

His eyes meet hers, holding them steady.   He glances back at the computer.

"Is this your ad? Wealthy retired actress seeks mature traveling companion?

 "It could be, Detective. Are you volunteering?"

47.
Slipstream
Rob McCrandall

Cory,

I hope you still remember how to read this. It's been years since we made the cipher. Hell, it's been years since we spoke.

Valicorp owns everything and has since 1981. Never heard of them? They're the most silent of partners, privately owned and operated by one Theodore S. Valitore, a first-generation Italian-American with an ego the size of California and enough money to make him untouchable. Through countless miles of red-tape and lobbying, he privately owns companies that are publicly traded every day. Never heard of him either? There are a million reasons, but I don't have time to put any down. Just understand that Valicorp is real and Valitore's are the hands that hold the strings of this world. Or so he likes to think. The one obstacle old *Teddy* couldn't overcome, will *never* overcome, is nature itself. Sure, he can pretend (and maybe even be deluded enough to honestly believe) that he holds dominion over it, but in the end, nature will always win.

All the alchemists and astronomers in history could only speculate on the wonders of the universe. The modern scientists scratch at the assumed surface of infinite knowledge and understanding like a dog on a door when it needs to take a piss. But nature holds its cards close, really goddamn close. Once in a while, it gives us a peek, but only a short window; just enough to keep us guessing about what's next, and coming back for more. We can pretend we do it on our own, in spite of nature, but in the end, we're just lying to ourselves.

Sorry to spew that bit of philosophical psychobabble, but I think it helps make my point. What I'm about to tell you is for your eyes only and is the absolute truth. I know we've had our differences in the past, but you're the only one I can trust with this and I know you won't go public with it. You can't.

I never believed in the soul or the afterlife or shit like that, which has always been a point of contention between us, but I do now. In fact, I know it exists. I'm not talking an out-of-body experience or a spiritual awakening. I'm talking about the very essence of *us*. I've seen it.

Do you remember six months ago when Prior Pharm built that research station in northern Alabama right at the base of the Smoky Mountains? They claimed some previously overlooked species of pine tree had finally been discovered and its sap had some miraculous medicinal power.   The cure for the common cold was finally found.   No matter how it mutated, one vaccination would stop it for life.   Remember? I doubt you got yours as I know you think those things are bullshit, but this one is legit, I swear.   But it wasn't suddenly created in some lab outside of a hillbilly town no one's ever heard of along a stretch of mining country.   No, Valitore finally decided his little drug company should reveal what it had been holding since the mid 90's.   A profitable diversion from what really happened.   Here goes:

A group of basics (you bet your ass those robo-drones are branded by Vali) were working as per their directives in a mine shaft some ten miles under the mountain, seeking some new vein of gold or something, when they broke through a wall into a tunnel.   The guys back in the control room made a couple calls and got permission to check it out.   They slipped into manual mode and walked those pieces of steel and wires a good mile and a half before the screens started to flicker and finally burn up.   Not just go blank, but full on explode into showers of sparks and plastic.   Of course, a recovery squad had to go in and get those fifty-thousand dollar husks out of that hole.   The footage from their suits was incredible.   The bots lay in a pile, all twisted and melted together.   Not a hundred feet ahead was something I can best describe as a stream.   Its official codename is the *River*, but we all call it the *Slipstream*.   I'll get to that.   Soon.   It has to be soon.

The stream was silent.   I mean pins could drop and echo for miles when next to this thing.   It glowed a deep, brilliant purple.   It wasn't water, Cory.   It ebbed and flowed down a narrow channel but never seemed to touch the stone around it.   One of the recovery goons stuck his hand in it.   His name was Eric Thorn.   Remember him?   A foreman who died in a tunnel collapse in Tennessee; that was his official CoD, but that didn't happen.   Still with me?   It gets weird here.

The anomaly was reported immediately and the team was called back to the surface for quarantine and medical surveillance.   No one knew what it was or what it did.   After three days, Eric started talking about seeing his birth and some other bizarre shit like he could relive his memories.   He talked a lot about his wife.   She died three months after they were married, only six months after they met.   The shrinks didn't know what to think other than he was losing his mind a bit.   Then a week later, one day after being released from quarantine, he was found dead in his bunk.   According to the autopsy, everything just stopped.   No heart attack, no stroke.   Nothing.   He just died.   The most natural of deaths: his body just quit.

In the weeks that followed, the first entry team was reevaluated and monitored while the Prior front was hastily constructed.   Once the top level was complete, six hundred basics were brought in to build what now is under that fully-functioning Pharma farce.   A fifty-thousand square foot structure to house the one thousand staff members.   Everything I just told you was explained to us under penalty of death.   Fortunately, I won't have to worry about their goons.   I just hope you're safe enough.   You'll understand.

Valicorp used its subsidiary companies to find intelligent, but seemingly pliable, single employees with no known close family connections. I was perfect. I didn't understand why an industrial gas sales manager was being promoted to a regional position within the newly partnered Prior Pharma, but I always was a sucker for the fast-track, wasn't I? I guess that's why I went into business instead of physics or teaching. The one thing those data-miners couldn't extract from their pool of personnel files, tax returns and general wiretapping (I did say they own everything, right?) were my interests. Cash, purchases, and real books. So ironically retro, I know. But it saved me. Saved the collective us. I'll get there. I have to. Three hours left.

We were all thoroughly examined inside and out, physically and mentally. We were assigned private quarters and told fraternization with other staffers was not only allowed, but encouraged. However, overnight stays in bunks were prohibited. I think we were sterilized chemically because the women don't have cycles and my production has a different consistency. I know, TMI, but I need you to understand. I spent four months down there before being released a week ago. I have to go back, but I need to finish. It's just so hard to put down. There's so much to tell you. What I know. What I've seen...

Shit. Alright. Focus. We were checked up and checked in and assigned new roles. Regional manager my ass. I was a lab rat at the mercy of the Company. They must have drugged us a little at first because we didn't get mad. Any of us. We just accepted what was being said and went straight to our duties. And after we touched the stream, we stopped caring about the lies and subterfuge. It was horrific and beautiful, Cory.

I'm getting a little ahead. Putting it in order is a bitch now.

After the second team, a group of brilliant research interns had gone down and walked into the stream, their progress was monitored. The scientists rationalized the unfathomable and began running tests on themselves. The third team to go down installed the atmospheric generators but never touched the stream. I guess they were the control group because they didn't report anything. Three of the second team (I think there were ten total) died as mysteriously as Eric did. In fact, they died *exactly* how he did. So Valitore decided to bring us in and perform some tests on what he thought was his new toy.

Cory, I need to tell you what it was that happened when anyone touched that stream. *The River.* Please don't think I'm crazy. Finish reading this letter and then destroy it. But someone needs to know. Wait, I pretty much said that already, didn't I? The words are coming so easy now even with the cipher. I'm rambling...

The River. Right.

I was a part of the fourth team.   Until us, the effects had been purely mental.   Not a hallucination, but I guess it could be considered akin to it.   A journey through the mind while the body stays behind.   But my team, three of us anyway, we were different.   Once we entered the stream, we could *feel* it move through us.   The second team theorized it was a physical modification of our DNA, but I don't think that's quite it.   It goes deeper than that.

The River flows forward, always forward.   To go back, upstream, takes a force of will like pushing a freight truck uphill with your hands.   To hold still isn't nearly as hard, but it takes focus.   The ones that died got lost and couldn't go back.   Back to where? I haven't told you what it *is* yet, have I?

It's time travel, Cory.   Real, honest, see-the-future time travel.   I'm completely crazy, right? NO!   The stream, nature's big middle finger, punishes those that wish to *use* it like a toy.   Or the weak ones.   One thousand went down... One hundred sixty-seven of us are left.   I don't mean still part of the experiment.   *Left*, as is in the rest are dead.   It wears on you.   Breaks you down.   It's just so damn easy to slide in...

Two hours; not enough time, but it has to be.   Remember how I said that I have seen the soul? It explains so much.   You see, when we let go and go into the *River*, we leave our bodies behind and drive through time.   I saw myself and others when we traveled together, and it was beautiful.   Just like the *Slipstream*, we were all transparent and purple, just generic shades of our physical selves.   That's how you look when you travel in time, Cory.   A ghost.

Most of us, anyway.   We were different, but I said that, right? If I just close my eyes I can see us playing with that stray dog in the park, the one with the glassy eyes... Focus.   It's getting harder to keep it straight. Time, that is.   The order of it all.   It's all at once now.   I have to finish before my shift.

My whole body can come.   Is that right? A Traveler, not a Spectator.   That's what old *Teddy* said.   We were Travelers since we could go, *whole*, anywhere we had the strength to go.   The rest could just watch it happen while we could make it happen.   I'll go back.   It makes sense, I swear.

The others, and us, at first, just closed their eyes for a second, basically a blink in some cases, and started telling stories from their past as if it just happened.   Unbelievable things from childhood like walking for the first time or their first word.   I mean, we shouldn't remember these things, and certainly not with clarity, but we all did.   It was easy at first to move in our own time, which is key.   If it happened during our life, we can't see beyond what we saw.   It's a law of nature.   It has to be.   We simply couldn't, can't see anything else.   We're trapped in our own skin, unable to communicate even with ourselves.

Where was I? I slipped for a day...but only a second here. That's how it goes. Here doesn't seem as real now... One hour, fifty minutes; I need to hold on just a little longer. No matter how far we traveled or for how long, it's only ever a second or less. But we could, and did, speak of our journeys with perfect clarity for hours afterwards. It's real, so much more real than here, which shouldn't be possible. I mean, this is now, right? Or am I just lost as to where *now* is? I'm losing my mind, Cory! This all stops tonight.

I can't say I'm getting ahead of myself anymore...since I've been there and back eighty-nine times. And that's just in this timeline... The Butterfly Effect is real, too, Cory, but it's not as big of a deal as we think. I mean, it is a huge deal if we kill Hitler before his rise to power (which didn't do anyone any bit of good, unfortunately) or save Kennedy (one-term president once the luster wore off and he was found to be no different than the rest), but it's so small in the grand scheme...

The Spectators were pissed when they saw the video. We went forward and back, as usual, but when we opened our eyes, we were different. Jerry had a scar on his face where a Roman soldier slashed him with a spear. He said it took a month to start to heal properly and another month to scar up like we saw it. In 0.65 seconds he went from handsome and clean shaven, void of imperfections on his playboy face, to ragged, worn, scruffy, and scarred from ear to lip. We got to live what the other could see. Whole bodies gone with us.

We could only go so far as Travelers. Any time before the planet was hospitable and any time after the end of life (It comes, but I can't spoil the end. Suffice it to say that we have plenty of time.). It's just another law of nature. Tara disappeared one day while she was traveling. The room stank of sulfur and burned hair. Her diary (another thing we are encouraged to have) said something about the extinction of the dinosaurs, so volcano or meteor are my guesses.

The Specs were jealous of our newfound ability, but as with everything else down there, it was kept to a minimum and the tests went on. We were forbidden from slipping unless it was our shift in the chairs, but no one could enforce it. By the end of the second month, half of us were dead or gone. Yeah, others started to Travel later on, but not everyone. I guess not all of us had what it took to make the final plunge.

I've seen how the universe started, all dust and the endless void of space. It was breathtaking and amazing at first, but after a couple hours I got bored and sped ahead a few million years. No matter how hard I tried, even as a Spec, I couldn't move beyond the planet. We're tethered here. Another law, right? And in these cases, the laws are absolute. No one could do it. No one can do it. Even before it took shape, the planet held on to us. Maybe there isn't anything else out there that's worth seeing.

Thirty minutes left. I fell asleep, an honest, dreamless sleep. It's the first time in three days, Cory. I feel stronger, more in control of the *now*, but it won't last. I have to tell you about the timelines and about the madness.

It feels like a lifetime since I started this letter. I don't have time to read more than the last few lines. Did I mention the Butterfly Effect? When we Travel, we make changes. We aren't *supposed* to be there, so any action changes something. Changes cause ripples, albeit small ones, but ripples nonetheless.   A new timeline is created. Kill Hitler? A plague wipes out millions of Europeans and a few Americans and Japanese to boot.   Stop the release of Detective Comics #1? Nightfox fights The Jester on the silver screen in the 80's.

Those are major events, but little truly changes in the world. We always woke up here, still a part of the experiment, still prisoners. But *we* were changed. We all knew what happened before the *River* but the world was no longer the same. It wears on you. The madness. How can one person keep track of these inconsistencies? Simple: we can't. We hold on as long as we can, but we can't survive forever. Even when we returned to undo our change, something subtle shifts. Hamburger Hut is known as McDonald's this time around...

Shit, losing focus.   My goddamned sanity.

I don't know if you and I know each other now; I haven't had the time to find out in this timeline, but I know where to send this.   We were close for years in my version of our childhood, but we fell out due to bullshit ideological differences.   I've lived a few days in a world where we were both given up for adoption. Separately. Others, we are best friends.   No matter what, though, we are always brothers. And one of us always grew up in the old house on Sebastian Avenue.   This will find its way to you.

During my shift tonight, I'm going to kill Valitore.   To stop all of this, he needs to be stopped, but it has to be *before* the tunnel is found.   Hell, before he ever rose to power.   Think what you will of me, Cory, but I'm going to kill him before he grows up. Then, I'll return to whatever version of "now" will exist for me and end it if I can. There isn't any other way.

I know I left so many questions unanswered, but please believe that, even with what I can do, there isn't enough time in the world to tell you what I know.   I tried, but I can't.   The basics will be here any minute.   I have one of my own, a reprogrammed gift from Jerry an hour before he travelled off for good.   It'll get this to you, and then it, too, will be done with.

Take care.
Your brother, Jack

****

The weary, strained eyes of the large man behind the mahogany desk lifted slowly from the scattered pages before him.   The well-dressed man sitting opposite squirmed slightly as the hardened gaze fell upon him.

"Mr. Seaton," the far smaller man said nervously, "I know it took a few days of work, but I promise that is the deciphered version. It was very complex. There were-"

"Eight layers of encryption, three of which used non-English characters and one no more than a series of childish runes, right?" Mr. Cory Seaton smiled as he spoke, causing the smaller man to squirm again.

"Um...Yes, sir. Exactly. But how did you know"?

Cory gathered the papers and tossed them in the shredder beside his desk before answering.

"Because I made it up a long time ago.   My brother Jack and I used to pretend we were spies sending messages across enemy lines.   Did you read this?" The small man blushed and opened his mouth to answer, but Cory continued. "Of course you did. You cracked the code, didn't you, Henry? Well, my brother died forty years ago."

Henry took a breath but, Cory again cut him off.

"I know what it says, but whoever this man is, he's sick.   I don't know how he found out about the cipher, nor do I care. I appreciate the time you spent on this, Henry, but forget about what it says. Whatever scam this bastard is trying to pull, I'm not interested. You're dismissed."

Cory watched Henry, shaken and confused, stumble his way out of the large office.   He inhaled sharply and turned toward the huge window overlooking the Chicago skyline.

I don't know how you did it.   It had to be you. You were born Samuel Jonathon Seaton and not even Mom and Dad knew I called you Jack.   I don't know if any of it is true, but I agree with one thing: nature's laws are absolute.   You just can't fight it.

Absently, he slipped the buzzing phone from his pocket and accepted the call.

"Yes, Sally? Oh...good. Tell me, how is the new Progress Industries building coming along in Alabama? It's almost complete? Fantastic. Please tell Edgar to start recruiting. Yes, for the project. Oh, and make sure to get the promotional materials into the right hands. The common cold doesn't stand a chance..."

48.
Soul Unicorn
Sue Ann Olson

I'm trying to have eyes to see
The light beyond my own reality
A light that shone where myths exist
But are they shadows from the mist
Of long ago and far away
In times of ancient distant days?
Or ages that just might have been
In differing realities?

I'm calling my soul unicorn
With the power of my horn
Who's to say what I really am
Unicorn, nymph, or human
Disappointing it might be
When we dip back to reality
Or what we have defined it to be

Where what we have to lose
Is less than mortal pain
But what truth truly gains
Cannot be easily measured
By comparing mortal treasure

Or the ways of which we're sure
For in the realms of light pure
There is no greater force
Than the song of love's true course
Following like a river to the ocean
As love guides us into the sun
Where mythical unicorns run
By the side of mighty dragons
Roaring fire that heals all strife
As the phoenix's song brings new life

All creations of the myths as one
Like your thoughts when love has won
In our future that was meant to be
In the value of the love we hold
Pouring on this earth of old
In the legends of my own
I can be my soul unicorn
Bringing magic to earth reborn
With the touch of my horn

49.
Stream of Consciousness
Wm. Bernan

"Jimmy's had nightmares for some time," Dad says, ashamed a Delaney could succumb to such deficiencies. AIDS, Leprosy, Smallpox, the Clap--anything but a perceived mental disorder, that would be fine.

My family's a clan of MENSA worshippers. The framed photo of Berrill and Ware, our Patron Saints, over the buffet in the dining room is the first clue. I'd have preferred Jobs myself, maybe Gates.

Anyway, they weren't nightmares, per se. Not in the I'm asleep, and this is a very bad dream sense. In the what the hell is happening to me sense, then, yeah, they were nightmares. I couldn't stop them from thinking what they wanted.

Not the family, anyway.

Their embarrassment started a few years ago, I was ten. One morning they found me in a full-blown panic attack following some kind of vivid dream, so vivid it crossed into my waking world. I awoke, staring up at the constellation of green-glowing stars I'd affixed to my bedroom ceiling (in the accurate positions of the southern hemisphere night sky over Australia in winter, which I couldn't otherwise see from Connecticut), and I couldn't move. The first shrinks pronounced an oversimplified and underwhelming diagnosis of sleep paralysis, which they say happens to all of us. Somehow, apparently, the higher functions of my brain ceased to slumber while the ones controlling my muscles dozed on peaceably; leaving me to scream and cry and choke and eventually to piss myself while I fought to move for a good bit of time without success. None of them connected the preceding dream to the immobility, but shrinks, I've since learned, generally aren't all that bright.

Truth is, I'd been regularly abducted by unknown somebodies for some time before that attack. I didn't understand it was abduction, per se, until the morning of the sleep paralysis. I'd just thought I was dreaming. A recurring nocturnal vision where I went to work, gamed my way through a shift in what I thought of as the Light Arcade and was home in bed by breakfast. Or, back in my body, I should say. See, they didn't really abduct people (or the kids they seemed to prefer) in ships and conduct medical studies like TV likes to tell us. They only needed our minds, which they made corporeal over there. Our natural sleep state is too easy for them.

They, and note I use the plural they as the beings' forms were as disparate as most humans, but I could just as easily use it, as they operated only a single collective-consciousness. A natural evolution once telepathy replaced language.

We operated in a skyscraper in a colossal city, horizon to horizon, unlike any I'm certain you've seen. A silver-gray glass-scape of oddly organic crystalline structures, as if constructing had given way to growing buildings. Glass-like, but lacking fragility. Almost like the walls, floors, ceilings, stairwells, elevators were all of a translucent diamond-metal amalgam of infinite strength, unlimited light, and inestimable beauty. The workers, initially a couple dozen of us, were young. The overseers were taller, appear to have been older, but the stretched grey-white hairless flesh, lacked any features that would hint at age.

I don't know what their daily duties were, but the bulk of the round room, encompassing an entire domed floor of the tree-like skyscraper, consisted of control panels not unlike a nuclear power plant, or Houston mission control. The young were placed in front of consoles with an oval aperture looking like a portal to another dimension. The overseers, I call them, maybe a hundred on our floor, some guarding us, watching, while most did whatever it was they did at all the other panels. An open space, like a round hockey rink seemed like wasted space in the middle.

Awake, I would have thrown a fit had anyone tried to jab me with a needle. There, it was natural to have needles in either arm, up by the crook and down by the wrists, as well as suction pads to the temples. I didn't know at the time my consciousness was away, they made it physical there. I think, like the movie, we were downloaded into avatars.

I was made to play what I thought of as "The Light Game" at a console I nicknamed the neurospectrograph--exactly what it sounds like, some kind of brain/light imager.

I apparently got very good at it, for pretty soon, I had fewer coworkers until there were only a few of us.

I faced the infinite portal, an aperture like a large 3D television through which was an almost infinite cosmic arc, no horizon, no edges. Not even a definite shape. At once it seemed convex, then concave, then no bounds at all. In it streamed, danced, and flowed untraceable beams of light, colors rebounding, sometimes blurred, sometimes distinct, always moving. As near as I can describe it, it was like all the neon in Las Vegas reflected in the chrome of an infinitely formless motorcycle exhaust, or simultaneously being inside and outside a blob of mercury in a rainbow. Staring into the light, everything disappeared. In a form of rapture my mind opened, absorbed, flowed, and I played, I think. Like a puzzle. Spectral connect the dots. Something like that. Lights would swirl, I would pull them into shapes like working taffy. They would pass right through my head into the world behind. When my shift was over I'd wake up in my own bed.

Then, that day when I was ten, they did something.   I didn't know if it was an accident or what.   A bad day at work, a shift hadn't gone well.   A colleague, a tan-skinned kid a little older than me, threw a fit.   He seemed possessed of a cognizance.   An individuality.   The unspoken something not tolerated there.   He screamed and shouted, trying to wake us, as if we were sleeping.   By the time his tirade started to register, the overseers had already wrestled him to the rotunda in the center of the office.   No one else seemed to notice, all following their routines by rote.   I left my station and ran to the rail, the diamond/glass/steel amalgam separating our workspace from the sunken floor under the dome.

The tan-skinned kid shouted, "Remember Reggie, it's Reggie...I told you!" as amorphous wedges of floor rotated like a Leica iris revealing a method of redistribution akin to a juicer.   Corporeal or consciousness alone, moot, the sound he made going through the Cuisinart was real.   It lasted maybe a second.

I understood--consciously subconsciously--that Reggie was really gone.   His parents would find a lifeless body in his bed, if they found anything at all.   The overseers must have sensed my discovery.   They weren't pleased.

That's when I woke in my bed, frozen, T-shirt and sweat pants soaked, capable only of thinking, breathing, screaming, pissing.   I'd never panicked before.   I mean full-blown grip of death panic.   Paralysis itself should be terrifying.   The knowledge that I could at any moment be dangling over a fifty foot Cuisinart still dripping bits of Reggie, that's cause for panic.

I wanted to tell somebody, but, in my family, that's a shortcut to an asylum.   So, initially, I stayed awake, fighting sleep for days.   Eventually it wins out, or they induce it.   They found me passed out in a leather chair in my father's library.

The needles hurt, unlike before.   The temple cups sucked at my brain like a vacuum.   New straps binding me to the chair chafed my wrists, knees, and ankles.   I fought, weeping in frustration.   They bound my head facing the portal, but I couldn't complete a single puzzle.   The strings of light, mad ribbons of random disorder I saw through the portal meant nothing to me.   Overseers stumbled around in rampant drunkenness.   Something was wrong.   They weren't happy with my work.   I just couldn't get what was expected of me, I'd lost all ability to play the game.   I couldn't stop thinking of Reggie.

I woke in my father's chair, paralyzed, pain coursing through every muscle, in a pool of excrement.   Apparently, that's what they do when they need you in line, short of shredding.

Agonized, tortured, wondering why I wasn't bits, I wracked my brain.

The shrink diagnosed the burns to my wrists and ankles a psychosomatic response to a particularly vivid dream--he supposed I'd grow up to like bondage.   The family was likely planning my accidental demise until the doc told Father that I was "inordinately gifted" to have a mind capable of pulling off a physical effect like that. Idiot. They put me on a benzodiazepine--supposed to help me sleep.

The overseers couldn't trust my work anymore. I no longer seemed to know what I was doing, I couldn't tune in. The blurs and colors; lines, ribbons, and strings, weren't puzzles anymore. They wove and drifted and danced, flowing out of some distant point, through the portal, blurring in a mad jumble past my head like some psychedelic 3D movie.

Again they were displeased.

I woke up, paralyzed, in a hospital bed. They'd said I'd had a seizure.

The new school I was sent to wasn't a mental hospital, officially, but that's about its function. Drug the kids, strap them down, no one allowed out of their cell without an escort. Maybe teach them something at some point. Rooms padded, corners rounded, tiny window to the corridor, everything a single shade of beige. Piss time, meal time, class time, drool, nap time, piss time again, sleep time. Locked doors. At least it allowed the family to say "he's off to a school for the gifted."

Fortunately I was allowed books. No outside contact, no laptop, no notepads, but I could read whenever the downers let up. Still the morning paralysis, which I was beginning to handle better; less screaming, more slow breaths, convincing myself it was just a dream. Unfortunately, it still had the loss of bodily function side effect. I could have hid the trauma from the Stewards nee Nurses, but we only had one jumpsuit, and mine needed frequent cleaning.

In the back pages of books, with a smuggled stub of pencil, I scribbled notes. The strict tablet cocktail, I couldn't fake the swallowing--they checked, slowed me, but still I tried to reason it out. Console, light, strings, Reggie, bits...? The chair. It always came down to the same thing. Why me? Why am I not bits?

At night I stared and stared into the psychedelic tie-dyed light riding bullet trains of smoke, drifting, flying, from the boundless portal past shoulders to somewhere behind me. I still couldn't make sense of any of it. What is it I used to do when I seemed to know what I was doing? The more clueless I felt, the worse the paralysis would be.

I drifted off to daydream, recalling my first dissatisfaction with games.

I built my first computer at age seven. No one could tell me why the original game of "Pong" was created, so I reconstructed it. Not to see how it was done, that was intuitive, but why people would think it's fun. I eventually mastered it as a two player, four player, and eventually as an eight way game on a hexagonal playing field. I played all eight players.

Distracted by "Pong" I overlooked a ray of white light attaching itself to my forehead. Harmlessly, an image of open space flooded my vision. A pinkish one followed. An intercepted command order. Lights started to organize, stream through me in a parade of random ideas. They flooded my consciousness. I sorted through so much chaff, catching snippets of history, identity, purpose. I began to understand who they were (it was), where'd they'd been, what they'd done, what they planned. Civilizations destroyed, planets robbed of anything they could use. Why they needed us. The insight--they needed me.

Effortlessly, demanding barely a hint, I bounced a blue tube of light off a red one. They momentarily joined into purple, then passing through, resumed each original course. Easy. I made it move. Manipulation, that's what I could do. They'd lost the ability. Surrendering consciousness to this absurd cloud at birth, they lacked the ability to impose order to their thoughts. Bodies idled, productivity suffered, intricate plans failed to develop.

I saw the stream of chaotic emanations no more as a psychedelic sputtering, but as a traffic cop would see vehicle congestion...at an intersection with an infinite number of converging streets. I picked out the most commonly travelled routes and streamlined them for better flow of traffic. Eased congestion. Made them flow faster, more efficiently. The world around me picked up pace, clicking along like clockwork, in an accelerated clock.

The constant threat of the shredder loomed but felt less immediate. I wasn't sure if I was doing right, wrong, or otherwise, but I seemed to be pleasing someone. I didn't wish to, but when I awoke I was able to stretch and yawn, rub the sleep out of my eyes. Better, I didn't need to be hosed off.

Daytimes, between hose baths, pills, meals, more pills, and what passed as classes, I wrote and re-wrote my thoughts. I stared at the acoustic tiles in my ceiling--twenty feet up to keep "students" from climbing inside. The speckled patterns, the white plains dotted and dented with dark shadowy dimples began to blur and fade to a white canvas to project my imagination on. I practiced manipulating the lines of light. What can they do? What could I do? Could no one else do this? This well?

Could I use them to escape?

Every once in a while, I thought I had it, I understood, but it escaped me.

The needles didn't hurt anymore. Work became simple. Within seconds of being strapped before the portal I had everything streaming through me fast, linear, efficient.

After a semester--apparently my sentence--I was deemed fit to rejoin the society of my ludicrous family. Somewhere along the way, I turned eleven.

I pulled every sticker off my bedroom ceiling when I got home. The flat white expanse made it easier to imagine. I tried and tried various manipulations of the lights from work. Twisting, bending. Gauging what would be the most likely outcome. Things I dared not try in the glass-scape. I forced my imagination to see deeper into the portal than I ever could. Tried to determine the source of the lights. Imagine what lay behind me and where they were rushing off to. I couldn't risk trying any of this at work, so every hour I had alone, I replayed a night's labor on my ceiling. Unfortunately, I got nowhere closer to understanding where they came from, where they were going. How to use them to escape. An idea hit me. Epiphany? But it was gone before I could catch it.

I was back in my own school. In the afternoons falling behind on homework, replaying last night's work. At work, I was phoning it in. I'd sit strapped to the chair, almost mindlessly making the lights cooperate, proceed smoothly with nearly no interaction, and half dozed. Until the next wake-up.

The next Reggie was a girl named Saffron. I don't know how I knew her name, I just did. She wasn't quite as gifted in the chair, so her sudden cognizance wasn't tolerated.

She spoke, shouted, cried. "I didn't mean to change them!" She saw in my eyes that I recognized. That was the most tragic part. She was cute, about my age, in a knee length sleep shirt covered in bears, pleading with me for help. She shredded slower than Reggie, more grinding. The rest of the shift the lines of light were harder to keep together. The needles once again ached.

The library at school still had a few quiet corners where a person could study in peace. I opened my laptop and used an alias to access the WiFi without leaving a footprint, another talent. Saffron isn't a common name, well not for someone with an obvious Boston accent. I quickly found the obit out of Stoneham, Massachusetts for the blond girl with pleading eyes. With a last name, it took no time to find her social network profile. Saffron McCarthy was beautiful when she smiled. She looked so happy. Her favorite quotes, Twain, Dickenson, someone named Izzy, chosen to be more funny than intellectual, but I liked that too. She wanted to visit Alaska, see the aurora. A hundred people had already posted tributes. I didn't.

My mind went erratic. Would have liked to have known her--saw her shredded--loved that smile--she begged me--Alaska--brown bears. I got mad.

The chair was cold. There was something wrong. I felt distrusted. The needles felt thicker. Hurt more.

The lights flowed at me. Erratic as always. I let them. I wasn't going to do their bidding. The suction cups sucked harder, the wind knocked out of me. I made lights move, and could breathe again. I arranged the randomness into streams, flowing through like efficient tubular rivers. Everyone seemed to ease. Everyone but me.

She went by Saffy.   She changed them?   Is that what she'd said?   Could I?

Suddenly I crossed them, all my lines, the needles hurt but I didn't care anymore.   I twisted them, spun them all, and made them into tartan ribbons, a wild rope of argyle braid. The overseers, a dozen in our space, millions in the city, stumbled, drunk and confused.   I whipped ropes of braided light over and through each other, back along their own lengths, tracing patterns like aerobatic smoke trails mock dogfighting then skywriting in Technicolor graffiti.   Overseers stumbled, crawled, clumsily struggling to regain their balance, groping their way toward me.   I changed a rope to black, thanks, Saffy.

Obliterating all color, obliterating a thought, simple as hitting delete.   Some of the overseers collapsed.   The nearest one struggled on.   I changed another rope to black, he and a few others dropped writhing on the ground, hands gouging at their temples with silvery nails.

I'd gotten it.   Finally.   I had them.

I restored the color, and the overseers began to recover.   I let them all stand.   I divided and merged all ropes until I had eight mass channels flowing through me, passing seamlessly, allowing them industriousness, life.

I felt the tension.   The unease.   Redder and redder lights streamed at me, I knew what it meant.   Thought has no language, only understanding.   They couldn't hide from me, I saw the plan of attack.   By coordinating their collective thought, they had no element of surprise.   They tried to rush.

Quickly I bent every ribbon, ninety degrees, up, down, left and right, none progressing beyond me.   Their world froze, no thought entering any of their heads.   Carefully I slipped in my own.

Undo the straps.

My head and arms were freed.   I looked around.

Release the others, send them home.

A half dozen kids fell asleep, their minds transported home, their last alien dream.

Alone in the diamond city with a few million abductors, I played the endgame.   Violent thoughts filled my mind, I unleashed.   Overseers flung themselves to the walls, some to the floor, forcibly thrashing, a battery of satisfying crunches.   Jimmy Delaney was here.   I left them panting, broken, pinning themselves in their place.   Next, I took on their core consciousness.

I shifted all colors, paler and paler.   Amplifying, distorting, thinking I knew what would happen if the source was hit by massive feedback.

The light colors disappeared first.   Pale blues and pinks.   The richer violets and ambers took longer to fade and for a moment I felt guilty of an intolerable cruelty or sensed I was being accused of it.   Finally, even the darkest red faded.

No hint of life came from anyone in the room, the building, the city.   Absolute blank.

The streams, the entire portal reaching pure white, I thought brighter, Brighter! Amplify. Supercharge.   An infinite fluorescence, brighter and brighter, blinding, until even I, who had control, could not bear to look.   I continued to increase the intensity.   More.   More.   Until, like that historic nanosecond at the Trinity test site, the light seemed to implode.   Total photonic reversal.   I let it go.

I sat in silence for I do not know how long.   I opened my eyes to the portal, but there was nothing.   I looked at my arms to see the straps, the needles, the chair, but they were gone.   I was in nothing.   No colored strands to manipulate.   No overseers or slaves or machinery.   No floor, no ceiling, no diamond-steel city.   Dimensionless.   The dimension obliterated.   I slept.

Family still thinks I have nightmares.   I let them…it gives me time to think.   Perhaps I'm becoming isolationist.   Good.   I've seen what happens when idiots share a collected consciousness.

My ceiling bears stars again.   An Alaskan solstice scene.   Complete with aurora.

For Saffy.

50.
Subterranean
John Grey

What shall I do?
I really don't want to do anything.
Where can I live?
One thing I know for certain -
this is not it.
So what do I desire?
More of this sun, this heat?
Unlikely.
My face lit up like a singer on stage?
No way.
So what do I desire?
Sex? To fill my belly?
How about just getting away
from every place and everybody.
I'm vulnerable here.
Someone could reach me.
The urgency is real.
Keep on the move?
Who can really do that?
And, besides, even if I did,
I'd still be in the public eye.
They say you can get lost

in a crowd
but I never could.
I want to be alone.
Solitude can keep a secret.
It doesn't talk back.
At least, not in any critical way.
And it's undemanding.
It doesn't have to be pleased.
So where do I go?
To the sewers?
Yeah, that's the best place for me.
Doesn't smell so good but nor do I.
Plenty of rats
but they're not human.
No family. No need for a job.
No relationships. No nothing
but the comfort of darkness.
So the subterranean it is.
I sit back.
Close my eyes.
And here I am -
somewhere within you all.

51.
Succubi
A.J. Huffman

Carrion bodies burn
to be entwined.   All flame,
no moth, our mouths
consume anything but silence.
Twin skins melt, merge, peel
apart for half a breath
before doing it all again.
We are needles, pounding,
piercing, forcing unnecessary
stitches.   We are bound
without tangible thread.   We flow
through midnight, eyes
fueled by blind desire.

52.
Susurros de Recurrencia
Franco Strong

She dreamed an endless, labyrinthine dream where shadows stretched over the abyss, where vivid colors sank into her skin, where the memories of the entire world were contained in a single drop of water that trickled down to the bottom of a forgotten riverbed. She dreamed because the liquid images were all she had left, all she could grasp with any certainty. Corrosive, dry years—along with too many days peering at the sun with her blue eyes—left her blind. Her vision had disappeared in gradual phases, like the moon, until the sliver of light finally faded and never returned. Muscles followed soon after, evaporated and useless in the perpetual drought of old age.

Yet the immobile darkness had its own landscape, its own dense valleys and open vistas for Quetzali to navigate. And in these unlocking, shifting, intertwining spaces her dreams were much more than simple reveries, they were her memories, pieces, fragments of a life that continued in a realm devoid of time and space.

She dreamed and remembered the days of spices, herbs, and roots, her young yet calloused hands pulling treasures form the desert soil and turning them into potions, remedies, and medicines. Those were days before the incursion of the intruders, the Spaniards, marched upon the land with skin white like cream and destroyed ancient cities only to rebuild atop the ruins.

In her life before the darkness she had been a healer, a woman of earthly medicines. The desert plains had whispered their secrets to her long ago and they still echoed faintly within the caverns of her dreams.

As the liquid images of her mind began to solidify, as she felt the sun against her skin, as the granule scent of the plains filled her nose, as she saw the receding horizon once again, her memories came alive...

Quetzali arrived at the entrance to a hut made of dried mud-bricks, her young hands armed with the ancient secrets of the earth. Her medicines were the last line of defense, the last barrier against the encroaching hands of death which consistently swept in like the western winds.

A man greeted and welcomed her in. He glanced over her with eyes that seemed like two shallow trenches dug up but quickly forgotten. The man wasn't too old, but his joints and neck moved slowly and deliberately as though every split second he mentally measured out his movements. The adobe walls were cracked and splintering, clay pots were strewn across the ground, some broken, others half-filled with rotting liquid and food.

"I don't leave her side," he said, "I'm sorry. I don't see much of the sun. Your hair, it's so bright."

Even though Quetzali already knew the answers she still asked: how long has she been sick? How often did she eat? Was there blood in her vomit? When was the last time she spoke? Are the blisters on her skin peeling off yet? When was the last time a Spaniard had been to their home?

After the man answered all the questions, Quetzali asked one more, "And your children?"

"They are gone now. Their mother lasted the longest. But even she hasn't opened her eyes in days."

The man led her to a small room, windowless, dark, a twin to the man's hollowed eyes. The man's life-partner, his spouse, lay huddled on a mat with a woven blanket pulled to her chin. Quetzali knelt and felt the sick woman's burning face. She told the man to fetch fresh water and food if he had any, and then to leave her alone so she could work.

The heavy, monolithic air tasted of sickness and made the scar above Quetzali's brow line ache a bit. She lifted the blanket to examine the dying woman. Her body was covered in leaking sores with blotches of skin that resembled creatures only found in nightmares. Nothing could be done for this dying woman, she was a breathing corpse, a human-sized piece of mucus ready to be dried out and then claimed by the desert sands just beyond the adobe walls. So many had already been taken, young, old, woman, man, child, the coughing-storm passed through the village with a blistering indifference, and it returned every year, hungrier than before. Quetzali had been spared, and sometimes she thought the plague had chosen her to be its eyes, to see and watch and remember all those who died. This sickly woman would be yet another, the herbs and medicine could do nothing except offer a few moments of comfort before another life slipped away.

Quetzali's hands worked some of the remedies onto the woman's boiling and blistered skin. Thick, coagulating human liquids covered the reed mat the sickly woman lay on. Quetzali started to clean the unconscious body.

The man, the sickly woman's life-partner, reentered the room with a clay pot filled with water and a few pieces of dried meat in his hands. "This was all I could find."

Quetzali nodded then said she needs to work here, alone.

"Can you help her?"

"With the blessings of the gods, maybe," she said. "Take this blanket, wash it."

The man gave one more pleading glance with his cavernous eyes before leaving again.

Using only the water of the clay pot, Quetzali washed the sickly woman's mouth, cheeks, and hair. A spectral echo of life returned to the dying face, but that was all. Her breath remained shallow, like ripples on a quiet lake. Quetzali patted more ointments, nectars, and pastes of dried leaves onto the swollen blisters. The woman let out a few unconscious moans, pure animalistic reflexes. The soul had already left the body, escaped though cracked lips and muffled breaths, and now it was wandering through the abyss, a lost murmur in the desert night.

Quetzali worked the dried meat between her teeth and spat it back into her hands before mixing it with a few roots she pulled from her leather pouch. Then she massaged the mixture into the sickly woman's mouth and made her swallow with a gulp of warm water.

"Rest," she whispered. "Let your soul find its way now."

After a short time the woman's breaths began to diminish like puddles of rain left behind after a storm.

Quetzali struck two pieces of chert together and ignited a small pile of sage. The scent and glimmer of light was for the lost souls, to help them find their way. She had done this too many times, ushered too many through the valleys of nothingness. She wondered if they'd be waiting for her when she died, a small army of souls smelling of burnt sage and eyes casting distant reflections of smoldering embers.

The soft glow died out, and the room reverted to obscurity as the earthy scent siphoned into the cracks of the walls. Silence arose. Quetzali knew that the woman had inhaled her last breath some time ago, that another bleak finality had arrived. A consuming fatigue descended upon Quetzali's bones, the same one that followed all the other nameless faces, but she clasped onto the small notion that the earth's immortal sin—suffering—had somehow been reduced, lessened. She uttered prayers over the lifeless body and reminded herself that her work was good, her hands were clean, that they would remain clean. Against the weight of the earth's cruel providence her own trespasses meant nothing, her hands were only there to gather whatever fragments remained, delicate and invisible.

A shuffle of approaching footsteps and muffled voices broke through the dense silence of the room. The man entered, followed by another man, taller, whose broad shoulders reminded Quetzali of tree trunks with eyes reminiscent of the leafless trees of a cold winter.

His low voice echoed between the small walls. "Get her away. She's done nothing here, nothing good flows from her."

The spousal husband dropped to his knees and cradled the limp body of the sickly woman. "She's dead. She's gone."

Quetzali's eyes scanned the room "Who is this man? Why have you brought him here?" she asked. "The work isn't done, I must finish."

The first man, the spouse, didn't reply to Quetzali's words, only cursing himself, the walls, this sickness, before muttering, "You've killed her. You came here to kill her, like the others."

"Yes," the tall man said, "She's killed them all. None make it alive."

Quetzali stood and faced the tall stranger and held his gaze. "You speak of things you do not know."

The tall man said nothing, only swayed slightly as though caught in a breeze.

The other man, the husband, shook the limp, sickly body, delicately, quietly.

"Do I know you, stranger? Have I wronged you? You come with venomous words," Quetzali said.

The husband, still clutching the lifeless hairs of his wife, spoke, "He found me. He came to me and warned me about you, about this. You leave a trail of death."

The tall man moved closer and added, "How many have survived? How many men, women, children, have been taken?"

"Sickness is sickness, it has no preferences," she said. "Its frigid hands reach everywhere."

"No, it doesn't take you," the tall man said, "It doesn't take them, the invaders of our lands."

Caresses of distortion lurched within Quetzali's mind. A warm sensation gathered, then slipped and stretched over her brow line. Her fingertips reached up to the scar beginning to tear open, the wound beginning to leak blood.

The tall man approached, looming over, "Blue eyes, from you mother or father? Or do you even remember where your blood comes from?"

Quetzali cursed and lunged at the tall man, but he easily grasped both of her wrists and held. The herbs and potions fell from Quetzali and scattered across the dirt ground.

The tall man spoke as though his tongue was coated in a thick poison and spat the heavy words, "Mother of the plague."

The vapors of the man's words lingered in her nostrils, but then the memory evaporated, her previous life vanished, and Quetzali was plunged back into her withered and blind body. The opaque dreamscape surrounded her once again, the steady ache of old-age lurked in her joints. She dreamed of a blackness that morphed into the night sky, empty of stars, then one, two at first, and slowly more gathered, points of light rupturing through the veil of darkness, then each star began to drip with light, until the brightness overflowed and fell out of the sky, down to earth, like tears forming into an ocean, and Quetzali felt herself sinking, gasping for air, drowning on the churning chunks of white foam. Then, through the waves, she felt the comforting and familiar sensation of hands, calloused yet young, holding her body, grasping her fingers, caressing her hair, and for a moment everything became calm once again.

****

If he peered at her face long enough, he sometimes saw the faint outline of the woman he had known in his childhood: blue eyes, skin carved by the sun, light-brown hair like the roots of the mesquite. His calloused hands caressed her gray hair, now brittle from a lifetime of soaking in sunlight. Her withered and blind body lay on one side, curled upon itself like a child. She opened her eyes—white with cataracts, two spheres of pure sunlight—then moaned, the sound reminiscent of a summer rainstorm over the barren plains. Her long fingers reached out and he held them, gently. Blood began to trickle from the scar cauterized upon her forehead.

"Grandmother, I'm here," he whispered in her ear. "Quetzali, it's your grandson, Surem. It's all right, rest now."

Her blind eyes lulled from one side across to the other, searching. The moans slowly subsided, but her fragile grip remained on Surem's fingers. Her lips moved, faintly, as though they tracing over an echo, and Surem leaned over, trying to make out his grandmother's words, but he only felt the subtle, distilled warmth of dying breaths against his ears.

There was little time left for her. Days ago the Spanish holy-men had come to give her the final Christian blessing, but the old woman still fought for life, almost as though she were mocking them and their feeble Christ-Child. No one else had come to see her though, none of her own people, none of her own tribe. It seemed as though the entire village had forgotten her, a stain scrubbed from their collective memory. Soon she'd join Surem's parents in the wasteland of the forgotten. He possessed only a few corroded images of his mother and father, spectral images devoid of faces. Their deaths had come suddenly when he was only a small boy, and the task of raising Surem had been left to this woman, his grandmother. Her austere, blue eyes had guided him through the lessons of becoming a man more so than any of those forced upon him by the Spaniard's schooling. She had knowledge of a time before the arrival of the crosses, whips, caballos, iglesia, and those thunder-sticks which can strike a man down in an instant, a time before the sweeping plague, a time before death. Even as she lay there inert, her blue eyes washed-out in white, he felt she still had more to teach him, that there were too many holes riddled throughout his mental landscape that only she could fill. If she had one more day with a clear mind and a voice that didn't crack like dead leaves. He dribbled a wet cloth upon his grandmother's peeling lips so the dead air wouldn't seize her throat.

Piled high against one corner of the adobe room were bones, hides, stones, each engraved with a tangle of symbols. Surem shuffled through them, examining, rearranging pieces, fitting one against the other. He recalled watching his grandmother as a young boy, her slender fingers scrambling over themselves to engrave the strange symbols, whether in the early morning light or the glow of the full moon, her lips silent, never releasing the secrets she so carefully etched out. Now, as she was dying, and Surem spent countless days beside her, he studied those engravings, desperate to find a remedy, a cure, something to regain lost time, lost health, a way to decipher those secrets that died in her shadows. It had to be somewhere in there, in those shambles of symbols, in a language he couldn't fathom.

He had asked her once, as a child, what they were for, what those enigmatic symbols meant. She only replied that they were for her memories, for the ones that she could never recover because they lay buried beneath the dry land, memories of a past, memories of a future. She forbade him to look upon the engravings and told him it was best to forget, to never see what she had gazed upon.

Surem pulled out a few more bones alongside another rawhide and looked them over. Desert sand clung to each crevice of the engravings, as though the earth were already reclaiming something. He carefully laid out the pieces, trying to reassemble the complex web of connections, his busy hands a pale, lost reflection of his grandmother's from years ago. The white cataracts of her eyes dripped with a veil of milky white. Surem's fingers worked to peel back the layers of gravel accumulated atop the years, to renew these echoes, to listen to the shadows of the desert—the ever-absent sea—whisper its secrets once again.

****

The tremors grow in violence until you are engulfed completely, like a great chasm has suddenly opened up to swallow you, a dead region between spaces. Then everything is dark and silent, except for the slight vibrations behind your ears. You cry out, just to drive away the silence, and you hear your own voice, tiny, frail, ready to crumble like the ash of a fire. The voice is that of a child, you, this lost child. It takes a moment for your mind to register that yes, this voice is your own, that you are nothing more than a slight youth. You try to move your arms, legs, torso, anything, but a cold pressure suffocates you, holds you down, renders your attempts less than useless. Your eyes gather nothing, only an infinitely long shadow that swallows the moments, a shadow that seems hungry to devour time itself. Your lungs cough up the vaguely familiar taste of earth and dust. You cry out once more, but this time to fill the void that has burrowed into your mind, into your thoughts. You have no memories, no recollections of a time before the darkness. A burning sensation creeps across your head and cheek. Tears soon follow, and you feel them fall from your face, claimed by the echoing nothingness that claims you. They were your tears, tears without memories and therefore tears like those of a newborn, plunged into the sublime terror of life, severed and separated from your own past.

****

Quetzali knew that she was dying, that she couldn't lay claim to her life much longer. Her soul was leaving her body through the pores of her ragged skin. She wandered through the barren dreamscape, a desert of forgotten time, as clouds gathered above. The wind blew stronger, rain fell to the ground. The storm coalesced into the images of another life, another memory of her youth...

She silently waited for nightfall and the cover of moonlight. Soon they'd arrive, all of them, nocturnal creatures of the night, with paws and snouts ready to unearth the sins buried beneath the dirt. She foresaw it, written there and inscribed in the symbols she had etched out in the bones and rawhides she kept, whispered to her by forgotten voices in the winds.

Her grandson, Surem, lay submerged in sleep, his adolescent body of skinny limbs reminded her of leafless tree branches. They were more than blood-relatives, more than simply grandmother and grandson, their existences intertwined within the prismatic, still waters of time. She uttered a prayer on his behalf, asking the gods for protection for both her and her grandson, before leaving her pueblo.

She crossed through the domain of earth and stars as she had done countless times before, but her tired hands weren't carrying the usual medicines and remedies. Instead they clutched a spear and a small dagger made of wood, sharpened stones, tied together with dried roots. She ran farther away, out to the dead lands, where the soil was too dry for life, the place where the village buried their dead. The earth cracked and sighed beneath her feet as though it had been waiting for her. Mounds of soil stretched out in every direction, forming an outline of the subterranean labyrinth of dead souls that lay beneath. How many had she put there? How many had she led along the journey just before death? How many sins could the desert hide, stored away and buried, but never forgotten?

She stopped and listened. The exhaling winds carried yelps, howls, and animalistic laughter of the beasts gathering in the distance. The sounds grew louder, closer, a sea of paws shuffled through the ancient gravel, descending upon Quetzali. Her hands gripped the spear and dagger as she silently mouthed one last prayer.

They were watching her, she sensed them, circling, a writhing mass of fur, saliva, and teeth. Their collective howl turned into an unwavering drone before dying down once again.

Then Quetzali heard their paws beginning to dig, scratching away the surface of those loose mounds of dirt which kept more than just the dead sealed within. Her eyes focused on a shadow in the darkness, one directly ahead, and she lowered the spear. Her arms jerked. The sharpened tip found its mark, plunging deep into fur and muscle, the fatal blow delivered followed by a yelp of pain and a string of soft whimpers. Her hands—almost possessed by another spirit—repeated the action again and again, the yelps of pain identical as three coyotes fell to Quetzali's feet. Warm blood trickled down the spear and gathered on Quetzali's fingertips.

An ocean of glimmering eyes and yellow fangs faced her, their hot breaths pressed upon the cool air of the night. The coyotes gnawed on the decayed flesh and bodies they dug up from the earth, their primal, ancient instincts subsumed by the night. The scent of saliva and death haunted her, a reminder of her failure and the bleak misery she had brought to these people, to this village. Soul after soul had been lost because of her, because of the blood which flowed through Quetzali's veins and kept her alive throughout the plague-ravaged years. These coyotes wanted to burrow into the past and remind her of the sins she carried, the burden of her existence, and the impossible atonement she craved every aching moment.

No, Quetzali wouldn't let these pack of beasts have their way. Her spear pierced through flesh once more, then again, and again. A set of jagged teeth punctured and tore through her own skin. She grunted and lashed out with the stone dagger, driving it somewhere into the attacking animal's neck, its final breath spilled into warm liquid upon her knuckles. From out of the darkness more fangs pierced and tore at the flesh of her arms, shoulders, legs. More fatal blows unleashed from her hands, but her attacks slowed, tired, the fatigue in her forearms turned her muscles to useless, dangling stones.

The blood of her wounds spilled out and mixed with that of the dying coyotes before the parched earth sucked down the warm bits of moisture, impervious of is origins, thirsty for more. The fangs became relentless, unforgiving, as though they were an extension of the night itself, thousands of razored teeth lined across the horizon, sown together by squeals and howls, a monolithic maw that precedes the absolute void. Quetzali staggered though the piles of whimpering coyotes, her bleeding body surrendering to the onslaught, collapsing onto the mound of loose gravel, waiting for the desert to claim her.

Face-down, her lips tasting the particles of earth, Quetzali whispered another prayer, urging the words to reach the labyrinth of bodies below. Finally, she could give her wretched blood to all those lost souls, to the desert, and her sins would finally be finished.

A small, indistinct glow appeared somewhere in the distance, approaching, splicing open the night of jaws and fur. The coyotes howled in pain as the light grew stronger, brighter, closer. It reached Quetzali, and she peered up and saw a silhouette with two eyes, human eyes, eyes that made her shiver because they were colder than a winter out in the open plains. She recognized them, they belonged to a man, tall, the man who knew exactly who she was.

The man waved a torch and his voice echoed, "Get up. These burial grounds are not your own."

Massive arms, the arms of a nocturnal giant, pulled Quetzali onto her feet. Her dry and bloodied hands still gripped the granite dagger, and in the smoky haze that enveloped her consciousness she lashed out, her hands still searching for flesh and fur.

The voice came through like an ancient command, "Stop fighting, stop struggling. It's useless."

Quetzali watched as the tall man used only the torch and his bare hands to beat down the advancing coyotes, grabbing coats of fur, throats, snouts, and heaving the animals to the ground, the reflection of the flame cast in the innumerable set of translucent, yellow eyes.

"We must defend them, these dead here, their memories. You have to help me," she cried, her desperate fingertips reaching out past the light of the torch and into the darkness searching for more animals to slay, more blood to let flow into the parched earth.

"These are not your dead. Not your ancestors. Not your people." His forearms lashed out at the wild, screeching animals. "It was you who brought misery and death. These coyotes only followed the scent, your blood, the wake you leave behind," the man shouted.

Quetzali's hands still prowled through the darkness, her blade slicing only the solid night-air. "I came to help. I foresaw it." Mocking howls of the coyotes descended against Quetzali's temples.

Palms—massive and unmoving—seized and held her, these hands and fingers which she intimately knew, their touch familiar. Her face met his in the epicenter of light and she peered at his eyes, two bottomless wells devoid of water.

"You don't know," she whispered to him, "You can't comprehend."

The torch-fire danced between the man's wrinkled lips. "They've whispered your secrets, they've revealed it to the land. The earth has already tasted your blood." Then he added, "You child of Christ. You Spaniard."

Those words burrowed themselves into Quetzali, into the scar that ran along her brow line, and the keloid skin seemed to unravel, and her blood, Quetzali's liquid sins, spilled onto the desert and the ground seemed only hungry for more.

Then the world seemed to be suspended, unmoving and placid. First the man disappeared, then the light, like disseminating ether. Then the coyotes followed too, their yellowed eyes extinguished. And then the mounds of earth crumbled, flattened, until nothing of the memory was left and Quetzali's body turned old and sour. She returned to the nocturnal, barren lands of her dying dreamscape. She found herself in the middle of a dry lake bed. It was a starless night, the horizon missing as though it had lost the ancient battle with existence. Cracks riddled the ground, and slowly they widened beneath her thin feet, growing larger. She tried to run and escape. but the gaps only opened further, just ahead of her fleeing steps, until a great chasm swallowed her into a frigid, timeless, eternally black moment.

****

The two crossed lines—sitting atop the Spaniard's iglesia— loomed above Surem's head. The wooden cross stood in defiance to that other god, the sun. The Spaniards had taught Surem that their Jesuscristo had risen from death after three days. But Surem thought that mattered little because the sun lived a daily death, plunging into the fiery evening-horizon, only to arise anew each morning.

The day had just begun as Surem descended the flight of stairs that led into the basement of the Spanish church. Other men followed, their faces like his, forlorn, deep-set creases, eyes which held invisible scars. Despite the perpetual shade the sun's slithering heat still reached the cramped corridors below.

With few words the men filed into a loose line, the corridors scarcely larger than the men's shoulders, and began their routine of passing bundles of corn, beans, and squash, storing them into the farthest reaches of the cellular chambers, those regions with small traces of relief from the omnipotent sun.

Disembodied calls of, "Wait!...Pass!...Hold!..." issued from the dimmest corners. Surem worked with his hands leading him, brushing against leathered-skin and callouses heavier than stone. The work was grueling, oxygen seemed to slowly siphon out of the corridors as breaths grew heavy, leaving Surem to inhale the sour perspiration of others. But the work here was better than being out in the fields, toiling beneath the unforgiving sun, where men constantly collapsed out in the open, choking on the purified light as the Spaniards gazed with indifference atop their four-legged beasts. And in these catacombs there were whispers, glimpses and echoes of a time before.

The subterranean network of passageways had been built long before the arrival of the Christ-God. The Spanish had erected their own temple atop the ruins of the old, the ancient gods had lost the battle against the Holy Trinity and were driven into hiding below ground, lurking in all that was left of their once towering home: subterranean passageways winding through stone foundations. At times Surem felt he was passing through the ancient gods themselves, but their voices went unheard, their whispers softer than smoke and almost forgotten. Surem possessed other memories though, more than just his own, those inscribed within the engravings of his grandmother, future memories that seemed to direct him as though her hands were present and guiding him.

As the other men worked, Surem slipped away and descended farther into the small network of corridors. He went searching for a hidden piece, one that his grandmother mentioned in passing, a stone that held the old and new worlds in place, a promise of new life amongst the ancient. He allowed himself to be guided by her aura, yet he thought of her back home, alone and withering away in a useless body. Her salvation could be found down here though, the fragments of a shattered existence could be reassembled. In his grandmother's engravings there were references to a clear stone, a sort of prismatic gap that contained all the memories of the world. This stone was the center-point, the epicenter, an exact middle that held everything together, right in the heart of the old temple. Through the convoluted mess of etchings and engravings that his grandmother had left behind, one message kept reappearing: a new life, a new salvation was to be found amongst the crumbled walls of the world, memories would regain a vivid existence, a return to a time and a place where sin and salvation meant nothing.

He stumbled through room after room with his hands groping across the darkness, at times stumbling over his own feet. The corridors seemed to open farther, bend, shift, unfold upon themselves, like a mute, slow dance of twisting walls. His fingers finally fell upon a set of stones stacked atop each other that formed a simple, unassuming arch. The stones were cold and his fingers blindly climbed upward until they reached the apex which was exactly even with Surem's eye-level, though he couldn't see it, only caress blindly. At the center of the apex lay a triangular stone, the one he had been searching for, the minuscule prism that contained the unforgotten memories, the stone that saw all and remembered all.

Surem pulled his hands back and his mind contemplated all the possibilities inherent within the triangular stone. He thought of his grandmother, of the words she'd never say, of the stories she'd never reveal, but they were here, contained only within this stone. He contemplated his own past and if it was also inscribed within those three points, running parallel to his grandmother's. Her life had always been shrouded in silence, unexamined, as was his own. Was he prepared to retrace those years that had passed so easily in silence? Maybe his grandmother never spoke of their past, joined and separated at times, because the keloid scars were better left closed than opened to bleed once again. For a moment he doubted his grandmother's engravings, the loose, convoluted shards that had no chronological order and only repeated the same notions in an infinite amount of series. No, her ghostly hands had guided him this far, led him to this place, this stone, there was no denying it now. Time wasn't ripe yet though. His fingers touched upon the center-stone once again. He needed them, the Spaniards, to be gathered above, witnesses to the new horizon that would accompany the crumbling of their wretched walls.

Surem left the black chamber and retraced his steps through the darkness, back towards the light of the sun, and joined the others just as their exhausting work came to an end. Every last bushel of harvested crop had been stored away, and the men began the trek out from their temporary tombs. Topside, the sun had already fallen below the horizon but its heat still clung to the air as though the sun was still claiming what it was rightfully owed. A few of the Spanish holy-men handed out meager portions of dry cornmeal, and Surem grabbed his small ration in silence.

Then a voice pierced the air and disturbed the comfort of the sun in freefall. Clouds of dust rose into the sky with more voices chasing, then surpassing, the upward flight. A Spaniard atop a four-legged-beast wrenched a worker from the crowd with a rope firmly set around the man's neck. Another Spaniard atop a beast proceeded to whip the bare back of the worker out in the open for all to see. The leather line traced out a curve through the evening air, and the separation between this world and a bleeding oblivion seemed to be concentrated on the very tip of the whip which split open naked flesh. The man cried out, and his voice hung in the air a moment as though it carried the collective pain of those gathered, a pain that only doubled as the seasons washed away. A screech of the whip, then flesh torn open, again, again, again. Then, just as easily, it was over, the man was released, free to internalize the pain as the land and the sun returned to their implacable indifference. The Spaniards rolled up their ropes and spoke in that slithering tongue of theirs before riding off atop their massive beasts.

Surem watched as the injured man lay motionless and bleeding, his prostrate arms embracing the ground, his blood offered to the arid soil, as though he were willing himself to become a part of the earth, as though his only desire at that moment was to become just another memory buried within the earth.

****

Your mind is a dry lakebed, a starless night, devoid of orientation. You have forgotten everything. You only know with a fleeting certainty that you are young, trapped in darkness, helpless. You try to push through the fog that has entangled your thoughts, your mind, your being. The buzzing in your head grows like winged insects in the early stages of flight. All you can remember is the terrible noise, the severed sounds, the great tremor that has fostered you, that created you, that has endowed you with existence, your very life has arisen from that single pulsation, a nameless daughter of a nameless calamity.

You try to move your body but your frail limbs are still held down by a great, dense, black pressure. You feel the tears fall from your face, down into a quiet expanse, and that makes you shed more tears because those intimate, liquid pieces of you are falling to the wayside, lost and subsumed by that void.

Suddenly, over your own whimpering voice, you hear traces of echoes, slight vibrations, stirrings of life beyond. You scream, a primordial scream, and your vocal chords are slowly shredded as you push them to the upper and highest registers possible. Voices, human voices float through the black and you listen, but there are others also, ancient voices endowed with the rasp of the endless sands, joining together in a quick succession then dying off once again. Through it all you hear that other voice, a human voice, calling out, and you answer back. Then a pinpoint of light pierces through the darkness, flickering, trembling, like the first star amongst the heavens struggling for life.

* * * *

Dreams escaped Quetzali for a long time, and she experienced nothing except her own approaching death in complete blindness. Her memories, too, had taken leave of her and fled from her dying presence. The drought that is old age had arrived with its slithering, choking finality. What more was left for a blind, immobile old woman? She was ready for her body to be reclaimed by the desert winds, for her impure soul to join the wasteland of the forgotten, to face all those souls with embers of burning sage within their eyes. Yes, they would be there, all of them, she could hear their calls already. The voices joined together in unison, a rolling chorus, and they sang of sin and atonements long forgotten, of one last memory...

It was a time of innocence, a time of beginnings, a time when the name Quetzali meant nothing to her. She had another name once, a Castilian name, taken from the Virgin Mother, the name given to her at birth had been Maria-Valentina. Small, adolescent hands gripped the stem of a vanity mirror, and she gazed upon the face of a child with round, reddened cheeks, a jawline and chin reaching out from a young neckline, brown hair with hints of infant-blond, and morning-blue eyes, the centerpieces of a child's face, a face she recognized as her own.

She was seated at a desk of mahogany-wood. Above, a small marble Christ presided over the young girl and the stifling heat of the small room. His stone body hung to the cross against the wall, His head downcast with a crystal and unwavering gaze. It was almost time to go see Him, the man who always watched and silently kept track of the world's sins. Those were the things that they taught her in Sunday school at the holy church, sin, atonement, impurity, salvation. They also taught her that she needed to look her best on the Day of the Lord, so Maria-Valentina softened her hair with a few more brush strokes then tied a blue ribbon atop her head. She peered up at the marbleized Christ, forever frozen in that moment of agony, His suffering a constant renewal, and she wondered if her appearance lessened His pain. At times she had to fight the urge to pull the suffering Christ down and whisper to Him that no one needed to die for her sins, that she couldn't stand the thought of anyone dying just for her to live. But her hands never reached out to Our Savior, Jesuscristo, and His presence remained on the wall as a simple reminder of all things.

A wispy voice called out to Maria-Valentina and then her mother appeared in the doorway. Lace hanging from a beige dress ruffled at her mother's feet. She spoke in a wet, Castilian tongue, "Are you ready, Mija? Vámonos. We'll be late."

Her father waited outside beneath the unforgiving sun, sweating, his great brow line offering the only vestiges of shade to his blue eyes, eyes that he had passed down to Maria-Valentina like water trickling downstream. The three walked together—father, mother, daughter—along the dirt path, the earthen ground wheezing and exhaling small plumes of dust beside their feet. Her mother spoke, her Castilian lips complaining about this miserable town, about the incessant heat of the land, how dry it was, how only savages could make a life here, how she missed home, España, its roads paved in cobblestones, the churches around every corner, and those evening rains of Madrid. Her father only nodded his head in agreement, saving his words for a later time.

Maria-Valentina had never been to her parents' homeland. She was a child of here, born in this parched earth which they called the New World, Nuevo España. Though whenever Maria-Valentina looked out across the plains dotted with beige boulders and the lethargic mountains in the horizon, this land, its colors, its people, appeared more ancient than anything else. It was España with its castles, grand churches, endless roads and endless lights that seemed like a new world to Maria-Valentina's young imagination, a foreign land built atop a dream.

As they made their weekly pilgrimage to the House of God they greeted others like themselves, castaway Spaniards, Spaniards who answered the call of The Church to domesticate a savage continent, but they also passed those that had already learned how to forge a life in this merciless land. A few of the indigenos bowed slightly while others kept their gaze focused on the cloudless distance, their forlorn faces and nocturnal eyes a stark contrast to the open sky. Maria-Valentina felt her father's arm guide her closer to him like she was the only precious treasure to be found in the desert.

The iglesia of Our Lord lay on the other side of town, and it slowly came into view along with its cross which loomed over the rest of the town's dismal buildings. No man and no building was allowed to rival His Glory. A steady, monotonous echo rang out from the church bells, prompting the family to hasten their pace. But Maria-Valentina noticed that the sound had no effect upon the passive faces of the indigenos. Maybe they were only accustomed to the whispers inherent within the empty plains and their ears couldn't register the alien, metallic chimes. Maria-Valentina had heard those whispers herself on quiet nights, when la luna left a ripple as it passed through the liquid night sky. Sometimes those voices called out to her by name, a different name, one she couldn't comprehend but undoubtedly knew was hers. She never spoke to anyone about the desert voices outside her windows, especially her parents. She told herself that some secrets were better kept buried.

Before passing beneath the arched doorway of the iglesia Maria-Valentina followed her parents' lead and crossed herself with holy-water and the bit of moisture felt nice against her warm head. The midday sun shined upon the stained-glass windows, and Maria swore that the brilliant colors came straight from Heaven. Her mother sat them close to the front because it was better to be closer to God's word. Maria looked back to the mass of indigenos standing outside the doorway, a sea of eyes and torn rags barely covering naked bodies. Their blood was still impure, they hadn't been redeemed by blessings so they were barred from His grace and His body.

The Priest took his place at the head of his parish and a hushed quiet settled between the walls. He only uttered a few opening words before an almost ephemeral tremor crossed over the ground, a yawn from the earth. A collective gasp escaped the throats of those gathered. The tremor subsided for a moment, the Father attempted to speak once again, but the tremor returned, stronger this time. The quivering earth grew more intense, turning violent, and the walls of the iglesia creaked in distress. Precious metals, candles, prayer-books fell to the tiled floor in echoing succession. The Father tried to yell over the crowd, urging them to remain calm because they were in God's temple, but his voice was drowned out. Maria reached out and clasped her mother just as the crucified Christ fell to the floor. Scattered cries for help bounced through the air as people scrambled to escape. The trembling grew into a consuming roar, as though the earth was splitting open within its innermost depth to reveal the gaping, mauling void that lay at the center of all things. Maria's father grabbed her and her mother, but a writhing mass of desperate bodies separated them from the doors that led outside to the safe, open air. Cracks spread through the walls and shards of stained-glass rained down upon the trapped victims, slicing the worshippers below with a thousand miniscule slashes upon their skin, crystal prisms of red, green, blue, yellow, lodging themselves within soft flesh.

Maria's blue eyes watched as the iglesia collapsed and crumbled around her, great pieces dropping from the ceiling and smashing into the poor, ensnared souls below. And amidst the catastrophe, a vague notion seized Maria that she had dreamt this calamity before, in another life, in another name, that a chorus of forgotten voices had already sung these scenes to her, those voices she heard out in the desert on silent nights. Her young mind tried to reach out and give shape to that mental landscape she envisioned before—somewhere she heard her mother' cries, she saw her father's outstretched hands—but the roaring seized her soul, a chasm of echoing nothingness seemed to open its jagged jawline and consume Maria, replacing her collection of memories with a dripping, black saliva.

****

A petrified sorrow sank into Surem's hands then slowly crept into the rest of his body, like roots groping through arid soil. Three days have passed—he counted each painted-sky fall into the evenings—yet he hadn't moved. He remained focused on that body which lay before him, inert, still, devoid of life: the body of his grandmother Quetzali. In her last moments, she exhaled simple, almost painless croons as though the eroding wind had already claimed her voice. Her opaque, crystalline eyes still lay open to the world, its sky, its horizons, its faces, a world she hadn't seen in years, a world she'd never see again.

He had left her body untouched after her last breath had fallen because there was no use, the vital spark of her soul had been lost to the wastelands of the remembered. It mattered little where her body lay, whether beneath a mound of earth or beneath the eviscerating sun, inevitably her flesh would be reclaimed and possessed once again by the desert sands. The raw, carrion stench reminded Surem that the process was already underway.

The trace amounts of moisture found in the morning air gave way to the stale, midday sun just outside the walls of the hut. Surem tried to recall time spent with his grandmother, but the only vision that came to him was that of her blue eyes and the way in which they seemed to comprehend the world differently than all the others of their village. What had those blue gems seen? What memories lay behind which injected her world with something unseen by others? And when her eyes had become blinded and sun-streaked what world did she inhabit, a place of perpetual light or immobile shadows? Or maybe she lived in the boundaries of both, a convergence of harsh oblivion and somber tragedy, a collapsed perspective of existence and oblivion in equal measure.

Pieces of her still remained though, in those scattered engravings of bones, rawhides, and colored stones she left behind. Surem stood, his back and knees aching, to examine the intricate web of symbols once again. They were his undertaking, a reconstruction of his grandmother's work as she lay dying. He had deciphered bits and pieces, enough to understand their full significance, symbols which conveyed notions of a return, a time without sin, a closing of circles, the collapsing walls of the new gods. Others needed to witness what Surem already knew, what only he possessed, the knowledge of the forgotten time was to return today—he had seen it, there, repeated in the engravings—three days after his grandmother's death.

Outside the foreign, metallic ring of church bells echoed through the distance and announced the day of worship for the Spaniards. They resonated, but the sounds seemed to transform over a great distance, change, take on another dimension, like a chorus of voices calling him. And those voices were almost familiar, like he heard them before, in another lifetime, voices that reminded him of childhood, but not his childhood, that of another's, someone he had known intimately well. They called to him, to be renewed, to be reclaimed, to be purified but never forgotten, whispers and voices. Surem uttered his own prayer before leaving his grandmother in the stale sunlight of the adobe room and walked outside, his first sunlight in days.

He made his way to the center of town and followed the dirt path towards the bells, the huddled masses, and the temple of the Spaniards. A sea of faces gathered outside, those like him, impure within the eyes of the Spanish and therefore barred from entering the Holy grounds on this day. But Surem didn't come to set foot upon the grounds of the Christ-Child. Instead he descended into the empty cellars below, to the foundations of the temple which lay beneath in total darkness. The chambers of the miniscule labyrinth were empty, and Surem groped through the dense silence that contained the hushed memories of the old gods. Their sterile presence seemed to guide Surem along, retracing those steps he had already taken, a preordained trajectory, returning him to the small arch and the stone that lay at the center of the old temple. His calloused palms hovered over and then stroked the cold walls until his fingertips finally touched upon the stone arch. His hands ascended to the top, to the apex where the triangular center-stone lay, the peak of the arch, and the granite felt tiny and fragile against Surem's palms. He sensed something after a few moments within the stifling black, a steady thrum and vibration emanating from the three points of the stone, like the hushed breaths that must precede life. Here were those memories, the forgotten records of the past, a transcription of everything that had been lost to the amnesiac hands of time, a promised renewal, salvation, his grandmother's salvation. It had only been three days yet he longed to see her again, to swim in the vision of her blue eyes. That's all he could remember of her with any intensity, blue eyes, calm, cool, the opposite of this boiling earth.

He dug his fingers into the cracks of the arch and clawed, pulling with his remaining strength. The stone remained placid, unaffected by the calloused hands around it. Surem kept pulling with taut shoulders and forearms, muscles which were accustomed to toiling in the ancient gravel, now yanking at this stone, wrenching the past from its subterranean roots, bringing it to light once again. And then it moved, in increments smaller than the invisible steps of the moon across the sky, and he could feel the stone almost loosen, and through the blind darkness he heard an inhuman echo growing, as though a deep chasm was opening and the dead gods were yawning at the bottom.

The stone finally broke free, yet after a few moments it did nothing, only a dead weight in Surem's hands. But the space it had come from, the apex and center of the arc, slowly became illuminated by something more pure than light. He peered into the empty, negative space and his pupils were bombarded with an onslaught of phantoms, apparitions, images. They appeared unsuccessive, simultaneously, in a single instant, but an instant that covered the solemn abyss across infinity, like a shattered crystal dragged through every point in time, then reassembled into a new prism with the images reflected through each fragmented piece, and he saw it all with an unwavering gaze: the roots of a cacti, a naked child paddling in the ocean, the stroke of a bird's wings, clouds, rains, a land of ever-changing dunes, boats filled with people darker than shadows, eyes staring through a slit in purple cloth, temples hidden beneath a sea of green vines, a bleeding coyote, hands inscribing a foreign yet beautiful language, flooded roads, dry voices, boulders tumbling into water, water droplets falling from frozen leaves, insects flying, insects crawling through the skeletal frame of a dead bird, men clashing, wood and metal and stone piercing flesh, the silent atrocity of a child frozen in ice with its eyes still wide-open, the breadth of a starving hunter, arrows that miss their mark, cities of pure light, fire, smoke, burnt flesh, lesions of the skin, a mother's hands, women with painted faces, oceanic waves, a tapestry of setting suns, the first light to pierce through the creosote branches, the vacant spaces between the sands of the desert...

Amidst all he saw, all those pristine images, he noticed a solitary figure pulling a child from a massive pile of rubble. The lonesome figure had eyes reminiscent of a cold, leafless winter. The figure's long jawline and overbearing brows were familiar to Surem, a face he had only glimpsed in the pale reflection of clear waters, a face he knew, a face he recognized as his own. The other eyes, the child's, were those of his grandmother's, he knew instantly. A bleeding scar was freshly carved into the child's cheek. Surem watched the figure—himself—take the child's hand, and they left the rubble and continued past a mass of injured people in a dusty village, voyaging into the open expanse.

The two—Surem's reflection and the child—crossed through the desert sands with thirsty mountains looming in an unreachable horizon. During the cold and indifferent nights the two huddled close together, their bodies kept warm by one another and nothing else. They finally made it out of the desert after many days, their path leading them to another tribe, people of the endless sands, like themselves, others who knew the hardships of a ceaseless sun. The two wanderers were welcomed into the village, and the child grew older between dried-mud walls. And Surem saw the figure's face—his own, a phantom of himself—keep a steady gaze upon the blue-eyed child, caring for her, teaching her a new language, urging her to forget her slithering Castilian. As the child matured, her skin darkened to the landscape, but her eyes always remained like droplets of the sky. She learned to heal, to make medicines, to mix remedies perfectly, to amplify the healing nectars found across the land. The solitary figure—his pale reflection, his ghost, his echo—loved the child. Even when the child grew sick, a small cough, a fever, and the child survived the sickness, but the illness took others, ravishing the village, a cough, a lesion of skin at first, a disease which crept steadily through the town, lurching, always hungry for more. The plague had arrived, and death left nothing untouched with her spectral fingers which slid down throats and gradually choked the life from all those infected. The child had brought the sickness to the people, she was the harbinger of the plague, her sins lay within her foreign blood, blood that boiled across the sun-soaked lands, blood that made her the mother of the plague.

Years later, during one fragile night, the reflected figure—Surem's own—abandoned the child and followed the light of the moon to live a solitary existence on the outskirts, across the borderlands. Alone, the figure grew tall, his voice deepened. He learned to only trust the call of the coyotes, the scents they picked up, their primal instincts that remained intimately attuned with the desert. His eyes absorbed every passing frigid winter, and his ears were haunted by the chorus stuck in the wind, the voices which sang to him of reminisces and remembrances, of memories and sins that could never settle into the desert sands.

Then the instant of kaleidoscopic images ceased, and Surem returned fully to the darkness of the subterranean chamber. He knew what he had seen, the memories that hadn't solidified into the past, memories that were yet to unfold. He inhaled the sublime horror of knowledge, of a certainty that contained every possibility and excluded nothing, the preordained and reoccurring finality that perpetuated itself through him. It was a glimpse of his origin, the architecture that condemned him from its inception, a prison of reoccurring time.

A guttural roar issued forth form the blackness, the earth shook as though it had been cleaved open to its very core, to the center where the void lay within everything. His mind stumbled over itself and wondered if this was the cry of the old gods, of those buried and forgotten, the roar of those who found a bit of life for a moment and were now dying a second death. Warm breaths of a monolithic, unseen specter descended upon his skin, chasing him as he ran from the labyrinth, his body slamming into hardened walls, scrambling, until he finally caught sight of light, ascending, up towards the sunlight, finally reaching the open air and loose gravel ground.

The roar and visceral tremors continued amongst masses of bodies trying to escape disintegrating walls. The foundations had collapsed and now the Spanish temple imploded upon itself. The two-crossed lines atop the Spanish iglesia fell and finally rested upon the barren earth alongside the rest of the collapsed structure. The tremors slowly throbbed and disintegrated into the silent horizon, and all that remained was a pile of rubble, fragments, debris which Surem recognized, ruins he had already seen, a wreckage which he witnessed once again, a catastrophe he had remembered from a time before.

****

Strong and calloused hands pull you into the full glare of the sun. Your light-blue eyes shutter in pain, but you are free, your frail body is no longer trapped within the consuming black. You focus on the man holding you, and you notice a sincerity in his brown eyes, but they also seem cold, as though they were made in the purest of winters. Your slender fingers move towards the pain upon your face and for the first time you feel the bleeding gash upon your head. You begin to cry, but the man holding you in his powerful forearms hushes you in a language you cannot comprehend, words that mean everything and nothing in equal measure. His voice is a voice you might have heard once before, but you are not sure because you cannot remember anything, only the blind, roaring tremors that held you, incubated you, then birthed you to the world. The man takes you away from the rubble which you recognize, if only vaguely. You struggle to pull from the negative spaces of your mental landscape—are you reborn, or is it that you've died again and this is yet another life, a different one, one with another name, another voice—and then you hear it, yes, something is there, you hear it within the crevices of your soul, the faint echo of voices that you might have dreamt once before in another life.

53.
Te Waka Wairua
Mercedes Webb Pullman

Look! A ghostly canoe approaches,
nomad roaming the ocean's grey waves,
oars in constant motion, tattooing the swells
with broken circlets of foam.
All who see them despair; ancestor ghosts
awake again because the oracle has spoken.
They approach close enough for you to hear
the clack and knock of oarlocks,
the crew of ancient sailors moaning.

Beware their words! Let them complain
in vain, tear their hair - they're ghosts,
jealous of their kin who breathe and sing.
Turn to the wall, do chores, scrape or sew,
mend nets, never forget they'll seize
you in a moment. If you listen
you lose, you'll be stolen, turned into rock,
locked offshore in a tidal bore
to act as a permanent beacon.

54.
Tea Time with Ghosts
Mark Hudson

In Wales, a new craze is shaking the nation,
giving people some investigation.
people are looking for something the most,
everyone in England is looking for ghosts!
Steve Parsons is your TV host,
who gets on television, coast to coast.
Cameras, gadgets, and blinking lights,
ghost detectors that will give them a fright.
Poltergeists, telepathy, and Ouija boards,
like fox hunts, the British flock in hoards.
Steve sports a Ghostbusters tattoo,
his ego is big, and he'll always scream BOO!
He claims that amateurs trample locations,
and ruin his ghastly reputation.
People sought sprits, ghosts and elves,
and believed the world ends in 2012.
Reflecting back in 2015,
there were no "ghosts in the machine."
I don't believe in ghost detectors,
but I do believe in angelic protectors.
The supernatural world can't always be seen,
but sometimes it appears on Halloween!
So I suppose in Britain, the spirits do rise,

just like some eyebrows, above seeing eyes!
What you see may be through your vision,
but don't believe everything on television!
Ghosts may exist, but I'm not afraid,
the ghost-busters worldwide always get paid!
Like child psychologists, making us tougher,
TV must work or the ratings will suffer!
Here we have "Invasion of the Body Snatchers,"
In England, they listen to Margaret Thatcher!
But the best British voice to hear is Charles Dickens,
read all his books, as plots start to thicken!
So England captured continents separated by water,
they need lots of writers to write stuff like Harry Potter!
Once again they've conquered us from coast to coast,
So are we still hiding cause we fear ghosts the most?

55.
The 3D Dead
Nick Johnson

Deep within the concrete catacombs of Gabor Labs, a renowned research institute just outside of Boston Professor Gilbourne was working feverishly on his new obsession. It was a project that eclipsed anything else in his life in its importance. The thirty-nine-year-old professor was conducting a series of experiments meant to bring back the dead by illuminating the alleged metaphysical forms said to inhabit a plane of existence inconceivable to the living.

For the last seven months, he spent every waking hour he could locked away in the lab. Breathing the sterile air and constantly immersed in the electrical buzzing emitted by the menagerie of machines he was working with.

He had recently lost his mother to cancer. His friends and fiancée thought this was just him avoiding grief by burying himself in work.

This was partially true. Gilbourne was a jovial and often playful man the glare from his glassy blue eyes when his mind lost itself in the cold void of its cold logic.

Medical doctors are advised not to get too attached to their patients so they can maintain a professional distance and keep themselves from being emotionally overwhelmed by their work. Physics was a field, which for some could also be psychologically breaking.

Being a physicist Gilbourne had become intimately acquainted with reality. He had some ability to grasp the finality of the infinite. He knew the mechanisms of the universe ran like machinery and its grinding gears were cold and indifferent to us. His recent confrontation with death forced him to think of the inevitable in the same logical terms of how he understood all things, and most frighteningly how he understood infinity. This was something Gilborune simply could not accept. He had to find a reason to believe there was something that linked life and death that there was somehow a way he could blur the line between the planes of existence and make one perceptible to the other. He had to do what few physicists are prepared to do. Take a leap of faith and light is where faith led him.

Light exerts a strange presence. It had mass but could still be everywhere and nowhere. Everything interacts with light and if a permanent human presence, a spirit for lack of a better term existed it too would have a form that interacted with light on some level. If he were to give form to phantoms, then the careful control and manipulation of light would be his only means of doing so. Holography is where he placed his hopes.

Gilbourne's lab assistant, Scott was a grad student just over a decade younger than the doctor himself. He was hardly passionate about the hypothesis. He thought of the doctor and his work as an amusing curiosity, but he was a reliable and competent lab assistant while also being the lowest bidder for the job. An important detail, given Gilbourne was receiving no university or private funding of any kind and had to pay Scott out of pocket.

Besides the far-fetched premise, there were more than a few glaring holes in Gilbourne's methodology. The pinpoint beams of light projected by holographic generators had to be set to specific points. Only if there was the presence of the deceased exactly where the lights were being directed would they be painted by the beams, or so the theory went.

There was no way for Gilborne to guarantee an aberration would place itself in the right position at the right time, especially given the possibility they may not even exist. The best Gilbourne could do was leave notes everywhere he went and just hope the invisible dead who may or may not be there happened to read them.   He had even taken to announcing to the empty hallway when he was about to perform his experiments on the off chance the silent corridor contained a wondering specter.

The night was going like most. Scott sat at the computer that controlled all the settings they could use to manipulate the lights. His attention was divided between a textbook, his constantly vibrating phone, and the control interface on the computer screen.

Gilbourne sat just opposite of him recording results. It was a chart with four long columns, the one at the far right filled with the word "negative." They were about two hours into their work today and naturally at this point Gilbourne's optimism was running low, so he decided to pass the time was small talk.

"Any plans tonight?" Gilbourne muttered in a halfhearted attempt at small talk.

"Sorry, what?" Scott said looking up from his phone.

"Are you doing anything after this?" Gilbroune asked again.

"Oh, meeting up with my girlfriend we're going to go to her apartment for a little dinner and a movie." replied Scott.

"I didn't know you had a girlfriend," Gilborune said.

"Oh, yeah been going out a while now I guess," Scott said dismissively.

"How long?" asked Gilbourne.

"Uh, about four months now I guess," Scott answered.

"Huh," Gilbounre grunted. There was a lull in the conversation. Scott returned his attention to his textbook and phone. Gilbourne was in no mood for silent contemplation though and endeavored to keep the chatter, no matter how inane going.

"What does she do?" he asked.

"Oh, uh she's getting her masters in communications."

Gilbroune grinned "Oh, that's a fascinating field." he sarcastically sneered.

"Uh, yeah," muttered Scott while pretending not to notice the doctor's snide remark.

"Has she learned to write an email yet?" asked an indignant Gilbourne.

"Hey, I thought of a name for this project," Scott blurted out. Hoping to quickly changing the subject.

"Yeah?" Gilbourne glared at him with crossed arms.

"Yeah, Dead Lights," Scott said. A large grin crossed his round red face.

"I don't get it," Gilbourne said flatly.

Scott's grin instantly vanished. "You know from the movie "IT" with the evil clown. He had his deadlights," he explained feelingly slightly embarrassed now that he was explaining the reference.

"Is that the one based on the Stephen King book? The one with Tim Curry and he's a killer clown that lives in the sewers?" Gilbourne asked.

"Yes, that's the one." Scott snapped, the enthusiasm returning to his voice.

"Never finished that one," muttered Gilbourne turning away and returning to his data.

A few moments passed and soon it was time for the computer to change the optical settings which it did automatically. In that immeasurably small fraction of a second everything humanity understood about consciousness and indeed, its very presence in the universe, changed. The lights refracted and diffused through the invisible particles in the air, the little crumbs of creation that were nothing, yet made everything and created the glowing almost transparent right side profile of an old man.

"Holy shit!" exclaimed Scott, his phone, shattering against the tile floor.

"Oh, my God it fuckin worked!" Gilbourne shouted. "Scott quick, adjust the lights so we can see more of him!"

"Yes, doctor!" Scott said as he snapped into action.

"Can he see us?" Scott asked.

"I don't know," Gilbourne said. "Excuse me, sir!" he blurted out.

The ghost turned and faced the astonished scientists. His full face was now constructed by the light. He was a very elderly man, with dark wrinkled skin and deep-set eyes swallowed by crows feet. He had a few wild strands of hair on his pockmarked scalp. He stood before the astonished scientists as a faintly glowing specter. The elderly aberration pointed to himself and his lips moved, but there was no sound.

"He knows we can see him!" announced Gilbourne. The old man's mouth was chattering, but no sound came from his lips.

"I can't hear him," said Scott. "We can't hear you!" he shouted at the old ghost. "I can't hear him," he repeated back to Gilbourne.

"Quick we need to hunt down the most sensitive microphones we can find!" barked Gilbourne.

Fortunately, the institution was one that received ample defense department funding and perhaps it was fate that a colleague had been working on a project that utilized audio capturing devices that could record conversations from satellites in space. It was only a matter of hours before they were able to give the mysterious visitor from beyond a voice, albeit a faint one.

The researchers had finally confirmed existence beyond death and naturally they had an abundance of questions.

In life, his name was James Kohler. He had fought in the second world war and had raised a family in a small town in upstate New York. The ghost had an infinite amount of time and just as much patience, and he allowed the two to interview him through the night. He couldn't remember how long ago he died, by his estimate it had been about twelve years, although it had been a long time since he visited his own grave.

"Can you see other ghosts?" asked Gilbourne.

"No, can't say I ever have. At least I don't think." The old man said in his labored and raspy voice.

"Wait, do you like being referred to as a ghost or should we think of something else?" asked Scott

"Eh, ghost is fine I guess," he replied dismissively.

Gilborune rolled his eyes at the question. "I assume you saw my notes. May I ask why you were hanging around this lab?" he asked.

"Well," said Kohler "being dead, I have nothing to do. Literally nothing. I don't get hungry. I don't need to sleep. I can't talk to anyone, so I've had time just to wander around. After a while, I was really looking for a way to pass the time, and then I remembered the atomic bomb."

"The atomic bomb?" repeated Gilbourne

"Yeah, it won the war, and I was always curious about how it worked, but raising a family didn't leave me a whole lot of time to learn about that kind of thing. So I decided I would just hang around the scientific movers and shakers to see where this world was going next. Then I found out about this place and decided it would probably be better than walking all the way to New Mexico."

"You know we do defense research here?" asked Scott.

"Yeah, it's not really a well-kept secret and being a ghost, it was pretty easy for me to get through security," James replied.

"Do you ever visit your family?" asked Gilbourne

"I went back to my house for a while, but eventually, my wife died. I was hoping she might turn up, but she never did, and the rest of my family is sort of all over the place. I figured it didn't make a ton of sense standing around my children if they couldn't see me and I couldn't talk to them," James explained.

The researchers fell silent as they contemplated the lonely existence of the dead. It was a fate that awaited them all.

"I tried everything to get them to notice me, but I can't touch anything either," continued James.

"What do you mean?" Asked Gilbrourne.

"Here, poke me with your pen," said James pointing to a pen in Scott's shirt pocket.

Scott took out the pen and poked the spirit. The tip of the pen passed right through James's transparent form.

"Oh, Wow," gasped Scott.

"Wait, if matter passes through you how come you don't fall through the floor?" Gilbroune asked.

"Don't really know. That would be a question for God. If I could just find him," retorted James.

****

The next day Dr. Gilbourne and Scott revealed their findings to an astonished world and Gilbourne and his young assistant enjoyed a meteoric rise. Their discovery got them instant notoriety, not just in the scientific community but massive worldwide fame.

They became instantly wealthy and scarcely a day went by when they weren't requested for an interview by the world's most influential media outlets.

Scott was quick to embrace his new found fame and fortune and all the decadence that came with it. Dr. Gilbourne, the man who had concocted the idea of illuminating the dead became ever more reclusive. It was nearly six months later that the two came together again. According to the experts, or at least people on television who have seen fit to include the word expert in their title, Gilbourne and Scott would be shoo-ins for a Nobel prize. The committee had reached out to the pair but hadn't received a response from the doctor. It was up to Scott to bring the hermit out and after some time he managed to do just that.

The two met in a restaurant in a downtown high rise that loomed above historic downtown Boston. It was an enclave for the elite of the East Coast. The tables were draped in ebony cloth and candlelight accompanied by a small orchestra that created a classical and comfortable ambiance. Even though it was the most exclusive spot in the city, the Nobel Prize nominees had no trouble getting a table.

The establishment was filled with politicians, business leaders, and those who just happened to have the money and influence to be there. They dined while discussing business deals, politics, and market trends. They were accompanied by friends, partners, wives, or mistresses. Some even dined and chatted with the glowing dead who had now been resurrected by a very expensive consumer holographic prototype. The rich had become immortal.

Scott's wardrobe had changed quite a bit. He traded the modest garb of the grad school student for a tailored designer suit. He had just finished ordering his first cocktail of the night when he saw Gilbourne by the Maitre D podium.

The haggard figure stood in stark contrast to his young colleague. He was a slouching disheveled mess. His face was unshaven, and he wore tattered clothes that were wrinkled and dirty. His now long stringy hair was graying and unwashed. His eyes were set in the middle of large dark circles and his skin, wrinkled from exhaustion and stress made him appear twenty years older than he had seemed just six months ago.

He shuffled over to Scott's table mumbling to himself the whole way. The other patrons who donned black ties and shimmering dresses murmured to each other. The doctor looked more like a homeless man than a world famous scientist.

"Doctor Gilbourne, how are you?" Scott said standing up to greet him.

"Fine fine," muttered Gilbourne before dropping into his chair. Scott still wearing his smile in the hopes of salvaging something from this encounter sat down too.

"So what's been going on with you? No one's heard from you in a while," He said in as congenial a tone as possible.

"Eh," shrugged Gilbourne.

"Did you get the invitation from the Nobel Committee?" Scott asked.

"Oh yeah, them. Yeah, I guess I'll go," sighed Gilbourne.

"Fantastic! We're going to be Nobel laureates!" exclaimed Scott "Another round over here, please." he called to the waiter. The doctor slumped in his seat looking far from elated. An awkward silence settled in and Scott took a sip from his glass. "Is something wrong doctor?" he finally worked up the nerve to ask.

"This whole thing is just weird," Gilbourne muttered.

"What do you mean?" asked Scott.

"Well, just look," Gilbourne said motioning to the illuminated specter of an elderly socialite sitting at a table, a full martini in front of her she could not even raise to her lips let alone drink.

"I don't understand. Thanks to our....your discovery, we no longer have to be afraid of death." said Scott. "We don't have to lose people anymore."

"Is that really a good thing?" snapped the doctor suddenly sitting up in his chair. "They're all around us you know. You're never alone. There's never any privacy. We can't miss anyone because they never leave us. What does that say about the value of life." Scott sat silent.

"You know why I started this whole thing right?" asked Gilbourne.

Scott shook his head. "I couldn't stand the idea of never seeing my mother again. She had just died of cancer, and the idea that she simply didn't exist anymore was too much for me. It wasn't enough to believe I had to see it and now that I did I'm not sure it's such a good thing. I don't know why it is so, but the dead are supposed to leave us for a reason, and now even after all this, I still can't find her. Which I can only take to mean she doesn't want to be found."

Scott took another sip of his drink. He had no words to offer the distressed doctor. It was their last meeting. Afterward, the dejected scientist returned to his home where he decided to join the ranks of the unseen dead. He disappeared forever into the lonely oblivion never choosing to reemerge in the world of the living as a holograph.

56.
The Die-Hard Fan
Jon Moray

"Here he comes. It appears Mr. Donnelly hasn't figured it out yet," said Boing, the flashy rainbow colored clad, classic red-nosed clown.

Roy agreed, with a flamboyant nod of his head. Roy, a mime dressed in black and white horizontal stripes and a white painted face, was Boing's enthusiastic apprentice. Roy was seated behind Boing in the lower level of a football stadium, home to the Philadelphia Eagles. The clown and mime were actually ghosts about to welcome a newcomer to the afterlife.

"He was only thirty-seven years old. No wife, no kids. Sanitation worker by trade. Abrasive demeanor. Obviously too dumb or absent minded to realize he's dead. Yep, that's him alright," said Boing, shaking his blue, bushy quaffed head in pity, while Roy mimicked uncontrollable sobbing.

Their subject, Darryl Donnelly, was angrily bobbing through the lower tier, making his way to the season ticket seats he shared with his brother on the thirty-yard line, twenty-five rows from the field. He finally labored through the masses and planted himself on the midnight-green, plastic planked seat, nipped by the December frost, under a blustery charcoal mist that covered the stadium.

"Well hello, Mr. Donnelly. Nice of you to join us today," said Boing, bouncing in his seat and clapping his hands.

Darryl looked him up and down and sneered, "What are you some kind of clown?" He turned away and focused on the field where the Dallas Cowboys were going through pre-game warm-ups.

"As a matter of fact I am. Or, I used to be…when I was alive."

"What the hell are you doing in my brother's seat? Where is he anyway?"

"Your brother is not here, Darryl. You're not here either. Well, not officially."

"Look, Bozo, the joke is over. Get your circus hanging butt out of here."

"My name is not Bozo. It's Boing," the clown stated, as Roy plucked a spring to accentuate the sound of his friend's name. "I am a ghost and so are you. You died in this stadium.   You were so drunk you ended up in the upper level and took a header over the railing when you flagged down your brother who was seated here.   I thought you stuck the landing,. However, the Russian judge only gave you a 7.8." Roy showed his displeasure over the score by throwing his hand up in a 'you've got to be kidding me' gesture.

Darryl clenched his fists and gritted his teeth. "Don't mess with me, clown. I am not in the freakin' mood."

"Look around.   See all the people in the stadium that seem translucent? Now look at me. I appear to you clearly, not as if I just came through a fog.   It's because when you are dead, the living appear as faint as ghosts. Most of the people in this stadium besides you, my sidekick Roy and I, are alive and kicking. We're as alive as the Eagles chances of winning a Super Bowl," joked Boing, as Roy exerted a comical knee-slap.

"What is he, your silent laugh track?" asked Darryl, thumbing back at Roy, still recovering from the joke.

"He is my apprentice. We are known as greeters to the afterlife. We are here to give you orientation and answer questions.   As for your brother, he can't bring himself to come back here, probably not until next season." Roy's attempt at a hug was met with Darryl's fist coming dangerously close to his face. Roy relented with a peace sign and a relieved wipe off his forehead.

"Just my luck, a clown, and a mime to welcome me to the hereafter. I don't believe this. You both are idiots. I'm getting security."

"Wait, try to touch the guy in front of you. Go ahead. Take a swing at him. He probably thought you were a wino anyway," dared Boing, as Roy, with raised eyebrows, looked over his shoulder.

Darryl skeptically turned away, bore down on the man's green ball cap and took a swipe that went right through his head as if he was shadow boxing.

"You missed, Sugar Ray," joked Boing, followed by another knee slapping, foot stomping response from Roy.

"You mean I'm dead? It can't be."

"It can and it is. You died last game against the Redskins. The game was delayed a half-hour so you could be carted out.   You were a true die-hard fan." Roy punctuated the comment with another visual show of amusement that now included drum roll tapping on Boing's seat.

"Could you do something about your stupid mute friend," asked Darryl, disgusted.

"Just be glad he isn't audible.   Word has it he died smiling." Roy confirmed the rumor with a nodding grin that almost split his face in half.

"I wouldn't doubt it.   He is freakin' annoying. Look, the game is about to start.   I would appreciate it if you two yahoos would leave me alone."

"Okay, okay.   There's the kickoff. We'll leave you alone...for now."

The Dallas returner received the ball at the five-yard line and took it the distance, bowling over the kicker for a quick score. The point after attempt was good and Dallas led 7-0.   The Eagles' faithful voiced their disapproval with collective booing and an array of colorful expletives that made Roy wince and cover his ears.   The ensuing kickoff placed the ball on the thirty-yard line and in front of them where the Eagles offense was gathering.

"What the hell? What are those fans doing on the field?" asked Darryl, perplexed and pointing at them.

"They are clearly ghosts.   You don't see anyone detaining them, do you?"

Four ghosts whose loyalties lay with the home team were jumping around as if they were in on the next play.   The Eagles offense broke the huddle and met the line of scrimmage.   The ghosts lined up between the left tackle and the wide receiver. The quarterback barked out a few audibles, received the snap and handed the ball off to the halfback going left.   The ghost fans formed a wall and collectively dove at the legs of two Dallas defenders and as a result, opened a gap for the runner and a big gain that netted twenty-five yards.

"Did you see that? Those ghosts did it," exclaimed Darryl.   "It looked like those two Cowboys lost their footing, but those phantom fans somehow made that play work."

"You think ghosts only hang around old Victorian houses?"

Darryl jumped up out of his seat and hastily headed down to the field.

"Wait, where are you going?" called Boing, rising to his elongated shoed feet.

"I'm going to help my team win," Darryl shouted, without looking back.

"That's the spirit!" cheered Boing, as Roy jumped to his feet and flailed his arms in celebration.

"Looks like our work is done here, Roy. Let's go and find our next subject."

57.
The Forest Beast
Moshe Sonnheim

The day dawned dark and dreary. The villagers woke to carnage. The necks of their watchdogs were broken. Their sheep were disemboweled. Their chickens were gone. The forest loomed forebodingly at the village edge. They dared not enter it at night, for fear of the Forest Beast. Now they feared even the day.

The Beast appeared shortly after the War. More precisely, its acts appeared. No one had ever seen it. They had heard its cries. They had seen its footsteps. They had seen the destruction it had wrought. Rumors were rife. It was an enormous wild dog. It was a werewolf. It was a survivor of one of the Camps. It was a ghost from one of the graves said to be buried deep in the forest.

These simple folk needed a savior. They found him in the neighboring town. He had come from nowhere after the War, but became a respected member of the community. As little was known about him as was known about the Forest Beast. But rumor had it that he had been an officer in an elite unit which tracked and killed escapees. He had enjoyed his work, and was ready once more to spring to the hunt. The fee was agreed upon, and he set to work.

First, he posted guards at night. Their necks, too, were broken. Then, he laid traps with metal jaws capable of breaking legs. The traps were torn asunder. One, however, had traces of blood; huge foot-or-paw steps led in the direction of the forest.

Delighted, he organized a search party. With great trepidation, the villagers entered the forest. The steps and blood moved deeper into the forest. As darkness descended, in the light of torches, they saw a huge figure limping rapidly, wailing in a tongue they remembered vaguely from the War. They turned and fled.

The "officer" pressed on alone. The figure turned. Too late, he recognized him.

The next morning, they found his body. His heart had been torn out.

The Forest Beast was never heard or seen again.

Except—once a year!

58.
The General's Leg
Moshe Sonnheim

Major General "Dapper" Don John Nichols lost his left leg to a Confederate cannonball at the Battle of Bloody Ridge, on the Fourth of July, 1863. He was one of 60,000 soldiers who suffered limb amputations during the Civil War.

Transferred to the Invalid Corps, General Nichols heeded once more the call to duty by the Army Surgeon General. The Army Medical Museum in Washington, D.C. was collecting specimens of "morbid anatomy." The General, without hesitation, packed the bone of his amputated leg (which he had kept as a memento of his injury), and dispatched it, along with the cannonball, to the Museum "With compliments of Major General D.J. Nichols."

Above and beyond the call of duty, the General visited his limb and cannonball every year on the 4th of July.

After a long and distinguished career in politics, "Dapper" Don died at the age of ninety-five. His leg remained in its display case alongside other shattered limbs, for others to view.

However, few visitors came to the musty museum to look at the carnage of the War. Until that is, two World Wars replenished the supply of "morbid anatomy."

Then, one day, a strange thing happened. A wounded WWII veteran, who also happened to be a Civil War buff, and knew "Dapper" Don's story, noted that the bone and ball case was empty!

The museum director and the police opened an immediate investigation. No other items were missing, and there was no evidence that the display case had been opened. There simply was no trace of General Nichol's memento! After a short period of public interest, the investigation was closed, leaving the mysterious disappearance of bone and ball "in limbo."

More than a half century passed. A young Orthopedic Surgeon, who had served in Iraq and Afghanistan, began a pilot study for his doctorate in Limb Surgery and Rehabilitation. He planned to build a database on the interaction of surgical techniques (flap/circular), timing and conditions of evacuation, and mortality rates. He would combine surgeons' reports of their operations (from the Civil War to the Iraq/Afghan Wars) with his own physical examinations of the amputees and their severed limbs (when available). This latter point raised logistic and ethical questions. He would need permission from surgeons, amputees, and their families. In the case of buried soldiers, he would need permission to exhume their bodies. Specifically with regard to the Civil War dead, for instance, he consulted family genealogies and succeeded in receiving permission to exhume from living descendants.

After all the above problems had been solved, Dr. Jonathan Brown began the grisly task of exhumation. The body of Major General "Dapper" Don Nichols was chosen at random.

To Dr. Brown's amazement, the missing leg was found in perfect condition on the General's skeleton.

Only the cannonball was gone.

A year later, at the Annual Reenactment of the Battle of Bloody Ridge, eyewitnesses swore they saw "Dapper" Don himself galloping forward with his men.

Suddenly, a cannonball ripped through the air, shattering the General's leg!

The next day, ball and leg were back at the museum.

59.
The Gigantic Pumpkin
Mark Hudson

Craig and Sammy were little eight-year-old boys who were wandering around the week before Halloween, being mischievous. They went into the local grocery store to get some candy before the week they went trick or treating. As they walked out of the grocery store, they noticed a bunch of pumpkins being sold outside. They saw one that was gigantic, orange with green spots, that looked huge and deformed.

"Hey, let's steal this pumpkin!" Craig said to Sammy.

"I agree!" Sammy said, between the two of them, they slunk off with the extremely heavy pumpkin.

As they began to get sweaty carrying the heavy pumpkin, they thought they heard sirens in the far-off distance. Feeling paranoid, they snuck onto the porch of the abandoned shack on Willow Road.

They ducked down on the porch, and saw the police drive by. The coast was clear.

Sammy said, "Boy, this pumpkin is too heavy to carry! I say we leave it here!"

They noticed a pumpkin that was carved with a scary face, and they noticed that someone left a carving knife.

"Let's carve a really scary face on this pumpkin, and leave it here!" they agreed.

They began to use their creativity to take turns decorating the pumpkin with scary attributes, when they heard a squeal or screech from the pumpkin.

They looked at each other in horror.

All of a sudden, the pumpkin collapsed and huge, bloody rats that were in the pumpkin emerged from the innards. Angered at the pokes in the sides of the pumpkins, they all climbed on Sammy and began to bite him.

"Help me, Craig!" Sammy screamed.

With shaking hands, Craig began to carefully stab the rats with the knife one-by-one, until they all lay dead by the side of the pumpkin.

Sammy was covered in rat blood.

Suddenly, a man came out of the door, looking like Lurch from the Adams Family. "What are you boys doing? You're going to clean this mess up, or I'll kill you!" Craig panicked, and plunged the knife right into the creepy man's bare foot. It pinned him to the floor on the porch, and he screamed in agony. The boys took off running, and never looked back.

That was the last Halloween the boys ever celebrated. But every Halloween, they hide under the covers, and hear the blood-curdling sounds of screaming rats and a screeching man who looked like Lurch.

60.
The Haunted Shoes of Peter Hurkos
Mark Hudson

Peter Hurkos was a Dutchman who fell off a ladder, and he woke up in the hospital, and had psychic powers. He died at age 77 in 1988. His two most famous cases were his work on The Boston Strangler case, and the Jim Thompson case.

He could touch an object that was at a murder scene and intuitively solve the murder. Although, he said he couldn't tie his own shoes. He was kind of a six-foot tall, clumsy Dutchman. He was not popular with everybody. He would reveal secrets about people they didn't want known about themselves. When it came to his psychic powers, he was right almost always. He helped police solve crimes. He eventually used his powers to go to Hollywood and work with celebrities. But when he got too greedy for money, that is when his powers began to run out.

Two mysteries that seemed rather unsolved were the Boston strangler mystery, and the Jim Thompson case. Albert Desalvo confessed to being the Boston strangler, and was put in prison for life. While he was a truly abusive person, it was proven that he was not the murderer who raped and strangled eleven women back in the sixties. He was in prison and signed a contract to have a movie made about him. But Albert was just a man who was desperate to be famous. He was eventually murdered in his cell. Some theories say that he was about to reveal who the real Boston Strangler was.

Jim Thompson was known as the Thai Silk king. He moved to Thailand to create a silk empire, which still exists to this day. But he mysteriously disappeared on Easter 1967 in Malaysia.

No one has ever figured out the answer to either case.

Harvard University, 1988

Jill, Stephanie, Isaac, and Fritz were four Harvard students specializing in psychology and neurobiology. Bored with their studies, they were getting a little off the beaten path and trying to investigate paranormal studies.

In other words, they wanted to be ghost-hunters.

They were very interested in psychic phenomena. Peter Hurkos had died, and they had managed to acquire a pair of his shoes. Doing experiments with telepathy, they hoped to solve the mysteries of the Boston strangler Case, and the Jim Thompson case. Their family had no idea what they were doing. Harvard seemed to be a network of brainy, wealthy students who were only interested in accumulating more money than anyone. The four would-be ghost hunters were not satisfied with this mundane pursuit. They thought if they could unearth the answers to these two mysteries, they could write a book and really become famous.

They had done a ton of interviews with local police, pretending to be doing research for their Boston research papers. They were able to get copies of records, but every cop said the same thing, "The mystery has never been solved. Nobody knows who the Boston Strangler was."

So Jill, Stephanie, Isaac and Fritz hoped to figure it out.

Jill was a beautiful blonde, who was the target for most of the football players at Harvard. Being science-minded, she liked soft-spoken men who could match her intellect. Stephanie was a red-head, six foot tall and in great shape. Isaac was a science wiz, often known as a mad scientist for his outrageous experiments. And Fritz was the rebellious one, who mainly got the group into all these studies. He seemed to have a rather dismal outlook on life, as if he already had seen some ghosts in his time.

This was before the days of the internet, so they didn't have Google Map, but they researched the area and located the apartments where the eleven murders took place in the sixties. They hoped to visit each house or apartment and find some answers.

The murders of Anna Slesers, Nina Nichols, Helen Blake, and Margaret Davis and Jane Sullivan seemed to be the most similar.

It had never been proven if there was only one murderer, or the crimes were copycat crimes. The aforementioned victims all had remarkably similar homes, which the police thought was a clue, but there weren't enough leads to figure it out at the time.

The victims were all senior citizens. Why would someone do such an awful thing? Some of the victims were nurses. Some thought the killer was a mental patient who hated nurses. But it was all speculation. And Peter Hurkos, the psychic, was stumped.

So the four would-be ghost hunters sat at a tavern on a Friday night, having a few drinks and planning their visits. They hoped to visit some of the old apartments, even though they may not be able to get in, and the gravesites of the murder victims. After they had finished their drinks, they drove to the first location. It was an abandoned building, with a lawn that wasn't mowed.

"Anybody have any hesitations?" Jill asked.

"It's now or never," Fritz said.

They snuck in through the gate, and found a stairwell full of cobwebs, and graffiti on the walls that looked like it came from the sixties or seventies.

They climbed the rickety stairs to where one of the victims had been murdered so many years ago.

They found the exact room where one of the victims had been killed.

There was a board over the room, which they knocked off and burst the door off its hinges. There in the room was a dusty bed, a dusty desk, and the whole room was covered in dust and filth, with ugly little creepy-crawly bugs everywhere, cockroaches, ants, spiders, dead mice, and so forth. Jill coughed and hacked as the disgusting nature of the room was obvious. They were visiting an old crime scene and they weren't supposed to be here. Their curiosity had got to them.

Jill exclaimed, "I'm going to have to do a little dusting if we're going to work here!"

"Oh, nonsense, Jill, we must try our experiment! Don't be a housekeeper now, the man who sold us Peter Hurko's shoes said they had special psychic powers and we could contact the dead. Where's your spirit of investigation?"

"Maybe I shouldn't have had so many drinks, I'm not feeling well!"

"We drink to have courage, and it doesn't hinder our scientific nature of inquiry."

"Well, let's try the shoes, and see what we can see."

They all sat around in a circle, and put the shoes in the middle of the dusty floor. They began to hold hands and meditate. They closed their eyes and asked the shoes questions. But the shoes didn't seem to be bringing any psychic waves into the room.

"This isn't working!"

"We've been had!"

"Now, wait a minute, let's not give up so soon. Are we going to give up that easily?"

"Wait a minute, do you hear that?'

"I hear something!'

"Look, there's a door up there, it might lead to an attic!"

"Open it up!"

Fritz got up on a chair, noticing a door with a latch on it. He dusted it off, and opened it up.

Immediately, a bunch of screeching, hissing bats flew out into the room, and one attacked Fritz and knocked him off the chair!

"Help me!" said Fritz.

It seemed the bat was trying to bite Fritz. Isaac grabbed the bat off Fritz's head and strangled it with his bare hands. But there were still a ton of bats coming out of the attic. Fritz leaped back up on his feet, and they grabbed the shoes and headed out of there, with flying bats hot on their trail.

They stood outside the building, gasping for breath. They saw the bats fly off into the night. Could they say their first experiment was a failure?

They weren't quite sure.

"Well, I'm not sure I'd ever want to go back into that house," Jill said.

"I don't think the experiment was a total failure. Maybe the shoe led us to the bats. Maybe somehow the bats hold a clue."

"Oh, come on don't give me that crap. What are we the Hardy boys?

There were bats and dead mice because it was an abandoned building. I say we go to the tavern and have a few drinks."

So they did.

The next day, or night rather, they went to the second house on their list. This time, the building was not abandoned. But it looked like it had been redone, as if to forget about the murders of the past.

They were standing in front of the building, wondering how they could get in. If someone was living in the same room, would they allow them access? And why would anyone want to live in an apartment where a murder had occurred so many years ago?

They noticed a back door was open, so they snuck in. They went to the place where the first murder occurred.

They could hear someone at home, watching television.

"Should we try to ask them some questions?" Jill asked.

"I don't think we should disturb them. We'll probably freak them out." Fritz replied.

"Maybe we can perform the ritual in the hallway," Isaac suggested.

"Let's try it."

They sat down in the hallway, in a circle, with the shoes in the middle of their circle. They began to meditate, listening for answers.

Suddenly they were interrupted by a loud voice. "What the hell are you kids doing here?"

They looked up and a custodian was staring at them. "I'm warning you kids, go away!"

The group was startled, but then Isaac ventured, "We're researchers from Harvard doing research on the Boston Strangler, trying to find out who he really was. You couldn't help us with our investigation?"

"You've got five minutes to get out of here, or I'm calling the cops! You should keep your nose out of other people's business! It's best to leave the past alone! Get out of here, now!"

Reluctantly, they got up and left.

The next day, they were sitting at their favorite hole-in the wall tavern, having a few drinks and contemplated their next attempt at unraveling the mystery.

"I think we need to make a pact, an oath of loyalty, because what we're doing might be illegal. If the police find out we're investigating paranormal activities, and we're doing it on our own without their consent, we could get arrested.

We should agree that if one person gets caught, we won't rat on the others," said Isaac.

"Well, what are we turning into criminals all of a sudden?" Jill asked.

"We're trying to crack a mystery that remains unsolved. Hurkos, as brilliant as he was, couldn't crack this mystery. But if we crack it, we'll be famous. We can write books and make lots of money. But we're really doing it to find out the truth. Or would you rather go back to Harvard, please our parents, and cater to wealthy know-it-all professors who enslave us with academia?"

"Well, that's true. I think I learned enough at Harvard for a lifetime! I feel totally brainwashed!"

"Well, I'm starting to have reservations about what we're doing," Stephanie said. "We're supposed to be college-educated, intelligent, sophisticated students with scientific, inquiring minds. And we're trying to investigate the supernatural with a dead psychic's gym shoes? I'm starting to get cold feet, no pun intended."

"Well, you can't back out now. We're all in this together. So far, our parents don't know what we're doing. They think we're attending class and studying to be what Harvard would prepare people to be; future leaders in the world of reason. I'm tired of thinking the way I've been taught to think. I am interested in the paranormal, and I think this pair of gym shoes will lead us to the answers. Peter Hurkos could go to a murder scene, touch a crime object, and solve the mystery with his psychic powers. But they say he couldn't find his own shoes, or tie his own shoes, but now we have a pair of his shoes. So I think these shoes have power. I think we can contact the dead to find out some answers. Now are we all in on this?"

They all tentatively agreed, but in each personality was a deeper sense of fear, that they masked from each other, not wanting each person to know that they were just college kids, used to restrictive lives, used to parents who demanded good grades, and all four experimenting with some of the temptations of college, drink, occasional drugs, and the free love that was prevalent at Harvard, not unlike any other institution in America since the sixties.

The next night they went to their next location. They crept through the alley, rats as big as cats scattering everywhere. They jimmied the door into the building they were trying to get into.

They found a room where one of the murders had been committed. It was empty, and similar to the first one they went to with dust and cobwebs everywhere.

They decided they had to work fast to do what they were going to do. They sat on the dusty floor, putting the shoe in the middle, and concentrated.

Suddenly, they seemed to be finally making a connection. They began to hear voices that sounded like someone speaking in tongues, although whatever they were hearing was undecipherable.

"I have to get out of here, I'm freaking out!" Stephanie said.

"You can't break the circle! You are ruining our connection!"

"I don't care, I quit!" Stephanie ran down the stairs.

The voices began to stop. The three sat puzzled, wondering what got into Stephanie.

"Well, we were really on to something. Let's continue without her." Isaac said.

"I'm going after her. I'm concerned about her." Jill said.

"Oh, come on! This is not professional!" Isaac screamed.
"Stephanie! Come back!" Jill screamed.

But as she stuck her head out the door, she noticed a police officer talking to Stephanie.

"What were you doing in that building!" the cop asked.

"Nothing!" said Stephanie, sobbing.

"You were breaking and entering a building! Is there anyone else in there?"

"NO!" said Stephanie, weeping.

Jill ran up the stairs, and told the other guys, "The cops are here! And they got Stephanie! Let's get out of here!"

They raced out the side of the building and somehow managed to get away. They even remembered to take Peter Hurko's shoes.

But Stephanie was brought down to the station for questioning. They couldn't get a straight answer out of her. Scared and confused, she made up a lie and said she was a Harvard student and felt a lot of pressure so she decided to "runaway" from school and hide. She was sent to a mental hospital for a psychiatric evaluation, and the psychiatrist did not detect any sign of mental illness. He simply stated that she was the "typical, stressed out, over-worked student," and her parents were contacted, and she returned home to Kansas, to her disappointed parents who had expected so much of her.

After Stephanie went home, concerned parents heard about it and began to contact college kids, making sure they were studying and not out breaking the law.

Of course, the parents of Fritz, Isaac and Jill were no exception. They contacted the school and asked to speak to their professors and get a report on their grades. They were alarmed to find out that they hadn't been seen in school in a while, and their grades, once excellent, were now an F in all areas. Each of their parents tried to contact them, but their scientific experimentation had alienated themselves from the real world.

It seemed like the newspapers and the media were on to them. Nosy neighbors had noticed sightings of four college students nosing around areas where the Boston strangler had once struck. The three remaining ghost hunters met at the local tavern over beers to discuss their next step.

"I think we are going to get arrested in Boston if we pursue this case any further," said Isaac. "But I'm still curious about these mysteries we're still trying to solve. Anybody up for pulling our money and going to Thailand, to investigate the missing Thai Silk king, Jim Thompson?"

"I heard they have great Thai stick there, too!" Jill added.

"Well, I can't return home at this point." Fritz complained. "My parents said I have let down the family. They say they've cut the umbilical cord."

"I say it is off to Thailand we go. How many college kids truly have the adventure of a lifetime?'

"We're having the misadventure of a lifetime," Jill groaned.
But they all agreed to go. They bought a plane ticket to Thailand, to the Cameron Highlands in Malaysia, where the Thai Silk company was founded by American Jim Thompson, who disappeared in 1967. The mystery was never solved, and the three head-strong Harvard educated scientists got off the plane, with great confidence in their mission.

"Want to get some Thai food?" Jill asked.

They went into a Thai restaurant and ordered some food. They asked the waiter if he knew anything about the Thai silk company.

"Thai silk company? Oh, no… you not investigate! Bad men buying silk stockings and wearing overhead, robbing businesses! Bad! You stay away…get killed!"

They looked at each other, finished their food, and paid their bill and left.

That night, the two men roomed together in a cheap hotel, while Jill had her own room. Jill had secured a bag of "Thai stick" showing that she wasn't joking about purchasing the potent drugs, although she didn't plan on sharing it with her friends.

They had all said their good nights, and Jill was busy taking hits of the Thai Stick. Pretty stoned, she fell asleep in her bed in what could only be called a stupor.

Meanwhile, in the other room, Isaac was sleeping, snoring like there was no tomorrow. Fritz had taken out the shoes, hoping to do a little research on his own.

He set up the shoes, lit a candle, and began to meditate. He began to feel a cold feeling come over him.

Meanwhile, as Jill slept in a tranquil stupor, a Thai custodian slipped into Jill's room. He had seen some Caucasian women before, but never quite this beautiful. He tiptoed up to the bed, admiring her beauty.

He got in bed with her, his heart racing. As Fritz meditated on the shoes, he thought he felt a ghostly presence. Suddenly the candle went out, and he heard Jill screaming!

He woke from his trance and bolted into Jill's room. There was a broken pillow on the floor with feathers everywhere. There was evidence of a struggle, and Jill lay on the floor, sobbing.

"What happened? Are you all right?"

"There….there was this man in my bedroom. And he got in bed with me. I woke up and he was trying to kiss me! He was ugly and his breath smelled like liquor. I fought him and he ran away. Oh, Fritz, I'm so scared!"

"Maybe we should wake Isaac and get out of here. I think this place is kind of scary."

"I think this whole country is scary. What was I thinking when I came here? I think I want to go back to the states tomorrow."

"Well, that's your decision. Hey, what are you doing with Thai stick? I thought you were just joking about that. Maybe you just hallucinated the whole thing. What, you weren't going to share?"

Jill laughed. "Would you like a hit?"

So the two began to smoke some of the potent pot, while Isaac slept like he was in a coma. Meanwhile, the same man, the custodian, snuck into the other room where Isaac lay sleeping. Tiptoeing around, he found both of their wallets, and quickly pocketed both, and tiptoed out as easily as he had come in.

The next day, Isaac woke up, to find that his wallet was missing, and so was Fritz's. He scrambled around madly, looking for the wallets. But they were nowhere to be found. He looked to see if Peter's shoes were there; they were still there.

He went into the other room, and was shocked to see his fellow ghost hunters in bed with each other, naked but covered and asleep, with a bunch of Thai stick bags sprawled all over the bedroom floor. Isaac assumed that Fritz had taken all the money from the wallets and purchased the weed, and double-crossed him. Besides, he had had a secret crush on Jill and now he was completely envious. He decided to take off with the shoes into the jungle and leave them with the hotel bill. And while he was at it, he stole the rest of the Thai stick weed.

He snuck out the back door with his belonging in his backpack, including Peter's shoes. He would be the one person to solve the mystery of Jim Thompson, and he would be famous.

Jill and Fritz woke up, and the first thing they noticed was that the weed was gone. They went into the other room, and thought that Isaac took his wallet and stole Fritz's wallet, and ditched them with the hotel bill. They were quite upset.

"Let's get out of here, Fritz!" said Jill. I think we should go back to the States!"

"Yes, I think Isaac really ripped us off," Fritz mumbled. "Do you have enough money to pay the hotel bill?"

"If I didn't spend it all on the weed," she said. "I hope they take credit cards."

They went and paid their hotel bill with a credit card, and left. Meanwhile, the custodian man, from a distance, watched from behind a tree.

Fritz and Jill headed for the nearest airport deciding to return to the States.

They were mad at Isaac, and weren't enjoying their stay in Thailand. Although, even though Jill had been terrified by the man in her room who was trying to have his way with her, she felt comfort in Fritz, and the two had become lovers.

She never knew why she hadn't noticed him before. He was there for her in her moment of need, defending her like a chivalrous knight. She felt safe from that stalker in the arms of Fritz. But Isaac had used the opportunity to steal their money and blow them off.

They couldn't care less if he rotted in the jungle.

They were able to purchase a return ticket to the states, and got home back safely. They moved to California, where they got an apartment together and eventually married. They didn't tell their families they ever went to Thailand, and it became a secret story they would never tell a soul.

Isaac walked in the jungle. He was now getting more and more lost, and frustrated.

It was getting to be night time. Where was he going? He began to think he heard voices coming from the jungle. Scared, he grabbed Peter's shoes and chucked them in the nearest ravine, thinking they were bringing him bad luck.

At this point, he turned a corner, and ran into that same custodian man.

He had a large machete in his hands!

"Not trying to investigate the disappearance of Jim Thompson are you?" the man smirked.

"Ah… no, I just seem to have gotten a little lost, that's all."

"Well around these parts, we don't like people nosing into our business. Jim Thompson is the most famous person to disappear. And anybody else who investigates disappears too. We like it that way!"

"That's nice!" Isaac said, and took off running in the opposite direction, running for his life, running as fast as his legs could carry him.

As Isaac began to run, he tripped and fell into a hole where his leg got fractured, and he became stuck in the hole. He desperately tried to get out, but he was completely stuck.

The man approached with the machete. "I could knock your head off right now, with the machete. But that wouldn't be much fun. I think I'll cover you in chocolate. There are plenty of creepy crawly things in the jungle. Huge red ants, tarantulas, you name it. And they all like chocolate, and if that doesn't kill you, the ghosts of the jungle will scare you to death.   So, I think I'll spread some chocolate all over your skin and watch the jungle creatures eat you. Nobody will hear your scream!"

        Sure enough, the wildlife began to eat the lure, and tarantulas began to bite into Isaac's skin. But that wasn't really what killed him. It was the ghosts he saw all around him, as his heart gave out to the fear that once was not known to such a brave, headstrong Harvard student.

61.
The Lady of White Rock
Mark Hudson

A Dallas legend, the lady of White Rock Lake,
is claimed by some to be true, not fake.
In the thirties, high school students told,
The version of the story that is most old.
Anne Clark wrote about the story in 1943,
it was published in a book of mystery.
Many versions came through the years,
As time went on, it raised more fears.
One says a couple was parked in July,
by the lake when the ghost came by.
She got in the car in a white dress,
and told them to go to a certain address.
She was completely wet, she made a mess,
But when they got there, the dad was depressed.
"My daughter drowned three weeks ago,"
He said with a definite degree of woe.
Another version talks about Neiman-Marcus,
the store where the owners would greet the carcass.
Mr. and Mrs. Guy Malloy saw a girl in distress,
who was wearing a Neiman-Marcus dress.
The couple, who seem to be really normal,
Never could believe in the paranormal.
But the ghost did the same thing like last tale,
She had drowned in the lake after taking a sail.
Rose-Mary Rumbley wrote in a 1998 book,
That other people have reported taking a look.
Another story states that on July 5, 1935,
Frank Doyle had a sister that didn't survive.
He found a suicide note in her hotel,
And some think she is the ghost as well.
She drowned herself in the lake which was sad,
And all these stories could've been a fad.
But do you dear reader, think ghosts exist?
Next time you're on a lake, look into the mist.
What you might find, gazing into the sea,
Is that all of us are headed for our destiny.

62.
The Loss of Abby
Lisa M. Scuderi-Burkimsher

Charlie's wife, Abby, diagnosed with cancer, was given six months to live, but it ate away at her organs in less than three. Charlie, stayed strong, but alone he cried and spent sleepless nights at home, the bed empty without her, while she laid in a hospital bed deteriorating. Her dimpled cheeks became frail and her once vibrant personality disappeared.

Charlie could still hear the ventilator pumping her breath until the last day when it flat lined and her distant eyes slowly closed. He held her cold hand and wept uncontrollably. Abby was gone and there was nothing he could do about it. The nurses stripped her gown; her body exposed for all to see until they placed a white sheet over her. At that moment Charlie's grief became inconsolable.

"My Abby! What will I do without you! I can't go on!" Flailing his arms and kicking, the security guards removed him from the room.

At Abby's wake, family and friends consoled Charlie with hugs and handshakes, but he was morose and light-headed from the tranquilizer the doctor prescribed.

Abby looked beautiful in the dress Charlie chose for her. She wore it on their twenty-fifth wedding anniversary. He still remembered that day in Paris when they visited the Eifel Tower. She looked lovely in blue and it matched the color of her eyes, serene and happy. She never wore it without the matching pendant he bought her. Now that pendant rested still around her neck and her white dangling pearl earrings sparkled in the light of the room. White and red flowers surrounded her coffin with a collage of family pictures. Their daughter Lily kept asking if Charlie was okay or hungry, but he touched her shoulder and nodded. She understood and let him be.

"You take the grandkids to Burger King. I want to stay here for a while alone with your mother before the evening viewing."

Charlie hugged Lily and his son-in-law Greg, gave his granddaughter Rose a kiss on the cheek, and patted his grandson Charlie on the back. He watched them leave, knowing later, when they arrived home, they'd have a full house and he'd go home to an empty one.

Alone in the quiet, Charlie walked up to Abby's coffin and placed his hand on her arm.

"Abby, it's Charlie. I miss you so much. Even in death you look as lovely as ever."

He put his head down on her chest and closed his eyes until a cold shiver on his arm jolted him backwards and he knocked over the prayer kneeler. He rubbed his eyes and took a step closer.

"Abby?"

"Yes, Charlie, it's me."

"It can't be. I watched you die." He stared without blinking, his eyes fixated on the figure before him.

"I couldn't leave this world without seeing you one last time. I need to tell you something and it needs to be said now. The cancer took my life, but you're the one suffering. You spent every moment at my bedside and endured many sleepless nights. My guardian angel showed me your future, but it can be corrected if you listen to me. I was given this chance before I leave to see you and I want you to listen. If you don't stop taking the tranquilizers the future shows you become an addict and lose your job. Our daughter tries to get you help, but you refuse and cut her out of your life and never see our grandchildren. You become severely depressed. Eventually you overdose and die. I can't let that happen. I'm gone, but you still have family and can find love again. You need to stop taking the drugs and sleep. Go back to work after my burial, otherwise you will end up alone and broken. Remember, I'm gone, but you're alive. Live your life."

Speechless, Charlie tried to touch her face, but a bright glow appeared and she backed up into it, her blue dress flowing before she completely disappeared.

"Was I dreaming?" Charlie shook his head.

A few moments later Lily and Greg came back with the kids. "Grandpa, we missed you." Rose jumped on his lap.

"Dad, you sure you're not hungry? We can take you somewhere before the next viewing starts. There's still plenty of time." Lily kissed his cheek.

"You know what, I haven't eaten all day. I would like that."

Charlie walked over to Abby's coffin, bent very close to her face and kissed her lips.

"Thank you. We'll be together again, but not yet." Charlie softly whispered.

63.
The Magic Ukulele
Mark Hudson

Part One: The Expedition

Gino and the expeditionary crew decided to take a rest from their excruciating journey through the rough jungles of Brazil.   They had two vans and lots of camping equipment.

They were on a quest for the Magic Ukulele, a ukulele with mythological powers that was rumored to exist.   Gino had come across the map in Hawaii, hidden in a cave.   The mostly Hispanic crew was led by Gino, and Gino was determined to get the Ukulele.   The Ukulele reportedly contained the key to immortality and god-like status.

They were sitting down eating pineapple enchiladas in a hidden grove.   The pineapple being added to the enchiladas was Gino's idea, seeing that he was Hawaiian.   The men brought lots of meat in freezers, and they also brought along grills.   They brought tons of water jugs, and overhanging limbs drooped over them as odd insects scrambled past their feet.   They were all sitting together, taking a well-deserved rest on their one-week journey.

"Hey, Pedro!" said Manuel, "You want to rub those rosary beads a little harder? I feel some bad luck coming our way!"

"No, no, no, señor! We are doomed! We'll never make it!"

"Quiet, you buffoons," growled Gino, well-known for his lack of manners.   "I'm not paying you for nothing.   Would you rather be in the oceans, chasing a big fat whale? You boys know this neck of the woods.   Brazil is not necessarily known as civilization.   If there is gold, you boys will get a share, didn't I say that? Would I lie?"

"But, senor, these forests are haunted! Nobody has ever come back! My Madre and Padre once wandered too close, they found a severed hand! And someone even wandered closer and found a severed head!"

"Well," joked Gino, "that is life, Brazilian style.   Come on, you sissies! I bet when you camped as kids you wet your sleeping bags, because you didn't want to go to the outhouse in the dark.   Do you want to be rich or not? Come on! We are starting to get on each other's nerves, but we still need to work as a team to survive."

They were not expecting danger, when a huge lizard, about as big as a cow appeared. They freaked out.   The big lizard grabbed one of the crew, Juan.

The men pulled out their guns and started firing; Juan was swallowed by the lizard and died.   The men hurled their stuff in the jeep and took off through the jungle.   The lizard chased the men, as they drove away.

"The creatures out here make the Galapagos Islands look like a pet store!" Gino said.

****

The next day, they found the ruins of the fortress where the Magic Ukulele was rumored to be.   It was buried so deep in the jungle, that it was no wonder that nobody had ever found it. It was obvious that the ruins were of an ancient culture's creation, unseen for centuries, As they approached the massive ruin, hyperactive monkeys jumped to and fro, bouncing off the top of the cave as if they were defending their territory.   They entered the cave and had to fend off the bats, which swarmed in multitudes.   There were remnants of some Latin American tribes with strange language written all over the cave, untranslatable to Gino.   There were cave paintings of unicorns and many other god-like creatures.   The men, led by Gino, entered the pyramid.

They held their flashlights tight, even though some form of light could be perceived.   As they walked in, a boulder fell from the roof and crushed some of the men to death.

There were only two men left, Gino, Pedro, and Manuel.   One man began to chicken out. "I don't know about this, Señor." he stuttered.   "I think I'm going to leave."

"You ain't going nowhere!" Gino stated, pulling out a gun.   "You're going to die!" He shot the man.

"Hey!" said the remaining man.   "You killed my brother!"

"And now I kill you!" said Gino, shooting his remaining worker to death with his handgun.

****

Gino followed the map to exactly where the Magic Ukulele was supposed to be, and there, in the middle of the room, was a giant structure where the Magic Ukulele should be,. Gino felt an adrenalin rush as if his greedy scheme were about to come together.   The room was lit by torches, and there was a great big Ukulele in the middle.

Gino was so pleased with his discovery.   He read the Latin inscription off of the map and the cave started to shake.   Rocks went crashing to the ground.   Out of the structure burst a purple unicorn holding the Magic Ukulele.   Gino let out a sigh of awe.   The unicorn sang:

"When it rains, it pours,

the Magic Ukulele is now yours,

and all the power it does hold,

is worth much more than gold.

You have solved this crazy riddle,

You gained much, you did so little.

As you hold the world in your hands,

Watch it follow your commands,

So take it, by its strings,

 be one of the kings."

The unicorn's voice was beautiful, reminding Gino of that ancient story of the sirens. Its singing haunted Gino, There was fire and a showering of rocks, and then it ceased. Gino had won the Ukulele. All he had to do was bring it back to his house in Hawaii so he could begin his experiments.

Part Two: Hawaii

Gino stepped out of the ocean, dripping wet, and squinting out at the beach in front of him. The sun felt good. He toweled himself off and sat down on his blanket. He felt the sun's rays dry him off, and he put his sunglasses on. He heard the merge of many different radios across the beach. The three different songs he heard at the same time made a cool sound. He closed his eyes and felt the sun dancing on his face.

"Gino, coming to the party tonight?"

His drink had an umbrella in it. He stuck the drink in his cooler, and he saw the ice melt in the blistering sun. The beach was soft and yellow, the water blue and even softer, and Gino could smell the smell of the fresh, pure water.   In the distance, he could see people surfing on the waves, and the waves were splashing everywhere. There were seagulls flying, and you could smell the sweaty bodies on the beach. Gino glanced at his friends, who were in the buggy.

"No, guys, I got something else to do tonight."

"What, a new woman?" they joked.

"Something along those lines,"he joked back.   He usually didn't miss any of the parties his friends threw.

Actually, he wanted to experiment with the Magic Ukulele that he obtained from the Brazilian jungle, and nobody knew that he had it. His friends looked perplexed.   "What could possibly be more important than the party?" they demanded.

"I'll tell you later.   Now if you'll excuse me, I'm going to head back towards my cottage." Gino picked up his stuff and trotted away, leaving his friends staring in

Disbelief.

When he got home, he drew the shades.   He put his answering machine on and locked the door.   He lit some candles.   He pulled the Magic Ukulele out of its hiding place and placed it on the centerpiece of his living room.   He pulled out the map.

"Ha, ha!" he laughed. "If I do the Latin procedure correctly, I will be elevated to god-like status!"

Little did Gino know that he was about to become a god of sorts indeed, but not in the manner in which he had planned.   Gino read the Latin inscription on the map, the second one, and sat back.   A grin spread across his face.

Nothing happened at first.   Gino waited.   Then, slowly, a ghost of a woman appeared out of the ukulele.   She was the most beautiful woman Gino had ever seen, even though he lived in Hawaii.   The spirit hovered above Gino.

"Wow!" said Gino, impressed.   He was not expecting this.

"I'm your genie," said the beautiful woman ghost.   "I will grant you one wish."

It didn't take long for Gino to say what was on his mind.   "My wish is to make love to you!" said Gino, drooling.

"Your wish is my desire! You're loved, baby! Ha! Ha!" said the woman as she turned into a demon, sucking Gino into the ukulele.

His body remained in the chair, like a zombie.

Part Three: The Other World

Gino lay sprawled out on the ground.   What just happened? He felt like he was getting over a terrible hangover.   This didn't look like Hawaii to him.   He groaned.   Where was he? He couldn't get up off the ground.   His body felt heavy.   He looked around.

He was suddenly aware that he was somewhere other than Hawaii. Everything in this new world was more purple than any other color. Everything was soft, and he could see a lot of flowers. He pinched himself and felt it. In the foreground, he could hear crickets chirping, and in the distant background, horse's hoof beats approaching. He still didn't seem to have the energy to get up. Suddenly, he looked to his left, and he saw a leprechaun no bigger than his hand. Gino silently vowed to lay off the opium.

"You must get out of here!" The leprechaun exclaimed. The leprechaun looked, well, like a leprechaun. He wore green and had a red beard and mustache that protruded from his face.

"Where am I?" Gino asked, suddenly awake.

"You have been sucked into the land of Rafalma, a magical land of non-human existence. I cannot explain any more than that for the Dark One approaches to execute you. Go on! Get out of here! You will hear from me later! Run!" Gino raced into the forest.

****

Meanwhile, in the forest, an ant-tribe strove through the murky swamp water. They were a race unto their own, dedicated to the preservation of their species. Five-hundred ants carried their leader, the king, on a half of a gas cap, the other half eaten away by rust. Where the gas cap had come from was a mystery, for there were no cars in this land.

The King barked orders from the top of his gas cap throne when the sweating ants spotted a half-eaten French fry. French fries were a rare delicacy for anybody in this land.

"French-fry! French-fry!" they shouted, letting go of the throne they carried and dropping it. This was a rare occurrence. The ant king slid into a puddle and drowned while the five-hundred ants tackled the gigantic French fry. "A paradise of food!" they all shouted in unison. Greedily, they began to devour the giant fry, it was at this point that Gino came racing through the forest, stepping on the French fry, killing all five-hundred ants. He was too busy running from the king. He was out of breath. He didn't know why the king was supposed to be his enemy, but he believed the leprechaun that he was. So he just kept running.

As Gino raced through the forest, a purple aura encompassed the entire environment. The forest was swamp-like, and there were huge puddles everywhere. Gino was more confused than scared. As Gino ran panting through the forest; you could hear the splish-splash of the water underneath his gym shoes. As he raced through the forest, his pants ripped, and a big hole appeared around his kneecap. Suddenly, he stepped in the wrong puddle, and his foot got stuck. He struggled to keep balance. He couldn't pull his foot out. Then a gigantic tentacle pulled him into the water. Gino felt his senses leave him as he disappeared underwater. As he fell into the water, his nostrils took in the smell of salty, dirty water. He got a ton of water in his mouth and had nowhere to spit it out. As he looked down, he could see a giant tentacle stretching all the way to the bottom of the ocean.   Now Gino was more perplexed than ever.   At the bottom of the ocean, Gino could see a mechanical mouth that looked like it wanted to eat him.   It seemed like the mechanical mouth was drinking in the entire ocean   The tentacle Gino was imprisoned by was connected to the machine.   The tentacle that engulfed Gino was slimy as a slug.   But Gino felt it grip him, and he couldn't get loose.   Gina felt panicked and wanted to find a way to save his life.

He thought this was the end for sure.   He awakened on this mysterious planet, or land, and had little or no recognition how he had gotten here.   He had been thrust into this realm, with no defense against his environment.

Just when he thought he couldn't hold his breath any longer, a giant swordfish sliced off the tentacle that was binding him.   It took less than ten seconds for the swordfish to cut the tentacle.

Not knowing how to thank a swordfish, Gino simply swam to the top of the water where he emerged from the puddle.   He burst out, gasping for breath.

As he lay on the ground, practically collapsed, it took him a moment or two to see that some sort of creature was standing above him, with hands on hips.   He looked like a cross between an ape and a bat.

"Hello." said the creature.   "I am Anthony ape-bat.   I am not here to harm you but help you.   I am the second one who has been sent to guide you through this dangerous land.   This territory is unfamiliar to you, I know, so come along.   There is much danger that awaits you.   You have overcome your first obstacle, the tentacle.   You must endure this journey if you are ever to return to your native land."

Gino was too tired to respond.   The ape-bat picked him up and carried him, and then spread his wings and they were off.   Gino gazed down at the forest below, and fell asleep.   Or at least shut his eyes, and shut out the environment around him.

Gino opened his eyes as they landed in a primitive looking village.   Gino was surprised at what he saw.   There were ape- bats everywhere, and they resembled a Brazilian tribe.   Straw huts made up the village.   Some of the ape-bats had bones in their noses, and there were some female ape-bats preparing some sort of stew.   Gino realized he was hungry.   They all had spears of some sort, and they wore no clothes, nor did they have genitalia.   Gino was wondering what to expect next when an elder of the tribe approached him.

"Hello, Gino," he said.   "I am the tribe wise-man.   Or wise ape-bat, if you prefer.   I will explain what has happened to you.   And when I do, you still won't really understand.   You see, the Magic Ukulele was a sacred object owned by the ancient unicorn race, little is known about the origin of this object.   But there was an evil unicorn named Cyrus, and he was a wizard.   A wizard unicorn, you say? Well, it gets stranger. He corrupted the Ukulele and put a curse on it. He released the dark powers of our sphere, and no one could tell well from evil.   This was the introduction of evil into our world. Our paradise was lost.   New races of creatures began to emerge. The unicorn became extinct. And no one could trust their neighbor. It is said that the soul of Cyrus lies in the Ukulele, because the good forces chased Cyrus. He has been stuck in there for a long time.   But then one of Cyrus's followers stole the Ukulele and put it on your planet, where we cannot go.   How the follower got to your planet is unknown.   And evil remains in our world until Cyrus is defeated.   He has been let loose on this planet as well as yours, and it's technically your fault.   You are the only one who can defeat him because you are human.   We cannot stop him. "You intended to use the Magic Ukulele for evil purposes, but now, our land depends on you.   You must help us."

Gino thought about this.   How did he get into this mess? It never dawned on him that by desiring god-like status, he was being corrupted by evil. He had been misled. And Cyrus had been the evil demon-spirit that had brought him into this wicked land, and the only way to get back home apparently, was to defeat Cyrus, making himself a hero in this cartoon world as well as returning him safely home. He knew he didn't want to be stuck here.   But what are the risks? Can I die in this fantasy world? Am I already dead?

"I'll do it!" said Gino, smiling at the elder.   "I've been an evil man, but I will join the powers of good to defeat Cyrus. It's the only hope I've got.   But what must I do?"

"When you read the sacred chant, you released Cyrus from his imprisonment in the Ukulele.   That is why his followers left the Ukulele on your planet.   He is probably loose on your planet. He has the power to destroy your planet.   You have to defeat

Cyrus's other half, his split personality resides in the King.   The King is the evil leader of this oppressed land.   If you kill the King, you can summon Cyrus's other half, and snub them both out of existence.   But you must act fast.   There's no time to lose! The King is searching for you as we speak."

****

The king heard these very words as he watched the scene from a crystal ball.   He growled.   He turned it off. "They will not win! I will not allow them!" he growled.

"I have been imprisoned for centuries and thanks to this fool, Gino, I have emerged.   I will not let him put me back in that cell.   The Ukulele remains in Gino's house, where my half has ventured out to see what havoc he can create. I hope he creates much, yet I must stay here to prevent Gino from fouling up my plans.   No one must stop me.   I will command my servants to seek and destroy Gino."

The King stepped out on a platform before his followers. They all bowed. He wore a hooded cloak over his entire body, and only had two glowing red eyes for a face. He looked like a stereotypical demon. All of his followers looked the same. They stood at attention like soldiers transfixed. As he stepped out on his platform, his followers got down on their knees. The king spoke. "Followers, take heed! Gino must be destroyed! You must not fail! Remember all the powers I promised you? Would I lie to you? Well, there's only one thing standing between us and glory, Do you know what it is? We must destroy Gino! Seek him and bring him back, dead or alive! Now go!"

Later that night, Gino was sleeping at the ape-bat's camp. Darkness enveloped the night. There were about sixty huts in a circular fashion surrounding the village. The woods around the village echoed with the sounds of the creatures of the night. Gino seemed to be sound asleep, but not really. He was aware of what was going on around him. You could say he was in a temporary state of relaxation, right by where the elders sat up, discussing things. He was not really in earshot, yet Gino could hear words. There was one guard watching the camp, with a sword held in one hand. He was completely alert and was prepared for trouble. Gino's dog, a pet the ape-bats had insisted Gino have, sat next to Gino on a pillow, and Gino could smell his dog-like odor. The dog had the largest neck Gino had ever seen on a dog, and he had short paws up front, and long paws on back. He looked more like a kangaroo than a dog. He spoke English and had a rather extensive vocabulary. But all the creatures in this land seemed to understand Gino's language rather well. Gino was lying on a straw mattress, and the atmosphere was rather hot, though damp, 'cause they were in a swamp. Suddenly, Gino's dog, Companero, nudged him.

"Wake up! The demons are approaching!"

Gino jumped off his mattress and burst out of his hut. Companero followed right behind. He ran to where the elders were standing. The elders turned to Gino. They seemed to be expecting him.

"Gino! There's no time to lose!" they said. "Get in this door in the ground, it leads to an underground passage! You are in grave danger here! We must hold off the demons, they are surrounding this village! It's you they're after! In the passage, there will be guides who will show you the way. Don't delay! Go! Hurry! Take your dog!"

Gino knew they were serious. Gino went down through the passageway in the ground, which went down a row of stairs. He heard them shut the door above him. Companero followed Gino. The earthly walls were lit by torches, and the walls and ceilings seemed to be perfected by skilled laborers. There was an arched quality to the design. There was nothing modern about this new land, although it seemed anything was possible. Gino walked on through the underground corridor, with no knowledge about how his friends the ape-bats were fending off the demons. He wished he could've stayed behind and helped fight.

So far, the tunnel went in just one direction.   Where it was leading to, Gino wasn't sure. Gino decided to consult his dog, Companero, about the scenario. He might know, after all, it was his accurate observation that the demons were coming, that's correct.

"So, Companero, where are we going?" Gino asked.

"Well, eventually, we're going to defeat the King." the dog said.   "But I think there will be stops along the way. You're not ready to do battle with the King. You're not properly equipped. But I have all the confidence in the world in you."

****

Meanwhile, the evil spirit of the Magic Ukulele had been released upon Earth.   It was double trouble for two separate realms. His spirit first entered a volcano, spewing forth lava on the island of Hawaii.   This was an unlikely occurrence, and the residents of Hawaii could not explain it. But his powers were only limited to the constraints of time, for he was a stranger in a strange land and not as powerful as he would seem.   He would've liked to appear in a form which could confront humans, but he could only remain invisible. Simultaneously, his other half peered into the crystal ball, watching his followers battle the ape-bats. This is what he saw:

The ape-bats were holding off the demons pretty well Some ape-bats lay on the ground, dying. The ape-bats were fighting with swords and clubs, yet the demons fought with their bare fists. The demons outnumbered the ape-bats by far. The ape-bats killed many demons, and one demon set the village on fire. The ape-bats were to lose their village and many men to Gino.

Meanwhile, Alandro, the elder, stood guard at the secret passageway where Gino had escaped.   He looked determined.   Several demons discovered Alandro guarding the hidden passageway. They approached him.

"Is that where the vile Gino resides?" sneered the demon, while several others made absurd grunting noises.

"Stand back, demon!" warned Alandro. He almost looked like a saint of this mystic land. "You shall not enter this passageway. I shall give my life for Gino."

"That you shall!" snickered the demon, pulling out a sword and killing the elder. All the demons laughed as the cadaver of Alandro hit the ground, glowing and disappearing into the air, the way all creatures died in this land.

****

Meanwhile, Gino and his dog ventured farther into the passageway. The leprechaun appeared with some magic potion for Gino. "Remember me?"' the leprechaun said "Well, the demons have killed Alandro, and they are coming into this passageway! The village is on fire, and the ape-bats have lost! You must take this magic potion, to ward them off!"

Gino took the potion.   He marveled at how the leprechaun appeared out of nowhere at the most opportune time.   The leprechaun then disappeared.   Demons approached, and Gino sprayed the potion on the demons, and they were gone.   It worked.   Gino reckoned if he sprayed some on the King, he'd be all set.   Gino was determined to defeat the King, in order to get home.   He decided to talk to his talking dog, to figure out some things.

"How far is this tunnel?   Do you know where it leads ?" Gino growled at his dog, never being fond of pets in his real life.

"What am I, psychic?" the dog joked, displaying his sense of humor.   "Just because I'm intelligent, does it mean I know everything?"

"Well, I'm sick of this world," Gino growled.

"But you won't be. Now you are. One day you'll miss us all. We're just strangers passing in the night. When you're married, with a mean wife, and bratty kids, you'll look back and be glad you had an adventure!"

"I always did hate dogs!" Gino growled." When I get back to Earth, I am not never having no pets!"

"Put a lid on it, Gino! No one on Earth has ever had the opportunity to have a talking dog. And you better get out the magic potion. Here come more demons."

Gino became alert, grabbing his magic potion." Do you think we'll be able to hold off these demons for a while?"

Companero turned to his master.   "Yes, but check your magic potion.   That stuff goes quick.   Make sure you've got enough to ward off the demons that will soon be on your trail."

Gino checked his potion.   "Oh, no! We're all out! Where's the leprechaun when we need him? Leprechaun? Where are you?"

Suddenly, a horde of demons appeared from the other side of the passageway. One of the demons approached Gino and Companero, an evil smile engulfing his face.   "We heard that! You don't have the magic potion to get rid of us! What good news! We will now accompany you to the King!Ha, ha, ha!"

The demons grabbed Gino and Companero, and hauled them to the end of the passageway. They walked over to a locked door, and the head demon conjured up a key, and it floated into the lock.   The demons led their prisoners outside.

Gino sighed.   "I guess we've lost the battle, Companero!"

Companero was being led by the neck.   Gino noticed a pinecone and wished he had the life of a pinecone, trouble-free.

The head demon let out a sound that was incredibly disturbing "We've got you, Gino! The king will be pleased with us. Ha,ha, ha, ha!"

Gino said, "I have hope that I will defeat you!"

Suddenly, a giant tornado appeared out of nowhere.   The demons let go of their captives, screaming in terror. "It's a tornado! Run!" The demons fled.

Gino didn't know what to say. "I guess demons are scared of tornadoes." The tornado stopped whirling around.   It was a giant snake.

The snake spoke.   "Hello, Gino. I'm Stanley Snake. Pleasure to meet you. I was told to tell you to take the raft over there by the lake to your next destination.   Comprehend?"

"Well, where is my next destination?" Gino asked.

"That is not for you to know.   At least not yet.   You are more than halfway through with your journey.   How do I know this? Face it, Gino, none of anything that's happened to you has made any sense, including your life on Earth.   Why, if it did make sense, it wouldn't be happening, right? If you were on Earth in your real life, you would be questioning events that were happening, but there would be no one to give you the answers.   Not that you're even the profound type to ask questions.   So what am I, the answer snake? Hell, I just pose as tornadoes. Now, get your butt over to the lake and get in the raft.   Don't dilly-dally. I have to go now, go over to Brubaker Hills, and scare a few more demons, pretend I'm a tornado.   Bye-bye!" The tornado-snake flew off into the distance, singing in a shrill, tornado-like, tone.

"So what, Companero.   Shall we go on to the raft?" Gino asked.

"Si señor, we must continue on our journey. It'll be over before you know it."

"Somehow, I don't mind getting in a raft," Gino remarked.   "Sure beats being in that underground passage."

The leprechaun appeared out of nowhere.   "Ha, ha! Thought I betrayed you, didn't you? It is I, with some more magic potion! Don't leave home without it! Use it wisely, Gino, for those rapids below you aren't called the Rancid Rapids for nothing! You'll soon find out why! So, see ya! Hee, hee!" The leprechaun disappeared.

"Cool! More magic potion! Let's go, my friend!" Gino and Companero got in the raft and took off down the river.

As they floated down the river, Gino spoke to Companero. "You know, this must be a dream."

Companero looked at his master. "You could say that, although, some dreams are real, Gino. Who is to say that your life in Hawaii wasn't a dream, and all this is real? You'll figure it out in time."

Gino looked thoughtful. "Well, I hope this is a dream. I mean, this raft seems real. If I pinch myself, I feel it. If I put my hand in this water, it feels real and in my wildest imagination, I couldn't have conjured up you, so this world must be real! But it sure doesn't seem real, and besides, I never believed in fantasy, anyway!"

"Well, maybe that's why you were summoned to this world, because you didn't believe. Stranger things have happened. You need to get more faith that you can conquer the unknown. Obstacles appear in everybody's life. Just think of this as a mental exercise, Gino,"

"Well, I mean, look at this, though. Tell me this isn't absurd! I'm sitting here in a raft with a dog that looks like a kangaroo with a long neck drifting down a river in a raft, and the rapids are named Rancid Rapids, going to the castle of the evil King to kill him to save fantasy land and the real world from mass destruction. Not only is that totally absurd, but I refuse to believe this is happening to me."

"Hold that thought, Gino. I think we're getting into rough rapids. Rancid Rapids if you will. I'm going to need you to row extra hard." They struggled against the rapids, and the water threw them onto the land, and the raft floated away down the river.

"Great, Gino! We're stuck on land! I should've known this would've happened. And oh-great! We're in the land of walking trees! Have you heard of this land? On this land trees walk around and eat you. Of all the places to be! This isn't a good place to be! But you know what? It's on the way to the King's. We're on the way. Let's go."

Gino looked at Companero, disgust written all over his face. "What do you mean, the land of walking trees? I've never heard of such a thing. I can't take this place anymore! This place sucks! Get me out of here! Walking trees! This is stupid."

Suddenly, a tree walked up. "Care for a game of badminton, and a feast of heavenly brains?"

"Get out of here, clown!" Gino screamed. The tree walked away, sadly.

Now, Gino, that was not nice.," said Companero, "He meant no harm. They just eat creatures, and they're harmless. They won't eat us without our permission."

"That's it, dog!" Gino punched Companero on the head so hard that his neck straightened out, and his neck looked normal.

"Thanks, Gino, my neck is normal!"

"Oh, shut up, dog!"

****

Meanwhile, Kirk, the leprechaun was returning to Wally Wizard to get more magic potion for Gino. Wally Wizard was a giraffe. Wally Wizard had a shack on the edge of the forest. Wally was more powerful than the king. He could've overthrown the evil king, but he had to let Gino do it as part of the plan. Gino had to defeat the king and fulfill his role as the chosen one In essence, by discovering the Ukulele, he became the chosen one.

Kirk entered the wizard's tiny shack. The giraffe had holes in his roof, so he could stick his head out, and no bed 'cause he sleeps standing up.

"How's it going, Kirk?" the giraffe said as the leprechaun entered the door. The wizard always has the potion ready on time. The leprechaun gets it to Gino because he can travel through air.

****

Meanwhile, Gino and Companero are venturing through the land of walking trees.

"We're almost there, Gino.," said Companero. "In fact, we are here. We'll camp here at the edge of the forest because the King's castle is on the other side. Tomorrow is your big day. "

"You mean tomorrow is the day I battle the king?" Gino asked."Yes, and you'll do. Now, get some sleep." Gino had a very strange dream .Gino dreamt that he and Companero entered the king's castle. As they entered, the demons were all serving hamburgers shaped like violins. This probably had to do with the fact that Gino's mother made Gino play violin as a kid.

Suddenly, the King said to Gino. "You can't escape power, look what I have here!"

Gino looked over, and the King pressed a button and a wall turned around, and there was a beautiful girl tied up to a machine which had tiny circular saws placed strategically around the girl's body parts. Suddenly, Gino wasn't smiling.

The king laughed. "This is your future wife. Beautiful, isn't she? If you don't join my dark region, I will press the button, and she will be disposed of. We wouldn't want that to happen, would we? For I am no longer the King, I am the Queen."

Gino was alarmed. The King laughed in a falsetto voice. "What'll it be, Gino? Make your decision now! I don't have all day, and you don't either!"

And then, in the dream, Gino telekinetically switched the girl with the king, (or queen,) so that the King was tied to the saw machine. Gino then telekinetically turned on the machine, and the wheel spun around and around while the King screamed in a high-pitched voice. Gino laughed, and then kissed his future wife while the King was splattered on the machine, blood shooting everywhere.

Gino awoke, refreshed. The sun was shining, and Gino felt renewed. "Wake up, Companero. Let's do this before I lose my confidence."

Gino and Companero entered the castle. The castle looked run down, like a ghetto castle. The door was wide open, as the King awaited their presence. They walked down the corridor and entered a giant court, where the King sat on his throne, with his demon guards standing in front of him. There was so much evil in the room, it was almost as if you could smell it. The King spoke.

"So we finally meet, Gino?"

"Yes we do, King.," said Gino. "Let's cut the chit-chat. I am here to return you to the prison of the Ukulele, and destroy the Ukulele so no one can ever use it again so I can return home."

"You can't defeat me, sucker! Ha! You're probably going to use magic potion to destroy me, but I have already created an antidote which repels the magic potion. You lose. You will become one of us."

"No, you lose, King. You were always a loser anyway. The wizard invented a time-traveling apparatus which enabled me to go back in time and wipe out your existence. In three minutes, you will have never existed, and I will be transported back to Earth, with no knowledge of this adventure. King, you are about to become a non-entity."

"Guards get him!"

"In a matter of moments, the king disappeared into thin air. So did the guards.

"So, I guess all's that ends well. Right, Companero? Companero?"

Gino went back to Earth, and the land of talking dogs and ape-bats lived happily ever after.

Gino awoke in bed with a start. He felt strange. Maybe he still had time to make the party. He felt like he'd been in a deep sleep. Why did he feel so tired? Oh, well. He heard a knock at the door. Who could that be? He answered it. A beautiful girl was standing at the door in a bikini. Gino wasn't sure if he knew her or not. She was blond, but her skin showed evidence of prolonged exposure to the sun. She was smiling, and her white teeth shined on her face. Gino was suddenly awake.

"Hi, Gino!" said the gorgeous blonde. "We were just wondering if you were going to the party. We've been knocking on your door, and you must've been sleeping. After all, what's a party without Gino?"

"Well, I guess I was asleep."

"Well, let's go, I'll give you a ride."

Gino enthusiastically agreed. He got in the car and off he went. As the car drove off down the path, a dog with a long neck and a leprechaun stuck their heads out of the bushes, watching their hero in gratitude and admiration.

64.
The Mayflower Incident
Victoria L. Scott

Agent Sacerdote Dato stepped out of the dimensional rift into a cold landscape, running a finger along the rough collar of the shirt he wore as the rift closed behind him with a pop. The collar itched and he didn't like it, but he needed authentic clothing to help him blend in. Therefore, his current body wore cloth called linen, made from some sort of plant-based fiber, along with wool and leather, which were both animal-based materials. *Barbaric*, he thought, and shivered under the brown wool cloak.

Sacerdote preferred the synthetics he usually wore on cold planets, but unlike prior missions where he just watched the subjects from afar, this time he had to make contact. Old Earth in what the later natives termed the 17th century was an extremely unpleasant and dangerous place, but because of the delicate nature of the anomaly, correcting the temporal error required more than a long-distance chronal fix. Predictably, Commander Egit had chosen Sacerdote for the mission, no doubt hoping the outspoken agent would not survive. Agents who interacted with temporally compromised subjects sometimes didn't.

Dato patted his torso, feeling his standard temporal repair kit in a thin pouch in a pocket on the inside of his dark blue wool 'doublet', which functioned, along with the linen 'shirt,' as a covering for Dato's torso. The folded cellulose sheet rustled in the outer pocket as well. He looked down. 'Breeches' made of brown wool covered his legs, and brown 'socks' and 'boots' covered the awkward appendages called feet. He frowned, looking at them in the snow. He missed his usual, elegant physical form.

The physical changes necessary to make him look like the sentient beings of the barbaric planet had been horrifying. Learning to walk on two legs as a simple biped had taken several time cycles, and his visual spectrum being limited to only three dimensions still made his brain ache. Absorbing the archaic language, cultural mores, basic biological functions, the flora and fauna of the planet and the appropriate macro and micro-expressions on top of the mission requirements and the temporal discrepancies to be corrected had been a pleasure in comparison to the physical adjustments. *But,* he thought, *the discomfort is temporary and the deception necessary.* If the *homo sapiens* discovered he was unlike them, his research had shown they'd kill him in any number of unpleasant ways. *Homo sapiens* were remarkably inventive in their methods of killing each other, however primitive and backwater their planet at that time was.

This time, Sacerdote reminded himself, *on this planet they are inventive. Not past tense. Keep that in mind.*

Dato looked around, taking in the dead aspect of the season called 'winter' around him. Grey-brown tree trunks and the brown stems of shrubs devoid of leaves poked out of a few inches of white snow as a cold wind blew past him.   He shook his head and sighed. His breath turned to smoke in the cold.

He stuck his hands in his pockets and trudged off, moving toward the newest settlement in the Earth region of New England in mid-December, 1620: the colony of New Plymouth, Massachusetts. As he walked Dato reviewed his knowledge of the subjects of his investigation.

According to the archaic Earth records, the *Mayflower* passengers, who differed from other humans in their perception of some supreme being, decided to leave their prior homes to seek another place to live. Dato didn't understand what sort of 'religious dissent' caused humans to brave travel in a wood cellulose container over a large body of salt water, but it seemed a minor detail. Upon their arrival to the Cape Cod peninsula they chose a site close to the seaside previously inhabited by a group of Wampanoag natives who had died in an epidemic. The passengers picked the location in part because they found the land already cleared for fields, and in part because it provided a good view of the surrounding countryside.   Strategically, it was a good choice. The colony of *homo sapiens* had thrived... eventually. Unfortunately, the first winter for the settlement had been grim, with nearly half of those who survived the sea journey dead before spring came in 1621.

Agent Dato mentally reviewed the names of those who had travelled on the *Mayflower*, and those who died that first winter. *I'll get a look at how much the sapiens have built from a distance, just as an initial check that everything is in its rightful place,* he thought. *Then I'll make my way into the settlement itself and see if I can determine the exact nature and source of anomaly, then set about fixing it.*

He crested the low hill that sat slightly to the north of the colony, taking care to keep to the limited cover of the tree trunks around him to avoid being seen.   The cellulose-based vessel *Mayflower* sat docilely in the harbor, its sails reefed. Dato couldn't believe how small the craft was and re-evaluated his opinion of the insanity of the people he was about to meet. The shallop, another smaller cellulose craft which ferried the passengers to land from the bigger ship, lay on its side on the beach, dusted with snow.

Sacerdote turned his attention to the settlement itself, then stopped and gaped.   Three long rectangular houses, their pointed thatched roofs covered in snow, stood finished in the clearing. Some colonists moved easily to and fro with various supplies while others focused on building a fourth long house. Muddy paths crisscrossing the settlement indicated a great deal of activity and a large number of people moving about.   The sounds of building drifted toward him, the saw noises and hammer blows even, robust, and mixed with the low murmur of conversation.

The settlement looked exceptionally primitive… And… successful.

Agent Dato leaned against an ancient oak trunk, its brown leaves rustling above him, and drew one hand over his face in dismay.

"God's wounds," he muttered, using one of the time-appropriate epithets he'd mastered. "Healthy settlers moving about, three buildings built, and another on the way." Dato sighed. "It looks as if nothing's wrong." He moved away from the tree. "This is more than just a minor anomaly," he muttered. "Nothing wrong means everything's wrong… and I've got to find out why." He closed his eyes and activated the database in his mind that provided current-time information to Dato's thought processes while he existed among the colonists. There was a moment of disorientation as the bio-circuits came on line. He opened his eyes and began his walk into the settlement.

He'd managed to come up with a cover story, of sorts, as he'd researched the time period and the beings who inhabited it. As a *Mayflower* settler noticed his approach, Agent Dato was glad he'd spent the time thinking it up. He also grudgingly admitted that Egit had been right about insisting on authentic clothing. The colonist – a male, as Dato was—stood next to a finished building, carefully watching the temporal field agent as he ambled up. He was a young lean-bodied sentry, bundled in dun-colored wool from head to foot as protection against the cold.   His boots had mud and snow on them, while his cheeks were rosy red, and his brown eyes bright. The male held a gun called a blunderbuss which sat uneasily in his hands. It was a laughable antique weapon so far as Dato was concerned, but he controlled his expression to keep his thoughts from showing on his face. It was obvious the young male was new to guard duty. *I do not want to give this male any reason to think me a threat*, Dato noted.

"Stand and deliver, sir," the young man said, blocking his way.

Agent Dato raised a hand in the manner he'd learned indicated a desire to do no harm. "Greetings, sir," Dato said, modulating his tone to indicate competence and wisdom, but not menace. He used the other hand to pull the cellulose document from a pocket, scribed with the visual form of the language he spoke. "My name is John Smith. I've come from the Jamestown Settlement to see how you fare here." He knew there was another settlement on the continent by that name, and had assumed mentioning it would make his presence more believable in New Plymouth. He'd hoped he'd not need to use the false identity, but he had no choice now.

The youth peered at the paper, brows furrowed.

"I do not have my letters, sir," he said. "You say your name is John Smith? From Jamestown?" He looked around Dato. "You came alone?"

Dato shut the paper and put it back in his pocket. "Best if you just call me Smith," he said. "I'm a traveler. I left my companions at a nearby Indian settlement and came here on my own." Dato reviewed his data and determined which sapiens – no, *man* - it would be best to communicate with. "May I speak to Captain Standish?"

The youth brightened. "Oh, aye, Master Smith. He'll be back from hunting shortly. Shall I have someone take you to Master Allerton or my Master Winslow until Captain Standish returns?"

"If you would please, Master….?"

"Soule, sir. George Soule at your service." The man turned, looked into the settlement and spied another young man. "Elias," he called, "Can you take this man to our master? He's come from Jamestown!"

Elias, red-cheeked and blue-eyed, nodded, smiling. "Oh, aye? Master Winslow is down this way, sir, if you care to follow?"

George smiled. "Elias Story will take you from here, sir," he said.

Dato stopped for a moment, scanning his knowledge once again. Elias Story had died in early December, 1620 according to the records, yet there the young man stood, very much alive. The realization deepened the agent's concern that all went too well in the New Plymouth colony. He nodded at George. "Thank you, Master Soule," he responded, walking past him into the settlement.

Elias waited patiently for Dato to join him.

"How are you, Master Story?" Dato asked, taking in the young man's obvious health. Elias also wore wool clothes of various brown and tan hues, though his were dirty from working, bits of wood splinters and bark stuck in the weave of his clothing. The two of them passed several people as they made their way to the Winslow dwelling, the other settlers noting the presence of a stranger, but not approaching him.

"I am well, thank you sir," he said politely. "So well they've put me to work on the roofs. Never've thought myself good at such work, but I'm glad to be of service."

"Indeed," the temporal agent said, looking at the newly constructed houses as they passed them. "How are those on the *Mayflower*, sick with the ague?"

Elias made a face as he remembered the time Dato had mentioned. "Oh, sir, to be sure, God has smiled on us. All those who were ill are recovered and here, working on establishing our new home. We were sore afraid many would die, but Providence saw fit to save us."

"It sounds like a miracle," Dato agreed, hoping 'miracle' was the right term for it, and feeling the bio-circuits confirm it. "Tell me, Elias. What turned the tide?"

Elias grinned, eager to tell the story. "Captain Standish and his party returned from an exploring mission. They became fevered, and we feared they'd die, but they awoke on the morn recovered, and the rest of us who ailed followed them into health." Elias stopped in front of the last building in the row of three and indicated that Dato should follow him in.

They stepped into a smoky room, rudimentarily furnished with several rows of beds, as if it were a dormitory. The floor was pounded earth, the walls wattle and daub, obviously newly finished. A blazing fire burned in the fireplace in the center of the building, warming the air against the December chill. A long table with benches around it sat near the hearth.

Agent Dato catalogued all he saw, and felt a chill run down his spine as he scanned the large enclosed space. It was a sensation new to Dato and apparently unique to humans. The interior of the building bore no resemblance to what he knew the Pilgrims built when they first arrived on Cape Cod. In the proper, unaltered history they'd constructed smaller, one family dwellings. What he saw was anachronistic in the extreme.

A dark-haired man faced the hearth, his back to the door while a woman worked at the table cutting softened pieces of ship's biscuit into a bowl. Their clothes were somewhat worn but well made, and like the others Dato had seen, they wore predominantly wool. A kerchief covered the woman's curly brown hair.

"If you please, sir," Elias said to the man facing the fire, "This gentleman here is Master Smith, a traveler from Jamestown. George asked me to bring him to you."

The man turned around as the woman looked up from her work. Both were clearly surprised by the presence of a visitor. "From Jamestown?" the man asked, looking the newcomer up and down. He was older than George, but not by much, Dato observed.

Dato made a low bow, relieved he didn't bobble the movement. "Pleased to meet you Master Winslow, ...and Mistress Winslow, I presume?"

Winslow met Dato in the doorway, his green eyes taking in Dato's unfamiliar face. "Elias, be off with you to climb a rafter," he ordered with a smile, and he put his hand out to Dato, who recognized the gesture as a greeting and shook it.

"A pleasure to meet you, Master Smith," Winslow said. "Please come in. If you give Elizabeth a moment, I'm sure she can find us some small ale to drink."

Elias bowed slightly to the men and departed.

Elizabeth smiled brilliantly and put down her work, wiping her hands on her apron. "I can do better than that, Edward, as you well know." She turned to Agent Dato. "Well met, sir. I rejoice that you have come to us safely. Surely it was a difficult journey. Did you travel all day today?"

"You could say that," Dato said, uncertain as to the best response. "Certain aspects of my travels today have been unusual," he temporized, "but I thank you for your hospitality, Mistress Winslow."

Edward Winslow indicated a bench. "Please, sit down, Master Smith."

"I'll get that ale," Elizabeth said, winking at her husband as she stepped around the table. "Back in a moment."

Dato sat down facing away from the door, suddenly uncomfortable. The physical signs between the two indicated Edward and Elizabeth were very much 'in love', which was an emotional state thought desirable by humans, Dato knew, though he didn't understand it. Dato also knew Elizabeth Winslow would die before summer came, a casualty of the illnesses the *Mayflower* settlers contracted that first year in the New World. Regulations forbade Dato from telling what he knew of the future, of course. For him, as a temporal agent, her death was written into the fixed point in time that was the *Mayflower* voyage and the foundation of New Plymouth. It could not be averted, no matter how much her husband loved her, or how full of life she seemed.

Edward Winslow moved to sit across from Agent Dato. He quickly put the thought of Mistress Winslow's death from his mind, for fear it would show on his face. The man, unaware of the his guest's deliberations, watched his wife breeze out of the house, then turned his attention to his guest.

"I must say, you have started out quite well here, despite the weather and the difficulties of your journey," Dato said. He hoped to craft a line of inquiry with Winslow that revealed what had kept the settlers from dying so far.

Winslow nodded. "Once we arrived and so many became ill, there was concern that perhaps God did not smile on our endeavor. But," he indicated the building around him, "now things proceed apace. The fourth building of our new settlement is to have two levels! At this rate, we'll have the whole colony built before spring comes."

"You've been fortunate," Dato agreed. "Elias told me the ague passed after the Captain and his men returned from a reconnaissance mission?"

"Indeed," Winslow agreed. "We were sore afraid we'd lose Elias, ill as he was, and Standish and the others were so poorly from their fevers, we feared to lose them too. We prayed for aid, and God saw fit to answer our prayers."

"I see," Dato said, certain the aid hadn't come from the supreme deity's intervention even if he didn't yet know its true source. "Have you noticed anything unusual in the area? Any odd stars or lights in the sky?"

Winslow frowned. "Tis a strange land to us, to be sure, but we've seen nothing in the Heavens to give us concern."

"Are you certain – "

The opening of the door and arrival of a burly figure interrupted the agent's sentence. Dato wrinkled his nose at the overwhelming scent of blood that suddenly permeated the room as the hair stood up on the back of his neck. He rubbed his neck, wondering how sapiens managed to have an uninterrupted thought from moment to moment with so many sensations to distract them. *Hair*, he thought in annoyance, *should not move on its own.*

Winslow's face lit in recognition.

"Captain Standish," Winslow said, standing up. "There's someone here you need to meet: Master Smith from Jamestown."

Standish and a large amount of blood? Dato thought. Alarmed, he turned to see if Standish was injured. What he saw stopped the words in his throat.

Standish stood in the doorway, childlike excitement coming off him in waves. In his bloody right hand, Standish held the savagely decapitated head of a deer, its eyes dark in death and its long tongue lolling out of its mouth. Coagulated blood covered the front of Standish's leather armor, dripping onto his trousers, hose and dirty boots. If it hadn't been for what Dato saw in the man's mouth, he might have thought someone had slit the captain's throat.

The military commander of the *Mayflower* expedition smiled broadly at Winslow and Dato, his mouth, beard and teeth covered in bits of deer flesh, hair and blood.

"It was good hunting, Edward," Standish said, obviously pleased. He took a moment to spit out some deer fur. "We ran down four deer.   I've got the others stripping the carcasses, and there will be fresh meat tonight for our guest!" He turned his bloody, ebullient smile on the newcomer. "Good day to you, Master Smith," Standish crowed. "You're well met in New Plymouth!"

Elizabeth Winslow stepped into the house behind Standish, a dark green wine bottle in one hand and three cups in another. She shook her head at the bloody figure in the doorway.

"I beg you, Captain Standish, step out of the house.   You're dripping blood on the floor, and I've no time for such foolishness."

Standish lowered the deer's head and looked contrite.   "Sorry, Mistress Winslow." He looked down at his bloody front, then wiped his mouth with the back of his dirty left hand.   "I was so pleased about our success I forgot my manners." He backed out around the woman.   "I'll get cleaned up." He looked at Winslow and Dato.   "I'll look forward to seeing you later tonight, Master Smith," Standish said, and bowing, the military commander left.

Dato watched dumbfounded as Elizabeth Winslow stepped over the blood Standish had left in his wake, came to the table and opened the bottle she held. She poured them each a cup of wine.

Dato recovered himself with difficulty and looked at Winslow. "He said he *ran down* four deer," he said. "Did he mean... on foot?"

"Oh, aye," Winslow said, untroubled.   He took one of the wine cups offered by his wife, and indicated the agent should do the same.   He did, but was too shocked to drink.

"'Tis the manner of our hunting," Winslow continued easily, taking a sip of wine.   "Do they not hunt that way in Jamestown?"

"Not quite," Dato temporized, his cup clutched in an iron grip as he flailed for an appropriate response.   "Mostly fishermen in Jamestown." He took a breath and plunged onward, looking into his cup as he smoothed his expression.   "Do all the men here hunt that way?"

Elizabeth took a sip of wine. "Not all the men are hunters, but those who do, hunt by running the animals down," she said.

Dato had a vivid mental image of precisely what the hunting had to have been like. He'd seen a variety of visual presentations on the various predatory life forms of the planet. He knew from his own struggles to master the physical aspects of his bipedal disguise precisely how difficult it would be for a human to run down a deer. The evidence on Standish's face clearly indicated what had happened, but he still had to ask. "He *bit* into the deer's neck, I presume, to kill it, rather than using a knife?"

Winslow beamed. "He did. Captain Standish is a fine hunter."

Dato's brain and bio-circuits calculated the overall impossibility of the historical Miles Standish, or any human, for that matter, running down a deer and killing it by tearing out the deer's throat with non-pointed, human teeth. He cleared his throat. "And you don't think that's... unusual?"

"We have always hunted this way," Winslow said, his face blank. "Always."

Dato swallowed his rising alarm and tried again. "Even before you came here? Back in Europe?"

"We have always hunted this way," Winslow repeated, his tone almost robotic. "Our skills help us survive in this place."

Elizabeth looked at Dato, her eyes glazed. "That is what we must do: survive," she intoned.

"I see," Dato said, trying to puzzle out the blank expressions on the human's faces. "I can't disagree with that, I suppose."

The Winslows snapped out of their fugue, smiled, and returned to drinking wine as if nothing strange had happened. Edward Winslow leaned toward the temporal agent. "Would you like someone to show you around, Master Standish? I'm sure you'd like to take our measure so you can tell our fellow Englishmen in Jamestown how we fare."

Dato nodded. *This is a way to look over the settlement in daylight,* he realized. "Yes. I'd like to see the whole settlement from top to bottom."

Winslow nodded. "I believe Master Priest would be available. He's been gathering thatch, but since the roof beams of the fourth house aren't fully up yet, he's at loose ends. Shall I take you to him?"

Agent Dato put his cup of untasted wine on the table, rose and took a step back over the bench. His knowledge of the list of passengers came into his mind, noting that Degory Priest was still alive at this point in time. "That won't be necessary. I'm sure I'll find Master Priest easily. Can you tell me one more thing?"

Winslow smiled, eager to be of service. "Certainly, Master Smith."

"How many have died since you arrived in Cape Cod?"

Winslow looked surprised. "Why, none, of course. Had you heard otherwise?"

Dato's stomach clenched uncomfortably, and he mentally cursed the odd biological reactions he seemed to be suffering from. "Ah," he said, "clearly I was misinformed." He pasted a smile on his face for his host's benefit. "I applaud you and your fellow settlers on your success so far, Master Winslow."

"Our success is due to God's providence, Master Smith." Elizabeth said.   "We're glad you came. I hope we'll be able to speak to you further."

Dato bowed slightly in a gesture he knew conveyed respect. "Thank you, Mistress," he said formally, and backed out of the house.

Edward Winslow turned his attention back to the fire in the hearth, swirling the wine in his cup while his wife returned to her work.

Agent Dato let the cold of the outdoor air wash over him. The brisk temperature cleared his head a bit, which only served to increase his concern.   The more he discovered, the more wrong things seemed to be. The proper time stream required the *Mayflower* settlers to lose half their number in the first few months. He wondered if Commander Egit had known the Earth mission involved fixing such a massive chronal dissonance before he'd chosen Dato for the job. *If he did, I wouldn't be surprised*, Dato thought grimly.

The temporal agent shook his head and started toward the house that was under construction. The settlers had built the outer frame of the building, the timbers standing upright as a group of several men readied other timbers to go up as more crossbeams. He recognized Elias on a newly erected crossbeam, barefoot and covered in woodchips as he worked with hammer and wood chisel.   He waved at the young man and Elias waved back, happily and comfortably sitting atop it, seemingly without fear despite its being twenty-five feet in the air. It all looked very normal based on his research, but then Dato noticed the settlers didn't have any ladders on the building site.

That is odd, he thought, walking closer. *These bipeds can't leap that high. How do they get the beams into place?*

At a word from the man who seemed to be the foreman, Elias nodded and hopped up on his feet, quickly walking to the end of the crossbeam. He dropped his tools to the ground. Then he leaned down, grabbed the upright timber that held the crossbeam, and crawled down to the ground headfirst like a spider.

Dato stopped in his tracks. He'd had an arachnid form on a prior mission, and remembered well the usefulness of the adhesive pads on the ends of the limbs. He also knew his own biped form did not possess adhesive pads, nor should the human settlers, yet Elias did. Oddly, the other settlers didn't react to the discrepancy at all, as if such super-human acrobatics were commonplace.

Elias regained his footing on the ground, grabbed his boots and moved off on whatever errand he'd been told to run. Agent Dato resumed walking, aiming for the bundled piles of thatch to one side of the building site that matched the description in his bio-circuits for the roofing material. An older man stood near the bundles with his back partially facing the agent, looking over the bundled reeds. Dato saw grey hairs interspersed amid the red in the man's beard and in the tufts of hair that stuck out from under the navy blue knitted cap he wore. Snow and mud covered his boots up to the ankles, and some mud spatters had reached up to the thighs of the man's canvas trousers. A leather vest covered the man's barrel chest, with the cuffs of two layered wool shirts evident at his wrists. He clutched a pair of gloves under his left arm, and scratched his head through the knitted cap with a work-roughened hand. Thanks to his intense preparation for the mission, Dato could read that the man's stance was tense and worried, which was unlike what Dato had seen in anyone else. *He knows what's happening isn't right*, he thought. *He's different from the others*.

"Are you Master Priest?" Dato asked.

Startled, the man nearly jumped out of his skin in shock. When he saw the temporal agent was a stranger, the fear was evident on his face. His breath came out in ragged gasps that made clouds of smoke around his face. Agent Dato put up his hands in a calming gesture. He'd thought the man looked tense, but this was more than just unease. Master Priest was strung tight with fear. "I'm sorry – I didn't mean to startle you," Dato said.

The man quickly regained his composure, but Dato saw tension thrum through his body.

"I am he, sir," Priest said. He tossed the gloves onto a pile of thatch. "You are well met in New Plymouth. I'd not expected an English stranger here so soon. May I ask your name?"

Dato held out a hand. "Master John Smith, from the Jamestown Settlement."

Master Priest shook the Doctor's hand warily, then released it. He looked down at his feet for a moment, obviously thinking. "How did you know to find us here? We've not been in this land long enough for news to reach Virginia, much less England."

Dato pulled out the sheet of paper and held it so Priest could read it, hoping to smooth the way. "When you didn't arrive in Virginia, we thought you'd been blown off course. I headed north in the hopes of finding you, as it says here."

Priest looked long and hard at the paper, his anxiety increasing. He rubbed his hands together nervously. "I beg your pardon, sir," Priest said, looking him in the eye, "but I don't believe you."

Dato quickly folded and pocketed the paper. *Perhaps I've found a key to the mystery*, he thought. "Tell me, Master Priest," Dato said, making his tone persuasive, "can we go for a walk? I've a lot of questions. I have the feeling you're the man to answer them."

Master Priest backed up carefully, shaking his head. "You are not who you claim to be," he said, and put one hand up in warning for Dato to stay away. With the other he grasped at his hip, feeling for the knife he used to cut the thatch. It wasn't there.

Moving slowly, Dato put his hands in his pockets and shrugged with exaggerated calm, focusing on keeping all physical messages ones of serenity and openness. He couldn't let Priest get away, and the man could see through deception. "You're right. I'm not John Smith. Not really."

"Why are you here?" Priest asked, taking a step forward, fists clenched. "Do you mean to cause us harm?"

Dato shook his head definitively. "No. I've come to check on things."

There were whoops and shouts behind him. Dato and Priest turned toward the noise. Two young men stood on a crossbeam, scuttling across it back and forth without effort or fear, hands and bare feet grabbing the wood with such surety their movements looked more insect-like than human.

Dato swallowed uncomfortably. It was disconcerting, seeing humans move like that, doing things he knew they shouldn't be able to do. He turned back to Priest, who watched for a moment longer with dead eyes as the men danced and laughed on the wooden beam. Then he turned a pleading gaze on the temporal agent.

"And..." he asked in a choked voice, "is everything going as it should, Master Smith?"

Dato shook his head slowly and sadly. "It isn't, Master Priest, but you and I are the only ones who think so. I'm willing to bet, were I to ask, you'd claim that what those men are doing is completely normal and always has been. Isn't that so?"

Priest brought a hand up to his mouth to stifle a sound. Dato couldn't tell if it was a sob or a scream, but it confirmed his suspicions. He stepped close enough to the man to put a gentle hand on his shoulder. "Come," he urged in a whisper, "let's take a walk. I need information and you look like you need a moment away from the settlement. What do you say?"

Priest nodded.

"All right then," Dato said, modulating his voice to sound reassuring. "Let's head into the woods over here." He indicated the woods to the right of the settlement. "We'll find a quiet place and see what we can figure out."

They walked in silence; the only sound that of the snow crunching underfoot. About ten minutes into their trek, Dato pointed to a downed tree partially cleared of snow and indicated to Priest they should head toward it. Soon both men sat on the horizontal trunk, surrounded by bare trees and snow.

"This all started after Standish and his men recovered from their fevers, didn't it?" Dato asked, not bothering with social pleasantries. It was a risky strategy, he knew, but the more he saw, the bigger the problem seemed to get.

Priest struggled for a moment, fighting with himself over how to respond. He looked at Dato in desperation. After a painful silence, the man nodded his head yes.

"I can break the compulsion you're under," Dato said.

"How do I know you can help me?" Priest asked, fear creeping into his face. "Why would you want to?"

"Because something is very wrong and I have to fix it. If you continue to fight this mental impulse to see the abnormal as normal, you'll be dead of an apoplexy in under a week. The cognitive dissonance you're experiencing is extreme. If I break the compulsion, I can find the source of the abnormality."

"What is a mental impulse....or cognitive dissonance?" Priest shook his head. "I don't understand why I came with you. You don't know me. We've only just met. What you say doesn't make any sense."

Dato closed his eyes and spent a moment culling the bio-circuits for what he knew about the man sitting next to him.

"You are Degory Priest, forty one years old," he said, his eyes still closed. "You were born in Devonshire, moved to London and became a hatter. You moved to Leiden with the other Dissenters. You married in 1611. Your wife: Sarah, and children: Marah and Sarah, are still in Leiden, since you didn't want them to risk the voyage here as you did. You had a bad cough before Standish's fateful return to the *Mayflower*, probably from going from the land to the ship and back in the shallop. And, though you've not been capering on crossbeams or using your teeth to rip out the throats of the local wildlife, you've noticed something is different about yourself, and you're worried what other changes are ahead." Dato opened his eyes. "I do know about you, Master Priest. I can help you if you allow it."

Priest swallowed, trembling. "How do you know these things about me?"

Agent Dato shrugged slightly. "It's my job." He put a gentle hand on the man's shoulder. "Surely you sense I speak the truth?"

"I do," he agreed. Priest wrapped his arms around his body. "I don't know why, but I do." He turned tormented eyes on the temporal agent. "I need help," he whispered.

"I can break the conditioning they subjected you to," Dato explained. "They did something to your thoughts. I can correct it."

"Tis witchcraft," Degory protested, shrinking away. "Your knowledge of my life, your offer to change my thinking.......such conjuring is the work of the Devil."

"No," Dato said, his voice and body utterly still. "I know you believe in such things, but I am not an agent of the being you call the Devil."

Priest's aspect became one of frightened despair. "Why do I trust you?" he asked in a croaking whisper. "You're not from here. You're different."

Dato looked at Degory for a long moment. He took a deep breath in and let it out slowly.

"Because," he began in a low, gentle voice, "as normal and commonplace as the voice in your head screams the way you live must be... a part of you recoils from it. You ask yourself if these are God's gifts, why do they trouble you so much?" Dato leaned over and looked the man in the eyes, hoping what he was about to say was correct. "You can't do what the others do, but you don't know why. What's worse, you worry what'll happen when you *can* do what they do. You're the only one among the settlers who wonders if something is wrong." He sighed. The agent stood up and considered the landscape he stood in. He looked at the human beside him.

Degory looked at Agent Dato, relieved. "I'm not mad, then? Something truly is wrong?"

Dato nodded.   "Yes. I've a suspicion as to the cause of the settlers' new abilities, but I need more information. You can help me, if you're willing."

Degory barked out a short laugh.   "You're not from Jamestown," he said.

Dato smiled slightly. "No."

"This will not end well."

Dato swallowed, feeling a slight chill pass down his spine. Degory, obviously a 'time sensitive', spoke more truly than he knew, and Dato was limited in what he could say. "Not right away, no... but in the end, yes.   That's the truth."

"If I do nothing, when my family comes here, they'll be in danger. Isn't that right?"

"Yes," Dato said, his tone definitive.

Degory looked at the woods around them.   "I want my wife and children safe, Master Smith.   If I help you, can you guarantee me that?"

Dato looked at his hands for a long moment, reviewing what he knew of the *Mayflower* passengers and their descendants. "Yes, I can guarantee your wife and children will live long, productive, safe lives."

"Work your magic, Master Smith," Priest said, covering his face with shaking hands, "and may God have mercy on my soul."

Dato pulled out his pouch of tools, and selected the two components that allowed the agent to see into the human male's mind, now calibrated to accommodate Dato's current human form. He placed the silver disk in the middle of his own forehead and handed the other to Priest, indicating the man should put it on his own forehead. Priest pushed up his knitted cap and did so. Dato closed his eyes and activated the devices, hearing Priest's gasp of surprise as a distant sound as he felt panic and terror bloom in the human's thoughts. Dato quickly enveloped Priest's mind and stilled the man's thoughts, detecting the block some other entity had applied to the human's fragile mind.

Dato lowered the pitch of his voice to resonate with the psychic field the device created between them. "They cannot hurt you here, Degory Priest. Remember. Remember it all."

Degory shook his head.

Dato projected his mind into Priest's, pushing against the block, but knowing his strength wasn't enough. He needed Priest's help. He didn't like what he needed to do next, but he had to draw on Priest's inner strength as a father.

"What did they do to the *Mayflower* children, Degory?" Dato asked.

"No," Degory whispered, horror in his voice.

"Can you imagine what they'll do to your daughters when they get here?"

Dato felt the play of emotions across Degory's mind. Horror turned to surprise, which became terror, fury, and finally the mental block crumbled with a burst of emotional agony even Dato felt. The agent reeled and managed to sit down on the tree trunk next to the human. His hand shaking, he took the silver disk off his forehead, ending the connection.

"They said they were angels," Degory said in a clear, strong voice, tears streaming down his face. He took off his own disk and handed it to the agent. Dato took it and moved to put both disks back in the pouch and put the pouch away. Priest clenched his fists. "They healed our sickness and claimed to be agents of God." Degory fumbled at his leather vest, undoing the buttons. Once undone, he pulled the vest off and threw it to the ground. Dato watched, uncertain what to make of the man removing his clothes. Then he undid the buttons of the wool shirts next, pulled them loose from his trousers, tore them off his shoulders, and threw them down.

A thin band of brown, pulsing as if it were alive, ran around Degory's chest. Dato's eyebrows rose in surprise and he felt what he knew humans called the 'stomach' drop to somewhere around his knees. Though it was a new experience, it matched the dismay he felt. He knew what the brown band meant, and it made the temporal anomaly issue he'd come to correct a moot point.

"I don't know what this is," Priest said, pointing at it, "but it's at the center of what the false angels did to us."

Dato knew what it was. He swallowed hard and put his hands in his pockets, letting the wool cloak cover his body, though suddenly he was very, very cold. He'd just become one of those temporal agents who died on a mission – the respiration and biological function between now and then was just keeping the meat fresh. The knowledge of his own demise in such a barren, pointless place should have filled him with some emotion, he knew – fear, fury... something... but it didn't. It had been inevitable the moment he'd stepped out of the dimensional rift, and railing against it was a waste of energy. He was a dead man. Period.

Degory picked up his shirts and vest. "Standish and the others came back to the ship wild-eyed and fevered," he said. "Nothing they said made sense and they wouldn't be still." He started to put the clothes back on. "We managed to get them to lie down, and started to tend them. Mistress Standish removed her husband's shirt in hopes of cooling him down – he was terribly hot to the touch—and that's when she saw the brown band on his chest."

"By then the genetic changes had already started," Dato said, his voice flat. "The delirium and high fever are symptoms of DNA manipulation."

"I don't know what that means," Degory said, confused.

Dato forced his mind to work. "Did the angels show up after that? All white, with wings and heavenly music? Ambrosial smells, a feeling of safety, warmth and peace?"

"Yes. The false angels appeared in our midst like a lightning flash. At first we were sore afraid, but with a wave of a hand, the fear left us. The false angels called us to them and we went, willingly, into their arms. We went to a white place, and that was the place of pain and oblivion." Degory sat down next to Dato. "You know these creatures?" he asked.

"Pelascans," Dato said, knowing he shouldn't tell Priest anything but deciding regulations no longer mattered. "Genetic slavers. They come to planets like this, modify the inhabitants and then collect the results to sell on the galactic market. It seems they've developed time travel capabilities."

Priest stopped buttoning his shirt. "Slavers? You're saying the angels changed us and intend to sell us?"

Dato nodded. "Pelascans. Yes. I think they're on the *Mayflower.* I have to get there tonight."

"What happens tonight?" Degory asked.

"That band around your chest does many things, Degory," Dato said. "It monitors genetic changes, it maintains mental conditioning, and it's a teleport beacon. Once night falls and the settlers are asleep, the false angels – the Pelascans - will teleport you back to their base to check on your progress." He looked at his hands. "I think it's almost time for the harvest."

"Harvest? God preserve us. What must we do?" Priest asked.

Dato looked at the human, surprised. "We? We don't do anything. I have to stop them."

"I don't know what manner of man you are, Master Smith, but you cannot expect me to leave this matter to you. The others..." he paused, frowning, "are too far ...changed... to offer assistance. I will help you. Tell me what to do."

The temporal agent considered the human beside him. It was against regulations to use indigenous beings in such a mission, but Priest was right: Dato needed the help. He reached into his pocket and drew out his pouch again, mentally cataloging every rule he intended to break. "Let's get that genetic manipulator off your chest."

Degory looked down at himself. "Then what?"

"Then," Dato said, "I give you a device that will reset the chronal signature here, and when the Pelascans start the harvest....I take your place."

Getting the brown manipulator off Priest's chest was a messy business, but Dato managed it without damaging it or the human very much in the process, though he knew it had been painful for the human. He used his own wound healing device on Priest to close the incision. Then he hung the writhing brown cord on a handy tree branch while he mentally reconnected himself to Priest with the discs again.

"My thoughts need more fixing?" Priest asked, brow furrowed. He touched the disc in the middle of his forehead. "I feel much better."

Dato closed his eyes and centered his thoughts, priming the bio-circuits for data transfer. "I'm breaking the oath I took thousands of years from now," he said, "by implanting time-sensitive information into your mind. You need to understand more about the world than you currently do if we're to succeed in getting time back on track." He opened one eye. "Do I have your permission?"

Priest paled visibly, but nodded. Dato initiated the transfer. His mind exploded in pain. He heard Priest drop unconscious to the snow-covered ground beside him from the psychic shock and a moment later, Dato joined him in oblivion.

The temporal agent woke a short time later, cold to the core, shaken awake by Priest. Yellow light flickered nearby as twilight descended. "I'm conscious," Dato said, teeth chattering. He looked his equally frozen partner up and down, both of them still wearing the discs. "No psychosis?" he asked.

"No," Priest said. "Just a headache. I made a fire. Come get warm."

They stood silently by the fire for a while, warming up as the world around them darkened into full night. "You're going onto the *Mayflower* to kill the Pelascans," Priest finally said, "using the thing you removed from my chest as a disguise."

"Yes," Dato said. "Once I've destroyed their link to this place, you'll need to correct the temporal anomaly. You know how to do that now?"

"The information transfer was successful," Priest replied. "I've already retrieved the device from your pouch and calibrated the settings. That will set history on the proper path again... but you'll be dead. There'll be no record of what you do here. No one will remember you... not even me."

"Perhaps I will continue on in your Heaven as a guest of your God," Dato replied evenly.

"With an increase in knowledge comes an increase in sorrow," Priest said, his voice devoid of emotion. "Knowing what I do now... I don't think I believe in God anymore." He pulled the disc off his forehead and handed it to Dato, who took it, then removed his own disc and put them both away. "You'll die tonight, I'll activate the device, the calendar will reset... half of the settlement will die from the ague and I'll die in January from pneumonia. Then due to their fear of the natives, my fellow settlers will prop my corpse against a tree to guard against Indian attack. I'll never see my family again. I'll not even have a grave... and there's no Heaven to hope for."

"Once time is back into its proper place, you'll not remember any of this," Dato agreed, "but when you die as you should, you'll still believe in your God and have hope of His Heaven."

"Ignorance is bliss," Priest said with a sardonic chuckle. "Something to look forward to."

Together they applied the brown genetic manipulator to Dato's chest, which was a messy, painful business. They went back to New Plymouth in silence and Degory Priest hid as his fellow settlers and Dato disappeared into thin air. Priest waited until he saw the *Mayflower* explode with a bright ball of orange-yellow fire in the harbor, brightening the area like a short-lived mini-sun. He wiped the tears from his eyes and activated the device to repair the time anomaly, whispering his wife's name as he obliterated that version of himself from the Universe.

After that, the rest was history.

65.
The Mummy Mystery
Mark Hudson

They found the body of a caveman frozen,
in the Alps, minus the lieder hosen.
They brought the body to an Austrian morgue,
the creepy mummy looked like a cyborg.
As the scientists studied the corpse's insides,
they discovered the world's oldest homicide.
A stone arrow in his shoulder was found,
revealing why he had no burial underground.
They also found injuries to the man's brain,
as if a boulder had given him a migraine.
Blood on his clothes and weapon showed DNA,
from four other people, that somehow stayed.
This mummy sheds light on history,
some say it's the oldest murder mystery.
No one can understand the motive to kill
this man who left a corpse on a hill.
How was his body preserved over time?
Does this reveal man's addiction to crime?
The scientists can study the forensic clues,
but murder mysteries govern the news.
How can the human race as a unit,
take this earth, and slowly ruin it?
Have we made no progress whatsoever?
Has peace just become a hopeless endeavor?
The mummy died in the mountains, by an arrow,
and he left with but his soul, like a pharaoh.

66.
The Mummy's Tummy
The Mummy Mystery Part Two
Mark Hudson

The Mummy's tummy gave scientists a clue,
the iceman from the Italian Alps reveals.
The scientists learned some things rather new,
about stomach ulcers, our bodies conceal.
The ice age might've made the stomach flu
something that came before inventing the wheel.
The Italian scientists know what to do,
studying this frozen skeleton so real.
The scientists work as a competent crew
excited, the project gives them a feel.
From Mother Nature they took someone who
had a frozen body available to steal.
When you die frozen, your bodies preserved,
and one day in the future, you may be observed.

67.
The Mysterious Call
Cynthia Marie Joyner

The phone rings in the middle of the night. An indiscernible voice speaks. "There is a car waiting for you outside your house. Get inside. You don't want to miss this." Your spouse rolls over, eyes squinting and says, "Everything okay?" What happens next?

As I look around my bedroom it's difficult to see. I sit up on the edge of the bed slowly peering around at the shadows on the walls, cast by the light of the full moon. As I stand and walk to the window facing the front street, still groggy, I notice an older car's engine just barely humming as it creeps down the street. Slowly leaving the cul de sac. Again at this point, being half asleep, I'm not sure if I'm dreaming or awake. I am awake. In fact, I'm confused about the last few minutes. I decide to start the day a few hours early and brew a fresh pot of coffee. I walk downstairs, almost silently to not wake my husband. Trying not to stir the dog, my feet barely touch the floor as I approach the kitchen. Funny thing is the French doors in the kitchen are wide open, with the sheers blowing in the brisk breeze. As I approach the doors puzzled, Brownie, my one hundred pound chocolate lab, runs in from the yard and almost knocks me down. At this point my husband is coming down the stairs, turning every light on till he reaches me. As we lock eyes, the kitchen doors slam shut!

The darkness was now turning to daylight. Since a thorough search of the house and yard turned up nothing, I decide to start breakfast. But my husband Dan just grabs his coffee and heads off to the office. I'm going through the motions of a normal day, but just can't shake the feeling of the strange night before. The day went by quickly and not feeling rested, I decide to turn in early. So exhausted, I fell asleep immediately. But soon awakened by what I thought was the phone ringing. As I look down on the floor, the phone is laying there. I then hear that strange sound of an old car drifting down the street. As I get up out of bed, I notice that I'm wearing my slippers. Confused and startled I jump back into bed, grab my husband and while holding him tightly drift off to sleep.

The next day I can't shake the feeling of confusion. Deciding to destress I decide to spring clean and tackle the attic. I start with the old cedar chest my mom left me. Not realizing this will be the beginning of solving this mysterious puzzle. After hours of dusting and sorting through stacks of old photos and clothing, the sun was starting to set. Dan had come home and was coming up the attic steps. This was a welcome break. As I start to close the lid of the chest, I notice a faded, folded picture. Upon pulling it out of the hinge of the lid, I realize it's a picture of my baby brother Bernie. He looks about seventeen. This just took my breath away, having lost him tragically in a car accident ten years prior. As my eyes swell with tears, I look at Dan and with lips trembling, whisper, "this is my baby brother Bernie, my only brother." Dan lovingly wraps his strong arms around me as we head downstairs. Not very hungry, we both nibble at some Chinese takeout and decide to turn in early. Knowing that I want the perfect frame for my brother's picture, I decide to leave it on my bedside table.

Falling asleep wasn't difficult after the previous restless night and a hard day's work. I drift off to sleep staring at the faded photo of Bernie smiling warmly pointing off in the distance. What seemed like just minutes later I was awaken by the phone ringing. As I tried to get my eyes to focus and my thoughts to come together. I pick up the phone. "Hello." There's silence. Just as I am about to hang up, thinking okay, wrong number or some idiots playing games. I hear a male voice!

"Adele, it's me, Bernie!"

I was stunned! Bernie my brother, my only brother who had since passed, was on the other end of the phone. I was unable to speak! Through my quivering lips, he spoke again!

"There is a car waiting for you outside, get in it, you don't want to miss this."

I jumped out of bed! By this time, Dan had woken up. He was trying to grab hold of me, as I was running down the stairs and out the front door. Stopped at the edge of the yard waiting for me was an older model red sedan. As I approached the car, the windows that appeared fogged, seemed to slowly clear. I am frozen with excitement, confusion, and fear. I hear the driver side door opening. As I stood there literally unable to move, I was contemplating running to my husband and the safety of our home; or waiting for well, the unknown.

I closed my eyes, took a deep breath and looking straight ahead, walked to the car. As I stepped off of the curb, I looked up and to my astonishment; I was looking at my brother! I felt my legs turn to Jello. My heart was pounding! I couldn't breathe, let alone speak. He looked at me, smiled, and put his finger in front of his lips as if saying, "Don't speak."

I am now in complete shock! He walks me to the passenger side of the car, and I get into the car. Still shaking and crying, I look back at my husband standing in our yard as we drive off. Still unable to speak I sit completely still. We drive on through the night. I don't know at what point I was actually coherent enough to comprehend what was happening, but as we drove, I realized that with each bit of pavement under the tires was a place, a part, of my life.

First our humble red brick childhood home, our elementary and high school, our grandma's and our old friend's houses. All leading up to the quaint country chapel where we were baptized, went to Sunday service, the place where I was married, and sadly, where my brother's funeral service had taken place. At this point, Bernie stopped his car, stepped out and walked to my side and opened the door. Again, I am in shock! Almost pinching myself to see if

I'm awake or dreaming? He helps me out of the car.

We walk through the mist down the cobblestone walkway that runs along the side of the church. No words or even gestures are exchanged as we walk. We come to the end of the walkway. I look up and as if it's possible, again, I am just in a state of shock, as I look around and realize that we are standing in the small church cemetery. But that's not all! We are standing at my brother's headstone! Yes, he and I holding hands, side-by-side, looking at his gravesite.

Just as I thought that I may be able to muster up the strength to finally speak to my brother, Bernie let go of my hand. He steps back into the mist.   As I try to approach him, thinking there's no way that I will let him go. He puts his right hand up, as if he's motioning me to stop. He then smiles so incredibly warmly and almost whispering, yet with a strong tone to his voice, says, "Adele, you are going to get the greatest gift of all!

At that exact moment, I opened my eyes to realize that I was at home in my bed, next to my husband! I jumped up to look outside for Bernie, his car, something! Just then my husband turns over in bed, hugs me and hits the button on the alarm to turn it off. I'm again in shock! Was it all a dream? Was it real? I sat on the edge of the bed, confused, sad, melancholy and missing Bernie. I didn't bring it up to my husband, because of the emotionally overwhelming, heavy-hearted feeling that I was experiencing. I chose to keep the experience locked in my heart, hoping that at some point, I would be able to make sense of it.

Several months pass without incident. No strange nightly calls, no odd dreams. Even the melancholy feeling that I was carrying around had faded. I still, every day missed my brother. But decided to keep my experience to myself. To consider the visit, or whatever it actually was, as the "Gift." I have to admit, I went to bed every night wondering if that phone would ring, that car would be waiting out front, would I again travel down memory lane and most of all, I wondered if I would have that chance to see my brother again. I kept holding on to the fact that even if it was a dream what a dream, what a gift!

Dan and I had been through a lot of ups and downs in our marriage. We both desperately wanted children. We weren't lacking anything in our relationship, in fact things were so good, and we were so in tune with each other, that it just seemed natural and right to share the Blessing of a child. We discussed, planned and dreamed of the day that we would bring a child into the world and complete our family. We even bought our home because it just seemed perfect to raise a family. It being an adorable two story cottage that has white siding, yellow shutters, a white picket fence, a huge fenced in yard and pretty flower boxes under every window. Not to mention the tree-lined cobblestone street with a park across the street. But not for lack of dreaming and trying, it just never seemed to happen.

As time passed by, Dan and I focused on building our business and even talked about turning our spare bedroom into a home office. We were enjoying our life together. We loved each other and seemed to have everything. But just like the empty place in my heart for my brother I longed to have a baby with Dan, It just didn't seem possible.

We finally just put that dream on the back burner. We just accepted the defeat of the dream. We worked, traveled and lived our life. That is until the moment that the phone rang, and I answered, "Hello." This time, it was in the light of day, and I was wide awake. The dream come true was my doctor calling to give me the news that I was pregnant. With this news, I felt my eyes fill with tears, and I trembled with heart filled exhilaration. I dropped the phone, grabbed my husband looked him in his eyes while also looking at my brothers picture. I softly whispered to my husband, "we are going to get the greatest gift of all."

Nine months later, on December fourteenth, my brother's birthday., Our son was born! Truly our greatest gift of all.

68.
The Mystery Creature
Mark Hudson

One day sitting in my writing group,
run by a therapist we discussed goop.
Kim noticed, "Outside these doors,
are some creatures roaming on all fours.
I see footprints and giant droppings,
around the grounds they must be hopping."
She thought it was a sign of Revelation,
I thought it meant, "Take your medication."
The therapist was equally perplexed,
he wondered if the grounds were hexed.
He said to me, "You own a guinea pig.
Could you figure out these droppings so big?"
So out I went to be the detective they wanted,
but there was no evidence the area was haunted.
The footprints were just probably rabbit's feet,
the therapist is the one we need to treat.
Perhaps he needs a brief stay in the hospital,
we should get him in as soon as possible.
After being around all of us crazies,
he sees what we see in the daisies.

69.
Panorama –
The Night Owl Superhero
Jon Moray

"Where do we set up camp?" asked Conrad, the eager college grad that just earned a BS in Wildlife Science.

"Just a few hundred yards more. My dad and I used to come here when I was a kid," answered David, Conrad's best friend in college.

"You said that a hundred yards ago. My feet are aching," complained Ralph, the less than enthusiastic of the three, bringing up the rear.

The trio had just graduated college together and decided to celebrate on a get-away-from-it-all camping trip in the woods and enjoy or brave the mysteries of the wild. Conrad and David knew they would have to do most of the grunt work since Ralph, the city boy, was clueless on outdoor survival. The Rambo movies were the extent of his exposure on how to survive without the basic necessities.

Nightfall cast an ebony sky surrounding a full off-white moon as they began to build their tents. Ralph was leery of the darkness and hastily pitched his tent improperly despite the ample glow of his bright lantern that sat on the leaf lined terrain. They finally settled in amid the smell of rotting wood and were huddled around a crackling fire when they heard ear ringing howls off in the distance. The truck was parked a mile west in the wooded parking area, so as the bays loomed louder, the city boy found refuge in his tent.

"C'mon out Ralph. It won't bother us as long as this fire is burning," called Conrad. The howls turned into growls and not just by one animal. Conrad yielded his rifle, and as he spun around toward the direction of the cries, a Gray alpha wolf leaped on him and forced him to the ground. Ralph emerged from the tent and his initial "oh my God" reaction had him racing like a thoroughbred towards the truck. David went for his rifle but was intercepted by a foaming-at-the-mouth wolf zoning in on its newly discovered five-foot-ten, one-hundred and seventy-pound prey. David's only defense was to make a run for it, and he took no time putting that plan into motion.

Conrad, bloodied and scraped, managed to kick the attacking grizzled Gray wolf off of him only to be met by two others biting at his limbs. The pack of five wolves surrounded him while his rifle lay out of reach. The sharp bites and the gradual loss of blood caused him to lose consciousness. The feeding frenzy was on when from the trees emerged a half dozen Great Horned owls, surprisingly to the rescue. The yellow-orange eyed night birds swooped down displaying an array of high-pitched shrieks and violently clawed at the wolves' heads. The inability to fend off the tuft feathered saviors sent the pack scattering. Conrad was only moments away from certain death until six unlikely heroes intervened.

The reddish-brown owls managed to lift Conrad off the ground by clutching each limb and parts of clothing in their talons. They carried him to the center of a huge deciduous pine tree with branches that spanned out horizontally, leaving a comfortable pad for Conrad to rest. They ministered to him using fluids that seeped from their beaks serving as an ointment for the open wounds. One of the owls clawed into its fur and then inserted it into the open cut under Conrad's left cheekbone, sealing the puncture. The poking and the fluid transfer continued for about twenty minutes until he regained consciousness.

Conrad instantly sat up only to be surprised by the six owls curiously peering down at him. His startled body spasm convinced the strigiform birds to stay a safe distance away. The owls took a watch on high branches as Conrad adjusted to his surroundings. As he became fully cognizant, he noticed a sudden dramatic improvement to his vision. He turned and witnessed crawling critters that could only be seen by a magnifier with the aid of lumens. His quick head turn rotated almost one hundred eighty degrees to his piqued jaw-dropping interest.

He was now bewildered with wonder as he adapted to his new bird-like properties. One of the owls hooted at him, and to his amazement, he understood it as an explanation for his transformation. Conrad tried to shake off the mind-bending reality only to battle the owls continuing communication to him. His attention now turned to getting out of the tree, and as he was attempting the climb down, the parliament of owls clutched his arms and flew him upward, about forty feet above the ground. They began to soar higher when suddenly, the owls released their clutches and left Conrad to fight gravity alone. He was falling at a rapid pace when his new instincts made him flail his arms as if they were wings. Feet away from grave impact, he began to slowly float upward through the arms of whistling outstretched branches. His shock soon turned to confidence as he glided effortlessly toward the night clouds. The owls joined him in celebration of his aerial discovery. As he continued his flight, Conrad noticed the pack of wolves attacking the jeep with his friends trapped inside.

Swooping onto the scene, Conrad zeroed in with aggressive animal bravado. The life-saving owls hung back to witness whether Conrad could handle the task on his own. Conrad didn't disappoint as one-by-one he grabbed each rabid wolf by the nape and hurled them like boomerangs into surrounding trees, rendering bone cracking sounds. Not wanting any further confrontation with the man turned super owl, the wolves hobbled away, disturbing the fallen pine needles and dead branches in their path. When all was safe, his friends exited the vehicle in awe of Conrad's supernatural power.

The father owl squawked off a final message and Conrad understood it as a warning not to display his powers for selfish exhibition. Conrad nodded thankfully as the owls flew off into the black wilderness.

"What was that all about and what the hell happened to you? Did I see you flying to the rescue?" asked David, demanding a plausible explanation.

"You're not going to believe this, but those owls rescued me and injected me with fluids from their bodies that enabled me to inherit their attributes," Conrad explained as he turned his head slowly one hundred seventy nine degrees to illustrate his point.

"Wow, how did you do that? I mean, you really are doing things an owl would do. This is too fantastic. Right out of a comic book," said Ralph, shaking his head in disbelief.

"Well, he always was into the comic books. Instead of Spiderman, he can become Owlman," added David.

Conrad looked at the moon as he massaged his chin in thought. "How about Panorama - The Night Owl Superhero?" he asked, with his hand slowly waving at the air as if he were reading the name off an intermittingly lit movie marquee.

70.
The Old House
Lisa M. Scuderi-Burkimsher

Dared by his friends, Matthew entered the old, nineteenth-century abandoned house. Cobwebs hung from the ceilings, with spiders awaiting their prey. The eerie silence, other than the creaking floorboards beneath his feet, gave Matthew chills down the nape of his neck. Nervous, he still continued. It was daylight, but the old, dark, heavy curtains, made it bleak, and dust filled the air, tickling his nose. He could hear Charlie, and Johnny chortling outside. Having just moved into town with his parents, and no siblings to look after him, Matthew was the outsider of the group. He wanted to make as many friends as possible, so he agreed to the dare.

"Any ghosts in there?" Charlie yelled through a broken window, startling Matthew into bumping a table with his knee. "You still have to go upstairs," Johnny told Matthew as he squeezed through the open space, pushing Charlie aside.

"I'm getting there, but it'll be a lot quicker if you two shut up." He used his flashlight, and walked up the wooden steps slowly, afraid if he went too quickly, they would break.

He ventured into one of the bedrooms. The floor was covered with dirt, and the furniture was thick with dust. The bed had no sheets, and consisted of just the wooden frame. Out of curiosity, he opened one of the dresser drawers. Inside, he found an antique pocket-watch, probably worth a fortune. He put it in his back jeans pocket, closed the drawer, and went back downstairs.

"Okay, I went in, and it's nothing more than an old house. Can we go get something to eat now, I'm starving," said Matthew.

"Okay, you made it into our circle of friends. Great job, Matthew. I didn't think you'd be able to do it. Let's go, I'm hungry too," said Charlie waving Johnny over to get a move on.

On the walk home, Matthew had a weight bearing down on him. It wasn't the watch, it was guilt. He decided he would show the watch to his father, and ask him what to do.

"Where's Mom," asked Matthew as he closed the front door behind him.

"She went to the store to pick up a few things," answered his father, Joe, thumbing through the newspaper.

"Dad, I have to show you something." Matthew pulled out the pocket-watch.

"Where did you get that," asked Joe, as he grabbed it from his son's hand.

"I found it in an old house nearby. Charlie, and Johnny dared me to go inside. I wanted to show them I wasn't scared, so I went in and found this in a drawer. I took it, dad. I thought I could pawn it for money. I'm sorry. I wasn't thinking, that's why I came to you."

"Wait here." Joe, ran upstairs, leaving a breeze in his absence. When he returned, he held an old photo album. The pages were stuck together, and falling apart. "Look at this picture of your Great-Uncle, Michael Carter. He's holding that same pocket-watch."

Matthew, wide-eyed, couldn't believe it. "Are you sure?"

"Look at the initials in the photograph, and on the watch. It has the same engraved initials as your great-uncle's name. It's his watch! My father told me he lived not far from here and owned a house back in the nineteenth-century. I had no idea it still stood after all these years. I haven't had time to investigate our family that lived here. Now I'll make the time. We need to keep this. It's a family heirloom. I'm glad you made the right decision, Matthew. You know you can always come to me no matter what. Friends are important to you, I know, but doing the right thing is even more important." He patted Matthew's shoulder and smiled. "Tomorrow, take me to the house."

The next morning at the old house, Matthew showed Joe where he found the watch.

"That's very strange. All that was in here was the pocket-watch, Matthew?"

"Yeah, nothing else. It was right there in that drawer."

"Well, the house isn't anything to look at. It's been empty for years, and decrepit. I wouldn't be surprised if I find out it'll be torn down, and the land sold. Let's get going."

"I'll meet you outside. I think I left my cell phone on the dresser." Matthew hurried and retrieved his cell phone. As he was about to walk out, he felt a sudden chill throughout his body. He turned, and a foggy silhouette floated through the ceiling into the unknown. If it was his Great-Uncle, Michael Carter, he hoped he was moving on, knowing the watch was where it was supposed to be, with his descendants of the Carter family.

71.
The Sensation of Flight
Matt McGee

The dreams started right after Robert and his wife moved into the new house off Mulholland Highway. It wasn't much of a house, more of a ranch stuck into the side of a mountain. The previous owner had put up a wood post entry gate; two poles pointed skyward and a weathered sign stretched across the top: 'Bar R Ranch.' Robert took this as a sign, literally, that they'd found their perfect retirement spot. Overlooking his former home at the LA film studios, he felt that he'd out-lived the game, ascended, that somehow he'd won.

The dreams always involved planes. He'd be on a peak, enjoying a breeze and a little sun when silently, out of a cloudless sky a plane would swoop straight into him. The planes never crashed; they'd just sweep through like a shark inhaling a meal and fly off.

He never saw them coming. He'd be gazing at the blue sky then BAM – a nosepiece straight to the ribcage. He wasn't afraid of flying. He loved travel and didn't have a fear of heights. He just, for some reason, kept getting hit by planes.

"I don't get it."

Robert turned toward his wife, Helene. She'd been gardening while he lay plopped in a lounge chair, the LA Times shading his eyes. He'd been digesting an article about aviators from the Second World War; they had higher incidents of vertigo than any other group.

"What don't you get?"
Helene had been kneeling in the soil. She leaned back on her haunches, butt against her ankles and surveyed the little plot she'd been tending for weeks.

"Everything I plant just withers. I don't get it. I'm not over-watering. The soil seems perfect. I put in a little mulch. Not too much of course. And the soil doesn't seem hot."

"Maybe it's the elevation," Robert guessed.

"Up here on Oat Mountain? Not likely. It's only," Helene rolled her eyes, "three thousand feet?"

"Almost four," Robert noted. "Pretty high for LA. Those plants," Robert pointed, "were probably raised in a nursery at sea level in Agoura Hills." Far off in the haze, the bustling suburb of tidy homes and manicured lawns served almost ninety thousand people. The nursery was a box store on the left.

Helene surveyed her withering perennials. "Maybe you're right. I guess the poor guys could be starved for oxygen."

Robert nodded. He loved being right. He went back to his paper.

"But if it's so bad why are we still breathing?"

Robert folded to the last page. "Plants and humans aren't the same. We can adapt." Robert set the finished paper down. "Well," he added, "most of us."

That night Robert was hit by a B-17 Flying Fortress. He shocked awake, still seeing the wide-eyed fury of the nose gunner's eyes. Shooting up in bed hurt more than being kamikazed by the Allies. Robert reached for his aching back and rubbed his thumbs where he'd pulled something.

Helene didn't open her eyes. "What's wrong?"

"Spasm or something."

"Getting old is terrible."

He flopped back down, his pillow still hot with the heat of disturbed sleep. He flipped it over.

"You ever have a recurring dream?"

"Like nightmares?"

Robert wasn't ready to admit that. "Whatever. Just some dream. You know, same place, same thing again and again only slightly different. Like you dream about, I don't know, riding a bike off a cliff. But it's never the same bike. Different bike, different cliff."

"You're dreaming about bikes?"

"No. I'm just saying, it's..."

He quit. He got out of bed. The first rays were already brightening the Southern California sky.

Helene patted his side of the mattress. "Come back to bed. I promise to protect you from bikes and cliffs."

Robert considered it. Then he shuffled toward the bathroom. "Almost morning. Might as well get on with doing something."

"What can you do this time of morning?"
Robert stretched. He didn't pull anything this time. "We're retired. Aren't we supposed to be racing other couples to Denny's, staking out our favorite booth, getting all worked up about Early Bird specials?"

Helene turned over. "Well if you go, bring me breakfast. Two sunny side up."

He smiled and mumbled 'I'll give you two, sunny side up.' But her eyes were closed and mouth slightly agape. A light snoring soon resumed.

Robert moved toward the shower.

Being fifty-two came with its problems but for Robert, narcolepsy was climbing the list. He showered, pulled on a spandex bike outfit and headed toward the garage. The movers must have left the bicycle somewhere in the back. He sat to survey the heap.

The plane he dreamt of was gray and covered in graffiti, dull and grainy as a ledge of the L.A. River. It must have been a glider the way it swooped in soundlessly from the blue. He'd just started to turn around when bam, there it was, like he'd never existed. This time, the pilot was a girl in a fashionable aviator's jacket. Not the real kind, but something turned out by Rodeo Drive.

Robert shocked awake. He was still in the garage, sitting on a dusty dining room chair. Helene had discarded the set four years earlier. Robert had suggested they give them to the studio's prop department, or, at least, a local black-box theatre. They always needed furniture.

Robert pushed himself up. How long had he been out? Couldn't have been more than twenty minutes. After years of sixteen hour work days, he was just profoundly tired. He wiped the sleep from his freshly showered eyes and scanned the clutter.

Unlike his contemporaries, Robert's knees were in great shape. 'In the long run, it pays to have a career with your ass behind a desk twelve hours a day,' he'd say. 'All you have to worry about is prostate cancer. And by the time that strikes you've used those parts about as much as you're going to.'

A pair of handlebars poked out from the back of the heap. Robert waded thru the clutter and pulled out the ten speed. He checked the tire pressure. He added a little with a hand pump. He tested the brakes. Then he rolled into the sunshine.

He typed a code into the security pad and watched the door close behind him. What do we need security from up here? All the demons we're hiding from are inside us.

Gravity pulled him down the driveway. Coasting was the closest he could feel to the sensation of flight; the bike whizzed beneath him, a narrow helmet and thin spandex layer the only thing between him and a severe case of road rash. Feeling the speed and wind, Robert closed his eyes. The nose of a B-29 was there. He popped them back open.

At the end of the long driveway, the security gate was still wide open. He and Helene hadn't figured out the code. He glided onto Stunt Road. It was a short climb to the peak; he hadn't been up the hill yet but, sure he could pull it off, he pumped his feet into the pedals. The crank was a good one; the guy in Agoura Hills who'd built the bike had raced the Tour de France.

A car whooshed by, a faded import of some sort. Robert thought to grab hold of the bumper and let himself be towed up the hill. It can't be that much further. When a light stabbing grew in his chest Robert hopped off; he'd push the bike the final six hundred feet. No shame there. No one up here to see, anyway.

At the top of Stunt Road, a bright red stop sign is poked into the crumbling hillside, the way a toothpick leans in a Monte Cristo sandwich. The thought just made him hungry. He focused on the last hundred feet of road as an ocean-scented breeze blew across his forehead, the kind that would cool the open cockpit of an old bi-plane. Up here, much of the Pacific was visible and Catalina Island was in sight. Robert rested beside the stop sign; to his right was a slight uphill and to the left, a gradual curve that drifted downhill and disappeared out of sight. He heard a woman's voice to the left. Robert coasted that direction.

A young couple with a tourist-style look stood beside a long, wood-framed map of the mountains. The young woman pointed at a red 'You Are Here' dot.

"Hey guys, what's up?"

Robert was met by curious glances and silence. He leaned his bike against the sign and walked over. The young man, about twenty, looked at the bike then back at Robert.

"Hey."

"Great view, huh? Wow!"

"Yeah. Did you ride a bike all the way up here?"

"Kinda," Robert panted.

"Why aren't you sweating?" the girl asked.

Robert felt his forehead. "Oh. Guess I never got much of a chance. I live right down the hill," he pointed. "At the Bar R Ranch."

"What's the 'R' stand for?"
The out-of-shape cyclist planted his hands on his hips and let his breath catch up. "Far as I'm concerned it stands for Robert. I'm Robert." He stuck out his hand for shaking.

The pair looked at each other.

Robert took his hand back. "What?" he asked.

Another breeze lifted from the Pacific. "Nothing. Just, we don't get a lot of bikers up here."

"Come up here a lot?" Robert's asked pleasantly.

The two didn't look at each other this time. The guy pulled out a cell phone. The girl turned away.

Robert wanted to smell his armpits. What the hell did I say? The couple turned and began walking up a narrow asphalt path cut into the side of the hill. Robert waited until they were out of sight; then he looked back at the bike leaned against the sign. If someone swiped it, well, it wasn't too far of a walk home. He was never going to be in the Tour de France, anyway.

The crumbling road the kids had climbed led to a small dirt trail, demarcated by a brown State Park plaque. He could hear the rustle of their footsteps on the trail. A head would pop over the brush and bob back out of sight again.

Okay, so he looked like a stalker. But Robert believed in signs and messengers. One afternoon during his years at Paramount he'd been reading a script about a group of old codgers who got together every Sunday to ride their motorcycles. He was thirty pages in, already imagining who he'd cast when a bike messenger knocked on his door; he signed the receipt, noting the Latino woman's faux-leather aviator jacket and the motorcycle insignias sewn into its sleeves.

He went right to the phone and optioned the motorcycle script. He even found the messenger girl and offered her a bit part. The studio never made good on his promise, as those things are often out of his hands. The film came out a year later, co-starring a former cast member of M*A*S*H*.

The movie flopped. Hard. It made up some ground as a TV Movie of the Week but the glittering promise of Robert's career never fully recovered. When he mentioned the 'sign' of the girl's jacket to Helene, she crunched a brow at him.

"Of course it was a sign," she said. "A sign to not do the picture. Those patches were fake, right?"

Now he was being led up a hill into who knows where by a couple kids who clearly loathed him. Or everybody. He couldn't tell.

He was getting closer to the sky. To his left, planes crisscrossed the Valley. He was almost on their level.

Wait. What the hell am I doing? On their level? Robert turned around quickly. Forget these stupid kids. I've gotta get back down. Fast. Then he stopped. He remembered the lesson Rick Moran had taught him as a budding studio exec:

Youth always knows. No matter what age a person may reach, a young mind will unknowingly point their elders the right way - if they listen. Robert turned and started climbing again.

Then it appeared. Over the top of the brush came a dull gray tower, rising like a dinosaur. Robert was like Richard Dreyfus in Close Encounters; he couldn't look away. A path led through a rusted chain link fence, torn by vandals. He spotted the kids climbing up a long, gray cement bunker.

The five-story tower stood atop the bunker, a mass of oddly shaped cones, squares, and one very large horn. Massive pipes twisted together with steel ladders and graffiti. The kids felt it with their hands, the cold steel of its spray paint coated ladders.

From atop the bunker, they watched as Robert scaled the sloped cement wall. The guy smiled; the girl nodded.

"Now you're working up a sweat," she called.

Robert kept climbing.

"Well, if he is with the government," said the guy, "he sure ain't trying very hard to chase us down."

Robert panted and clawed at the cement. His fingertips become raw. He was almost there.

"Government?" he said. "Is that what you thought? You thought I was some kinda narc?"

"Well, look at it from our perspective," the girl said. "We're just about to climb up to this abandoned missile base..."

Robert froze. "Missile base?"

The girl stood quietly. "Didn't you know?"

"No," he said, "I didn't."

The girl nodded. "We're about to climb up here and along comes this guy shows up who looks like some kinda government agent."

Robert stepped to the top of the cement bunker, puffing hard. He surveyed the view. "Not with the government. Movie exec. Retired. The only agents I've ever dealt with are thieves, representing actors and directors. They come to pick my pocket."

Robert tilted his head as far back as it would go. The tower was the queerest structure he'd ever seen. Forgetting the graffiti, the structure itself seemed to be some kind of old world fortress, its design long since replaced.

"It's like some kind of Spielberg thing." Robert caressed the tower with his eyes. "Did you say missile base? As in nuclear missiles?"

"Nike," the young guy started. "Decommissioned in the 80's. For a while LAX used it to direct air traffic."

"Giving signals to planes," Robert mumbled.

"After that, it was just a big make-out spot for a long time. People call it The Top of the World. You can see everything up here."

"People say it's haunted," the girl added.

Robert held in a laugh. "Haunted."

The girl pointed five stories into the sky. "Well, that's one of the legends. Some people call it The Tower of Lost Angels. It was like a Lovers Leap. There was this one girl I heard about, she was a bike messenger trying to make it in Hollywood..."

Robert wasn't listening anymore. His eyes were following a small Cessna turning in from the Pacific. He imagined someone leaping from the tower, maybe on acid, maybe just distressed from not realizing their dream, now just trying to get out of the way of an incoming plane.

"... she tried to land a good role and never, you know, whatever, so like a lot of people she came out here and tried to fly," the girl was still talking. She spread her arms, made a few maneuvers. "They'd jump from up there, have a moment of bliss, then..."

"...splat," the guy said.

Robert nodded. Splat. A breeze lifted the girl's hair. She slid her arms around her boyfriend.

"I've been having nightmares," Robert admitted. "I'm up really high. Usually on a hill. And a plane comes crashing into me. Every time."

"Same plane?" the guy asked.

Robert shook his head. "Always different. Last night it was a Flying Fortress."

"And this has been happening every night?" the girl asked, engaged.

"Every night."

She titled her head. "Did you say you'd just moved in?"

Robert nodded. "My wife is probably wondering where I am right now. Didn't exactly have pockets to bring a cell phone."

"Doesn't matter," the guy said, "they don't work up here no how. Don't ask me why," the kid said. "All the way up here on a former government site? The highest peak in the county, and we can't get reception? Ironic."

"This thing is right behind my house," Robert thought aloud.

"Every night?" the girl repeated.

"Huh? Oh, yeah. Every time I fall asleep."

"And always a plane crashing into you?"

"Yes."

The girl thought half a moment. "I don't mean to be rude, but..."

"Go ahead," Robert said. He clasped his hands behind his back, the official posture of the studio exec. To show one's hands was to, well, show one's hand. Robert lifted his chin as if expecting a blow.

"Did you have other ambitions?"

Robert wasn't sure. "Ambitions?"

"Like a vision. I mean, did you want to be something else other than a studio exec?"

"Well," Robert said somewhat absently, "there were those years in The Crotch."

"Oh man," the guy said, "I'm not sure I even wanna know what kind of movies you were making."

"No, no, not that. There's this place - down where the 101 and the 134 freeways come together. The Hollywood Freeway is jammed in too just for good measure. And beneath all these arteries is a square mile of cheap apartments. Every actor getting off the bus from Omaha falls into The Crotch. It's all they can afford. To the west is a pool of small theatres where they get their chops. And over to the east, Hollywood. Anyone who wants to make it usually ends up in that neighborhood."

The couple nodded.

"Some people never leave." Robert sighed. "I came out here with a really good script in my suitcase. Really good. But everyone knows you don't start at the top. I did crappy extra work, just getting used to sets. Didn't make any money."

"Maybe you didn't give it enough time."

"Eleven years. So I tried to be a director. I only went so high with that. So, I took my business degree and became part of the studio system. Worked my way up as far as I could go. But despite what they tell you, there's a glass ceiling for men, too."

"So you became part of the studio system."

"Yes. And I got to my peak. I wasn't the head of a studio but the view was pretty damn nice. The million dollar annual salary got to be a good way to live."

"Even though…" the girl stopped.

Robert dared her. "Even though…?"

"Even though you never got where you wanted to be? I mean, all those things. Did you hear yourself? 'Only so high.' There's 'a ceiling.' It 'never took off.'"

"Not following."

The girl swallowed. "This plane that keeps crashing into you. It's your fear of success." Robert didn't change his expression. He took a moment, then he turned around to leave.

"I didn't come up here to be psychoanalyzed."

He'd only taken a couple steps when the girl spoke up. "And yet here you are, right? Having climbed all that way, winded and sweaty, and that's good enough for you right?" She looked up at the tower. "You're not going all the way, are you."

"What the hell are you talking about? 'All the way?' You know I've only lived here three weeks but I do know that this is the highest peak in the Santa Monica Mountains. And we're on a bunker of some kind of old missile base that looks over everything? I'd say I've done pretty well."

"You failed."

"I'm sorry?"

The girl looked apologetic. "You failed. Not as an earner. Or an executive. I'm sure you made some wonderful films or shows."

Robert thought of the motorcycle movie. You can still find it on DVD. "Damn right I did."

"But you've failed that struggling actor. That director inside you. You never starred in a smash hit. You weren't celebrated at Cannes. So you settle for a million dollars, buy a house in the hills..."

Robert was quiet. Then his mouth slowly opened.

"Settle for a view of the clouds from the ground rather than the sensation of flight."
The young couple stood quietly. "That's pretty good," the girl said.

Robert looked at the ocean and the LA skyline on its left. "It's from the script I wrote."

"The one that never got done."

Robert nodded. There was a long moment when the wind filled everyone's ears.

"Well," the girl finally said. "Looks like it's time for you to leave."

Robert nodded. He started down the steep cement ledge. Ten feet away he looked back.

"When I finish the script and make the film," he pointed up at the five-story tower, "I'll come back and finish this."

"Invite us to the premier!" the girl smiled. The guy waved. Robert descended the bunker. He couldn't believe he was climbing a platform that had once been ready to launch nukes. He remembered those tense days and felt relieved to have outlived them. Back on land, Robert slid back thru the fence. The bike was waiting where he'd left it.

He pedaled onto the pavement and let gravity take him back to the Bar R. He wasn't sure the brakes could handle the downhill, and for a moment he felt himself gliding out of control, too fast, with only a thin helmet and thinner coat of spandex to protect him. He'd be alright. He was never more sure of it.

He'd coast past a bed of wilted flowers, dropping the bicycle wherever it landed. It simply didn't matter. Then he'd go in to tell his wife they were moving back to the city. In his script, he would add the character of a bike messenger. The right actress would show up.

They always did.

72.
The Shadowman
Vanessa Matheny

"In ground breaking news today, residents of Pleasantville Memorial Hospital's Psychiatric ward have mysteriously awakened. This puzzling phenomenon has everyone confused. The reason being is because for the past fifteen to twenty years these patients have been in a catatonic state. Now suddenly, they're all talking and walking around confused as to why they are in a psychiatric ward. This sudden awakening even has the doctors baffled. No one can pinpoint or explain the cause of the arising. Due to this recent development, all of the staff is no longer needed in the psychiatric ward. For many of these patients it has become a joyous reunion with their loved ones and for some they have woken to a tragic realization of great loss. Some would call this a singularity event while others are simply calling it heart wrenching. Please stay tuned for further details. This is Pamela Stone reporting. Stay tuned for your local weather."

I stood with my mouth hanging open as I watched the local news reporter spill the day's event. Pleasantville isn't exactly newsworthy town. In fact, the small town hasn't had any real "big stories" worth getting excited about since my father was a reporter over fifteen years ago. The population of 1,500 has lain dormant of any type of scandals; for a reporter, that can kill anyone's career faster than cancer.   Sure, I've gotten your occasional domestic violence cases, your small town burglaries, a handful of infidelities, and a few strange cases that ended up being pranks by a gang of teenagers called the Teenhood. But I have yet to capture the greatest story of my career.

While my eyes were glued to the TV, I tried to remind myself why I chose to stay in ole' boring, Pleasantville instead of taking a high-rolling reporting job in New York City. It wasn't until my boss snapped me out of my stupor that I was reminded of why I stayed.

"Hey, Aiden, you know that big break of a story you're always looking for...well there it is." My boss said gruffly as he pointed to the TV. "In fact, isn't that the facility your dad is in?"

My short term memory loss came flooding back as I realized that it was, in fact, the same ward my father was in. "Yeah."

"Then why are you still standing here? Don't you have some investigating to do? And oh, don't let anyone look down on you just because you're a short, curly haired geek."

"Right back at ya, Pillsbury Dough Boy!" I retaliated.

I grabbed my notepad and pencil, threw it in my bag and rushed over to Pleasantville Memorial. I wasn't quite sure what to expect. My father has been in a catatonic state for fifteen years unable to speak, walk or show any mobility. Even though the news report stated that all patients in the psychiatric ward are up and about, I was skeptical that my father was one of them.

I stepped off the elevator onto the psychiatric ward and right into a swarm of chaos. It was unusually packed with people aimlessly going in and out of various rooms. I headed straight for my father's room only to find it empty. His bed looked like it hadn't been slept in and a suitcase was lying open waiting for it to be filled. I emerged out into the traffic of nurses and wondering patients. I quickly made my way to the front desk and asked, "Excuse me, where might I find Frank Matthews?"

The nurse smiled and said, "Hi Aiden, your father is waiting for you in the activities room."

Dumbfounded, I questioned, "Waiting for me?"

Again the nurse plastered on a big smile, "Aiden, your father is awake and he's been asking for you."

I immediately made my way to the activities room and when I arrived, I saw my father frantically looking for me. When our eyes met a wave of emotion came crashing down on me. I had to swallow them down so as to not make a fool out of myself. The last thing I wanted was to be on the front page of the Franklin Times, where I work. "Breaking news, Aiden Matthews is crying uncontrollably like a baby and having a mental breakdown, a perfect place to have one."

My father rushed over and embraced me. I hadn't been in his arms in so long. It was so good to see him like this. It almost felt as if he had never gone away.

"Aiden, my son!"

It was exhilarating to know that my father recognized me. Just prior to him falling into the catatonic state, he lost his memory of who I was. He could barely remember who he was, where he was, and the day.

"Wow, Dad...I don't know what to say except I'm so glad you're better."

"Better, boy, I haven't felt this great in years. Where's your mother and your sister?"

I looked to the ground. I didn't want to have to be the bearer of bad news so quickly into our reunion.

"Is there something wrong, Aiden? Is your mother okay?"

Again, I choked down the emotions. "Um, Mom died about four years ago."

My dad ran his hand a crossed his forehead and down to his chin as pools of tears emerged. "How… how did she die?"

"…Of a heart attack."

"And your sister?"

"Ever since Mom died, Torey and I haven't exactly been on speaking terms. I don't know where she is."

My dad looked at me with red-filled eyes and hoarsely choked out, "I'm glad you're here." He pulled me into his arms again. My dad quickly pulled up a chair and sat, "Just how long have I been in that deep chronic state?"

"About fifteen years."

I could tell the news of everything hit him hard. His shoulders were bent and when I looked into his brown eyes, he looked lost. I didn't blame him for feeling unsettled with the news. The man did lose fifteen years of his life, no memory of anything, as if he had died. Any person in their right mind would feel overwhelmed in knowing they'd lost a big chunk of their life that they could never get back.

The reporter in me immediately went into action. I pulled out my notepad and pencil and asked, "So Dad, can you tell me what happened to you? Why you're awake after all these years?"

My dad leaned back in his chair and grinned, "A reporter hey? Just like your ole' man."

I grinned and said proudly, "Yeah and I feel this story could be the one."

My father returned the smile and said, "The one "eh", the one that every reporter searches for in hopes one day becomes "the one."

I smirked and continued, "Can you tell me if there was anything unusual when you woke up?"

My father leaned forward and placed his hand on my knee and said, "Son, I think it's time to go home. I've been in here long enough. I'll answer all your questions at home." He slapped my knee and stood.

As we were heading toward the doors a Nurse was nearby, "Excuse me, Nurse Betty, can you tell me anything about today's events? Do you think it was a change in the medication the doctor's gave the patients?"

My father chuckled and informed, "I'll go pack while you interrogate."

"Um…" Nurse Betty began as she eyed her patients wandering around waiting for their family members. She placed her hand over her mouth as she was overwhelmed at the sight.

I pulled her over to a more private area and helped her sit, "How about we start from the beginning. Give me all the details. Don't leave anything out."

"Well, the day started out just like any other day. I filled my cart with my patients' medications and was just about to go into Henry's room when I saw him get out of bed. I thought I was going to pass out from fright. That man hasn't moved in over eighteen years. I've had to do physical therapy with him every day so his muscles wouldn't deteriorate so fast. And then… one by one, patients were coming out of their rooms. It was as if the dead had awakened."

"Aha, now did you see anything unusual prior to the people waking up?"

Nurse Betty shifted her eyes to think, "Now that you've mentioned it, I did see a shadow run across the hallway and then I saw a woman who quickly fled toward the elevators."

I sat up straighter. A witness, that's great.

"Can you describe this woman to me?"

"It all happened so fast. I think I saw a flash of blonde hair maybe. That's all I can remember."

"That's okay Nurse Betty, you've been very helpful. Just one more question, did the doctors give the patients any new type of drugs within the past few days, weeks perhaps?"

"If you ask me, I think it was aliens. They've infiltrated our people, like invasions of the body snatchers." Lionel, a paranoid neighbor of mine, said in my face.

I rolled my eyes, "Lionel, really?"

"Maybe we shouldn't close down the psychiatric ward just yet." Nurse Betty said jokingly.

"Yeah, you might want to rethink that."

Nurse Betty leaned in and whispered, "About the medication, I would normally get fired for telling anyone this, but since I no longer have a job anyways… the medication I am supposed to give the patients every day are nothing but vitamins. Now that's a story worth writing about. Doctor's charging family members big bucks for "vitamins." Here these poor family members are thinking that their loved one is being given a revolutionary drug to help them live and one day recover from this catatonic state, but in reality, the doctors are making a fortune off these poor families."

I raised an eyebrow, "Oh really." I quickly scribbled that juicy bit of information down.

My father returned to my side and asked, "Are we ready to blow this Popsicle stand? No offense, Nurse Betty. You've been a great Nurse, I think."

She gave my dad a slight kiss on the cheek and said, "You've been a great patient, Frank. Stay out of trouble."

"Will do."

****

It was painful to see my father walking around our house as if he was in a stranger's home. We casually sat down on the couch. "Dad, I really want to know why you are awake after all these years, don't you?"

"Not really, son. I'm just glad to be awake."

"Can you tell me just how it happened to you? What took place at that moment?"

"It's hard to say really. It was like someone had pulled up the shades and it was bright again. I could see, I could feel and I could move. And my memory of who I was came rushing in like a tidal wave."

"Did you see or experience anything unusual before or after you woke up?"

My father beamed as he looked at me, "It wasn't what I saw but more of what I felt."

"And what did you feel?"

"It felt as if someone was pouring warm oil over my head all the way down my feet."

"Did you happen to see a shadow perhaps or maybe a blonde haired woman?"

My father took a few moments before he answered, "I did sense someone was there but I couldn't make them out."

I felt like I was getting nowhere. I thought I would have more success if I went back to the hospital and talked to more of the patients and doctors. But I knew that had to wait until morning.

****

I wrestled with sleep and I had won, by not sleeping a wink. Too many thoughts and questions rolled around in my head. Even though I was happy my father was awake and back to his old self again, I wanted to get to the bottom of why suddenly everyone on that ward woke up. I was bound and determined to crack this story wide open and have it eloquently served on a silver platter to my boss.

****

I spent all morning questioning the staff and a few of the patients who were still waiting for their family members to pick them up. It was a total bust. They all said the same thing. They saw a shadow and possibly a blonde woman fleeing the scene.

My cell phone rang, "Yeah."

"I don't know what's going on but this town has gone completely nuts!" My boss said as he was trying to catch his breath.

"What do you mean?"

"Within the last three hours I've received ten anonymous tips on various events that have taken place. Either everyone has gone mad or bizarre aliens have taken over our town."

"Really Ted, not you too, you know that aliens don't exist."

"Okay then explain how a two-year-old drowned in a pool, EMT personnel did everything they could, covered up the child and placed him in the back of the ambulance, and five minutes later the child sit's up and asked to go play... in the pool no less. I'm going to need you to come to the office and get these files. I wonder if these cases are linked to the awakenings."

My heart thumped wildly as I was elated to finally be busy with a real investigative story. I wanted to be the one to put Pleasantville back on the map and make the Franklin Times big again. I just needed my Mojo.

I ran into Mel's diner to get a cup of coffee before I headed to the paper. As I was waiting for my coffee, I noticed a beautiful piece of origami sitting on top of a receipt. I picked it up and asked Helen, the waitress, "Do you know who left this?"

"No, it was some blonde-haired woman who I haven't seen around here, and I didn't catch her name."

I looked around the diner.

"She left a little bit ago."

There was only one person I knew who could take money and turn it into a beautiful piece of origami, but it can't be, Libby's dead.

I took my coffee to go and headed straight to the paper. "Whatcha ya got for me, Ted?"

"As of right now, I have eight cases and the phone keeps on ringing." Ted handed me the files.

As I read the cases, I was astonished as to the types of cases they were, if that's what you would call them. I personally would call them paranormal activities. One file stated that an accident was avoided because the vehicle miraculously passed through the other one leaving everyone intact, no dents or fender benders. All the witness saw a shadow hover over the two vehicles and a blond woman fleeing the scene. Another file stated that Harold, the cook from Mel's diner, severely burned his hand and by the time he got to the hospital it was completely healed. Another anonymous tip gave a report of a fisherman who caught a net full of fish within five minutes of putting it out. The thing about that particular report is the fact Pleasantville's Lake Kahoota isn't primed for fishing. And even more of a peculiar report was a two-year-old boy who supposedly was dead is now alive. However strange these cases were, I was excited to have my whole day to investigate.

I headed to the Manson Family to question the parents and the two-year-old boy who allegedly was raised from the dead. "Mrs. Manson, could you tell me exactly what happened here."

Mrs. Manson wiped her eyes as her hands were shaking, "I told Billy to stay away from the pool until his sister was able to take him swimming, but you know Billy, he's not one to listen. The next thing I know, Shelby was screaming. I ran out and saw my baby's lips were blue. I quickly called 9-1-1 and then I tried mouth to mouth..." she paused and wiped at her nose.

"And then what happened?"

"The paramedics tried everything to bring him back but nothing was working, so they called his time of death." Mrs. Manson burst out in uncontrollable sobs.

"I'm so sorry you had to experience such trauma today. Can you tell me what happened after that?" I pressed.

Mrs. Manson took a deep breath and continued, "They covered him up and placed him in the back of the ambulance. I had to see him again and say good-bye so I hopped in the back, pulled the cover down. His lips were still blue. He was lifeless and cold. No color to him at all and then..." she paused and looked at me as if she had seen a ghost. "The whole ambulance filled with a warm, shadowy hue. I felt at peace. I heard a voice that told me to close my eyes. I heard a gasp and when I opened my eyes, Billy sat up and asked to go back into the pool."

"Hmmm… so you say you saw a shadow?"

Mrs. Manson nodded her head, "Something like that, yes."

"Can you describe this shadow?"

Mrs. Manson narrowed her eyes and said, "How else do you describe a shadow—it's dark, ghostly. Aiden, do you think I'm making this up or that I'm crazy?"

"No ma'am, it's just that others have seen this shadow and I would like a little more detail as to what it may look like. Was it in the shape of a person?"

"More like a blob."

"You didn't happen to see a blonde-haired woman around the premises by any chance?"

"Well, I did hear a voice and when I opened my eyes, out of the corner of them I did see a woman leaving the ambulance, but I don't remember if she was blonde or not."

"Do you mind if I ask Billy a few questions?"

"I suppose, but make them quick he's had a rough morning."

"Billy, glad to see you're alive little man, so can you tell me if you saw a shadow?"

Billy shook his head yes, really big.

"Can you describe it for me? Was it in the form of a person?"

Billy shrugged his shoulders and said, "It was friendly."

I raised my eyebrows in curiosity, "Friendly? How do you know it was friendly?"

"Because it told me that it wasn't there to hurt me but to make me feel better. When it touched me, it tickled and I was able to breathe better."

"So the shadow had a voice? What did it sound like, a woman's voice or man's?"

Billy shrugged his shoulders again, "I don't know. I heard it in my head. I'm tired."

I jotted some information down in my notes: It must be telepathic. And if that is the case, could it be… an A.I, artificial intelligence? Whoa… what is going on in this town?

****

My next stop was the Hiltons Farms. According to the file, an anonymous tip was called in to report that all of Widow Agatha's water jugs had turned into olive oil. As I was approaching the farm, I saw Agatha joyously jumping up and down. "Good morning Ms. Agatha. I see that you are having a happy day."

"Oh yes, yes, yes. Lookie here, Sonny, I've got me the best kind of oil you can have."

I looked inside the water jug and sure enough, it was oil.

"Why would someone put oil in your water jugs, Ms. Agatha?"

She shook a finger at me and said, "Oh Sonny, I have been worried about food and in great need of oil, and with this drought, my crops are dying and I don't have a way to pay for my food, or my bills, and I'm on the verge of losing the farm. With this oil, I can sell it for a pretty penny!"

I got out my pad of paper and started asking questions, "Do you think maybe it was a prank from the Teenhood? You know, they have been doing a lot of pranks lately."

Ms. Agatha squared her face and with a parental voice scolded me, "Sonny, that would be one expensive prank for anyone to pull off and who would want to do that? I have at least fifty water jugs filled to the brim with oil."

"I suppose. When did you last see the jugs filled with water and then to oil?"

"I filled the water jugs myself at seven o'clock and when I went to grab one to fill a trough, it poured out oil instead."

"Okay, let me ask you this, at any given moment, did you happen to see a shadow?"

Ms. Agatha squeezed her chin as she pondered on my inquiry.   "What comes to mind is that when I sat the last water jug down I felt as if someone was in my barn and I ain't talking about the horses or the pigs either. I literally felt a presence."

"Did it say anything to you?"

She cocked her head to the side and said, "It wasn't like I heard an audible voice, but a knowing."

"...A knowing?"

"Yes, like a knowing that everything is going to be okay, not to worry. I shrugged it off and went about my chores."

"Did you happen to see a blonde woman walking around your farm?"

Ms. Agatha smiled brightly and said, "Why yes, I invited her in for some tea just before I went to fill the water jugs."

My eyes widen. Great, a small break in the case. Someone had seen her. "Can you describe her to me and tell me why she was here so early?"

"She was the most beautiful looking thing ever. She had blonde hair, soft blue eyes and a bit of an accent that I couldn't quite place. As to why she was here so early, I'm not sure. She started asking questions about Manny."

I swallowed nervously. It couldn't be. Libby died in my arms. It has to be someone who just so happens to look like her, talks with an estranged accent and folds money into origami. And why would she be interested in Manny? "Did you happen to catch her name?"

"No Sonny I didn't. She was kind of in a hurry."

"Did she say she'll be back or where she came from? Where she's heading?"

"I'm afraid we mostly talked about was my troubles. Nice young girl, polite."

"Thanks, Ms. Agatha, for your time. Enjoy your oil." I said lamely as I looked at my next case file.

****

I drove over to Lisa Gibson's home. The report shared very little detail about her mugging. I thought these series of events seemed random, possible acts of kindness from a wannabe hero who lurks in the shadows. And just maybe the hero is a blonde-haired woman. But still, the questioned remained, how did the psychiatric ward patients become awake?

I knuckled knocked the door and waited for a few moments until Lisa answered.

"Hi, Lisa."

"Aiden," Lisa said shyly. "Would you like something to drink?"

"Water would be great unless all of your water has been turned into oil too?" I said mockingly.

Lisa just looked at me blankly.

"Never mind, so it says here in my file that you were almost mugged this morning? Can you tell me about it?"

Lisa cleared her throat and grabbed a tissue, "I was walking home from my shift at Mel's diner when I turned down the alleyway and three teenagers with knives ordered me to stop and give them my purse."

I shook my head angrily and pointed out, "The Teenhood, eh?"

"I believe so." she said quietly.

"Go on."

Lisa licked her lips and said softly, "Then I threw my purse at them and they started coming toward me. I told them to take the purse and let me go. Then, just as one boy was going to charge a knife at me, I saw something so amazing, possibly even heroic."

"And what was that?"

"I saw a huge shadow overcast an entire building wall and then it split into two huge shadows."

The way she was telling her story, I had to scooch to the edge of my seat. I was ready for her to tell me she saw Spiderman, but what she said next blew my mind even more than seeing Spiderman.

Lisa scooted to the edge of her seat as well. She leaned forward and whispered, "I hope you don't think I'm crazy, but these two shadows simply growled like a lion, removed themselves from the wall and chased after the boys. The boys screamed like girls, dropped their weapons and my purse. And let me tell you, I booked it home. I was so thankful for the shadows saving me. I thought I was going to die."

"Did you happen to see anyone else around you?"

"No, I don't believe so why?"

"A young, blonde woman perhaps?"

"No, but I did get the sense someone else was there with me and a few moments after that feeling I heard the sound of high heels."

I looked to the ground and studied the carpet as I was trying to think of the connections to all of this wildly, bizarre chain of events. The blonde-haired woman couldn't possibly be the hero, the shadow or shadows are infiltrating each situation themselves, so what does this woman have to do with it and why is she at just about every scene I've come across?

****

At each stop, my questions received stranger answers by the minute. And how was this connected to the awakenings… I still did not know? All I did know is that a shadow was running around town helping people in unearthly ways and it's sidekick was a blonde-haired woman.

My last stop of the eight cases took me across town to the very edge of Pleasantville.

Jonas, an elderly man who was a war vet, blind and homeless for as long as I lived here, is claiming he can see.

"Jonas, how's it going?'

Jonas had a big smile smeared across his face, "I recognize that voice anywhere. Aiden! I can finally put a face to the voice; of course, you sure don't look like your voice."

"Yeah, I get that a lot…" I mumbled out of humiliation.

"So, how very exciting for you now that you can see-," I stated as I held up three fingers.

Jonas laughed and said, "So you don't believe me either, Mr. Smarty Pants who's holding up three fingers.

I laughed, "So how did this great thing happen?"

"I was just sitting here waving my cup around and I felt something wet hit my eyes. I wiped them off on my shirt and I could see."

"Did you see anybody or sense anybody come up to you and touch your eyes?"

"Um… no, but I felt a mist and then there was this pungent smell of frankincense. I did feel a brief moment of the sun on my face, but then a cloud had covered it and gave me shade."

The shadow, I thought. "After you regained your sight did you happen to see a blonde-haired woman?"

"…With soft blue eyes?"

"Yes." I said excitedly.

"She stood at the end of the block, smiled and waved at me."

"Did you happen to catch her name?"

"No she didn't talk, just stood there and waved. I looked down and in my cup was a couple of thousands of dollars. See…"

I peeked inside the cup. "Good for you."

I left for home to process it all. Study my notes and ask my father for help. I was more confused than when the day started.

****

I plopped myself down at the kitchen table and shared every detail about the investigations, "This is a tough case, Dad."

"Every good reporter knows that you need to find the common thread. You find that, and then you'll get your answers."

I put my head down on the table and mumbled, "I know what the common thread is. It's the shadow and the mysterious blonde-haired woman."

My father scooted closer to me and said with enthusiasm, "Find them and you'll solve this story."

Right at that moment, my cell phone rang, "Yeah, this is Aiden."

"I have the answers you've been looking for."

"Lionel is that you?"

"Yes. I have to meet with you in person and alone." Lionel said with fear in his voice.

"What's wrong with you? You sound paranoid."

"Someone or something is stalking me."

I rolled my eyes at my Dad and continued, "Fine, where?"

"Behind Mel's Diner, and come quickly."

****

The sun was slowly giving up its light as I walked behind Mel's to meet Lionel, but when I arrived, Lionel was face down on the ground as if dead. I ran up to him and checked for a pulse, it was faint. I called 911. I frantically checked his pockets for his information he said he had, but nothing. Clenched in his hand was a piece of paper and lying next to him was a card that had an image of a serpent on it.

After the paramedics arrived, they informed me that they found a snake bite on the left side of his neck.

"Last time I checked, we don't have any poisonous snakes around here, do we?" I asked one of the paramedics.

"No, not that I'm aware of and nothing I've seen like this. These are big bite marks."

"Is he going to be okay?"

"I certainly hope so."

I looked around for evidence of a snake home-, but found nothing other than a brown-haired teenage boy peeking over a huge garbage dumpster.

"Manny is that you?"

He looked scared out of his mind as he was holding his head and not wanting to come out.

"Manny, did you see what happened?"

"You're going to think I'm crazy."

"No Manny, I'm not. Not after what I've heard all day."

"I'm not sure what I saw was even human. It appeared to be male with ghostly, sunken-in eyes and it was wearing black ratty clothes. It came up from behind Lionel and shape-shifted into a black snake, bit him and then the snake turned into vapor."

My eyes widen with disbelief. I wasn't sure I could trust Manny's story. He ran with the Teenhood and they got into all sorts of stuff, telling lies, and pulling off crazy pranks. Unless he was a good actor, Manny appeared to be seriously frightened.

Manny took off running while I unraveled the piece of paper. It read, "Answers are in the Ancient Book. 52 Aimly Street. Rebecca."

I screwed up my face, "What does this even mean?"

I headed toward Aimly Street and found the house. When I approached the door, I noticed it was slightly opened. I looked at the note again and called out, "Rebecca?" No answer. I walked into a sitting area and there she was, reclining. "Rebecca, it's Aiden Matthews from the Franklin Times. I'm here to ask you some questions."

There was no response. I came around to the front of the chair and she looked as stiff as a board. I felt for a pulse and was glad to find a faint one. At her feet was a card with a snake on it. What is happening? Do we now have a villain who is silencing my sources, but why?

Dangling from her hand was a gold, heart necklace. I quickly called 911 and then my boss.

"Ted, my sources keep coming up comatose, unable to speak."

"Yeah, I've been hearing over the CB dispatch radio that our anonymous sources have been found in that comatose state with, oddly, a card that has a snake on it by them."

"It must be Venom."

"...Venom?"

"That's what I'm naming him since it fits his calling card."

"Oh, so now we have a villain? Isn't it bad enough that we have a shadow acting as a superhero with a blonde-haired sidekick?"

"Well, you know what they say; every superhero battles a supervillain."

"Are you even close to solving this story?"

I sighed heavily, "No, this story is getting weirder by the hour." I paused as something caught my attention, "Hey Ted, I'm going to have to call you back, I think I may have found something."

Against the wall was a wooden podium. On top was a huge book. The cover was made out of mahogany and beautifully carved. The title read The Ancient Book. It was locked and appeared to need a key to open it. The lock was in the shape of a heart. I quickly thought of the necklace Rebecca was holding. I opened it up and a pungent smell of old, musty paper socked me in the nose. The fibrous paper was thick as I turned to the beginning.

I read out loud, "long ago, Ancient of Days, the King of all, came down in lowly form. Miraculously born of a virgin, he fulfilled all prophecy. He came to seek the lost souls of his kingdom and to bring them back to right standing. The King, being the light into the world found that his people loved the darkness instead of light because they were afraid their evil deeds would be exposed. However, he was pleased to see some lived by the light and recognized their King. The King knew that whoever lives by the truth comes into the light, so that it may be seen plainly that what they've done has been done in the sight of their King.

"For the King declared: -'"The people living in darkness have seen a great light on those living in the land of the shadow of death a light has dawned.-'"

"But in order for this prophecy to come true, the King, the Creator of his people, had to die and suffer on their behalf to make things right; to take his people out of the darkness.

"For it is written in the Kings Chronicles, '"-For God so loved the world that he gave his one and only Son, that whoever believes in him shall not perish but have eternal life."

I paused from reading and whispered, "All of this can't be about... Him is it? He's the Shadow?"

I turned several pages and continued, "Woe unto you peoples of the earth, for I have hurled down the serpent of old. He goes around seeking whom he may devour, steal, kill and destroy."

I slammed the book closed, "...Venom? I need to find the blonde woman, she knows something."

Just before I was about to leave the paramedics showed up. "Another snake bite?"

"Yep!" I yelled as I ran out of the room in search of the woman.

****

Night was now upon me as I jogged my way through the lowly, city lights. A loud clanging noise caused me to stop dead in my tracks. Before me stood the freakish being Manny had seen earlier.

In a demonically, raspy voice, it said, "Those who seek the truth don't like what they find, it only leads to bondage of the soul. I am warning you. Leave the truth to be undiscovered and you'll live. Press forward and you'll end up like the others."

The hideous creature made a seething sound, instantly shape-shifted into a snake and started to slither its wormy way toward me. I was completely immersed in fear. My breathing was labored as I baby stepped backward into a lowly lit alleyway.

Out of nowhere, a gust of wind blew. The snake stopped and moved its head frantically back and forth as if it were indecisive as to where to hide. Instantaneously, the snake turned into vapor and was gone. An enormous shadow emerged and covered what light there was in the alleyway.

"I hear you are looking for me, Aiden?" The Shadow asked.

I circled about trying to find where the voice was coming from. "Why don't you come out and stop hiding in the shadows?"

"I am not the one hiding, Aiden. It's you who is in the darkness and that is why you see me as nothing but a shadow."

"I don't understand?"

"Exactly, I am light to those who believe in me, but to those who don't believe, the god of this age has blinded the minds of unbelievers so they cannot see the light, and therefore remain in darkness."

"Are you the Supreme Being talked about in the Ancient Book?"

"I am."

"So you're the one that's behind these supernatural events?"

"I had help."

"...The blonde-haired woman?"

The Shadow didn't answer.

"Why are you doing all of this, for what purpose?"

"You see, Aiden, soon I'll be coming to collect my people and bring them back to their real home. It's imperative for me to reach all of my lost sheep, as I like to call them. I love them and if they don't come unto me, they will perish a horrible death. They will be separated from me for all eternity, all because they are lost to their own demise and are afraid."

"Afraid of what?"

"Many things really... the unknown, not wanting to believe in a real Supreme Being that they have to answer to, skeptical of my powers, and some even think I'm just an ancient myth or a legend."

"This is just crazy," I mumbled underneath my breath.

"Is it Aiden? At least believe the evidence of the works themselves. The question is, do you believe?"

I certainly couldn't argue the evidence of my father being awake, but there was still something in me that needed more. "Answer me this... why was my father and the others in a catatonic state in the first place?"

"I tell you the truth, the Serpent, and his demonic imps, have authority on this earth to kill, steal and destroy. That is all I can say for now. All your questions can be found and answered in the Ancient Book."

Then the Shadow took off faster than the Flash.   "Wait!" I yelled.

I tried running after it. As I rounded the corner, I bumped into someone. All of my adrenaline left my body as I stepped back to see the blonde woman, my ex-girlfriend from college standing before me. "Libby? But how? You died in my arms."

I saw a flicker of light in her eyes as she smiled, "I did, but I was brought back to life and not by man's doing."

I was speechless, twice in one day, and that never happens to a guy like me. "W-What are you doing here?" I stuttered out of shock.

"I'm here for Manny?"

"Manny, why?"

"He's my brother. After I supposedly died, the state automatically took Manny and placed him in the foster care system, since both of our parents are gone. I managed to find him here in Pleasantville and have come to bring him home with me. I also learned you lived here."

"You never told me you had a brother, in fact, you never told me much about yourself when we were dating."

"Because I soon realized that it wasn't going to work out between us."

I lowered my head, "Because I didn't believe in the way you did... this whole Supreme Being with supernatural powers that guides you, protects you and obviously heals you."

"Yes." Libby said smiling. She took a step closer to me and continued, "Quite the series of "paranormal events" wouldn't you say, Aiden? And as a reporter, I'm sure this is getting all of your attention. In fact, one would say this could be your biggest story yet."

"Yes, I suppose so. So then answer me this, why have you've been spotted at every incident?"

"To try and find Manny. I was on my way here when my car almost collided with another, but thankfully, a miracle happened and that was avoided. I then went to the Hilton Farms because I heard that he and a gang of teens were running around there, but no such luck. I ran down to the marina to see if anyone had given him a ride off shore, but again, nothing.

"I thought I would try the hospital since Manny had been through a lot, I thought just maybe he might be there, but he wasn't. I knew if I went to the diner, I could get answers. People love to talk and gossip and what better place to get information than your local diner. I learned that Manny was being fostered by the Manson Family, but he wasn't there either. I was on my way back to the diner when a girl was being mugged and that's when I saw Manny. I yelled out for him, but he took off. I followed him all the way to the edge of town where he was hanging out with an old man who couldn't see. Needless to say, Manny was in shock to see me, but after I explained everything, he's ready to come home with me. Does that answer your question?"

"No. I still don't understand what all of these unnatural events have to do with anything and how you're involved."

Libby smiled and placed her hand on my shoulder and said, "I'm simply the Shadow's, as I hear you like to call him, his hands and feet. I placed my hands on the people and asked for his power to manifest on their behalf. I also asked him to show himself to you, because I knew it would be the only way you would believe. All of today's events were about you and those who don't believe that there is a real superhero out there fighting their fight, protecting them, guiding them, healing them, loving them, and wooing them into a personal relationship that will ultimately lead to everlasting eternity."

"You're saying He did all of this for me? He woke up my dad for me?"

"Yes."

"...because you simply asked?"

"Yes."

"...but why?"

"To show you that He's real and that He loves you, Aiden. Aiden... He is really real!"

"What about this creature that's been turning into a snake, biting people and putting them in a comatose state, how does it relate to all of this?"

When Libby explained who Venom was and his ultimate plan, I was flabbergasted, and yet I found myself angry. I knew I needed more answers and I knew just where to get them.

"It's good to see you, Libby. Maybe later we could continue catching up."

She smiled and said, "Of course. Just one more thing before you go."

"...yeah?"

"The Shadow... He has a name. It's Yeshua Yahweh."

"What kind of name is that?"

She giggled and replied, "You're the investigative reporter you figure it out. I'll give you a clue, it's Hebrew."

****

I was given permission to take the Ancient Book home with me to further my research. I found it to be rather compelling and the truth! I had spent several hours compiling my story and in the end, I patted myself on the back and submitted it.

The next morning when I arrived at the paper, Ted stood on a chair, snapped the new, crisp newspaper in his hands and cleared his throat, "Alright people, here it is hot off the press! The story we've all been waiting for.

"The SHADOWMAN by Aiden Matthews:

"In light of recent anomalies, many have been wondering if aliens have landed or if there has been a disturbance in the force. I say it's both.

"Wouldn't you say it's true that the world wants to believe in superheroes? Everyone desires to be rescued in one way or another. Why else do we go around idolizing fictional characters from comic books, watch movies and play dress up? I mean, who doesn't want to be a superhero? But here is an interesting fact; all of the fictional superhero's we know are based off of the attributes from the greatest superhero of all time. One that is actually real and lives among us, I'm talking about the Shadowman.

"He is the Supreme Being that has always existed. In fact, he's the author and finisher of the beginning and the end. The universe is his castle, a city in the sky and those who believe in Him belong to the sky, so therefore, there are aliens among us. The Supreme Being is a mighty force that brings signs and wonders, such as raising a boy from the dead, miraculous healing of a hand and eyes, manhandling vehicles and giving protection, and sparing a woman's life to get a teenage boy's attention. He is the One who supplies a desperate plea to help save a farm and multiply oil and fish. And most importantly, one that is close to my heart, He is the one that awakens those who are asleep.

"Written in an Ancient Book, the Supreme Being states, '"-I am the light of the world. Whoever follows me will never walk in darkness, but will have the light of life.-'"

"Up until now, He was nothing but a shadow until I believed in him and now I see him as what he truly is... Light!

"I find it reassuring to know that he is the only superhero that can truly offer you immortality. One who can offer you hope and a future full of prosperity.

"Where is your proof in all of this you may ask? The answer lies in what the Supreme Being stated to me, '"-...at least believe on the evidence of the works themselves.'"- And in His book he further quotes, '"-Very truly I tell you, whoever believes in me will do the works I have been doing, and they will do even greater things than these, because I am going to the Father.-'"

"If we believe in Him, we too can possess the same power as He and be his sidekicks. An old friend taught me that. Thanks, Libby, for sharing the truth.

"But there is a price to pay and that's giving up the darkness and acquiring an adversary like Venom. A real life villain who's objective is to deceive you into believing lies about the Supreme Being, to kill you and to see you rot in an eternal, fiery abyss where it is so hot that one's tongue will long for a single drop of water from the finger to cool it off. His goal is to silence you from sharing this truth and from hearing the truth.

"So I pose this question, what side do you want to be on when the Supreme Being leaves his throne to collect His people and will you be one of them?

"Again He quotes, "I am the way and the truth and the life."

"So today, I declare we have a real live superhero among us, but I now call him the Light Warrior, but his real name is Yeshua Yahweh, Jesus Christ who saves!"

The room was dead quiet after Ted stopped reading, which caused my heart to pound as I was nervous to know what people were thinking.

My father slowly started clapping and then others followed.

I breathed a sigh of relief as Ted slapped me on the back. "Well, that was interesting. Certainly wasn't what I was expecting, but I think I can believe it to be true."

****

We all went about our business as usual. As I watched Libby leave with Manny, I knew that Pleasantville would never be the same, and I was encouraged to know that through her help, I captured the greatest story... My story.

73.
The Short Cut
John Grey

You go home via the graveyard,
with mud on your pants leg,
gravel embedded in your soles,
a twig of willow in your hair.

You go home via the graveyard
head full of doleful dates on a stone,
the cold eyes of a wingless angel,
a lurking, looming mausoleum.

Some things scrape off
or comb out easily.
Others stick around
now they've got you in the mood.

74.
The Surgeon
Charlotte Mielziner

Perhaps one assumes my moment of rebirth was blasted by a dazzling surge of lightning while my creator, dramatically screamed to the heavens, "Life! Give my Creation life!" The reality was quite different. The good doctor, may he rest in peace, equipment so primitive, gave but one blast to my system and then for weeks, a tiny trickle of electricity equal to that of a normal human body ran through me, steadily feeding my physiology with the signals it needed to mend the myriad connections.

How much luck merged with the doctor's skill I can still barely fathom. That I am a compendium of over twenty various parts all found with blood type O+ still amazes me. The fact that none of my incisions became septic and that circulation was restored to each part must be credited to his obsessive cleanliness and attention to detail. God is not the only one to have performed a miracle.

I agree. The possibility of my existence is so improbable it is the stuff of gothic horror, is it not? True, but, this infinitesimal level of probability actually happened generations ago before even a true comprehension of the Herculean effort was understood. I stand here, today as proof.

Now we will finish the refinement my creator would have given me if he'd lived. Your work in reconstructive plastic surgery is nearly as legendary as the good Doctor was in reanimation of inanimate tissues. By the way, I enjoyed your paper in *Lancet* on advancements in non-steroidal therapies for scar removal. It was cutting edge, if you'll pardon the pun.

You're quite welcome.

Because of my obvious alarming appearance, I have so little chance for polite conversation. Please allow me to babble on as you work, it takes my mind off the procedure. I'm simply anxious to see the final results. Perhaps this is why most surgeons would prefer their patients under sedation.

Thank you...you're too kind.

Consider my left hand, the fingers smooth and long, nails arched and thin; a sensitive hand meant for the arts, music or sculpture. I often imagine it was the hand of a classical pianist, well known for his innovative interpretations of Liszt. Yes, Lizst of the demonic, pounding chords of Faustus. This hand could stretch across the keys of a fine Boesendorfer, feel the song within and give it voice. Or perhaps that of a violinist, who made his instrument cry to the heavens. Upon hearing its sweet voice, the angels themselves would weep.

Compare the left hand with my right. So different, with strong, blunted fingers, age spots, callused palms and a curious scar on the ring finger. It has strength, but not gentility, coarseness, but not refinement. This is the hand I prefer for... well, more menial tasks.

In the beginning, consciousness came slowly. What I remember is pain, all-encompassing white hot pain. It racked my body and pounded me with its only reality. How long did I lay on the table unable to move, to voice my agony? Imagine needing to scream and having no mouth. It seemed as long as it takes a waterfall to etch away the threshold to a picturesque cascade. Be reassured, what your laser scalpel has inflicted on me is not even a prick from a rose.

My first recollection other than pain feels as recent as if it were yesterday. I heard music like it was echoing in a cave, drifting softly into my consciousness. I became aware of someone standing over me, assessing my vitals, quietly making notes and humming the loveliest song I've ever heard. It was melancholy and sweet. I clung to it like a lifesaver to a drowning man.

As if clarity rode in on the descending chords of the song, I began to identify new sensations. I felt the brush of a cool, wet cloth on my face. The hands holding it were gentle, even loving. I fought through a fog of confusion for awareness to find it's source.

I opened my eyes and slowly focused on my creator. To me, he was beautiful. He lifted my head to sip some cool water. Even though I was as massive in size and strength as you see me now, I was helpless in his arms. He tended to my needs in those next weeks with the care of a lover. He was my universe, my light, all good came from him.

My brain tested its new connections, synapses fired and signaled movement. I began to stretch, flex and extend my limbs and the good doctor was there by my side. Coordination and balance had to be learned anew. Like a teenage boy who grows overnight, my brain needed to adjust to the capacity and range of movement of my limbs. The doctor celebrated my first halting steps like a proud parent, perhaps he was.

That wretched little assistant Igor, perhaps the most famous hunchback since Quasimodo, limped through the laboratory incessantly. Remember, at that time research such as this was illegal and considered evil, diabolical. Today, cutting edge research has the backing and protection of drug companies more powerful than governments. Malpractice suits pale in comparison to being burned at the stake by an angry mob. I, his greatest success had to be kept secret from the world and this scheming, greedy man was the only one who knew. The secret was vulnerable.

Like a child, I feared the night, fire, the unknown and the hunchback. My frustrations grew and anger deepened, but so did my curiosity. What worlds lay beyond the walls of the laboratory? Where did the doctor go when he passed through those doors? I yearned for knowledge one hundred and forty years ago just like today. I am driven to learn, explore and live.

While I experienced love and nurturing from the Doctor, the hunchback was the opposite in every way. At first, I couldn't understand taunting, but as my language comprehension grew, meanings became clear. Tripping me as I tried to navigate the narrow stone steps to my chamber grew to threatening with a torch and beatings with chains. You may doubt it listening to me now, but speech came much later and I was unable to verbally protect myself or plea for help.

When that little troll threatened to reveal my creator's miracle to the townspeople, I silenced him. The secret had to be kept. It was actually easy. His twisted spine, a symbol of his life, was straightened in death. My life force fed off his energy as he died by my hand, the power was exhilarating. Yet, he did what I cannot. He died.

Yes, you're right, I don't appear to have aged since the day I was reborn. How reanimation kept me from the degenerative effects of time is another mystery the doctor will unfortunately never explain.

Whenever possible, I explored the halls of the castle and found the first woman I ever saw. She was captivating in mauve satin and lace. She moved with a grace I had never imagined. Simply to be near her I conquered my fear of the night. How was I to know she was my creator's fiancée?

Instinctively, I knew she mustn't see me. As she slept, I came to her room to touch her hair and breathe in its lavender scent. I knelt in adoration at her bedside. Wanting to honor her, I softly hummed the sweet song the doctor sang when I first became aware. It was the only gift I had to give. My heart flew when she smiled in her sleep. I wept with love and a tear fell on her cheek and awakened her. She saw me and a scream began to fill her fragile throat. I had to stop it before it got out and so my first love ended tragically.

I carried her lifeless body to the tower. I begged the same power that gave me life to bring her back, but my prayers went unheard. All that she was or ever would be was gone. I had taken a life in anger and now I had taken a life in love. Having been created from death, were all my relationships to end this way?

From the windows I glimpsed a world beyond the castle walls and it was to there that I escaped. Torn between curiosity and terror, I found the door and freed the latch. The night air washed across my face, cleansing me of my sins and calling me to the world. I stumbled into the courtyard, dizzy with freedom and awed by the sheer openness. I thought the stars in the sky and the lights in the houses of the village below were the same. For a long moment, I stood arms out, drinking in the vastness of simply being free.

Straining to listen to the sounds of the night, I heard music floating up the hillside from the village. Not the sad, sweet melody of the doctor's, but bright, happy and inviting music. Reaching out, I went forward not to fame, but infamy.

Need I tell you how I fared in the village? That man fears what he does not know has been written about by philosophers for generations. The villagers looked into my eyes and saw a man without a soul. As the townspeople pursued me, I panicked and ran to my only sanctuary and that act brought wrath and vengeance upon the Doctor.

We were tried by fear, found guilty by ignorance and executed by bigotry. But, I couldn't die again, I could only suffer. The emotional pain of losing my father, my very creator, eclipsed the physical pain I had felt as my body rebelled at being awakened.

For all these years, I've lived a solitary existence. I protect the secret. Secluded and rejected, I've searched the world and never encountered another being like me. Never known acceptance by society, nor the smile of a woman. I read, learn and observe unseen and unknown. But now, through your surgical expertise, I can at least cosmetically appear to be the intelligent and sensitive creature I am. You give me hope.

There is a lovely sidewalk café in town west of the park. It's a charming place well known for their homemade brioche. Oh, you know it. I yearn to spend an afternoon there, drinking tea, reading poetry and watching passersby with no one taking more note of me than any other casual, however large patron.

You are finished? Let me see. I've anticipated this for so long. Yes, this is much better. Excellent scar minimization, I must say. I'm nearly handsome. Your reputation is certainly deserved. You were well worth what you asked, but really shouldn't have pressed me for my story, because as you now know, I must keep the secret. Your fate was sealed when you made me relate my beginnings in exchange for your services.

You see, I am a miracle of science reaching to the time when man first questioned his universe, explored his limits, but found no inner peace. For my creator to reanimate a concoction of cadavers was a tremendous leap of faith so far past it's time it has yet to be replicated. His secret must be kept.

My life is a metaphor for whatever theory the sages wish to posit. It could be Man's struggle against ignorance, his inner need to create, the immorality of egocentrics, the futility of playing God, you name it and this humble tale fits. I prefer to see it as an example of how shallow is our veneer of civilization. Oh, the tyranny of humanity.

Samuel Morse once asked, "What hath God Wrought?" I am not the product of God, but that of one man who wanted to emulate his own creator. I am a calculated culmination of my parts. I am of Man and by Man, but never will I be for Man. I am quintessential nature verses nurture in action. I am the Monster. Call me Frankenstein.

Dear surgeon, don't struggle, your passing will be indelicate if I must use both hands. Sadly, it truly seems that all my relationships end this way. You will always have my deepest gratitude and apologies.

Lie still now, lie still.

75.
The Wind Whistle

Influenced by the short story, "Oh, whistle, and I'll come to you, my lad" by English writer M.R. James.

Mark Hudson

There was a professor named Parkins,
we hear about him, our story darkens.
An archeologist, he was British,
there wasn't much that made him skittish.
He was going for a trip to the East Coast,
little did he know he'd see a ghost.
He was warned not to stay at the Globe inn,
but he laughed it off with a big old grin.
When he arrived, he dug into some dirt,
and found a whistle, and put it in his shirt.
It had a Latin inscription he could read,
he blew the whistle, and a spirit was freed.
That night, he laid wake in his bed,
with terrible visions going through his head.
He visualized a figure running on the beach,
he was trying to escape, but he couldn't be reached.
The window cracked open, and the wind blew through,
Parkins couldn't sleep, the terror that he knew.
The next day a boy was running down the street,
screaming in terror, fleeing in retreat.
He claimed he saw a ghost in Parkins window waving,

Parkins simply thought the boy was misbehaving.
That night he tried to sleep, but the bed sheets were moving,
Parkins was scared now, nothing needing proving.
He thought he'd jump from the window, trying to escape,
the ghost appeared right there and met him at the drapes.
Fortunately a man walked in, and scared the ghost away,
Parkins didn't die but he's been scared to this day.
M.R. James was a story teller with a skill of scaring you,
that Hollywood and Stephen King cannot even do.
The son of a clergyman, an unlikely one to write,
stories that are creepy, and bring a sense of fright.
But God created good and bad, I heard that Sunday morning,
and sometimes bad things we see are our final warning!

76.
Theodore's Surgeon
Mark Hudson

The surgeon specialized in plastic,
but when Theodore came it was drastic.
Theodore had a face rather scarred,
the surgeon accepted his plastic credit card.
But Theodore's face brought him revulsion,
the surgeon began his other compulsion.
Looking for flesh to cover those wounds;
he drove his car and went out to the boons.
He arrived at a graveyard at night,
the mortician inside gave him a fright.
Because he looked like a zombie like Theodore,
and the mortician slammed the mausoleum door.
The surgeon tried to escape out the back;
but there was no back door to take steps retract.
And the zombie walked closer to him;
its face contorted, distorted, and grim.
And with flesh falling off its face,
said, "Can I have a kiss?" it was a disgrace!
Whether the zombie was a his, her, or it,
he grabbed the surgeon, transferring zits.
And the zombie took the surgeon's flesh away,
just so he could see the light of day.
Now the surgeon is part of the zombie club,
his skin falls off if you give it a rub.

77.
Tryst With The Succubus
John Grey

What's a man to do?
My visitor is
a naked Venus
of sensual curves
of skin, carnation pink.
And yet I know she is a demon.

Lush ruby hair
falls below her shoulders
but a hideous snake
wraps around her thighs.

For every soft inviting whisper
a breath from my ear
there's a hiss
out of her nether regions.

This could be the consummate in pleasure
or the ultimate in damnation.

What's a man to do
but what he has always done.

78.
Uxoricide
Bob McNeil

During a Thursday, around three forty-three in the morning, a female and male sauntered towards the driveway of her Spanish Colonial-style mansion. The woman, Neala Desdemona Johnson, was blonde, in her thirties. Her appearance was comparable to the models found in *Playboy*. Her male counterpart, Rod Silverman, who was younger than she, favored an actor, Johnny Depp. In an attempt to convey his libidinousness, the male stopped and put his arms around his girlfriend's waist. This effort at warming the woman to the proposal of having sex worked. Under her red leather skirt, jacket and shoes, she felt a lot warmer. And Rod's blue Italian suit felt tighter, much tighter.

Mansions were common to Rod Silverman. Being the son of an investment banker father and an art curator mother, he was used to wealth. Irrespective of his family's moneyed existence, as a young, rising model, Rod was getting riches of his own. Among the profits of appearing in fashion magazines and going to trendy clubs was dating attractive, wealthy divorcees like Neala.

Over to the right of Neala and Rod, crouching behind some shrubbery, the forty-seven-year-old African-American former football star Orello Johnson was wearing a ninja outfit. Disguised by his black cotton Balaclava Ninja mask, anger monopolized his expression.   Sans his gear, he had short dark coiled hair, straight features, oval eyes, somewhat narrow lips, broad shoulders, bronze skin and an Olympiad's musculature. Certain women thought the man was handsome. His awareness of these females made his ego rival the Rungrado May Day Stadium for largest mass.

Unheard by anyone else, Orello whispered, "I should take the blood from her fake breasts, breasts that I bought for her. I am the man who inflated those trailer tires and parked them in my mansion."

Upon amassing an armory of anger, Orello emerged and unsheathed his head.

"What, what, what drug made you come here, Orello?" Neala screamed. Cold, pale fear encased her from skeletal pillars to the flesh covering her.   Letting her fingers unify into fists somehow made the woman resuscitate her composure.   The girder for steadying her logic was in place as she continued speaking, "I thought the court explained your visitation rights to you. You can see our daughter and son on the weekends."

Asleep and oblivious to the fight below, two olive-skinned children with sandy hair were in the right wing of the mansion. Their little bodies, which had the attributes from both parents, were content.

"Pray, puta, pray!" Orello's reply had all the rancor of a Rottweiler before chewing on its prey.

"Hey, uh, uh, don't call her that!" Rod tried to posture like a defensive lineman, but the boy knew that if a fight started, Orello would defeat him.

"Shut up, sex toy. Your trampish hole and I have some probing to do. Does this boy know that you drove him in my Charcoal Gray 1969 Ford Bronco? Does this boy know that you're gonna screw him in the house that I pay mortgage on? Does this boy know that you spend my one hundred six thousand dollars every four weeks?"

"Yeah, I'm a trampish hole, but not your trampish hole anymore. You will never screw me anymore and that's causing your rage. Well, you had this hole for a whole long time. Some days I was your pleasure and other days I was your opponent in a boxing ring. Did you feel like the Heavyweight Champion of the World after beating a woman, Orello? Other than bringing grief, what else are you going to give our relationship?"

Each word that she lunged turned into a shank stabbing Orello in the abdomen. Psychosomatic pain or not, either way, it hurt as if it were a real weapon. Enraged by her, Orello wanted the discomfort of the scene to cease. Walking away was not enough, he wanted blood. Orello wanted to see the submission of defeated fighters. His psychopathic need, the desire to ingest violence, wanted a couple of servings.

Evil was never birthed out of nothingness. Orello's family proved that aforementioned concept to be incontrovertible. All Johnson men were large. Ranging from the tall and muscular to the stout, they were huge. What they possessed in size, they lacked in compassion for women considerably smaller. Bullying diminutive females was yet another trait these men possessed. Johnson men were known for abusing women. The clan pounced on insecure women. A specific Johnson son named Orello saw his father abuse his mother. That fight left bruises upon his psyche.   The bruises metastasized into a murderous adulthood.

With a quick motion, Orello stabbed Rod with his Bowie hunting knife.   The blade rammed through the trachea of the Hollywood-model-handsome male. Gurgling sounds, instead of other pained utterances, came out of the victim.   Akin to a cocaine high, Orello felt exhilarated.

Before she could run or scream, Orello grabbed Neala.   Stifled by his left hand, her howl was hampered.

"As opposed to screaming, why don't you say this? 'For giving my boyfriend a means to meet God, thank you, Orello.'   You won't repeat those words, will you? Even though you won't praise the gift that my knife gave your man, I am going to give you the same prize.   But, first, speak your last words, say them."

"What will you do with our d–d-daughter and s-s-son? Don't deny Sandy and Justice a relationship with their mother.   Leave before the police arrive.   I won't tell them that you stabbed Rod.   Orello, besides thinking about our babies, I am concerned about your other children from your first marriage. Consider Arnette and Jordan before you do another thing right now."

"Arnette and Jordan are adults now.   They hate you.   Praise for killing you, not criticism, is what I will get from them.   Frankly, as for our kids, being six and seven, they won't remember you after a while."

"Imagine our kids' lives with you in prison then put the knife down."

"You're merely another wallet-sucking parasite."

"Your cynicism will prevent you from hearing this, how-however, I did love you.   I profited from your love, never the money.   Baby, even after the abuse started, I thought my heart could love you so much that your evil would weaken and go away. No matter how much love I gave, you still found reasons to beat me.   Honestly, if I didn't divorce you, Orello, I would have killed you.   Much as I desired your death, I didn't try to kill you.   Two things prevented me from murdering you: our children and my hope that our relationship would become something beautiful.   Please, Big O, don't kill any chance for our reconciliation."

Believe it or not, Neala was expressing some truth, despite what Orello thought.   For a corn-fed 19-year-old Indiana girl, armed with dreams of being a model, L.A. was like paradise.   So, between waiting tables and auditioning, Neala thought success was a tip away. Some fifteen years ago, at The Datura Club, when she met Orello, her whole spirit knew they were going to be media town's hottest twosome. And, yes, around the beginning of the relationship, she did love him.

Years later, she saw that love get tackled until it hurt.

A single portion of the plea was false as a faked orgasm and that was the part about any future reconciliation. Neala would have sooner French kissed Charles Manson than date or remarry Orello again.

A combination of cocaine, steroids, CTE (chronic traumatic encephalopathy) and genetics prevented Orello from comprehending Neala's statement. Exceeding all else, the weapon in his hand was able to communicate Orello's response. Quicker than his mind's ability to realize what he was doing, Orello's arm swung as if it were a scythe mowing grass. Known for its sharpness, the metal went straight through the victim's neck. There was no way of concealing the sanguinary act, Orello realized. Blood shot out and stretched to greet his clothes. The knife was the bartender and it was serving blood. Unsinewed as a dishrag, Neala fell and a plasma pool widened around her outstretched body.

Soon, though, once the satisfaction of killing his ex-wife dissipated, elation died. Not much later, it became dread and nausea. Fear's cold hand grabbed the killer's spinal column.

Leopard-legged and madness-motivated, Orello ran into the darkness. Among his goals, not getting caught for his monstrous act was paramount.   Through sidestreets, the murderer made his way to his new home. About half a mile separated him from his desired sanctuary. Midway to his destination, Orello reminisced about being the first NFL player to rush for more than 2,000 yards in a season. Considering that he was now much older and his stamina had changed since the mark he set during the 1973 season, the former running back was pleased with the amount of strength his legs still possessed.

Orello entered his residence which looked like a place that Elvis would have enjoyed calling home. Although it was large enough to accommodate two jumbo jets, Orello preferred his former home. Expensive divorce proceedings made him lose the other house to Neala.

Disrobing in the dark and thinking about all that took place, the murderer scrutinized his actions. Garments and the weapon went into a plastic bag. The evidence was going to be put in a place as unattainable as Amelia Earhart, Jimmy

Hoffa and D.B. Cooper.   Sneaker prints on the carpet were vacuumed away. Inspired by a childhood spent watching Basil Rathbone on television, Orello mused that he could stump Sherlock Holmes.

Later, in his bedroom, numerous glasses of screwdrivers with a little juice could not remove Orlello's conscience.   Emotion-sedating pills, the kind that could make an elephant sleep, were also unable to remove the disturbing murder from his dreaMs.

****

Yes, I killed my wife! Yes, I killed my wife!" Orello cried out.   Remorse was a touchdown vulture that stole his demeanor.

"From the first news report, I knew you stabbed that woman.   Unfortunately, by a jury of your so-called peers, you were deemed innocent of that charge.   Double Jeopardy prevents the judicial system from putting you in a court for that case ever again.   This time, however, the State of Nevada will make these unrelated kidnapping and robbery charges placekick your prick into the penal system for a long, long bid."

Orello did not know who spoke to him.   He opened his eyes and found out he was not in his home at all, but he was in a 6 by 8 grey prison cell, wearing blue inmate garb.   The voice belonged to a Corrections Officer in a green uniform.   A middle-aged, tall, muscular white male with short auburn hair was standing outside of the prison door.   He was in front of the bars looking at Orello.   There, on his cot, Orello realized what transpired.

"Whoa, I was having a real serious nightmare, man.   Check it out, um, what I was yelling wasn't true.   I had nothing, nothing to do with Neala's, you know, you know, murder."

"Bad dreams aren't all you have to worry about today, football hero.   Your court case is being called again.   Make sure you wash yourself well because the jury is going to screw you." The guard walked away from Orello's cell.   A blitz of laughter struck the walls and bars of the building.   Inspired by the officer expressing his appreciation for his own humor, co-workers and other inmates stormed with their chuckles.   From afar, Orello could still hear the guard speaking.   "Try to understand this, sports star, pretend today's New Year's Eve and you're the only available toilet in Times Square.   Justice is going to piss on you.   Court TV will let everyone see you get wet. Disappointingly for all the abused women out there, you're not going to get a lethal injection, or what I call the 'Juice.'"

Denied comfort, a need to satirize another inmate's sorrow was on par with escaping.   Humor was a tunnel to a freer place.   Everyone in that section of the prison enjoyed lampooning the once venerated football player.   By laughing at Orello, these criminals and officers felt better about their parts in the melodrama.

Disorientation was exiting with its fog in tow.   Memories of situations that brought Orello back into the judicial double arm bar pin maneuver were appearing. The criminal remembered that after fifteen years of freedom, he made a life-defeating mistake.   In a Las Vegas' Auction House, with a gun in his hand, Orello confronted men who allegedly stole some of his valuable possessions.   Since he stopped the auction in an illegal manner, Orello was arrested.   That June, he was charged with a load of felonies.

Imprisoned by the realization that his somniloquy confessed to a form of unlawfulness while facing another form, Orello sat up on his cot.   Right then, his desire for cocaine made him imagine the taste of the white powder on his tongue.

That guard returned to the cell.   For a while there Orello thought he was hallucinating, because it looked like Neala exited the Correctional Officer's body the way steam would from soup.   Previous to disappearing, the apparition, dressed in a miniskirt-short ivory-colored tunic, turned, smiled and laughed.   It was the type of laughter that people would associate with villains.   Hearing the manic cackle gave Orello the feeling icy stalactites were forming on his spine.

****

Entering that courtroom with an infamous murder case in his past did not make the accused criminal look nicer.   There was a full meal of reasons to hate Orello Johnson.   Each person in that room chewed on some reason or another.   Nervous about the setting, the defendant fidgeted.

Compounded with all the legalities Orello had to battle, there was Neala's ubiquitous being standing next to the jury box.   Later, she was standing beside Judge Janis Copper.   Other times Neala stood a foot away from the bailiff.   No matter where the ghost stood, she laughed throughout the long trial.

"Can you hear and see her?" Orello whispered the query to Criminal Defense Attorney Harvard Moldova.

"Who?" The middle-aged white lawyer in the pinstriped suit replied.   Indeed, Harvard did not know to whom Orello was referring.   In addition, he wished for another client.

"Neala is standing over there and over there at the same time. Look over there to the right and left of the judge before Neala changes her position again," Orello whispered.

"Are you trying to get an insanity plea?" Harvard asked. Nervously awaiting an answer, the brown-haired lawyer stared at a client who made him feel hatred.

"Insane, no, I am not insane. I was just saying that some of the women here look like Neala." A plea bargain for Orello to stay in an asylum would separate him from his children and his assets. His plans would be tackled. Sure, seven hundred fifty milligrams of Depakote and about four hundred milligrams of Theophylline would make the prison bid bearable, but deadening his senses would prevent Orello from getting the ultimate touchdown--freedom.

"Members of the jury, have you reached a verdict?"

Nervous about the setting, Orello continued tapping his brown slippers and biting the cuticle of his thumb. He wanted supernatural strength so he could race to a time before meeting his wife. If time travel were possible, Orello thought, he would jettison back to a time when he was loved by the American media.

"Yes, your honor, we have." Harder than an assassin's demeanor was the expression on the young, pale woman as she spoke, "Guilty, your honor." Neala exited the woman's flesh triumphantly.

His countenance became melted chocolate. All the flesh on his face dangled in a mass of sadness. Muscles that once maintained his structure buckled. Orello collapsed. His body and existence met the floor.

"Now, you're gonna rot," Frank, the father of Rod Silverman, screamed.

Age and despondency tormented the Silvermans. Every day the two conditions stabbed another part of them. Frank's green eyes appeared murkier and sadder since the murder trials. His square jaw, which once gave him an appearance of a strong leading man, now hung as if the floor beckoned it. Over the course of the trial, his dark and full collar-length hair became grey. In his case, it was not the natural aging process. The loss of his son siphoned all vivaciousness from his being. Frank, in his sixties, could have passed for a man ten to fifteen years older.

Another victim of this siphoning process was Rod's mother, Cheryl. Called the Elizabeth Taylor of the Hamptons, Cheryl's beauty was admired for many years.

Losing her son and finding alcohol turned her cinematic sultriness into a network of decrepit wretchedness. Wrinkles, warts and a disposition that would befit Edward Albee's Martha replaced the woman Frank married.

Undeterred by their divorce after the murder of their son, they attended all of Orello's trials together.

Right alongside the Silverman family was Neala's older sister, Daphne Ensler. Both were stair step children, a mere year separated them. There, at age forty-eight, the auburn-haired buxom woman would sell her eyes and arms to get her sister back. Loss was an exclusive concern for the senior sibling, especially now since the murder of a family member and the death of her parents, Lars and Janet. On the day Orello stabbed Neala, he ran the blade through that farm couple. A little less than two years passed and both the mother and father died of heart attacks. Daphne's heart was dedicated to her son, twenty-year-old Christopher, her husband, Jack, the contractor, and her career as a writer. Daphne's books on domestic violence were acclaimed.

United, the Silverman family and Daphne Ensler stood in clothes befitting a funeral—Orello's funeral.

Turning towards Frank, Orello saw the ghost of Rod Silverman appear, wearing the same type of tunic that Neala had, but his covered both knees. The ghost wore the expression of an individual who wanted to slaughter his slayer. If Orello were beef, Rod would have served the slices to sewer rats.

Even scarier than Rod's expression was the presence of a brown-haired angelic woman with white wings and a yellow robe. None of the other apparitions scared him as much as the presence of this ethereal female. Maybe she was the devil, Orello thought. Yet, unlike any other known description of the fallen angel, she was not what the ex-football player expected. Materializing when she wanted, the creature was instructing Neala. Towering above everyone in the courtroom, she glared at Orello. Perhaps she was awaiting her moment to kill, the ex-football player concluded.

****

Orello returned to inmates and corrections officers tormenting him with words that felt like a bump and run. Such discomfort that was created by critical quips was not quite as painful as the visions of Neala, though. Without a logical schedule, the slain woman often appeared in Orello's cell and laughed. Sometimes she was accompanied by Rod and that winged figure. Under those aforesaid circumstances,

Orello awaited his next court appearance in two months.

Had Orello known how strange it sounded to others outside of his cell, he would not have yelled at his ex-wife. Testimonials from convicts and corrections officers agreed on this observation: Orello argued with a woman who was unseen and unheard.

In particular, there was this outburst from Orello that an inmate remembered. An unnamed eavesdropper said Orello bellowed the following: "Neala, Neala, appearing just to disappear won't help you win this game. Stay so I can explain things to you or hide like a scared girl. Either way, I am going to win. I am Orello Johnson. Don't you understand that in 1966, when your little ass attended grade school, I rushed for 1,709 yards, got me twenty-two touchdowns and earned the *Heisman Trophy*, the *Maxwell Award*, and the *Walter Camp Award* all during that same year? Hell, in the Rose Bowl, just three years later, I ran 171 yards. Plus, I got an 80-yard TD run. What's a pale as bird poop phantom gonna do to this brother, huh?

"I played the pig on the gridiron. America cheered me. America revered me. The reverence was a treasure in my bank. My name became success. My persona became a multimillion dollar advertisement. Back when America transmitted racism through rabbit ears, I was on TV. In people's homes, I was selling waste and they guzzled it like they liked it. Spread out on the big scene movie screen, I was a buffoon with the stadium-wide smile and audiences wanted more helpings of my trash.

"Soon I am going to play a role that's better than being in a franchise. This role is going to give me the Oscar for bedding that Lady Justice Broad."

"Next to ants, you're a giant. Next to an ethical man, you're dirt," Neala stated before her figure materialized.

"What's a ghost gonna do to this brick house, huh?"

"Yo, Orello, shut your hole or I'll show ya who's goin' to knock your brick house down. Ya sound like you're crazy talkin' to yourself," an unseen inmate yelled from another cell.

Not a soul but Orello could hear Neala speak. Realizing that his responses were what the inmates overheard, Orello imagined cement drying on his lips.

Left with nothing else to do after Neala disappeared, Orello tried to sleep, but even that provided torment. Since his incarceration for his wife's murder, Orello had nightmares about castration, not just anybody's castration—his castration.   Nighttime hours, rather fittingly it seemed, were now reserved for new horrific scenarios to play in Orello's mind.   The drama that played throughout his nightmare showed Orello tied to a bed and all the women he abused cheered as Lorena Bobbitt and Neala cut off his genitalia with knives.   Every night there was this sensation of metal slicing him.

Besides the vision of the mutilating duo, there was another sorority that prevented comfortable sleep.   His need to nod was interrupted by seeing Velma Barfield putting a toxic chemical in his meals.   A lot of reveries were spent being chased by ax-swinging Karla Faye Tucker.   Sweat formed all over Orello after watching Betty Lou Beets and Aileen Wuornos shoot at him.   Sleep was a murderess.   Nauseated, nervous and pained, Orello rarely got more than three hours of sleep per day.

****

"The judge is getting ready for the game, Mr. Sports Hero."   Those words were the alarm clock and calendar that alerted Orello to the date and time of his court case. It was two months to the day since his last judicial ordeal.

Whether it was an appropriate analogy or not, Orello saw himself as the team captain standing in front of a blackboard, drawing diagrams and preparing to defeat the other team.   Further contemplation on the subject of his pending court case made Orello come up with what he believed was a good game plan.   He envisioned himself mesmerizing the judge.   Based on all accounts, Orello was effective in getting field goals on females.   Even going back to his youth, the opposite sex wanted the athletic male.   Success increased the man's appeal.   Orello figured by letting his charm run with the ball, the female judge would personally lead him to the parking lot.   During Orello's shower and dressing ritual, the idea became erotic.

****

"Is there anything that your client would like to say before sentencing?"   The forty-something-year-old judge asked.   Her approach to the case was much like the ponytail holding her black hair—severe.

"Your honor, my client would like to make a statement."   Earlier Orello told his lawyer that he had some words to impart.

"You may precede, Mr. Johnson."   Only Orello could hear Neala's cackle.

"Ma'am, I'm a simple former athlete.   There's no law degree hanging on my wall at home.   Ignorance is the reason why I decided to do an unlawful thing. Someone told me about an auction that was going to take place.   Also, I heard that my stuff, stuff that was stolen from my home was going to be sold.   Sure, now after learning about the law a little, I understand that I shouldn't have gotten a gun to get my things.   Nor should I have held the thieves against their will at the auction house. Emotions, such as anger and hate, inspired a reaction before I could think about the best action."   Midway to the end of his monologue, Orello thought he made the judge wet.

"Your honor, let me say this, I am sorry about my unlawful act.   Certainly, you can understand that I was trying to regain my own possessions from some thieves. My approach, though a little too hardcore, was well-intentioned.   Whether some would call me a criminal or not, all I wanted was my own stuff back."   Convinced that his monologue was working, Orello started to plan a release party, complete with strippers, hookers, celebrities, booze and drugs.

"This state was always my favorite.   A lot of my football fans live right here in Nevada, and I have always been good to my fans.   Nothing would ever make me do anything against this area."

"Mr. Johnson, you have two minutes before sentencing."

"Okay, try to get into my motivations and you'll understand why I handled the situation the way I did.   Thank you for allowing me to speak in this honorable courtroom."

Talking got Orello out of myriad personal dilemmas in the past.   As a result, he was convinced that his voice made eggs sizzle.   Unless the judge was a blind and deaf lesbian, her body should be lava, Orello thought.

"Thank you again, your honor."

"You are welcome.   I hereby sentence you to thirty-four years."

Nine years before the possibility of parole became a mantra in Orello's head. Over again the sentence echoed.   He had to serve all those years in state prison before being eligible for parole.   The judge might as well have shot Orello.   There was, of course, the possibility of an appeal.   No matter the legal option, the process of fighting the judge's decision would take something that Orello did not have— patience.

There, as per usual, Frank Silverman was in the audience taunting Orello with condemnation.   Orello's acquittal for the murder of Neala Desdemona Johnson and Rod Silverman was a dagger in Frank's heart.   Granted, the Civil Court passed a judgment against the former athlete for two wrongful deaths, but it could not make the Silverman's pain of losing a son stop. $66.6 million dollars that the parents were supposed to receive did not alleviate the lamentation either.   Consistent excuses as to why the complete amount could not be paid pushed the blade further into Frank's psyche.

Ritualistically, beside Frank, Cheryl and Daphne stood.

It was the civil case that forced Orello into questionable business choices.   He made a porno film, wrote a book about his wife's murder and did personal appearances, etc.   The celebrity could not let people sack his fortune.   So, desperation became his defensive line.

"The Devil is going to bake your hide," The Silverman patriarch cried out.

Consistently absent, Orello's four children saw no reason to attend any of the court proceedings.   As far as they were concerned, after Orello was arrested, he died.

Anna Simpson, dissimilar to her children, watched all of Orello's courtroom problems on TV.   Wearing a red floral Muumuu, red processed hair in rollers, surrounded by cherry soda cans, barbeque potato chips and a remote control, her pudgy physique was orgasmic while watching the defeat of her abusive ex-husband.

A Hispanic bailiff, who was about the size of a kick boxer, took Orello out of the courtroom.   The bewildered criminal turned to Rod's father and stared.   That uncommunicative state was caused by the presence of three afterlife figures.   Overhead, unseen by all except Orello, Neala, alongside some befeathered female and Rod, cheered repeatedly.

****

Once the case concluded and the lawyer told Orello they could appeal the decision, the cell seemed even smaller.   Handicapping this jurisprudential game, Orello knew that no appeal would overturn his predicament.

Later that evening, psychotropic drugs were administered to help alleviate the sensation of cleats and knives piercing Orello's brain and lower extremities.   The pills were prescribed because it was deemed that he was suicidal.

Somewhere around twelve thirty in the morning, his ex-wife returned. The abusive spouse knew that the woman who bore his child would trek his way once more. Orello wanted Neala to haunt him.

"Now I guess my sentence will be spent being haunted by you."

"Why would I share another portion of my immortal life providing a source of escape from your loneliness? No, you're going to detox from your favorite stimulant—attention. Get ready for withdrawals from the warm love of women, football fans and your children."

"Please allow your spirit to forgive. Please give me that."

"You're right. I should give you some things. Here's the first thing I will give: information. Recent reports have proven that a woman is beaten every nine seconds. That calculation inspired me to give you a gift. Right at the point some malevolent man hurts a woman, you will feel the blows upon your body. Punches and slaps some unknown woman endures will affect your flesh. Why should women suffer unaccompanied by your presence? Aside from being suicidal, you will experience discomfort a prison doctor will believe is psychosomatic."

"Your gene pool was as worthless as pigeon crap on a porch. Until I came into your soon-to-be-on-food-stamps life, you were a liability. How could you have such powers?"

"Try to work past your stupidity and listen. That night you stabbed the life out of me, I saw a Goddess."

"Did you get high before coming here?" A titter accompanied the question.

"She called herself Nemesis. This Goddess and her minions hunt men like you."

"What kind of weirdo name is Nem-ee-sis?"

Annoyed with the process of answering Orello, Neala's eyebrows illustrated her anger before she continued speaking. "My wounded form, which you created, angered her. She said, 'Get up, Gaelic girl. Your parents dubbed you a champion and a champion you will be.' For my promise to become a fighter on the side of her legion, I was given abilities.

"Far from this dimension, in a stratospheric area reminiscent of ancient Greece, fifteen of my post-mortal years were spent training. Taught by Nemesis and other ancient mystics, I learned about bilocation, dematerialization, levitation, metempsychosis, mesmerism, psychokinesis, radiesthesia, telepathy and a lot more. Thankfully, this ghost of an abused woman was given powers by those omnipotent sources. I was using those powers to get you in this prison."

Binocular-eyed and confused, Orello stood and listened. Neala's words were unexplored constellations. Lost in her utterances, Orello could not believe how much his former wife had transformed. Besides the powers the creature gave her, Neala's IQ increased. His former simple country girl morphed into some kind of Mensa member.

"Above all, being vengeful was not a simple lesson. My folks taught their belief in forgiveness. Unlearning that concept was the hardest.

"Rod wanted justice to come down on you with the force of a mudslide. Repeated pleas on my part gave me the right to administer your sentence. Albeit simple, my first attempt at attacking you was by storing a meaty suggestion in your mind. Over and over, I repeated these words: 'Take your gun and get what someone got from you.'

"Easier than waving flesh in front of a piranha, you enjoyed the bait."

"I'm sorry!"

"Ah, Orello, your anguish is the best dish for me."

Coinciding with the final vowel, she disappeared in way that would perplex Houdini. In her place appeared Rod Silverman and the other outer worldly lady.

Frustrated with the amount of time Neala used for her revenge, Rod's interest was his family. Rod was also exasperated by Nemesis and her associates. He was mystified by these beings, living in levitating jewel-encrusted Grecian buildings. From their ancient ceremonial clothing to their arcane rituals that were on par with witchcraft, Rod disliked their oddness.

Instead of yelling at Orello, Rod wanted to punch him and watch his frame become bloody pieces of dismembered flesh. Almost Herculean impulse inhibitors suppressed Rod's vengefulness. Incapable of expressing his rage, he let Nemesis speak.

"Orello, certain people say I am a demon and others call me a saviour. Neither description matters," Nemesis stated in a synthesized and genderless voice. "What concerns my existence is seeing parasites like you suffer. All of my ethereal resources are dedicated to a single goal—the destruction of brutish beings. View your torment as you would a tragic play. Moreover, know that Neala and I will enjoy your every upcoming scene."

Before Orello could respond, the figures disappeared. Defeated, he tried to understand his fate.

"I'm sorry! I'm sorry!" Orello yelled while feeling invisible fists pummel him. Doubling over as a result of the attacks, he felt bruises form. Again, being consistent with Neala's plan, the protuberances were imperceptible to everyone else. "I'm sorry," Orello screamed once more.

"Yeah, you're sorry for being such a sorry has-been." Approximating the style of a stand-up comedian, the guard paused for an audience reaction. Bolstered by the sound of inmates laughing at his put-down, the correction officer continued his critical jokes about Orello. "Don't be sad, Superstar. You'll have your football memories to enjoy tonight. The guard quipped outside of Orello's cell. Laughter that was coming from all sides of the isolation ward became louder than the 1812 Overture. The guffawing made the sobs Orello emitted inaudible in the Lacrimae Rerum Criminal Compound in Nevada.

A prison that was normally known for misery was pleased about accommodating its newest inmate.

79.
Vacation
Lisa M. Scuderi-Burkimsher

Glen dozed off at the wheel of the car.

"Glen, look out!" Lydia yelled and grabbed the steering wheel guiding it back onto the road before he swerved into the other lane. "I'd like to make it to Las Vegas. I told you I'd drive the rest of the way."

"I'm so sorry! Look, the sign said there's a motel up ahead, let's get a room and rest. You're right, I can't keep my eyes open, and I could use some food, too."

As they pulled into the parking lot, a car zoomed right past them; tires screeching.

"What the hell!" Glen yelled out the window, but the car was long gone.

"My heart is racing. What a lunatic," Lydia said.

Glen rang the bell at the front desk. A tall woman with brown hair and too much pink blush approached. "Hi, I'm Laurie, can I help you?"

"How much for a one-night stay?" Glen asked.

"It's one-hundred-fifty a night."

He pulled his credit card out of his wallet, and when he placed it in her hand, he felt a sudden chill in the air.
Glen took the key. He and Lydia, exhausted, slowly walked to their room. Inside, it was simple with dull ivory curtains, an end table with a lamp, pen, white writing pad, and a television set with the old-fashioned, large back.

"No high definition TV in this place," Glen said.

"Who cares. We're here to sleep and then hit the road," Lydia said as she took off her sneakers.

Glen plopped down on the bed and closed his eyes. He mumbled, "Joseph", his son who had died in a car accident two years ago at twenty-two-years-old. Joseph was struck head-on by a drunk driver. The impact killed him instantly. Glen never got the image of the wreck out of his head, and how he'd cry well into the night. Lydia would say he was hysterical, but she was too. At the wake, Lydia spent hours at the coffin touching Joseph's hand and praying. Glen and the family let her be. It was her way of dealing with the grief. Glen and Lydia drowned themselves in their work and rarely spoke of their son.

After awakening from a sound sleep, Glen rubbed his eyes, looked out the window and saw it was dark out. His watch said eight-fifteen.

"There's a diner next door. Let's go get something to eat," Glen said.

Lydia stretched her arms and nodded in agreement. "I'm starving."

The diner was empty except for one waitress and a cook they heard rattling pots in the kitchen. "Hi, welcome to the Carolina Diner. I'm your hostess and waitress, Sue."

The woman waved Glen and Lydia to a booth and placed two menus down. They were so hungry, they ordered their drinks and food immediately, and Sue said she'd be back momentarily with their drinks. Glen eyed the place. The paintings on every wall were of black wilted roses. Dim chandeliers hung over the tables, and in the half hour they'd been there, no other customers came in. He noticed Lydia glancing at the walls, but didn't say anything. He could tell by her fumbling with her purse, she wasn't comfortable.

Glen stood. "I'm going to see what's going on. This is ridiculous. How long does it take to cook two burger platters?" Glen strode to the kitchen and peered through the swinging door. No one was there. The strangest thing was the whole kitchen didn't have a morsel of food. The stainless steel counters were spotless, the pots he heard rattling were nowhere in sight, and there wasn't a dish or utensil anywhere. "What the hell is going on here?" He went back to the booth where Lydia was applying mauve lipstick.

"We have to go. Neither the cook nor the waitress is here, and there's nothing in the kitchen. I went inside to see if there was anything to eat in the refrigerator and it was empty. I have no idea where they went. What kind of diner doesn't have food?" Glen was puzzled, creeped out, his heart raced, and sweat dripped down his neck.

"I'm frightened. We should just leave this place and drive on until we get to Vegas. We'll have plenty to eat and drink once we get there," Lydia said her legs and arms trembling.

"I'm with you, let's go."

Back to the motel, the clerk, Laurie, wasn't at the front desk.

"We'll leave the key on the counter after we get our things from the room."

When they got back to the motel room, a newspaper, that hadn't been there before, sat on the end table next to the pad and pen, opened to the front page. The headline read: "*Murder-Suicide at Carolina Motel*." A picture of Laurie, the waitress, and what must've been the cook, stared Glen and Lydia in the face. It said Laurie Simmons was married to the cook Jonathan Simmons. They owned the hotel and diner together. Jonathan had an affair with the waitress, Sue, who was also Laurie's best friend. When Laurie found out, she murdered them both in the motel lobby, then shot herself in the head. The place closed down and never reopened.

Glen and Lydia looked at one another. He tossed the newspaper down; they grabbed their bags, and ran to the car. He glanced back at the motel as he sped out of the parking lot. Laurie stood at the door, grinning and waving. His heart pounded as he stared at her. He never saw the oncoming truck.

"Glen, watch out!" Lydia screamed. But it was too late.

80.
Voodoo Museum
Mark Hudson

A voodoo museum is owned by Jerry,
and let us just say it's a little scary.
In the heart of New Orleans,
every day is Halloween!
The practicing Catholic runs the joint,
showcasing voodoo is the point.
Voodoo is popular in the French quarter,
voodoo priestesses on the border.
The museum is full of masks and skulls,
a little bit scary, but not quite dull.
People sold him skulls for his museum,
And people come from all over to see 'um'.
They show how to do voodoo by a wish,
With poison extracted from a blowfish.
The museum is visited by the curious,
leaving religious people furious.
Voodoo comes from the African slaves,
and haunts people even in their graves.
A school went on a recent tour,
And the children couldn't take anymore.
The eight graders were a little scared,
a little nervous, hardly prepared.
Seeing all those flickering candles,
was a little more then they could handle.
"Can we go now?" a student said in a small voice.
They were certainly fortunate they had a choice!

81.
Werewolf Cane
Mark Hudson

Stuart was working out at the Y,
a man came in with a wolf man cane.
He wondered if he could believe his eyes,
as if he might be going insane.
He asked the man, in hope of a reply,
"Are you a werewolf, can you explain?"
The man responded, "You might say I try,
but I'm a fan of horror films that entertain!"
Stuart laughed as if he would die,
so naïve to expect wolf's bane!"
And so the movie fan did not surprise,
a real werewolf would never exercise!

82.
When He Saw They Were Dead
Allen Kopp

His name was Edgar Delong and in 1921 he was fifteen years old. He had an accident in his sleep and they wouldn't stop laughing at him. They called him "baby" and said he ought to be ashamed of himself. They kept it up all day. Finally, he went and got a shotgun they didn't know he had and, at seven minutes after four in the afternoon, he shot both of them in the chest, his mother first and then his father. When he saw that they were dead, he went up the stairs in the old house to the attic. He found a rope, climbed up on a table and tied one end of the rope to a rafter and the other end around his own neck. After pulling on the rope to make sure it would hold at both ends, he stepped off the table into the void. As he strangled to death he said, "This is the thing I've always wanted."

It was written up in all the newspapers. People loved talking about it, recounting and embellishing all the details. The house where it happened stood vacant for years and was said to be haunted. Weeds grew up in the yard. Small boys threw rocks at the windows. The front porch began to sag. People claimed to hear demonic laughing coming from the house, gunshots and screams.

Finally, a man bought the house and fixed the sagging porch, the broken windows, the missing shingles and the peeling paint. He lived with his large family in the house for more than twenty years. Then there were other families after that to put their imprint on the character of the house. The day would come when the only people who remembered Edgar Delong and what he had done were the superannuated.

Edgar Delong still existed, though, in the world the living cannot see. Every day in the house his mother and father laughed at him and every day he went and got the shotgun they didn't know he had and, at seven minutes after four in the afternoon, shot both of them to death, first his mother and then his father. Every day he heard the startled cry from his mother right before he shot her and the strangled shout from his father. Every day he climbed the creaking old stairs to the attic, tied a rope around his neck and hanged himself. Every day he relived the whole thing, even though he was dead. Every day the same, the days unending.

More than eighty years after the death of Edgar Delong, a writer named Charles Delong rented the house for the summer. He was the grandson of Edgar Delong's father's brother and, so, a cousin of Edgar Delong. He had grown up hearing the stories and, when he began researching and writing a book about sensational murders, he knew he had to include a chapter in the book on the Delong double murder and suicide. He believed that by living in the house, if just for a few weeks, he would feel close to Edgar Delong and would understand him a way that no other living person could.

The house proved a wonderful inspiration to Charles Delong. While he didn't believe in ghosts, he did believe that something of Edgar Delong remained behind in the house. Using newspaper accounts and photos of the day, along with family reminiscences and his own grandfather's diary, he wrote an inspired and chilling account of the crime, to which he added a personal slant. "I am related by blood to the murderer," he wrote, "and am writing about his crime in the house in which it occurred."

He finished his book ahead of schedule and was sure it would be a success. He sent it off to his publisher and began working on his next book, a novel and a complete departure from crime. He still had a couple of weeks on his lease in the Delong house—which technically hadn't been the Delong house for decades, although he still thought of it in those terms. He stocked up on groceries and planned to spend a quiet time alone.

Except that he wasn't alone. Edgar Delong, his murderous young cousin, was there in the house with him, watching him, standing behind him, sometimes touching him on the shoulder or the back of the head. Edgar Delong would make himself known to Charles Delong when he believed the time was right.

The house had a soporific effect on Charles Delong. He took to taking naps on the couch in the afternoon, hearing only the ticking of the clock, the wind outside rustling the trees or the faraway barking of a dog. One afternoon during one of these naps he was made to see the thing that happened every day at seven minutes after four. He thought he was dreaming as he saw Edgar Delong emerge from the back of the house bearing a shotgun and walk with it toward his parents as they sat in the room they called the parlor. His mother drew back instinctively and gave a startled cry when Edgar shot her. His father began to stand up and emitted a strangled shout as the bullet entered his chest.

After he had killed them both, Edgar Delong turned to his cousin Charles Delong and said, "It's always the same."

Still believing he was dreaming, Charles Delong said, "I don't understand."

"Every day the same. They laugh at me and I keep killing them but I can't make them stop."

"None of this is real," Charles Delong said. "You're a figment. You don't exit."

"Maybe it's a figment to you. To me it's real and I can't stop. I want to stop. I want you to help me to stop."

"How can I do that?"

"Let me come into your body so I can have the means to leave this house."

"No, I would never do that! It's impossible!"

"I can make you see it every day. Live it every day. As I do."

"No, it's out of the question!"

"You wanted to know what it was like to be me."

"You're a murderer. I don't want to be you."

"We're cousins. We're the same blood."

"No!"

"I'm going up to the attic now and hang myself, as I have thousands of times before. I want you to come along and watch."

"No!"

"I think we've reached the point where there's no longer a choice," Edgar Delong said and raised the gun and shot his cousin Charles Delong squarely in the chest.

The body of Charles Delong wasn't found for five days. When the police were called in to investigate and were unable to find a murder weapon or a motive, they deduced that the murderer was somebody that Charles Delong knew and had willingly admitted into the house.

And so it continued. Every day at seven minutes after four in the afternoon, Edgar Delong shot and killed first his mother and then his father, after which he climbed the stairs to the attic and hanged himself from a rafter. The only difference now was that he had his cousin Charles Delong there to experience the whole thing with him. Without end and *ad infinitum*.

Contributing Authors

A.J. Huffman

A.J. Huffman has published eleven solo chapbooks and one joint chapbook through various small presses. Her new poetry collection, *Another Blood Jet*, is now available from Eldritch Press. She has three more poetry collections forthcoming: *A Few Bullets Short of Home* from mgv2>publishing, *Degeneration* from Pink Girl Ink, and *A Bizarre Burning of Bees* from Transcendent Zero Press. She is a multiple *Pushcart Prize* nominee, and has published over 2200 poems in various national and international journals, including *Labletter*, *The James Dickey Review*, *Bone Orchard*, *EgoPHobia, and Kritya*. She is also the founding editor of *Kind of a Hurricane Press*.

www.kindofahurricanepress.com

Allen Kopp

All we see or seem is but a dream within a dream. Allen Kopp lives in St. Louis, Missouri, USA, with his three cats. He has had over a hundred short stories published in such diverse publications as *Midwestern Gothic Literary Journal, Dew on the Kudzu, Gaia's Misfits Fantasy Anthology, Bartleby-Snopes, The Grey Wolfe Storybook 2014, Write to Meow 2014, Danse Macabre, Creaky Door Magazine, Penmen Review, Zodiac Review, Abandoned Towers Magazine, Superstition Review, Necrology Shorts, A Twist of Noir, Skive Magazine, Short Story America, Intellectual Refuge Journal, Santa Fe Writers' Project Journal, Wilde Oats, Diverse Voices Quarterly, People of Few Words Anthology, Belle Reve Literary Magazine, Literary Orphans, Best Genre Short Stories Anthology #1, Death Head Grin, Spasm Valley Paranormal Horror Anthology, Dysfunctional Family Story: An Anthology, Offbeat Christmas Story: An Anthology, Churn Thy Butter* and many others. His Internet home is: **www.literaryfictions.com**

Briana J. Weiss

Briana J. Weiss is a recent graduate from university and a Midwestern homebody. She's loved reading and writing for as long as she can remember, and hopes to one day write her own fiction novel. Her past experience includes being an Editor/Editor-in-Chief of her university's literary magazine *Prairie Winds*, and earning first place in the *Agnes Hyde Writing Competition* for poetry.

Brittney Corrigan

Caitlyn Mancini

Caitlyn Mancini born and raised in Ann Arbor, Michigan graduated from the University of Michigan with a BA in English and a sub concentration in creative writing. Caitlyn started her writing journey at the age of seven, coming up with fantastical stories and characters, including a children's series at the age of twelve inspired by her sister Laurynn. Caitlyn continues to live and work in Ann Arbor.

Her first book, *Project S.K.I.E.* was released earlier in 2016 (Grey Wolfe Publishing), and the second in the series is set to be published in 2017.

Charles R. Stern

Charles is a psychologist practicing in the Detroit area since 1980. He has also taught at every level of education during his career.

He is the author of *Juxtaposition Paradox* (Grey Wolfe Publishing, 2015) and his new novel, *Finder In Hellworld*: *A Love Story* (Grey Wolfe Publishing) will be released in early 2017.

Edward Ahern

Franco Strong

Franco Strong takes his inspiration in equal measure from his philosophical studies and the almost ceaseless sun of the California/Mexico border.

H.R. Boldwood

H.R. Boldwood is a writer of horror and speculative fiction. In another incarnation, Boldwood is a *Pushcart Prize* nominee and was awarded the *2009 Bilbo Award* for creative writing by Thomas More College. Publication credits include, *Short Story America, Bete Noir, Everyday Fiction, Toys in the Attic, Floppy Shoes Apocalypse II, Pilcrow and Dagger, and Sirens Call.*

Boldwood's characters are often disreputable and not to be trusted. They are kicked to the curb at every conceivable opportunity. No responsibility is taken by this author for the dastardly and sometimes criminal acts committed by this ragtag group of miscreants.

In another incarnation, H.R. Boldwood can be found writing as Mary Ann Back, whose collection of short stories *Dead Reckoning*, published by Grey Wolfe Publishing, is available at **www.amazon.com**.

Madame Zelda first appeared in print and on Podcast (#6) at www.pilcrowdagger.com

Jane Sloven

Jane Sloven is a retired psychotherapist and attorney who lives in Portland, Maine with her husband, Joe, and pooch, Benji. In addition to her clinical articles, her short stories and essays have been published in print and online: *Rufus and Rascal*, two short stories, and *Ralph*, an essay, appeared in *Write to Woof, 2014*, by Grey Wolfe Publishing; *Chocolate, a memoir*, appeared in *RiverPoets Journal: Tales from the Matriarchal Zone*, and *Tara at the Mall* appeared in *Chicago Now*.

Mark Hudson

Mark Hudson is a freelance artist and writer who studied creative writing at Columbia College in Chicago, and has been taking art classes ever since. He writes almost every day, to the point of insomnia and eye exhaustion. He is currently writing from a library where he just worked so hard on two poems that he needs a cup of coffee. He thinks that everyone has a story to tell, but a writer is someone who puts the pen to paper.
Grey Wolfe Publishing is one of his favorite places to work with.
He resides in Evanston, Illinois.

Matt McGee

Matt McGee writes short fiction in the local library until the staff makes him go home. The Stunt Road Tower really exists, is definitely thought to be haunted, though good luck getting there; it is currently guarded by armed security that won't give their names or purpose. It is still viewable on Google Earth from high above, like a plane soaring overhead.

Mercedes Webb-Pullman

Mercedes Webb-Pullman started writing in 2007. She gained her Diploma in Creative Writing from Whitireia, 2009, and graduated from IIML Victoria University with an MA in Creative Writing 2011. Her work has appeared in *Turbine, 4th Floor, Swamp, Reconfigurations, The Electronic Bridge, Otoliths, Connotations, The Red Room, Typewriter Kind of a Hurricane Press, and Cliterature*, among others, and in her books. The latest, *The Jean Genie*, explores the work of Jean Genet. She lives on the Kapiti Coast, New Zealand.

Michael Berton

Michael Berton is the author of *Man! You Script the Mic.* (New Mitote Press) published in 2013 and the recent poetry collection, *No Shade in Aztlán* (New Mitote Press). He has had poems published in a variety of publications including *The Cracked Mirror, Moonshot, Otoliths, Fireweed, Sin Fronteras Journal, Pacific Review, Gargoyle, Blaze Vox, Snow Monkey, Legends: Summer, Perceptions, And/Or, REM Magazine, Cirque Literary Journal, Volt, The Blinking Cursor, Hinchas de Poesia, Do Hookers Kiss?, Yellow Medicine Review, Fourteen Hills, 2016 Texas Poetry Calendar* and others. He lives in Portland, OR.

Moshe Sonnheim

Dr. Moshe Sonnheim, a native Philadelphian, lives in Jerusalem, Israel.
He is married to Jolene, a Dutch Child Survivor of the Holocaust, and they have two
married daughters and nine grandchildren.

Dr. Sonnheim is a retired Senior Teacher of Social Work with several academic
publications and two short stories, *Somewhere Else* and *Lacunae* to his credit.

At the age of 83, Moshe has finally returned to his "first love"—creative writing.

Norbert Gora

Norbert is a twenty-five-year old poet and writer from Poland. Many of his horror and science fiction short stories have been previously published. He is also the author of poem, *The Feathery Immensity of Blue*, which was a part of an English-language anthology of poems and short stories, *Contemporary Writers of Poland*.

Sue Ann Olson

Sue Ann Olson grew up in Connecticut writing her stories with the help of a secret magic window which allowed her to see all of the way to alternate dimensions and distant galaxies. She has held various jobs, mostly clerical and secretarial, except for stints as a pre-school teacher and a bookstore cashier. She has a degree in Anthropology from the University of California, Los Angeles. She is divorced and has two teenage daughters. She is currently attending Wayne State for a Masters in Social Work. She still has that magic window which lets her see into those mysterious, alien universes to tell the stories of their people through her poetry, children's books, and science fiction fantasy stories.

Vanessa Matheny

Vanessa lives in Michigan with her husband of twenty-three years and together they have raised three beautiful children. She is a devout follower of Jesus Christ and loves to serve Him. She enjoys serving in her church and working with woman through an inner healing ministry.

"Never in my wildest dreams did I think I would become a writer. In high school, I hated to write. In fact, I was horrible at it. It wasn't until the Lord healed my heart from many wounds of the past that He gave me the desire to write. He has taken my victories and turned them into stories. My heart's desire is to touch heaven and change earth for the Kingdom of God one story at a time."

Vanessa's first novel, *Out of The Darkness and Into The Light* (Grey Wolfe Publishing) was released in 2015 and won the Bronze Medal in the *Moonbeam Children's Book Awards*. The second book in her series will be released in mid-2017.
www.VanessaMatheny.com

Victoria L. Scott

Victoria L. Scott teaches Social Studies, Latin, Steampunk Studies and Quilting to middle schoolers at a private school in Southeastern Michigan. She has studied Shakespeare in England and at *The Folger Shakespeare Library*; communicated extensively in spoken Latin at Latin Language immersion camps in Kentucky, Michigan and Massachusetts; and studied Roman History and Archaeology in Rome and environs as a student of the *American Academy* in Rome. She is an avid quilter and Steampunker who enjoys *Doctor Who*, walking her dog Red 'the Wonder Husky', and writing.

Victoria's first novel, *The Odin Inheritance* (Grey Wolfe Publishing) was published in 2015, and the second in the series is expected in 2017.

William Doreski

William Doreski lives in Peterborough, New Hampshire. His latest book is *City of Palms* (AA Press, 2012). He has published three critical studies, including *Robert Lowell's Shifting Colors*. His fiction, essays, poetry, and reviews have appeared in many journals, including *Massachusetts Review, Notre Dame Review, Worcester Review, The Alembic, New England Quarterly, Harvard Review, Modern Philology, Antioch Review, Natural Bridge*. He won the *2010 Aesthetica* poetry award.

Wm. Bernan

Wm. Bernan is an author of historical and paranormal fiction from Portsmouth, NH. His associations include the Seacoast Writers' Circle, The Portsmouth Writers' Salon, and the New Hampshire Writers Project. His novelette *The Last Bone* can be found in the recent 18th Wall Productions anthology *Those Who Live Long Forgotten II*

www.ingramcontent.com/pod-product-compliance
Lightning Source LLC
Chambersburg PA
CBHW080722020726
47503CB00010B/2754